in and out of the book on the Island of Peeg in a balloon

JONATHAN GATHORNE-HARDY

Illustrated by Nicolas Hill

OVERLOOK DUCKWORTH
New York • Woodstock • London

This edition first published in the United States in 2006 by
Overlook Duckworth .

NEW YORK:
The Overlook Press
141 Wooster Street
New York, NY 10012

WOODSTOCK:
The Overlook Press
One Overlook Drive
Woodstock, NY 12498
www.overlookpress.com
[for individual orders, bulk and special sales, contact our Woodstock office]

LONDON:
Duckworth
90-93 Cowcross Street
London EC1M 6BF
inquiries@duckworth-publishers.co.uk
www.ducknet.co.uk

Cataloging-in-Publication Data is available from the Library of Congress

Book design and type formatting by Bernard Schleifer
Printed in the United States of America
ISBN-10 1-58567-798-1 / ISBN-13 978-1-58567-798-6 (USA)
ISBN-10 0-7156-3671-5 (UK)
1 3 5 7 9 10 8 6 4 2

JANE'S
ADVENTURES

JANE'S ADVENTURES

Contents

Jane's Adventures
in and out of the book

To my sister Rose

1. The Book

JANE CHARRINGTON stood beside a large cupboard and watched Mrs Deal dashing about the kitchen. She made so many unnecessary journeys that Jane knew one of them would lead to the cupboard. Then Mrs Deal would say,

'Now, don't get in my way. Off you go and play.'

But even this was better than having nothing to do, so Jane stood and watched.

After four minutes Mrs Deal decided she wanted a new duster. Patting the grey bun on the back of her head, she trotted over to the cupboard.

'Boo!' said Jane.

'Good heavens! What a start you gave me!' said Mrs Deal. 'Now, be a good girl and run along. I've got quite enough to do as it is.

'But I'm so bored,' said Jane. 'What shall I *do*?'

'Now, now, now,' said Mrs Deal, 'I haven't time for larking about,' and opening the door she shoo'ed Jane out.

Mrs Deal was a small thin woman with grey hair tied in a thick, wispy bun. She was always worried and always busy. Jane's father, the thirty-fifth Earl of Charrington, said it gave him a thrombosis just to look at the woman.

But it was in fact really his fault that Mrs Deal had such a lot of work (which, it's true, she enjoyed). Lord Charrington was extremely rich and the very fact of being so rich seemed to keep him busy all the year round. There were frequent trips to London; men would come down with suitcases of papers and cheques for him to sign, and about twice a year he had to go to America. When this happened—as it just had—he always took Lady Charrington with him, and before they went the twenty-five indoor servants, the eighteen gardeners, the six game-keepers and the three chefs would all be sent on holiday. Left behind were Jane and Mrs Deal. Mrs Deal was in charge of everything, and as a reward and because Curl Castle was so large, she was paid the wages of four people during this time (£50 a week).

Because Curl Castle *was* large. It was, in fact, one of the largest in the world. Every owner for hundreds of years had added a new wing or turret or courtyard, and now the castle half filled the Cornish valley in which it stood. Special vacuum cleaners with powerful engines, and seats for the drivers had been built to clean the miles of carpet.

But if Mrs Deal had too much, Jane had far too little to do. She had now been alone in the castle with Mrs Deal for a week and done every possible thing she could think of except one. And that she planned to do after lunch. It concerned a distant tower which was supposed to be haunted. A little girl had gone into it two hundred years before and never been seen since—or not seen alive. But on dark and windy nights her transparent ghost had sometimes been seen walking silently down the dark corridors, with a candle in her hand.

This story had frightened Jane for years, but since it was a warm July day, since she was now twelve, and since she was going nearly mad with boredom, she had at last decided to find out what happened behind the thick oak door which separated the haunted tower from the rest of the castle.

When she had finished lunch she changed into jeans and an old shirt. Then she took a small satchel and put into it a penknife, some chocolate, a torch with an extra battery, two bandages, some Dettol ointment and a handkerchief. Lastly she went to the vacuum cleaner cupboard on the first floor and in a few moments was roaring away down the long, empty, carpet-covered corridors with the satchel bouncing at her waist.

All too soon she reached the door to the haunted tower. She looked at it for some time, her heart beating. It was at the top of six steps, looking very innocent and covered in small brass knobs. After a while, clutching the penknife in her right hand, she very slowly climbed the steps. At the top she stopped again, then putting out one finger she gave the door a tiny push.

To her horror it swung open at once. At first, all she could see was darkness. Too frightened to move, Jane stared into it, expecting at any moment to see the dim figure of the ghost.

Gradually, however, she saw that she was looking up a narrow, winding staircase, and, feeling a little calmer, she took out the torch and began to climb slowly up it.

It was obvious that no one had been there for years. The dust was so thick on each step that she sank into it up to her ankles. Before long she reached the top, and once again was faced by a door covered in brass knobs. But this time it was firmly locked and no amount of shoving would make it open. Half disappointed, half relieved, Jane was about to go back, when her eye was caught by something high above the door, just under the ceiling.

It was a large round hole, and sticking out of the wall all the way up to it were iron bars about a foot apart. At once Jane began to climb up and in a moment she had reached the top, to find that the hole was just big enough for her to squeeze through.

She was in a very high, completely round room. Though the shutters were closed on the windows, one of them had broken open and it was possible to see quite clearly. All round the walls there were very high shelves filled with books, and it was on top of one of these that Jane was now kneeling. Below her she could see a desk, a large globe of the world and, in the middle of the library out of her reach, some tall wooden steps on wheels. However, rolling onto her tummy and sliding her legs over the edge, she managed to climb down.

The dust at the bottom was even thicker than on the stairs, and when she walked it puffed up round her in great clouds, making her sneeze. The first thing she did was to open all the shutters and the windows.

The room, she now saw, though high, was really not very large. Looking around, she noticed that on one of the chairs there was a doll dressed up in curious old fashioned clothes. But before she could pick it up her eyes were caught by something lying in the middle of the floor. It was a book, and even though it was half covered by dust, Jane could see that it was the largest book she had ever seen in her life.

From top to bottom it measured about five feet and it was at least four feet across. Its cover was of solid black leather half an inch thick, with a title written on it in gold, but in a language Jane couldn't read.

Bending down, she put her fingers under the cover and heaved; though it looked so heavy it opened easily enough, almost as though someone inside had given it a push.

At first there were just seven blank pages, but on the eighth the whole page was taken up by an enormous picture. It was of a square in the middle of a town. The square was full of people all standing and staring at a raised platform. On the platform an old man in a purple cloak was kneeling with his head over a basket. Beside him stood a huge ugly man holding above his head an enormous axe. The picture was drawn in great detail and in bright colours. It looked so real that Jane felt quite frightened.

The same was true of all the other pages. Each consisted of one vast picture, some with a few lines written underneath in the strange language, some without. Turning them over, Jane found one which particularly interested her.

It showed a prison cell, quite bare except for a low wooden bed. High up on another wall a tiny, barred window let a thin stream of sunlight fall onto a table in the middle of the cell. On the table was a half-empty pie dish, a plate of butter and a full glass of wine. In one corner a young man was crouched by the wall trying, it seemed, to write on it with a fork. Every inch of the picture had been minutely and carefully drawn. Jane could see that on the neck of the young man, below his untidy yellow hair, there was a piece of plaster.

To see more closely exactly what he was doing, Jane crawled on hands and knees to the middle of the picture. As she did so she suddenly saw that about a foot to her left a small piece of paper had been stuck into the edge of the book. She could see that it had something written on it and though the writing was very brown and faded she could just read it:

> *Shut eyes, do not look,*
> *Close your pages on me Book.*
>
> *Turn again, oh Book now turn,*
> *Back through your pages I return.*

I wonder what it means, thought Jane, and almost without thinking she closed her eyes and said aloud in a dreamy voice—
'Shut eyes, do not look,
Close your pages on me Book.'
The moment she had finished the most extraordinary thing happened. The pages of the Book suddenly began to feel soft and fluffy like cotton wool and at the same time the whole picture on which she was sitting turned milky white. The pages grew softer and softer, Jane felt first her feet, then her legs sinking into them, she struggled, reached out to grab the edge of the Book, and then all at once she felt herself slip into a blackness beneath her and go falling, falling, falling.

Someone standing in the library at that moment would have been amazed to see the vast cover of the Book slowly rise up, as though lifted by an invisible hand, and slowly shut itself, apparently squashing the little girl inside completely flat.

2. The Tunnellers

JANE opened her eyes and found that she was standing by the table in the cell she had been looking at a moment before in the Book. She was still holding the piece of paper she had found and, without looking at it again, she folded it up and pushed it into the left-hand pocket of her jeans. A few feet away, with his back to her, the young man was still crouching by the wall. He had not noticed her and she could see that he was chipping with his fork at one of the large stone blocks. He was wearing a loose grey dressing-gown.

After a while Jane coughed and said,

'I say, excuse me.'

The moment she spoke the young man gave a loud scream, sprang to his feet, and holding the fork in front of him backed nervously away.

'No, no,' he said very quickly and loudly. 'I didn't . . . I promise . . .' But seeing Jane he stopped, looking rather surprised, and then said in a quieter voice.

'Oh, I beg your pardon, I thought you were someone else.' He walked over to the table and picked up the glass of wine. When he had drunk some of it he turned and looked at her.

'That's better,' he said. 'Goodness what a terrible fright. But who are you? How did you get here? Have they put you inside too?' He smiled at her.

'In a way,' said Jane, thinking it would be better to explain about the Book later on.

'I wonder why I didn't hear them bring you in?' went on the young man. 'I suppose I didn't notice. It's true I'm becoming very absent-minded.' He brushed his yellow hair out of his eyes and looked worried for a moment, then said, 'Are you one of us, a Tunneller, I mean?'

'Yes, in a way,' said Jane.

She didn't know what a Tunneller was, but had decided that the young man was so nice that she would like to be with him and his friends whatever they did.

'What were you doing over by the wall?' she asked.

'Trying to escape,' said the young man. 'I thought if I could get that big stone out I might find a tunnel.'

'But it would take you years,' said Jane. 'Look, you've only made a few scratches on it. How long have you been working?'

'A week,' said the young man gloomily. 'I know, I'm hopeless. The trouble is, I was never taught to be an escaper. But I had to do something. They don't let you read here, you know—it's called Ordeal by Boredom. I'm surprised, really, they've put us together.'

'But have you tried any other way?' said Jane. 'Picking the lock or the window?'

'No,' said the young man, 'but it's no good. The window's too small, and you can't pick a lock without hairpins and I haven't any hairpins.'

'What about the bed?' asked Jane.

'The bed?' said the young man.

They looked at it together. It was really just a long wooden box, with a mattress and some grey blankets on it. The young man went over and tried to move it. After some moments puffing and pulling he stood up. 'Screwed to the floor,' he said, staring crossly down at it. Suddenly, however, he dropped to his knees and began to fiddle at its end. 'I wonder . . .' he said, then a moment later, 'Hand me the knife off the table.' After several minutes twisting and poking, he made a pleased noise and with a hard tug pulled off the end. 'There,' he said, holding it up to Jane. '*Not* so hopeless, after all.'

They both knelt and stared into the small black space. 'I can't see a tunnel,' said the young man sadly.

'We can't *see* anything,' said Jane. 'It's far too dark. Look, I think I can just squeeze through. You keep guard.' And before the young man could say anything she began to wriggle under the bed.

'All right,' she heard him say, 'I'll put back the end.' Then, as he did this, his voice became muffled but she thought she heard him say something like 'I'll whistle if there's any danger.'

When Jane had disappeared the young man sat down at the table and began to finish the pie. He had been doing this for about two minutes when there came a tremendous clattering and banging on the door. It flew open and a huge red-faced man with a beard, a green uniform covered in medals, leather boots up to his knees and with a machine gun dangling from his belt, burst into the cell.

The moment he appeared the young man sprang to his feet, leapt onto the bed and putting his fingers into his mouth gave six or seven piercing whistles.

The red-faced man stopped, his face suddenly be coming redder than ever.

'What the devil are you doing?' he shouted. 'Are you mad? Stand to attention this instant!'

At once the young man stepped off the bed and walked back to the table.

'I'm sorry, Major Wilkinson,' he said. 'I've been in rather a nervous state this morning.'

'Going mad, eh?' said Major Wilkinson. He gave a deep laugh. 'So the Ordeal by Boredom is beginning to work, eh? Well, it doesn't surprise me. Now, is there anything you want, which you can have, and that means it is no good asking for books, paper, ink, musical instruments, cards, soap . . .' He droned on and on, but when he had finished the young man, instead of saying nothing, felt he had to keep the Major talking in case he should hear some strange noise coming from under the bed.

'Well, I wonder,' he said slowly, 'I wonder if I might have some hairpins?'

'Hairpins?' roared Major Wilkinson, once again staring in amazement at the young man. 'You really *have* gone mad. What the devil do you want hairpins for?'

The young man was always startled when the Major shouted and without thinking he said, 'Why, for the young girl, of course. She needs them for her hair.'

'Hair? Girl?' shouted the Major, looking wildly round the cell. 'What girl? Where?'

'Ah, you wonder where she's gone,' said the young man, beginning to lose his head. 'Quite natural. Well, she slipped under the bed for a few moments to look for her hairpins. That is, not the bed, but out of the door when you came in. I saw her ask one of your men to take her to the matron. So I expect the whole thing will be quite all right,' he went on in a soothing voice. 'The matron will see to the hairpins and we can all relax.'

But the Major was not to be calmed. Instead, with a cruel smile he unhitched his machine gun and advanced upon the young man. 'So you think you need hairpins?' he said. 'You think there's a little girl under the bed, do you? Well, I'll show you, I'll show you!' And before

the horrified young man could stop him, he'd raised the machine gun to his shoulder and with a series of deafening explosions fired twenty bullets straight into the bed. Then, laughing loudly and shouting over his shoulder, 'After the Ordeal by Boredom comes the Ordeal by Bullets,' he crashed out of the room.

When Jane had squeezed herself under the bed she had opened her satchel and taken out the torch. At first all she had seen were pieces of fluff and some dead flies. But then, feeling about with her hand, she had found a ring sunk into the floor. It lifted easily, and when she pulled, a small trap-door opened before her. In a moment she had wriggled through.

It was then that she heard above her the shrill whistles of the young man and the thumps as he jumped on the bed. However, she shut the trap-door quickly behind her and set off down the steps leading steeply downwards. On either side were high damp walls, and every now and again sharp corners, as the steps bored deeper and deeper into the castle. Jane followed them for five minutes and then decided she must go back and get the young man. She had just reached the trap-door and was opening it, when she heard the terrible noise of the machine gun and with a zipping noise two bullets shot close past her and went smack, smack, smack down the steps.

Jane got such a fright that she nearly fell backwards, but when nothing else happened she picked up her torch and pulled herself up through the trap-door.

No sooner was she under the bed again, however, than she heard above her the most piteous noise. It was the young man crying. Through his sobs Jane could just hear—

'Oh it's my fault, my fault . . . are you dead? Oh, oh, oh . . . You brute, Wilkinson, brute! brute! brute!'

Jane listened for a while, then she shouted up,

'I'm quite all RIGHT.'

At once the crying stopped and a moment later Jane was clasped in the arms of the young man, who was amazed and delighted to find that she was still alive.

Jane told him what she had seen and, though it was now well on in the afternoon, they decided to escape at once. The young man stuffed a pillow in his bed to make it look as though he were asleep there, and after wrapping up the rest of the pie and putting it in the satchel, they set off.

Jane went first and was soon waiting at the top of the steps. The young man followed and together they started down the steps.

After a little way Jane kicked something which rolled ahead of her like a pebble. Turning her torch downwards she saw a small flat object gleaming up at her.

'Must be one of Major Wilkinson's bullets,' said the young man. 'Why not keep it as a souvenir?'

Jane picked it up and put it in her pocket. After this they walked for a long time. Sometimes steps turned into a tunnel so low that they had to crawl. Sometimes the steps went upwards for a while before continuing down; and several times they must have passed quite close to rooms in the prison because they could hear through the walls the sounds of voices and the tramping of feet, but at last, just as Jane's torch was growing dim, they saw ahead daylight shining through a narrow opening.

The tunnel had ended some way down a mountain. Spread out far below them was an immense valley from which she could see feathery pencils of smoke rising straight into the still, clear air. Down its length curled a distant river shining silver and grey in the early evening light. But she only looked at the view for a moment. Far more interesting was the scene in front of the tunnel.

Immediately before them was a flat open space around whose edge grew a number of small bushes and trees. At a far corner there were parked a number of large cars. In the middle, round three bonfires, sat and strolled a group of perhaps fifty men wearing the same bright green uniform as Major Wilkinson.

'Oh, no,' whispered the young man as they both stared out. 'We're trapped.'

'Who are they?' whispered Jane.

'They must be from the castle,' said the young man. 'Look, do you see those boxes with long wires stretching from them? They are tunnel detectors for finding tunnels underground. We'll be lucky if they don't discover us.'

'What shall we do?' said Jane. The young man said nothing, but continued to stare anxiously out in the fast fading evening light. At last, putting his mouth close to her ear, he whispered,

'Listen. We have one chance. Do you see those bushes which grow away from us to the left? Well, they reach almost to the line of cars. When it gets a little darker we must try and creep round and then make a run for the nearest car. I only hope I can drive it.'

They waited for ten more minutes and to keep up their strength Jane gave them both some of the chocolate. Then suddenly the young man whispered, 'Now!', and slipped out of the passage mouth and crawled quickly to the first bush.

It was a long and painful journey. Several times Jane felt sure they must be discovered. Once she kicked a stone so that it rolled noisily down a little slope. Once they had to pass so close to one of the sentries that they could hear him softly humming. And once, just as the young man was darting across a small open space between two bushes, one of the sentries cried 'HALT!' in a loud voice and turned round pointing his gun. The young man stopped, and luckily it was now dark enough for the sentry to think him, as he crouched trembling in his dressing-gown, just another bush, because he soon turned round and they saw him light a cigarette. After half an hour of crawling and stooping and running and wriggling they came to the last piece of scrub.

Before them was a wide gap of forty yards, then the cars. They stared in silence until the young man whispered.

'We'll have to chance it. When I say "go" run as fast as you can for the nearest car. Ready?'

'Yes,' whispered Jane.

There was a short pause while the young man looked towards the camp fires, and then all at once he said 'Go'.

They were off. In the darkness Jane seemed to be running very fast. From the right came the noise of the soldiers. Ahead of them the cars grew nearer and nearer. They were more than halfway across when suddenly Jane caught her foot against a large stone and before she could stop herself had fallen flat on her face, letting out a loud yell as she did so.

Immediately a great many things happened at once. There was shouting from the camp. The young man, who had been running in front of her turned round and came running back. And hundreds of powerful torches shone fiercely out of the darkness. There came the sudden sound of guns and almost at once the young man said 'Ow!' very loudly and clutched his left arm. Then he scooped her up with his right arm and she was being carried at great speed towards the car, her ears filled with the rattle and crash of firing guns.

Luckily the door of the nearest car was open. The young man threw her in, then jumped in himself. For a moment they lay there panting. Jane, beginning to recover from the shock, was now suddenly much more frightened. Before, though nervous, she had somehow felt that nothing would happen to her. But now she realized that these men were dangerous. They could, and would if possible, kill her. Kneeling up on the seat she looked anxiously out of the back window.

'Oh, do be quick,' she said. 'They're coming.'

'I'm sorry, it's my arm,' said the young man. However, he pulled himself up and began to push and twist at buttons and switches. Jane stared out, watching the little, running figures with their waving torches come closer and closer. Luckily the car was covered with thick steel plates and had special glass so that the bullets just bounced off.

'Quick,' she said.

'I *am* being quick,' said the young man, feverishly pressing knobs and pulling levers. Jane heard the wind screen wipers begin to swish.

'Damn!' said the young man.

'Quick!' said Jane.

But just as the first soldier was ten yards from the car, the engine gave a sudden roar, the headlights blazed ahead over the valley, and with a jolt it shot forward and in a moment they were careering down the twists and turns of a steep and terrifying mountain road.

Their troubles were still not over. After five minutes the young man said in a weak voice, 'Look, I feel rather faint. Do you think you could steer the car for a while? I'll work the brake with my foot. We don't need to change gears going down hill.'

'I think so,' said Jane. 'I've sometimes sat on my father's knee and steered. I'll try.'

So the young man moved over and Jane slipped into his place. She found it, in fact, quite easy. The steering was specially made so that the lightest touch made it turn, and after a while she began to enjoy spinning the huge car round the steep corners.

Down into the night they sped. The young man didn't faint but sat silently holding his arm, down which Jane could see, in the light from the dashboard, a dark stain was spreading. After a while, however, they began to hear some way behind them the noise of distant hooting and the sound of guns being fired. Quite soon the inside of the car was lit up by the flash of pursuing headlights as the enemy began to gain.

'We'll have to change places again,' said the young man. 'We're not going fast enough.'

They did so, and the car went faster than ever, swaying violently from side to side and going so wildly round the corners that sometimes they skidded within inches of steep precipices. But the pursuit still gained and now on straight bits of road bullets once again went smack against the steel plates.

Suddenly, after turning several sharp corners, there appeared in the headlights a vast tree growing on the left-hand side of the road. Though she saw it only for a moment, its strange shape reminded Jane of a question mark. But when the young man saw it he stopped the car at once.

'Quick, get out!' he said. 'I know where we are.'

They scrambled out, and he leant inside to let off the brake. The car moved slowly forward. Then faster. And faster—until with a rush and a great bounce it disappeared over the edge of the next corner and fell with echoing crashes down the steep cliff. Immediately Jane and the young man turned and stumbled towards the tree, to throw themselves flat in the high bracken which grew around its roots.

They were just in time. In a moment the enemy soldiers came

whirling round the corner and went rushing by, shouting and yelling and firing guns into the air.

'Now, let's rest a bit,' said the young man, 'and after that I'm almost certain that quite close to here is the entrance to one of our main tunnels.'

'And first,' said Jane, 'I'll look at your arm.' She gently pulled off his dressing-gown, and turning on her torch (into which she first put the spare battery) she looked at the wound. There was a lot of blood, but as she was not a squeamish girl she wiped it away with her handkerchief and then bound it tightly up with one of the bandages. After this they ate the remains of the pie and finished off Jane's chocolate.

At last, feeling much better, they lay back in the bracken and looked up at the stars. After a while the young man said, 'You know, there is one thing I don't quite understand. I don't think Major Wilkinson knew you had been put into my cell at all.'

'I know,' said Jane. Then, suddenly deciding that she must tell him everything, she said, 'You see, the thing is, I'm not *really* a Tunneller at all.'

'You're not?' said the young man. 'What are you then? Surely not one of *them*?'

'Oh no,' said Jane. 'No, well, you see, it all happened like this.' And then she told him everything, about Lord and Lady Charrington, about how lonely she was in their enormous castle with Mrs Deal, about the haunted part and about the strange book she had found in the old library. He was silent for a while when she had finished, then he said, 'I see. I understand now. You're one of those. I wouldn't have thought so.'

'How do you mean, "one of those"?' said Jane.

'Oh, it doesn't matter,' said the young man. 'You'll find out soon enough. But of course you may not be, in fact I should say you weren't. Even if you are, it doesn't really matter. But I can't tell you. You have to find out from one of them. But perhaps you'd like to know about the Tunnellers?'

'Well, I'd particularly like to know about what you mean by "one of those",' said Jane. 'But if you can't tell me, tell me about the Tunnellers instead.'

'Well,' began the young man. He explained that they were in a country called Kloffus. Some years before, Kloffus had been invaded by its much larger neighbour, Klofron. Many people had been killed and soon the little country had been defeated. However, Kloffus had not given up. After the final battle most of the population had retreated to the gold and silver mines, of which there were a great many, mostly dug deep into the mountains. Since then they had spent their time tunnelling, and now almost the whole of Kloffus, or rather the whole of the underneath of Kloffus, was full of tunnels. When the people of Kloffus felt themselves strong enough they would break out and recapture their country for themselves. The Klofrons, of course, knew that some tunnels existed but they had no idea how many, or where.

'And that's just the trouble,' ended the young man, 'because my job is planning where tunnels should be. When I was captured I had a map of a whole new area of tunnels in the south. It was in code, naturally, but they will soon find out what it means and then we shall have to fill in about forty miles of brand new tunnel and start again.'

'Well, we'd better go back now and try and find the map,' said Jane.

'Yes, but not alone,' said the young man. 'The prison is too well guarded.' He stood up and pulled Jane to her feet. 'I'm almost sure,' he said, 'that near here is a tunnel entrance. Look for a clump of bramble bushes on a little hillock.'

It was very dark now, and as they searched they kept on stumbling. In the end they discovered it among some gorse bushes.

'*Gorse*,' said the young man, as he poked about. 'Of course. I'm afraid the entrance will be very small, but it will only be for a few yards.'

It *was* very small. When he pointed the torch, Jane thought it looked no larger than a big rabbit-hole, but before she could suggest widening it the young man had knelt down, pushed aside some pieces of gorse, and disappeared.

Inside it smelt of earth. She could see nothing and could only just breathe. From ahead came the noise of the young man scrabbling and occasionally a muffled 'ouch' as his bad arm brushed the walls. Suddenly she saw the light of the torch again and almost at once the tunnel widened above and around her. The young man was waiting for her.

'We've joined the main junction tunnel to Mahmelg, the capital,' he said. 'And that means—yes. Look over there.' He pointed to their right and Jane saw that stretching away into the darkness were several rows of narrow railway lines. On two of these was something like a long steel sausage.

'A tunnel car,' said the young man. 'Come on, climb in.'

There were two seats, one behind the other, covered in soft rubber and very comfortable. The moment they were in, the young man said, 'Ready?'

'Yes,' said Jane.

'Hold tight,' said the young man. There was a loud swooshing noise, and Jane was pressed back into the rubber cushions. As the sausage shot forward a single headlight lit up the tunnel down which they raced.

It was a long journey, but Jane remembered little of it. Now that they were at last safe she suddenly felt very tired. The gentle swooping motion of the tunnel car as it went up and down, the faint hum of its engine, soon lulled her into a deep sleep. She was asleep when the car stopped, she slept through the amazed greetings of the young man's fellow-Tunnellers, and still asleep she was lifted out, and put into a large soft bed in the chambers of the Chief of the Tunnellers himself. She did not even wake when his kind wife undressed her and wrapped her in a shawl.

'We must recapture the plans as quickly as possible.' It was the Chief of the Tunnellers speaking, a large man with a round, kind face and yellow beard. Jane had been woken by his wife, who had brought her breakfast in bed. After Jane had finished it, the woman had said that if she felt rested would she get up and go to the meeting being held to discuss the loss of the plans. When Jane had arrived at the conference room—cut, like all the rooms, out of the solid rock—she had been introduced to the Chief of the Tunnellers, who had shaken her by the hand and said 'Well done, my girl.'

Also in the room were about five other men and her nice young man. He was dressed in a handsome purple uniform like everyone else, but his arm was in a sling and he still looked rather white. He was lying on a low couch and when he saw Jane he gave a grin and waved to her to come and sit beside him.

'Sit beside me,' he whispered. 'I've told them all how brave you were and the Chief wants to give you a medal.'

'As I was saying,' said the Chief, 'the sooner we get the plans the better. How long would it take them to understand our code, Kronin?'

'About two days, sir,' said the young man.

('Kronin,' thought Jane, 'so that's his name. I must remember to tell him mine.')

'We must attack tonight,' said the Chief. 'Now, what method?'

'I suggest, sir,' said one of the other men, 'that we enter by the same tunnel which Kronin escaped from.'

'Excellent idea,' said the Chief. 'Can you remember it, Kronin?'

'Certainly, sir,' said the young man.

'I'm afraid there can be no question of Kronin leading such an expedition tonight,' said a tall, distinguished looking man sitting on Jane's right. 'His wound is septic and will almost certainly lead to a fever.'

There was a pause, then the Chief said, 'I see, doctor. You're quite sure of that?'

'Of course I can do it,' said Kronin furiously, 'I'm perfectly all right. Look,' and sitting up he waved his wounded arm at the company. But the pain was too great. He turned even whiter, beads of sweat appeared on his forehead, and with a groan he fell back into the cushion in a faint.

'You see?' said the doctor, getting up and moving to his patient. 'The bullet has shattered his bone. I absolutely forbid it.' He felt the young man's forehead, and then, while Jane watched anxiously, signalled to some attendants to carry him out.

'Very well,' said the Chief, 'in that case we will have to think again.' There was a silence while everyone looked at their knees and thought. Then all at once, to her surprise, Jane heard herself saying,

'Excuse me, sir. But I could show you the way. I think I can remember it exactly.' Everyone looked at her and there came a murmur of admiration. Jane blushed. Then a large smile spread across the Chief's face, 'I believe you could,' he said, 'all right then, now let's discuss plans.'

'There is just one thing,' said Jane timidly.

'Yes, my dear?' said the Chief.

'You don't think that the green men may have found out we escaped and be guarding the tunnel and kill us all when we appear?'

'They may,' said the Chief, 'but it's a risk we'll have to take. The Castle is too strong to attack from outside and we haven't time to dig a new tunnel.'

The rest of the morning was spent in planning the attack, which was to be guided by Jane. She had been given the rank of Colonel for the occasion.

They set off at eleven o'clock that night. First went the Chief and Jane, followed by one hundred and fifty soldiers in fifteen of the largest tunnel cars. Jane had been given a revolver, which she had strapped round her waist. The tunnel cars travelled at enormous speed, and soon they were all gathered round the tree shaped like a question mark. All the Tunnellers leapt out and began to change the wheels, putting on soft rubber ones so as to make no noise on the road.

The Tunnellers' cars went almost as fast above ground as they had on their lines beneath it, and it did not take long to reach the fiat space halfway up the mountain where Jane and the young man Kronin had first seen the enemy. Jane guided them to the tunnel and then the Chief took charge.

'I shall go first,' he said in a quiet voice, 'followed by Colonel Jane. I should like Captain Crispin to bring up the rear.'

Up and up and up. Jane wondered if she could ask the Chief to carry her but decided it was not the kind of thing a Colonel could do. Behind her came the steady tramp, tramp, tramp of three hundred feet. After two hours, Jane and the Chief were standing in the empty cell from which she and Kronin had escaped only the day before. The Chief went and shook the door.

'Too strong to break,' he said, 'call for the Lock Picker.'

'Lock Picker, Lock Picker, Lock Picker!' Before long a fat little man with red hair was pushed panting up through the hole in the bed. He had a large leather bag in his hands in which Jane saw, when she came closer, lots of different sized hairpins. After looking at the lock for a few moments he selected one of these and began twirling it in the keyhole. 'Good man,' said the Chief.

After a few minutes there was a soft click from the door and it swung open. At once Jane and the Chief hurried through and then stood on one side and let the soldiers stream past them. To every third soldier the Chief whispered instructions and then in groups of three they ran off in different directions. In ten minutes the last of the one hundred and fifty had run off into the darkness and then, before she could ask him what she should do, the Chief disappeared too.

Before long the Castle was in confusion. Lights were switched on and switched off. The air filled with shouts and shots and the sound of running feet. And as she hurried along the corridors, Jane would have to jump behind doors to avoid angry groups of men racing past after one another, or fling herself flat on her face as bullets went whizzing above her head. Several times she passed rooms full of green-uniformed men tied tightly hand and foot and gagged with torn pieces of sheet.

She had just passed one of these rooms and was creeping down some steps some way away from the main fighting, when all at once the lights went out again. Jane stood quite still, then very softly began to tiptoe on down the steps. After each step she stopped to listen, but now even the sound of the firing and shouting had died away. One step—stop; one step—stop; one step—stop; she had reached the bottom and was about to feel her way forward, when suddenly an arm shot out of the darkness and she felt herself seized and lifted off the ground. The arm closed round her neck, another gripped her stomach and a deep voice hissed into her ear 'Don't struggle or I'll kill you.' At the same time the lights went on again.

She found herself looking into a huge red face, with a thick red beard. Out of the beard came great hot breaths smelling of onions and wine and rotten meat. 'Well, well, well,' said Major Wilkinson (for it was he). 'Well, if it isn't a little girl. Well if *that's* all we're fighting, an army of little girls, there's nothing to worry about.'

'Put me down, you filthy beast,' said Jane.

Major Wilkinson squeezed her neck and then moving his arm from around her stomach gave her hair a sharp tug. 'Don't you "filthy beast" me, you brat,' he said.

Pulling her hair always made Jane furious. 'Put me down *now*,' she said, 'your breath smells disgusting, revolting, ough!'

Major Wilkinson's face grew redder than ever and he began to squeeze her so hard that Jane thought he might be going to squeeze her to death. But just then the sound of firing broke out in the distance and at once he tucked her roughly under his arm and set off at a run down the corridor. 'I haven't time to bandy words with you,' he said. 'I'll either have to kill you or lock you up.'

He ran on for some time, with Jane jolting uncomfortably up and down on his belt, when all of a sudden he stopped outside a door, pulled a key out of his pocket, unlocked it and threw her in. As she fell through the air she heard him lock the door and shout 'No one will look in here, you brat. I hope you break your legs.'

She must have fallen about twenty feet, but she landed on a large pile of something quite soft and soon she sat up and slid off the pile onto the floor. Then she took her torch out of her satchel.

She was in a high, small room with the door right at the top under the ceiling. She at once saw how lucky she was not to have been badly hurt, because the stone floor was quite bare except for a pile of what looked like sails, made from some red material, neatly heaped in the middle. The room was high for a purpose, because hanging on all the walls were long, thin pieces of wood and hundreds of strings and cords and wires. Nailed to one of the walls was a piece of cardboard with 'LOOK OUT KITES, LIFTING WEIGHT 5 STONES *ONLY*' printed on it.

Jane did not look round for long. Still furious at having her hair pulled, she dashed up the steps determined to catch Major Wilkinson. The door was locked, but taking out her revolver she put it close to the key hole, closed her eyes, and pulled the trigger. There was a fearful explosion, the gun jumped violently in her hands, but when she opened her eyes the lock had been completely shot away and the door opened the moment she pushed it.

Once in the corridor she set off at a run to the left, guessing that Major Wilkinson would hardly have gone back the way he had come.

She needn't have hurried. When he had re-locked the door, Major Wilkinson had walked very carefully, stopping every few steps to listen. Jane had run down the corridor and one flight of stairs when she came to a long straight passage. At its far end, creeping close to the wall, she saw the green back and vast green bottom of her enemy.

'Stop!' she said, 'stop, you disgusting, cruel, beastly man!' Then closing her eyes again, and clasping her revolver in both hands she once more pulled the trigger and once more felt the gun leap and crash.

When she opened her eyes a little cloud of smoke was drifting away. Her arms ached. And at the far end of the passage Major Wilkinson lay stretched upon the floor.

At once Jane was filled with horror. 'Oh dear, I've killed him,' she cried; 'oh how awful, how awful.' And throwing the gun away she ran as fast as she could to the motionless figure.

But, in fact, Major Wilkinson was almost all right, When Jane had pulled the trigger the gun had been pointing at the ceiling and the bullet had hit first this, bounced to the floor, bounced back to the ceiling, and had gone on from floor to ceiling, ceiling to floor until finally, moving now hardly any faster than a stone from a catapult, it had bounced off the ceiling onto the top of Major Wilkinson's head and so knocked him out. When Jane reached him a large bruise as big as her fist was swelling from the middle of his head. She had not looked at this for more than a moment when suddenly three Tunnellers appeared round the corner. These promised Jane (whom they respectfully saluted) that they would tie up the Major and take him to the other prisoners.

'How's the battle going?' asked Jane.

'Very well, Colonel,' said one of the men, 'but it takes a little time to winkle the devils out.'

In fact it took until seven o'clock in the morning. By that time the last of the Klofrons had been placed under guard. What was more, the Plan of the Tunnels had been found locked in a box in Major Wilkinson's office. It was clear, from marks on it, that the Klofrons had not yet succeeded in discovering the code.

Now everyone was drawn up on the roof of the Castle. Tired, many of them bruised and battered, they all looked happy in the light of the rising sun.

'Gentlemen,' said the Chief, 'brave soldiers of the Tunnel, I am very proud of you. But before we return underground, I want to single out one of our number for special praise. And that is our new young Colonel here.' So saying, he laid his hand on Jane's shoulder and gently brought her forward. Immediately the air was filled with cries of 'Hear, hear!' and 'Bravo!' Jane blushed and looked at her feet.

'But for her,' went on the Chief in his embarrassing but kind way, 'our venture could never have succeeded. It was she who boldly guided us to the secret entrance and she who captured, single-handed, the chief officer of this prison, the notorious and evil Major Wilkinson. I have decided to reward such bravery with the highest reward we Tunnellers possess—namely the Order of the Golden Epans. Step forward, Colonel!'

At this speech, renewed cheering broke out and several men lifted Jane upon their shoulders and carried her towards the Chief. He was smiling broadly and holding in his hands the magnificent scrolls and ribbons of the Order of the Golden Epans.

But before he could pin it to her shirt, there came a loud shout and bursting through the door which led back into the Castle, his face white, his arm still in a sling, ran the young man Kronin.

'For God's sake, Chief,' he cried, 'we must fly. All may be lost.'

Immediately an excited murmuring broke out among the men and the three holding Jane put her down. The Chief held up his hand. 'Be quiet,' he cried, then, 'now what's all this about, Kronin? And why are you not in bed?'

'Just after you left,' Kronin said, 'I woke up feeling much better. I stayed in bed till six o'clock this morning and then I took a spare tunnel car and drove it up here. Imagine my surprise when I found, at the entrance to the passage, over two hundred Klofrons gathered round it in the very act of entering. I immediately charged them with my car and managed to scatter them. Then I blocked the hole with my car and hurried up here to warn you.'

At once the Chief began giving orders. 'Good Kronin,' he said, 'you have done well. 'Captain Crispin,' he added, 'take ten men and some gunpowder and go and block the tunnel into the cell before the Klofrons succeed in moving Kronin's car. Sergeant Trindle, double the guard on the prisoners.' The Chief then walked to the edge of the roof, followed by Jane and Kronin and looked over. After a moment she heard him mutter, 'As I feared.'

Looking down, she saw why. Already the bare ground at the foot of the Castle was swarming with hundreds of Klofrons. And every moment more and more of them scrambled up over the steep sides of the mountain.

'We must get help,' said the Chief, 'give me a signalling pistol, someone.' At once a soldier handed him a short pistol with a huge fat barrel big enough to hold a cream bun. Into this the Chief put a large round bullet, which indeed looked rather like a cream bun, pointed it above his head and pulled the trigger. Immediately the bullet shot upwards and burst into a small red cloud high in the air above them. Five times the Chief did this and each time looked anxiously out over the valley. At last he said, 'It's no good. We're too low.'

'What are you doing?' said Jane, unable any longer to control her curiosity.

'Look over there,' said the Chief and pointed across the valley. Jane looked, and saw that he was pointing to the distant mountains which rose beyond it. High as they were in the Castle, the mountains were far higher, and in the early morning sun she could see great stretches of snow glistening on their mighty peaks. 'Among those mountains are our main look-out points,' said the Chief. 'If any of us want help when we are out of our tunnels, we fire one of these red bullets and at once a tunnel is dug to the place where the bullet has been fired from. Unfortunately this Castle is so placed that another mountain is between us and the look-out points. If we were higher it would be all right.'

It was then that Jane had the idea which nearly cost her her life.

'Quick,' she said, 'come with me.' In a few moments she had brought him to the room into which Major Wilkinson had flung her. She opened the door, turned on the lights and pointed excitedly to the notice on the wall. 'There,' she said, 'isn't that the answer?'

The Chief looked at the notice in amazement. 'Goodness me,' he said at last, 'enormous man-lifting kites.' Then his face fell, 'but they can only carry five stone,' he said, 'and none of us is as light as that.'

'Yes they *are*,' said Jane, her heart beating.

'Who?' asked the Chief, 'I weigh fifteen stone.'

'Me,' said Jane. A gasp of admiration came from Kronin and from the little group which had followed them down from the roof. And the Chief himself seized her by the hand and gave it a hard squeeze, saying, 'Brave girl. It's what I would expect from a winner of the Golden Epans.'

After that all was bustle. Ropes and struts of wood were seized from the walls and huge stretches of the tough red material were unfolded on the floor. Soon the largest kite that Jane had ever seen was standing on the roof. It was fifteen feet high and ten feet across, and in the middle, among the stout wooden struts, was a small chair. 'For me,' thought Jane nervously.

But there was no time to be afraid. The Chief pressed a signal revolver into her hand and three round bullets, explaining how it worked. 'Don't fire it until you see me fire one from down here he said. 'That will mean you are as high as we can get you. And don't worry. These kites are very safe.' Then he suddenly bent forward, picked her up and kissed her. The young man Kronin did the same, and Jane saw tears in his blue eyes. 'Good luck, little girl,' he whispered.

Jane thought 'I haven't told him my name,' and then they were helping her into the seat. She shut her eyes and gripped the arms of the chair.

'One—two—three – NOW!' shouted the Chief, and at *now* ten men bent their backs and with one heave hurled the kite high into the air. For a moment it was motionless, and everyone wondered if it would crash back onto the roof. Then the wind caught it, blew it sharply across to the right, and the next instant it was soaring up into the sky, pulling the rope after it and shuddering a little to the buffets of the air.

Jane kept her eyes tight shut and held her breath. She felt she was going up in the fastest and most unsafe lift in the world. There was a roaring in her ears and her hair was blown in all directions at once. But gradually the upward rush of the kite became slower, the shuddering less violent, and she felt able to look about her.

The view was terrifying but wonderful. Away to her right rose peak after peak of the distant mountains; to her left was a vast plain with a tiny blue line at its end which must have been the sea; and below her feet, no bigger now than a teacup, was the Castle, with the thick black rope rising from its roof. This rope was quite tight and Jane could hear a deep humming as it vibrated in the wind. As she looked down a large white bird flew between her and the ground, brushing the rope with its wing tips.

Just after it had passed, there came a tiny puff of smoke from the Castle and a small red cloud appeared about sixty feet below her. Immediately, Jane took the signal pistol in both hands, pointed it up through the top of the kite and pulled the trigger. Far above her a little red cloud blossomed in the sky. But when she looked across the valley to the mountains there came no answering signal. Nor was there any after the second. And when the third red cloud had been blown away and there was still no sign, she was about to drop the pistol in despair, when all at once, from the top of one of the distant, though not the highest peaks, there rose a slender column of green smoke. The signal! And they had seen it from the Castle. Looking down, Jane could just see tiny figures jumping about and running around the roof with excitement.

It was at this moment that disaster struck the kite. The Klofron soldiers had watched its rise into the sky with amazement. 'Surely,' they thought, 'no one expects to escape by kite.' But when the little red signal clouds began to puff above it they guessed that the Tunnellers were calling for help and at once began to fire their rifles and revolvers, hoping to bring it down or kill the person in it. The kite was far too high for any of their bullets to reach it, but just as the Chief was ordering it to be pulled in again, a stray bullet hit the rope and with a twang cut clean through it.

At once the kite gave a fearful lurch and started to plunge downwards. There came a groan of horror from the watchers on the Castle and a cheer of triumph from the Klofrons. Jane was flung forward and only saved herself by dropping the pistol and clinging with both hands to the wooden seat.

But the wind so high in the sky was very strong indeed and the rope still dangling from the bottom of the kite was very heavy. After falling for a few seconds, the kite was suddenly seized by an extra powerful blast of wind and in a moment was soaring up into the air again, carried in its gusty arms. The Castle was so far below that she could hardly see it. A little group of white clouds appeared on her left and then seemed to float downwards as she sped up past them. Now she was level with the tops of the highest mountains, now rising above them. 'Perhaps I'll be blown to the moon,' thought Jane, beginning to enjoy herself even though she felt frightened, 'or Mars.'

But the higher it rose, the stronger blew the wind. It deafened Jane with its roaring and made it difficult to breathe. And as she watched, one of the smaller struts broke with a snap and was instantly whirled away. And then another, and another, and then the wind caught a strip of red material and tore it off with a great ripping noise. And suddenly, with a loud cracking of wood and a flapping of stuff, the whole kite was torn into shreds as though by a giant claw, and Jane was flung out into the air and began, with terrifying speed, to fall back towards the earth, turning over and over, head over heels, down through miles of empty sky.

'I shall be smashed to pieces,' she thought, as a cloud rushed past, 'I shall bounce and bounce and bounce,' as she shot down level with the tops of the mountains. 'Perhaps I'll land in a deep river,' she said as a startled bird flew out of her way.

And then, as the ground came racing up to her, as she saw now trees now clouds in her spinning fall, she suddenly remembered the piece of paper she had found in the Book so long before and had stuffed into the pocket of her jeans. In a moment she had pulled it out, in a moment opened it and held it to her face, and just before she hit the ground, when she could actually see the rocks and stones and little bushes of the hillside rushing towards her, she cried at the top of her voice:

'TURN AGAIN, OH BOOK NOW TURN,
BACK THROUGH YOUR PAGES I RETURN.'

Her fall was checked. The air around her turned milky and felt more and more like cotton wool. And she started to rise upwards almost as fast as she had just been falling. She was saved.

3. The Flood

AT ONCE Jane guessed what had happened. And when she sat up she found, as she had expected, that she was sitting on the open Book in the old library. It was night, but there was enough light from the moon for her to see the high bookshelves, the desk and the library steps. She could also just see, when she looked down between her knees, that the picture of Kronin in his cell was no longer there. The page on which she sat was completely blank.

It did not take her long to climb out of the library, and hurry back to the vacuum cleaner. She pressed the starting button, turned on the headlights specially put in by Lord Charrington so that Mrs Deal could do the carpets at night and was soon whirring down the mile-long corridor. She had almost reached the end, when all at once she saw in the headlights an enormous pool of water. Before she could brake, the cleaner raced into the middle, sending great waves whooshing up the wall on either side, and came to a spluttering stop.

For some moments Jane sat doing nothing, amazed. It was completely dark, because the lights of the cleaner had gone out when the engine stopped. In the silence she could now hear the gulping and swirling of water as though the Castle were slowly sinking into a lake. What could have happened? Perhaps Mrs Deal had left all the baths on by mistake. 'MRS DEAL,' she shouted, MRS DEAL, WHERE ARE YOU?' But there was no answer.

'I shall have to wade,' thought Jane. She took off one shoe and sock and dipped her toe in. Luckily the water was only a few inches deep, so she took off the other shoe and sock, rolled up her jeans and, shining the torch ahead, set off. Under the water the carpet felt cold and furry, like stiff moss.

Quite soon she came to the place where all the corridors on the first floor joined a large landing running round the front hall. It was light here from the moon, so Jane turned off her torch and moved over to the balcony, hoping to feel her way to the main stairs.

But at the balcony she saw the most extraordinary sight. Instead of stopping at the edge, the water on the landing continued straight on. The entire hall was filled with water. That meant, thought Jane, that the kitchens must be flooded, and the drawing-rooms, dining-rooms, sitting-rooms, cellars, even, perhaps, the gardens, the whole valley. And as her eyes grew accustomed to the moonlight she could see floating on the water a fleet of familiar objects: Lord Charrington's wooden shoe-trees, a sofa, lamps, chests, tennis rackets, a tea cup, tables and, suddenly, Mrs Deal's Wellington boots.

At the sight of the boots Jane began to feel frightened. What had happened? Where was Mrs Deal? Was she drowned? And then, tired, alone, cold, wet, hungry, Jane began to cry. 'Mrs Deal,' she sobbed, 'Mummy, Daddy, where are you? What shall I do? Help me, help me, help.' But again there came no answer except the gentle swish of the dark water and the bumping sound as bits of floating furniture knocked together in the hall.

It was at this moment that a door opened just behind her and a bright light shone out. At the same time a well known voice said, 'Is that you, Lady Jane? Goodness me, whatever have you been doing? I found a vacuum cleaner missing and you know your father doesn't allow jaunts on the cleaners.'

'Mrs Deal!' cried Jane. 'Oh darling Mrs Deal,' and splashing across the carpet she flung herself into Mrs Deal's arms. 'Oh Mrs Deal, I saw your gumboots and I thought you'd been drowned.'

'There, there,' said Mrs Deal, 'there, there, you know quite well I'd never let myself be drowned, you silly gumption.' But encumbered though she was by a hissing hurricane lamp, she swung her arms round Jane and lifted the little girl up to give her a dry, gentle kiss. 'Stop your crying,' she said, 'all's well that ends well. And now up you come to the nursery floor. The water is still rising and we'd best get you some supper.'

When they reached the nursery, Mrs Deal pulled off Lord Charrington's duck-shooting waders which she was wearing and, while she dried Jane in front of the fire, explained what had happened.

Apparently the little dam at Combe Reservoir had broken on

Wednesday night and the waters had at once rushed into Curl Valley and flooded it. Luckily it was only the small reservoir and the Authorities said the water would go down in a few days. 'They offered to take me off,' said Mrs Deal, 'but I refused. I've telegrammed your father and asked for instructions. Now you, my girl, must have something to eat and then off to bed.'

Jane had some bacon and eggs and then Mrs Deal gave her a wash and tucked her up. However, before Mrs Deal blew out the candle, they had one small argument. She was folding up Jane's jeans when a small, flat object dropped to the floor.

'What's this,' said Mrs Deal, picking it up.

'A bullet,' said Jane.

'Nonsense,' said Mrs Deal, 'a bullet in Curl Castle indeed.'

'It's my bullet,' said Jane, 'and please give it to me.'

'Certainly you may have it,' said Mrs Deal, 'but a bullet it is not.' She looked at it a moment and then, smiling down in a kindly grown-up way, gave it back. 'I would say it was dentist's filling from a particularly large tooth,' she said; 'probably from your grand mother, old Lady Dorothy Charrington, who was famous for the size of her teeth. Yes,' she finished, 'that's what it is. A large filling from one of the largest of old Lady Charrington's lovely back teeth.' And bending down Mrs Deal kissed Jane softly and dryly goodnight.

In the morning they had a breakfast of baked beans and eggs, and tea with condensed milk. Mrs Deal had managed to move nearly all the food from the store room into the nursery before the ground floor was flooded and now about four hundred tins were neatly piled there. There were also some bottles of wine which, Mrs Deal explained, they might need for medicinal purposes. Mrs Deal had also rescued a primus stove and plenty of paraffin.

When Jane looked out of the nursery windows, the hot sun was shining onto the gleaming water which stretched all round them to the curvy hills of the little valley. Everywhere, most of their trunks out of sight under the water, the tops of the trees stuck up like vast floating bushes. She could see the ropes of her swing, which was hung from a high branch of a cedar on the lawn, suddenly disappearing under the surface and when she looked down at the drive underneath the window she could see the dim wavery black outline of a car standing at the front door, completely covered by water.

During breakfast they discussed plans.

'The water has been rising,' said Mrs Deal. 'I don't know what we should do, I'm sure. Still no word from your father.'

'We must rescue things,' said Jane. 'First precious things like pictures and all the tables and then things like blankets and food and nails and gunpowder. No,' she went on, 'perhaps the gunpowder and the nails and things first. We may be here for weeks or months or even years. Have we any weapons for killing food, etc.?'

'Weapons my foot,' said Mrs Deal briskly. 'Luckily the telephone is still working and I rang the Post Office this morning. They said the water should be going down by this evening. You've got too much imagination, my girl. But some of the nice Chippendale we ought to carry out of harm's way, and all the pictures.'

Jane's first move was to the summer room, where were stored all the games and fishing nets and flippers she played with in the summer. Here she found two Li-Lo's and a rubber dinghy. She blew them all up, tied them together, and then started up the corridor, towing behind her a bobbing convoy whose rubber colours were bright in the morning sun.

She would tie her fleet outside a room, wade in and carry out whatever seemed valuable and pile it onto the Li-Lo's and into the dinghy. Then she would slowly drag the whole load back and heap it at the bottom of the nursery stairs so that Mrs Deal could help her drag it up.

After a quick lunch of potted shrimps, ham, mashed potatoes and tinned peaches and condensed milk, they continued their work.

Jane, however, soon grew tired of collecting furniture and pictures. Not only was it very hard work, but also there was so much left in the myriad rooms, galleries and cupboards and bathrooms of the first floor that it seemed quite pointless to continue. Without telling Mrs Deal, therefore—who was in any case far out of sight and sound in the distant East Wings of the Castle—she set out to gather more practical objects.

First she went to Lord Charrington's gun room and loaded a Li-Lo with cartridges and guns. Having stored these in her nursery cupboard she went to the Forestry room. Here her father stored the ropes, axes, choppers, cutters, nails, etc., which were needed for all the work on the estate. Nearly all of these Jane took and locked in her toy cupboard, which was very large. She also took eighteen large, sealed tins of best quality gunpowder. This her father used for blowing tree stumps out of the ground. The tins were very heavy and only three could be safely loaded into the rubber dinghy at a time. And from her father's study she collected three bottles of gin and put them in the toy cupboard. Mrs Deal's plan of medicinal wine was sensible, but Jane felt that for a real emergency spirits might be needed.

And all the time the water rose. Inch by inch it climbed until the bottom, then the second, then the third of the wide nursery stairs were covered. It loosened the wallpaper from the walls so that it floated out in a broad frieze, like curiously coloured seaweed. First it came to Jane's knees, then her thighs and finally her last trips had to be made sitting in the dinghy, pushing aside, as she went, the chairs and tables which had floated out of the rooms and were making aimless, slowly twirling journeys by themselves down the flooded corridors.

It was late evening when Jane decided that she had done enough. She made a last visit to the Forestry room and loaded up with some more gunpowder and a large box of wind-and-rain-proof matches. From everywhere came the sound of gently bumping furniture as sluggish currents moved it about, a steady dripping and running and sucking noise, and all along the walls and ceilings there was the flickering reflection of the evening sun off the water.

Jane steered round a waterlogged sofa, and turned the corner into the last bit of corridor before the nursery stairs. As she did so she heard Mrs Deal calling:

'Lady Jane? Lady Jane? I need help. Please come and help me. Lady Ja-a-a-a-nne.'

'Coming, Mrs Deal,' shouted Jane, and began to paddle the heavily weighted dinghy as hard as she could. 'Coming.'

As she came out of the corridor onto the landing round the main hall she saw the most odd sight. Across the other side of the hallway, and a quarter way up the nursery stairs, Mrs Deal had propped herself against the banisters. Above her, and held in place by her thin, straining shoulders, was a vast grand piano. By some miracle of wedging and shoving she had managed to push it well clear of the water. Now, defeated by its immense weight, she could go no further, and was only just able to keep it in place.

Jane paddled towards her. 'What are you doing, Mrs Deal?' she called. 'We'll never get that up the stairs. Let it slide back.'

'We can't,' panted Mrs Deal, 'your mother's favourite Steinway. Ruin the keys. Just get it a little higher then we can tie it out of harm's way.'

'But it's huge,' said Jane.

'It's slipping,' said Mrs Deal suddenly, in a weak voice.

'I'm coming,' said Jane, paddling as hard as she could. 'Hold on.'

But she was too late. Even as she watched, the piano, with a tiny twang from its strings, began to move. 'Oh dear,' panted Mrs Deal, forced down a step. 'Twang' went the piano. 'Oh dear,' cried Mrs Deal. And then, before Jane's horrified eyes, the piano began to bump noisily down the stairs, faster and faster, its strings jingling and jangling and tingling, sweeping Mrs Deal irresistibly before it, until with a final ringing of disorganized chords it surged into the water and floated swiftly out into the middle of the hall, where it spun slowly round and round, bobbing gently. Of Mrs Deal, there was no sign.

'Mrs Deal, Mrs Deal,' cried Jane. 'Where are you?'

She need not have worried. When the piano swept into the water and through the balcony, Mrs Deal was carried with it, clinging to the keyboard. Once in deeper waters, she let go and at once sank to the bottom, dragged down by the weight of Lord Charrington's rubber waders. Now, peering down into the still clear depths, Jane saw her shake these off and in a few moments rise to the surface not far from the piano and swim energetically to the gap in the balcony.

'Are you all right, Mrs Deal?' said Jane, paddling up to her. 'I thought you'd gone to a watery grave.'

'Nonsense,' said Mrs Deal, 'ever since a girl I've been a good swimmer. What a lot of trouble this water's giving us—and the mess!' As she spoke, she twisted the long tresses of grey hair that hung round her shoulders from her undone bun. 'Now up we go,' she said, 'it's dry clothes for me and a good hot supper and bed for you.'

Jane waited until Mrs Deal was changing her clothes, then hurried down to carry up the rest of the gun powder and hide it in her toy cupboard. She also dragged the dinghy up and left it outside the nursery door, just in case.

They were both tired, and after a dinner of chicken, tinned peas, and condensed milk, they went to bed. Though it was not enough of an emergency to reveal the gin, Jane suggested Mrs Deal have some glasses of medicinal wine. This she did.

As she fell asleep, Jane found herself wondering if she would ever have another adventure in the Book. She decided that, if the waters went on rising, she would go to the tower next day and just make sure it was, as she thought, really one of the highest in the Castle and so quite safe.

She was woken at six o'clock by the early morning sun shining onto her face. She lay sleepily for a while, and then all at once decided it would be more fun to get up and go for a quiet paddle in the dinghy before Mrs Deal was awake.

At once she sat up, put on her dressing-gown, swung her legs over the bed and—*felt water*. Water! An inch deep all over the nursery floor, water gently creeping higher and higher through the night, filling the house, burying them—water! Jane seized her boots and splashed over to the door. Once more she saw a flooded corridor, the round rubber dinghy floating some way down it. She hurried back and opened the window. It was true. The water had silently risen a whole storey during the night; in the distance, only the very tops of the trees now waved above the surface.

At once, all was bustle. She woke up Mrs Deal who, without even waiting to take her hair out of curlers, rose magnificently to the occasion. 'First we must have breakfast,' she said, 'then carry as much as we can up to the roof. There's no telling where this will end.' Jane agreed.

They both dressed; had a quick breakfast of boiled eggs and tea; and then started to carry essential provisions up to the roof.

It was after the second of these journeys, when they were in the nursery loading their arms with tins and blankets, that the sudden chugg-chugg-chugg of an engine made them both hurry to the window.

Out in front of the Castle, steering between the tussocks, which was all that remained of the tall trees on either side of the main gates, a small motor boat was speeding towards them.

'Ahoy!' shouted Jane. 'Ah-o-o-y, ahoy!' The young man who was driving swung his motor boat round and stopped just under the nursery window.

'Good morning,' said Jane, 'what's happened?'

'Cracks has appeared in the big dam at Combe,' said the young man, 'been a lot of big leaks. But they say she'll hold. I've been sent to take you off of here. And I've a telegram for Mrs Deal.'

'Oh dear, where are my spectacles?' said Mrs Deal, fussing in her apron pockets. 'That will be your father. Now give me the telegram, young man.' He rocked his boat close to them and handed over the yellow envelope. Mrs Deal tore it open and together they read:

'Stand fast. Report position. Full instructions following. Charrington.'

'Well, that's that,' said Mrs Deal. 'I'm afraid we can't come with you, young man. There's far too much to do here, as his Lordship knows.'

'But I've particular orders,' said the young man in a worried voice; 'I was told "rescue all inmates of the Castle".'

'Only people who are in trouble need rescuing,' said Jane, 'and we are not in trouble. We will stay in the Gazebo on the roof till the waters go down. And my father quite agrees.'

'I only take instructions from Lord Charrington,' said Mrs Deal; 'or Lady Charrington,' she added.

'Or me,' said Jane.

'Now then, my girl,' said Mrs Deal.

'Well I don't know,' said the young man, 'I've had me orders. But they say the dam will hold. I think I'll go back and if it looks any worse come straight back. Well cheerio. Mind you stay on the roof.' And with a wave of his hand, he turned the motor boat and went roaring straight as an arrow over the fountain, between the topmost leaves of the gate trees and was soon gone.

They had little time to worry about his departure. The noise of the cracking of the big dam spurred them on, and soon the pile of tins and blankets, beds and bottles began to fill the eight-sided Gazebo on the roof.

By twelve o'clock they had carried up almost more than the Gazebo could hold.

'Now you run along and play awhile,' said Mrs Deal at last, 'and I'll get this lot sorted out. No sliding on the slates, mind. We don't want the rain getting in.'

Jane, however, had other plans. She hurried down the stairs again and went straight to the toy cupboard. The water on the nursery floor had now risen above her knees, but she had been careful to put the tins of gunpowder, the wind-proof matches and the gin on a top shelf.

It took twelve journeys to carry them up and hide them in a small wooden shed where the Castle chimney sweep kept his brushes and rods. It was well out of sight of the Gazebo, but Mrs Deal had already begun dusting and Jane could have driven an elephant across the roof without her noticing it.

When she had carried everything up, she went down one last time to get the dinghy. It had floated all the way down the corridor and was now gently bobbing about at the far end. Jane squelched up to it over the spongy carpet, swung it round and was about to return, when all at once she heard a distant rumble, at the same time the water in the corridor surged up her legs and then fell back, as though the Castle had been tilted. Nervously she looked back over her shoulder out of the window. And there she saw a sight so frightening that, as she afterwards said, terror turned her knees to jelly.

Not half a mile away, where Curl Valley opened out into the wider Inkpen valley, a great grey cliff, seeming hundreds of feet high, its mile-long top sparkling and breaking in the sun, was racing towards the Castle. And as it came, hurtling ever faster, its rumbling grew to a roar, its roar to the rocky bellows of the most terrible earthquake, and the walls and ceilings and floating furniture and Jane herself began to jump and tremble as though with huge million-ton feet a giant were charging up to crush them into pieces.

The big dam had burst at Combe. As Jane had come down the stairs, a great crack had suddenly leapt from its bottom and shot two hundred feet to its top. As Jane had squelched up the corridor, the main reservoir had begun to burst through and workmen had fled for their lives. And as she had turned to take the dinghy back, the whole dam had crashed to the ground, a mountain of grey, turbulent, angry water had sprung forth and swept irresistibly into Curl Valley.

She just had time to fling herself into the dinghy and take a tight hold of the side ropes, and then the huge wave dashed against the Castle.

The walls stood firm—all except the North Wing, which was instantly washed away. But the windows did not. There was a moment's pause, an inky blackness while the waters whirled outside, and then with a crash a thousand casements broke and the deluge poured in.

The first terrible wave knocked Jane unconscious for a minute. The dinghy was engulfed and pressed down under the weight of water. But in a moment it had bobbed to the top and Jane found herself racing down the corridor on the surface of a deafening river. But it was a river that was rising. From all sides other rivers spouted from the doors of all the rooms, and soon, bouncing off the walls and spinning in the eddies, Jane was speeding along just below the ceiling.

Just before she was crushed against the top, the corridor ended in a short staircase to the floor above. In a flash the dinghy was lifted up it by the surge of water, and then went hurtling down another corridor, bounding round corners, whirling past pictures, which were buried even before she had passed them, and soon was once again just below the ceiling. Jane had to crouch low to avoid the chandeliers, soon she could touch the ceiling, then was forced to lie flat and holding her breath, heard the sound of the dinghy scraping the ceiling as it was driven higher, and felt a cold rush as water was forced over the sides; and then, just as she was expecting to be drowned, there was a loud crash and the dinghy shot forward into darkness and began to rise rapidly upwards.

What had happened was quite simple. The combined weight of water, Jane, branches and furniture had been too much for a thin wall at the end of the corridor on the third floor. It blocked the corridor off from an old staircase which led up to the roof, and when it had broken let Jane and the dinghy shoot through. As the old staircase filled with water, so up rose Jane, carried safely on its surface.

Carried safely, and carried ever more slowly. Because now the worst was over. The waters from the broken dam, sweeping past the Castle to fill the whole valley, had begun to find their proper level, and by luck this was just below the level of the roof. After five minutes Jane found that she had stopped rising and as her eyes grew accustomed to the darkness she saw before her a small door, secured by a simple bolt. She opened it and sunlight streamed in. Before her was the roof, and in a moment she had stepped out onto it and pulled the dinghy out behind her.

4. The Explosion

THE view from the roof was desolate and strange. On all sides the sun-lit waters stretched to the enclosing hills, but now no tree top, no gatepost, chimney or wall poked above their ruffled surface. Only the roof of the Castle, like a vast, strange raft floating on a grey sea, gave comfort to the little girl. The tower which held the old library with the Book rose highest above the surrounding flood. And when Jane walked to the balustrade, she saw that the water whirling only a foot or two below the gutters was black and dirty, thick with branches, pieces of gate and fence, and other more horrid things.

The entrance to the staircase which had so miraculously saved her life was not far from the Gazebo. As she drew close to it, she shouted 'Mrs Deal, Mrs Deal—I'm all right,' and began to look forward to telling about her adventures.

But Mrs Deal had worked herself into a positive frenzy of dusting and cleaning and mopping up, and was far too busy to take any notice. In its first rush the wave, only about sixty feet high despite its terrifying appearance, had swept into the Gazebo. Mrs Deal was now busily mopping it out and at the same time cooking lunch on the primus stove. She had also, Jane was surprised to see, put on several large jerseys, gloves, an overcoat and wrapped three dusters round her neck, even though the sun was shining as hotly as ever outside.

'I've had a *terrible* adventure,' cried Jane, bursting excitedly into the Gazebo.

'I'm sure you have, dear,' said Mrs Deal, speaking calmly and not for a moment stopping her mopping and dusting, 'and I've caught a terrible cold. Now get those wet clothes off, there's enough water about without you adding to it; we must get something warm inside us as soon as this broth has cooked.'

Though Jane felt disappointed at not being able to tell her story, she knew better than to try and talk to Mrs Deal in a dusting mood.

During lunch Mrs Deal's cold grew rapidly and visibly worse. She sneezed a great deal, blew her nose, and began to talk in a thick, hoarse voice. This sudden collapse did not worry Jane. Mrs Deal often 'went down' with something, and soon recovered.

After lunch, however, when Mrs Deal gave five enormous sneezes all in a row, she thought it would be kind to give her some gin. She therefore fetched a bottle from the chimney-sweep's shed and filled a tumbler with the watery liquid. 'Here, Mrs Deal,' she said, 'I think in this emergency you should have some spirits. My father always says they are very good for a cold.' Mrs Deal took the glass gratefully.

'Dank you, my dear,' she said in her new, hoarse voice, 'dat 'ould be very kind.' And spluttering a little, and pausing twice to sneeze and blow her reddening nose, she soon finished it.

'More?' asked Jane.

'No dank 'oo,' said Mrs Deal, coughing, 'dad will do. I'll have some bore ad dea-dime.'

'But what shall we do *now*?' said Jane.

'We mud wait till we are rethcued,' said Mrs Deal mournfully, 'there's nudding for it.'

'But what will my father say?' said Jane. 'Oughtn't we to stick to our post till the water goes down? Why, I think it's a little lower already.'

'Nudding for it,' repeated Mrs Deal, her voice getting slower, 'if we had a plug we could pull it out. But the water will day and day and we can't do nudding. Furniture ruined. We mud wait dill they come wid a boat and a thtretther,' she added, so low that Jane could hardly hear her.

But she wasn't in any case listening. Because when Mrs Deal said 'Plug,' the most wonderful, brilliant, exciting plan had sprung into her head. 'Plug.' *That* was the answer—*pull out the plug*!

Of course, she couldn't tell Mrs Deal. Even ordinarily she would have been most unlikely to agree to Jane's simple but dangerous plan. Now, weakened by her cold, dizzy with gin, she certainly wouldn't. Luckily, however, Mrs Deal had fallen asleep. It was the work of a moment to cover her warmly up with some blankets, and slip outside.

Once there, she became very busy. First she carried the dinghy over to the balustrade, lifted it onto the water, and tied it firmly to the edge.

Next she hurried to the chimney-sweep's shed and one by one carried three tins of gunpowder and lowered them gently into the dinghy. Then she put the wind-and-rain-proof matches in her pocket and wrote a short note to Mrs Deal.

> ' Do not worry. I have gone to blow up mushroom
> tunnel. Back in time for tea or supper. Don't fuss.
> Love, Jane.'

Then she climbed over the balustrade, settled herself in the dinghy and cast off. At once the currents which were still moving in the flood waters caught hold of the dinghy and in a moment it was moving rapidly away from the Castle.

Jane's idea was this. Many years before, her father's great-grandfather, the thirty-second Lord Charrington, had decided to grow mushrooms in Curl Valley and sell them in France. To make this easier he had dug a long tunnel beneath the hills at the end of the valley so that it should join with the sea at the other side. Unfortunately he had died before his scheme could be tried, and the tunnel, because it used to become filled with salt water at high tides, had been blocked up with bricks at the end nearest the sea. It must now, Jane realized, be full of flood water, and if she could blow up the bricks at the sea end then the water would pour out. Just, as Mrs Deal had said, like pulling a plug out of a bath.

But she could already see that it was going to be harder than she had thought. Luckily the currents seemed to be sweeping her towards the far end of the valley. But even then, though she paddled as hard as she could, and though the long rim of Curl Castle roof soon grew small behind her, the distant hills seemed to be no nearer. Jane was strong for her age, but gradually she grew more and more tired. The dinghy began to move slower and slower. The wide grey waters stretched all round her, and, though she knew it was foolish, she suddenly began to imagine strange monsters moving in the trees and fields buried underneath.

Just when she was about to give up in despair, a light breeze sprang up. Soon it freshened to a wind and before long the dinghy was being blown merrily over the small waves with Jane resting against its rubber sides.

Even so, it was four-thirty before, with a gentle thump, she reached the shore. She climbed out, tied the dinghy to a nearby bush, and unloaded the gunpowder.

It took her two hours to carry the three heavy tins, one at a time, to the top of the valley. Two hours which left her boiling hot and exhausted. But reach it she eventually did. Suddenly the hill fell away in front of her and at its foot was the peaceful, sparkling sea. After a while Jane sat up and turned to look down at the valley behind her. This, too, looked peaceful in the slanting rays of the sinking sun. From side to side, from end to end, the waters of Combe Reservoir filled it, making a vast, almost circular lake. Birds glided in the air above it and some landed on it. And these waters had already begun to clear. She could see an oblong, dark patch where the branches of Currel Wood must have been waving in the slow currents; a light patch where the cornfield was; and a wavery, pale ribbon which was the road to Inkpen winding away under the water. Only in the middle, like a huge, irregular tray covered in chimneys, turrets, towers and roofs, the top of the Castle broke the surface.

The downward journey was very much easier and faster than the journey up. Jane reached the bottom in an hour. At half past seven, she was standing before the bricked-up entrance to the tunnel.

The mushroom tunnel was nine feet high and ten feet wide, and the bricks blocking it had been built five feet thick to withstand the batterings of the winter storms. But in the very middle at the bottom, where some bricks had crumbled away, the sea had scooped out a small, smooth cave, about two feet deep.

Into this Jane pushed her way, shoving the tins of gunpowder one by one in front of her. She lay two of them side by side, and then opened the third tin and, as she had often seen her father do, poured a large mound of black gunpowder grains in between them. Next she crawled backwards pulling the open tin with her, so that a black trail led from the tins inside the wall out onto the beach. Once there, Jane lifted up the open tin and, holding it between her knees, walked slowly backwards letting the gunpowder trickle out in a wavy black line.

After she had gone some way down the beach, she turned up the hill again. There was no knowing what might not happen when the explosion came and she would be safest if she went quite high up.

At last she felt she had gone high enough. She dropped an extra dollop of gunpowder on the ground, and then slowly went back, putting down more gunpowder wherever the black trail looked thin. It was a quarter past eight when she finally reached the blocked up tunnel again.

She crawled in and put the last tin beside the two others. Then she covered them quickly with some rocks that were lying around. For some reason she was beginning to feel rather nervous; the sound of the sea seemed somehow frightening behind her, and when she stopped to listen she thought she could hear the noise of the flood waters moving in the black tunnel behind the wall.

Without waiting to pile more stones, Jane backed out of the hole and ran as fast as she could along the beach and back to where the trail of

gunpowder ended. There she sat down, panting, and pulled the wind-and-rain proof matches out of her pocket.

Below her, the sea lapped on the shingle, its silvery surface ruffled by a gentle wind. The hillside rose above her, very black and very still.

'Wow!' thought Jane.

But she did nothing. What would happen when the gunpowder exploded? Perhaps the whole hill would collapse. Her father had always said it was dangerous. She would be buried in an avalanche.

Very quickly, as though getting into the sea on a cold day, Jane lit a match and touched the little pile of gunpowder at her feet.

At once, with a fizz, it was off. A bright but small flame went running down the hill. Sometimes it went out of sight and Jane thought it had gone out. Then it appeared again farther down. Now it had reached the beach, now was running along the shingle, now turning up towards the tunnel. And then, craning round the boulder behind which she was crouching, she saw the flame disappear inside the hole. There was a pause, a silence, and then suddenly a bright, shooting flash of orange light and the most tremendous, rocking, crashing EXPLOSION Jane had ever heard. It shook the ground and threw her flat on her back. And behind it, even as she fell, she heard a deep, rumbling, terrifying roar.

When Jane stood up again, the most extraordinary sight met her eyes. The front of the tunnel and part of the surrounding hill had been completely blown away. And from the opening a great gush of water, thick and solid, was spouting out into the sea.

It had worked! Jane was so excited she found that she was jumping up and down and shouting. Then she sat and watched while the flood waters rushed from Curl Valley. Sometimes she saw tree trunks thrown out, once a farm cart, and once, for three minutes the water suddenly stopped altogether and then, with a great spurt, a whole haystack shot like a bullet out of the hole, landed, and slowly floated away.

All this was slowly beginning to turn the sea a dark brown colour, and gradually the chunks of hay and branches of trees and other pieces of flotsam and jetsam covered it like a strange fleet. But it grew too dark to see these, and then difficult to see the long, thick hosepipe of water springing out of the bottom of the hill, soon Jane was sitting growing colder and colder and now suddenly very tired, listening almost in a dream to the endless crashing and splashing of the water.

All at once, however, she heard a different roaring, and saw coming swiftly towards her along the beach a great pool of light. In a few moments she saw that it was a helicopter with powerful searchlights shining down. When it came opposite the tunnel it stopped and, hovering some fifty feet in the air, began to swing its search lights in wide arcs along the beach and up and down the hillside. Suddenly one of these beams struck the place where Jane was sitting and at once, though both blinded and deafened, she sprang to her feet and began to shout and wave.

The helicopter saw her. Its engine noise softened and it sank swiftly to the ground. The next moment a fat, jolly-faced man came clumping up the hill. 'Well, you've caused us as much trouble as a sack full of monkeys, young lady,' he said when he'd reached her, 'you and that Mrs Deal. But I don't know but what you may have done a good job.'

He took her hand and led her to the helicopter. The next instant they were roaring up into the sky (rather like being in the kite, thought Jane). But, exciting as the journey was, she saw very little of it. She was so tired after the day's adventures that by the time they had risen up above the hills she had fallen asleep.

For three days the tunnel gushed, slowly emptying Curl Valley. People came from miles around to see the extraordinary sight and take photographs. By the end, when the water was no longer leaping out but racing like a river and gouging a deep channel in the shingle, over three thousand people had come to see it.

After three days the valley was empty enough for them to return. Mrs Deal who had been put to bed in her hotel bedroom, also said she felt strong enough to travel. And so on Wednesday morning, accompanied by the fat pilot, Jim, they all set off for Curl Castle in a Land-Rover.

It was a difficult journey. By no means all the water had left the valley and on all sides there were ponds and puddles and little rivers; often the road was completely covered. Several trees had been uprooted by the force of the in-pouring water, and from all the others hung festoons of grass and hay and other flotsam swept into their branches by the flood. (Luckily the farmers were all on holiday too, so no one had been drowned.) And everywhere there swirled a delicate, cold mist as, in the hot July sun, the valley slowly steamed itself dry.

But the Castle itself was an even wetter and sadder sight. As they swished up to it over the sodden lawn, they could see that all the windows had been broken and several small pieces of furniture had floated through them and then, as the waters fell again, had been deposited all over the flower bed. Smashed drainpipes hung loosely against the walls, with torn creepers drooping beside them.

But when they got inside they could hardly believe their eyes, so terrible was the confusion. The air was cold and dank, water dripped and oozed and trickled from everything, wending its way down stairs and walls to form pools and lakes in all the rooms and corridors; and all over the place, stacked in untidy, sodden heaps, lay the precious furniture, the bedclothes, brushes, pictures, vacuum cleaners, gumboots, suits of armour, in fact everything that had filled the Castle for hundreds of years.

When she saw it, and thought not just of the dusting, but of the mopping and mending and drying it would all mean, Mrs Deal sank onto a nearby sofa (though immediately springing up again when, like a large sponge, it sent jets of water in all directions), Mrs Deal leant weakly against a dripping wall, and began to moan. 'Oh dear, oh dear, oh dear, oh dear . . .' in a faint despairing voice. And Jane herself, though interested in the disaster, wondered what on earth they were to do.

Luckily, however, Jim at once took charge. 'First,' he said, 'we must make a list of what we'll need. Then I'll get on the blower to camp and see if the CO can send some trucks out with some of the boys. Now you cheer up, Mrs Deal,' he went on, 'you have a cup of tea and you'll soon be as right as rain.' Though it seemed a tactless comparison in the circumstances, Jane liked him for his kindness, and Mrs Deal at once brightened.

They squelched their way up to the roof and while Mrs Deal bustled about with the primus stove, Jim and Jane made a long list of what they would need: oil for the central heating, all the servants to return at once, food, mops, cloths, dusters, buckets, carpenters, window-menders, builders—the list soon covered several sheets of paper. Then after they had finished their tea, they each took some of the list and went to separate telephones to send telegrams and instructions. The great battle to restore Curl Castle had begun.

At first Jane was very busy. All her toy-cupboards had to be gone through and everything ruined by the flood thrown away. She made out a list of all the new clothes she would need. She wrote a long letter to her father and mother describing exactly what had happened, with a lot of pencil drawings showing Mrs Deal falling down the stairs under the piano, she (Jane) blowing up the tunnel, the helicopter, etc.

But after a week she suddenly realized that she hadn't anything very much more to do. The servants were too busy to talk, and had also left all their children behind with relations, so she still had no one to play with; the builders and decorators and insurance men were interesting to watch for a while, but only for a while; and Mrs Deal had started, once the first rooms were dry, on a frenzy of dusting so violent that it was dangerous to approach her. Jane decided that the time had come to pay another visit to the Book and this, on the Wednesday after they had returned, and after a large and delicious lunch, she accordingly did.

5. More Adventures in the book

THE journey to the old library took very much longer than it had the first time. The vacuum cleaners were all at the menders, and even if they hadn't been, all the carpets had been taken up and hung out to dry. It was a gloomy walk after she left the workmen, the only sound her footsteps echoing on the damp floorboards and from the ruined, dripping rooms.

After an hour she reached the familiar, brass-knobbed door. Once again it swung easily open, once more she found herself on the dark twisting staircase. A few moments later she was standing in the library again.

At first she thought it was all the same. But in fact, she soon noticed that two rather strange things had happened. The first was that the steps, which she was quite sure she had left under the hole after her return from the Tunnellers, had been moved back into the middle of the library.

However, the possibilities of ghosts—or worse—which this at once suggested were so worrying, that Jane quickly turned instead to the Book. And here she got another surprise. Because instead of the square in the town, where an old man was about to be executed, which she was almost sure had been the first picture last time, she now found a very detailed drawing of some mermaids swimming about on the edge of a waterfall. Nor, as she turned the pages, could she find any trace of the picture of Kronin, though once a glimpse of some high mountains reminded her of the Tunneller's country.

She looked at several pictures—one of spiders, one of some large bats flying across a lake, and one of what looked like a giant's grocer shop—but none of them looked quite safe. Then all at once she came on one which seemed to consist entirely of flowers. They were so bright and cheerful, so soft looking, that she felt nothing could possibly go wrong in a land which had such lovely things in it.

Rather nervously Jane crawled out and sat beside a large poppy. Then she took the piece of carefully folded paper out of the pocket of her jeans, and said very quickly:

'Shut eyes, do not look,
Close your pages on me Book.'

At once the thick paper began to turn into that cotton wool which Jane remembered before. The picture faded and became milky, and her legs began slowly to sink. She held her breath and shut her eyes, and once again, had there been anyone else in the library, they would have been surprised to see the giant cover of the Book rise up and close swiftly down, driving the little girl like a nail into the page.

Jane found that she was sitting on a small bank covered in big bright flowers. Beside her grew the poppy, quite as large, if not larger than it had seemed a moment before. When Jane stood up it was level with her chest, and each red, tissue-papery petal was the size of her hand.

The bank was at the edge of a wide, moss-covered track twisting through a forest of enormous trees. From many of the higher branches long creepers dangled to the ground and everywhere, on the creepers, the large green leaves, swooping among the giant flowers, millions of gaily coloured birds chirruped and called, filling the air with their song. There were also other noises coming from the forest which she thought might be monkeys. 'Perhaps,' thought Jane, as she set off down the track, 'I'm in the jungles of Africa or South America.'

Certainly it was warm enough. A faint mist rose from the soft damp moss and Jane soon rolled up the sleeves of her shirt. Though the track was very flat and smooth (she thought it odd there were no stones) she had to clamber over lots of branches. After an hour of walking in the hot sun, she decided to rest. She had hardly sat down on a fallen tree when she began to have the curious feeling she was being watched. She looked about her, but could see nothing but the birds who twittered everywhere. And then, just at her feet, she heard a gentle click—click— click—click, like a tiny pair of knitting needles.

She found that one of the smallest birds she had ever seen was perched beside her, staring at her with bright, black eyes. It was the size of a small bumble bee, with shiny blue wings and a pointed beak like a pin. It was so light that it hardly bent the stem of grass on which it swayed. And it seemed completely unafraid of Jane, because when she slowly stretched out her hand it hopped easily on to her little finger and perched there as she lifted it to her face.

'Hullo,' said Jane.

Click—click went the bird.

'I suppose you *are* a bird,' said Jane, and then because she had been feeling rather lonely and wanted to go on talking, she went on, 'Do you know where I could get a drink? I feel so hot and thirsty.' At once the bird, or bumble bird, rose swiftly into the air and poised hovering in front of her face. Then it darted off again and all the time made such a clicking with its pointed, pin-like beak, that she soon realized it wished her to follow. She, therefore, set off after it down the track.

They had not gone far when the bumble bird turned up a little path to the left and, after following this for a while, they came to a little glade. It was filled with tall white lilies, whose large waxy flowers pointed upwards like wine glasses. The bumble bird balanced on the nearest of these and when Jane came up, she saw that the flower, indeed all the lilies, were filled with a pale liquid the colour of weak tea. The bumble bird now made dipping movements and clicked rapidly at her.

'All right,' said Jane. And bending forward she tipped the flower into her mouth.

It was delicious. Jane was reminded of a very fresh melon, only sparkling and not too sweet. She drank six flower cups and was just about to drink the seventh (out of greed, not thirst) when suddenly she began to feel very drowsy. She gave a great yawn and turning to the bumble bird she said 'Aaaaaaah—dear bumble bird, I think . . . must just . . . goodnight,' and lying comfortably back into the moss, shut her eyes, and in a moment was fast asleep.

The bumble bird flew down close to her face, hovered there for a few seconds, then shot into the air and flew at great speed into the trees.

Jane was woken some hours later by a delicate pecking on the nose. It was the bumble bird again. But when she had rubbed her eyes and sat up, she saw that standing watching her was a boy of about her own age, leaning calmly against a tree. When he saw that she was awake, he smiled at her and said, 'Did you have a good dreamless sleep?'

'Very good, thank you,' said Jane, 'but I think I was put to sleep by these flowers. What are they?'

'Surely you've seen Deluna before,' said the boy, 'we take them every night to stop dreams. What do you take?'

'When I can't sleep my mother gives me an aspirin,' said Jane, 'if I still can't sleep they give me two aspirins. Ten aspirins,' she added, 'is a fatal dose.'

'Ah well, I expect in different parts they have different names,' said the boy, 'but you don't know my name. I'm called Tamil and I live half an hour away in Fluffball.'

'My name is Jane,' said Jane, 'and I live in Curl Castle.'

'Curl Castle?' said Tamil, 'I don't think I've ever heard of that village. But of course the jungle is very large. You must have travelled a long way. Why not come and spend the night in our house. Where are you going?'

'Deal Village,' said Jane, 'miles away. You won't have heard of it.'

'Miles?' said Tamil, 'surely you mean hours?'

'Oh, not hours,' said Jane quickly, 'weeks away, months, years I think. Yes, at least eight years away.'

'Goodness,' said Tamil, looking at her with admiration, 'eight years away. They never told me the jungle was that big. You must talk to the Aged. He will be very interested.' Jane felt that the conversation was getting out of control, so she said, 'Let's go to your house now. I'm beginning to feel rather hungry.'

As they walked, she was able to look at him more closely without appearing to stare. He had a kind, rather thin face, with fair hair and black eyes. His skin was a deep brown from the sun and he was quite naked except for a strip of light green cotton tied round his waist.

It was plain that Tamil was also thinking about her because all at once he said, 'Curl Castle and Deal Village. Do tell me why you are going such a very long way.'

For a moment Jane didn't answer. As with the Tunneller Kronin, she felt rather nervous of explaining exactly how she had arrived. At the same time what she had said seemed likely to lead to more and more embarrassing questions. She particularly didn't want to meet the Aged, who sounded like a very grown up grown-up. Also, like Kronin, Tamil seemed gentle and kind. So she stopped and said 'Look, I'm afraid I didn't exactly tell the exact truth about Curl Castle and Deal Village.'

'Oh?' said Tamil, 'why not?'

'Well, the thing is,' began Jane. And then, as quickly as she could, she told him everything that had happened.

When she had finished, Tamil looked at the ground and said slowly, 'I see. Now I understand. I think I won't tell my mother and father, not of course that they'd mind. I'll just say you're a traveller.'

'How do you mean "You understand"?' said Jane, 'am I odd or something? What do you understand?' As with Kronin, she had the impression that her arrival through the Book meant something to him which he didn't want to tell her.

'Oh, not odd,' said Tamil, laughing. 'You're very lucky, really. But I don't really know very much about it. In any case you'll find out sometime and it's certainly nothing to worry about.'

And with that Jane had to be content, because Tamil went on to say that it was getting late. As they walked, he told Jane about his country. It was called Tree Land, but was in fact not really 'land' at all. Tamil explained that the trees they saw around them were thousands of years old, but most of what they saw were only the tops of those trees. What had happened was that the trees grew so close together that when branches fell they got caught and entangled with other branches before they reached the ground, these in turn caught other branches and soon a sort of floor had been formed many feet above the ground. Seeds had landed in crevices of this floor, had grown into flowers, then died, to rot down gradually into earth. More seeds had fallen, more branches, and over hundreds of years the floor had grown many feet thick, able to support whole trees on its own, and these too had fallen, rotted down and made the floor even thicker and stronger. Then sometime long before anyone remembered, Tamil's ancestors had climbed up the giant trees from the jungle below and had found this sunny land, full of richly growing flowers and no enemies, and had lived there ever since.

'Do you mean that we are really walking on a sort of platform?' said Jane in amazement, looking down at the solid-looking earth and moss of the track at her feet, 'you mean that somewhere underneath is a gap and then below that the real earth? But we might fall through.'

'Oh we'd never fall through,' said Tamil, 'it's far too thick for that. The Aged says it is fifty feet thick even at the thinnest part, and it is all bound together by roots and huge old tree trunks.'

'But what happens down at the bottom, where the trees grow from? Who lives there?' asked Jane.

'Nobody knows,' said Tamil. 'To tell you the truth I wouldn't ask anyone if I were you. We aren't really meant to talk about it. If you do ask people they look very frightened and quickly change the subject. I'm about the only person in our village who isn't frightened—well, me and my friend Mayna. One day when we are bigger we are going to climb down one of the holes and explore. But it's very dangerous. There have been men who have explored but none have ever come back. The name of down there is the Land of Dreams.'

While they had been talking the track had gradually been widening, and now it opened into a large clearing. All round the edges were about thirty little houses made from large leaves plaited together. In the middle was a much larger house, standing on stilts and made out of tree trunks. 'That's where the Aged lives,' said Tamil.

The village was a peaceful and happy sight in the evening sun. In front of each little house sat women sewing and talking, and everywhere little brown children were playing and laughing.

'First you should pay your respects to the Aged,' said Tamil.

'Oh dear, must I?' said Jane. 'I feel so shy.'

'Well, not tonight then. But before you go. It's our custom. Now, come with me and meet my family.'

First Jane was introduced to Tamil's mother, a smiling woman with her fair hair tied in a bun and a rather large nose. Then she met his five little sisters. His mother gave her a bowl of grey, porridge-like stuff, with some syrup and pieces of very good fresh bread and jam.

After this, though she longed to go on asking Tamil questions about Tree Land and the Land of Dreams, he said she should go to bed.

'We get up with the sun here,' he said, 'and go to bed with it as well. So you see it is already late.' Then he showed Jane where she was to sleep, which was in a large wickerwork hammock swinging from the ceiling in a tiny room off the main one. She said goodnight and had just settled herself in it with a blanket over her, when a shape blocked out the dim light from the door.

It was Tamil's mother. 'I've brought you some Deluna,' she said, 'in case you dream. Tamil said you wouldn't need it, but there's no need to waste your own remedies while staying with us. Come drink it up and you'll have a lovely, dreamless night.'

Jane thought it would be rude to refuse, so she thanked Tamil's mother and once again tasted the sweet, pale liquid she had drunk from the lilies. A few minutes later she slipped into a deep and, as it turned out, completely dreamless sleep.

The next morning, as they wandered among the paths and long, narrow fields which surrounded the village, Tamil answered Jane's many questions about Tree Land.

'I don't see any rivers,' said Jane, 'or fountains or ponds. How do you get water?'

'Look,' said Tamil. He ran a few steps down the path they were following to one of the many banks of dark green moss which were at its edge. Stuffing his hands into it he pulled off a large chunk and then squeezed it. At once water poured onto the path. 'That's one way,' he said, 'the other is the water plants, which are like the Deluna lilies only bigger and filled with water.'

Although Tamil told her a great deal about Tree Land—about its peaceful peoples, it's animals, the great rains which sometimes swept it—there was one thing he did not speak of, and after a while

Jane decided she must ask about it.

'If it worries you, Tamil,' she said, 'of course, I'll quite understand. But I would like to know a little more about the Land of Dreams.'

For a moment she thought she saw a shadow of nervousness cross his face, but he answered quickly enough. 'Well, the thing is I don't really know any more than I've told you. This other land may not exist—it's only a sort of legend really—a story. But it's true that explorers have gone to find it and have never returned. It's true, we're not allowed to talk about it. And it's true that in secret parts of the forest there are deep holes which lead no one knows where. If you like, I could show you one after lunch.'

'Oh please do,' said Jane, 'yes, in fact I'm getting quite hungry now.'

Lunch, consisting of hot, sweet black porridge and some sugared violet petals, was soon over. Tamil told his mother that he was going to take Jane for a walk in the jungle and, after collecting his friend Mayna, they set off.

Mayna was shorter and fatter than Tamil, with a happy smiling face, and as they walked he skipped ahead and came running back, laughing and making jokes. But as they plunged deeper and deeper into the jungle, and as the paths grew narrower, the light dimmer, even he became quiet. Soon all three were struggling in silence through thick undergrowth.

They had pushed on in this way for about half an hour when Tamil suddenly stopped and whispered, 'Listen.'

Jane could at first hear nothing, but then very faintly came the sound of running, or really dripping, water.

'We're nearly there,' whispered Tamil.

A few more clambering steps, and then the bushes suddenly stopped and they were looking down into a small hollow. There was not much light, but in the middle of the hollow, Jane could see the blackness of a deep hole. From out of this hole rose the trunk of a huge tree, and from its depths came the sound of trickling water they had heard a moment before.

'There you are,' whispered Tamil, 'that's it.'

'Have you ever tried to get down it,' said Jane, 'I mean even a little way?'

'No, no,' said Tamil, 'it's far too dangerous. We've only been here twice before.' Looking at them clinging to the bushes at the edge, staring down with wide eyes, Jane suddenly realized that both the boys were very frightened.

'But it looks easy,' she said, 'look, you can see that the branches of that tree going down in the middle could easily be climbed.'

'No, no,' said Tamil nervously, 'far too dangerous. Look, do you see that steam coming from the hole,' and as he mentioned it Jane could see that there were faint wisps of steam rising sluggishly in the dim

light, 'it must be very hot down there. You'd probably be boiled alive.'

'Or eaten by huge ants,' said Mayna, 'or squashed by worms. Look, we'd better get back. It's already late.'

And then Jane made up her mind. 'Listen, Tamil,' she said, 'I'm going to explore that hole. I can quite easily get to the edge by those roots and things and then jump across to the tree. You know it's all right for me. If there is any danger I can just say the magic words and return home. If there is no danger then I can really find out what happens down there.'

'No you can't, you mustn't,' said Tamil.

'Now don't worry,' said Jane, forbidding though the hole looked. 'If I don't come back in ten minutes go and explain to your mother that I decided to go on with my journey.' And before the boys could stop her, she had leapt lightly down, stepped from branch and root to the edge of the hole and then jumped easily onto one of the branches growing out of the trunk of the tree. 'Goodbye Tamil, goodbye Mayna,' she called, 'see you soon.' And before the nervousness she already felt could get too strong she at once began to climb down into the dark, earth-smelling hole. As she disappeared, she heard faintly from above her, 'Goodbye Jane. Be careful. Goodbye.'

At first Jane found it quite easy to climb down the tree. There were a great many branches and footholds which, although it soon became completely dark, she easily found by feeling; and for some reason the earth through which the tree rose never came very close to the trunk. The air was warm and damp and the earth smelt rich and rotten like a forest floor in summer time. 'It must smell like this to worms and moles,' she thought.

But as she climbed deeper the trickling water began to pour onto her in little rivulets. Soon she was soaked to the skin. The earth pressed closer and closer and she had to push her way down through dead branches and matted, sweet-smelling leaves. Several times she became completely stuck and only the most violent kicking and jumping enabled her to get any further.

It was when she became finally stuck, that Jane realized how unlikely Tamil's story was. Another world *underneath* Tree Land indeed! All she had done was to burrow deep into the ground in this boggy hole and now would either have to remain there till she drowned or suffocated, or say the rhyme and return to Curl Castle. Furiously she gave a kick at the criss-crossed branches and earth around her feet.

To her horror, with a sudden cracking and rush, they disappeared. One moment they were there, the next Jane felt the ground fall beneath her. Wildly she grabbed at the tree, for a moment held to a slender, slippery branch, then as it snapped felt herself falling into deep, dark, space—falling . . . falling . . . falling . . .

6. The Land of Dreams

JANE dropped like a stone for about five seconds; then to her surprise she found that she was falling more and more slowly. The air around her was becoming thicker and thicker until very soon it supported her as though she floated in an invisible sea.

Jane also realized that she was moving. The air nudged and buffeted at her back, and once her hand touched a slimy tree trunk sliding past. The current gradually grew stronger and before long she was being carried through the darkness quite fast, the air swirling between her legs and turning her slowly over and over like a leaf in the wind.

Although it was not unpleasant, Jane was relieved when she saw it growing lighter ahead. Soon tall tree trunks began to appear on either side, looming out of the fog which was blowing Jane between them. It became lighter every moment; now Jane could see the ground below, now see she was floating down towards it. The fog became a mist, the mist melted away, and suddenly, light as thistledown, she landed on her feet again. Looking back she could see only a deepening fog, with the trees rising straight up until they disappeared into the darkness; but ahead, she saw the edge of the jungle, with sunlight shining through the trees and beyond, the green of meadows. Fifty steps, a small ditch to be jumped, and she was out in the sun, suddenly surprised at the noise of birds.

After a pause to wipe off the mud which still clung to her sandals from forcing her way through the floor of Tree Land, and to wring as much water from her clothes as she could, Jane hurried off towards a distant hill.

The countryside was surprisingly English, with little fields and hedges not unlike those round Curl Castle. After half an hour, Jane turned to look back at the jungle. The trees rose, straight and branchless, so high into the sky that she had to tilt her head back to look towards their tops. But these, and therefore the second level which was Tree Land, were hidden far above the clouds.

She was now beginning to feel extremely hungry. She had just reached an oak tree growing in the middle of the fourth field she had crossed. It was surrounded by little oak apples and Jane suddenly murmured to her self, 'I wonder if I could eat oak apples.'

'Of course you could,' said a voice behind her, 'if that's why you are here.'

Very surprised, Jane looked up. Sitting on one of the branches was a short, but extremely fat little man wearing a bowler hat. Next to him sat an equally fat little woman in a large, old-fashioned, orange bathing dress. The man was in pyjamas and dressing-gown. As Jane continued to stare at them, the woman said, 'Introduce me to the young lady, Mr Henry.'

'Of course, dear,' said Mr Henry, 'how remiss. I would like you to meet Mrs Forth, my wife. My dear I would like to introduce you to Miss . . . Miss . . . Miss . . .?' He inclined his round fat head politely towards her and lifted his bowler hat.

But Jane's manners had completely disappeared with amazement. 'How ever did you get up there?' she said.

'Ah, you think we are too fat?' said Mr Henry quickly, 'granted, granted. We are fat, very fat, but we're also incredibly light. Observe.' And pushing him self off the branch, Mr Henry rose lightly into the air and then very slowly floated down until he came to rest beside Jane, where he continued to bob up and down like a balloon in a hot drawing-room. Looking up he called to his wife. 'Show her, my dear.'

At once a silly but pleased expression spread over Mrs Forth's round face. She too propelled herself into the air, but on her way down, merely by raising one plump, pink leg, she turned a complete somersault.

'How extraordinary,' said Jane.

'Hardly extraordinary,' said Mr Henry, 'this is what we want. This way we combine the cosiness, the jollyness, the warmth and lovely, rubbery softness of being fat without any of the disadvantages. We never get breathless, my wife's feet never ache, furniture never breaks and we eat and eat and eat. All because we are so delightfully light. How much do you think I weigh?'

Jane looked at him. A ton? To be polite she said, 'Fifteen stone.'

'I weigh two ounces,' said Mr Henry grandly, 'we both weigh two ounces. Now hold out both your hands.' Then Mr Henry turned to his wife, 'Come my dear, let us show this nice young lady some more of our little games.' And with a 'hurr-up' they both leapt daintily into the air and came lightly down on Jane's out stretched palms. Neither of them seemed heavier than a hard-boiled egg. With a gentle movement, Jane threw them both up into the air, and when they had once more bobbed to rest beside her, said 'But how do you do it? Does everyone round here do it?' '

Only if they really want to,' said Mr Henry, 'why we met a man the other night, well how can I describe him? He was as thin as a bootlace. Now, he wanted to be heavy. Every step he took he sank up to his thighs; we saw him break a large rock into fragments just by sitting on it. Now, you want something to eat. Why not try the oak apples or a branch? What would you like them to taste of?'

'Fish fingers,' said Jane.

'Well, try one,' said Mr Henry.

But before Jane could bend to pick one up, there came a faint cry of 'Mr Henry' from some way off.

While they had been talking, a faint breeze had sprung up and this had carried Mrs Forth a considerable distance out into the field and was rapidly carrying her farther.

'Mr Henry,' she called, 'we shall be late for breakfast.'

Mr Henry, who had only kept his position by holding fast to one of the branches of the oak, from which he now waved like a large flag, turned his head and cried 'Coming, my love.' And then said hurriedly to Jane, 'She's quite right. If you're late for breakfast you never catch up. Well goodbye, Miss . . . Miss . . .?'

'Jane,' said Jane, not bothering about Lady.

'Goodbye, Miss Jane.'

'Goodbye,' called Jane, as, releasing his hold, Mr Henry was swept away, his dressing gown billowing around him. She watched him join his wife and then saw them hand in hand begin a series of huge, slow leaps, the last of which must have taken them up into some stronger currents of wind, because they were almost immediately blown out of sight.

Although it seemed odd that they should worry about being late for breakfast in the late afternoon, unless of course they had a long way to travel, Jane now felt too hungry to worry about Mr Henry and Mrs Forth. In stead she picked up one of the dead branches lying at the foot of the oak tree and took a dainty nibble from one end.

It did not surprise her to find that it tasted exactly like one of Mrs Deal's best fish fingers, only cold. '*Hot* please,' thought Jane; and at once had to drop the branch as it began to sizzle in her fingers. She soon found that by concentrating she could make anything taste of anything. Grass of chicken, bark of chocolate, earth, poured from her cupped hands, became milk as it entered her mouth. After a large and varied meal of chicken, chocolate, ham, cheese fingers, fish fingers, summer pudding, milk, bitter lemon, sherbet, roast mutton and chewing gum, Jane set off again in the direction of the hill.

The field was surrounded by a high hedge full of gaps. On the other side of it was a grassy path which, though it twisted and turned seemed to lead more or less towards the hill. Jane decided to follow it.

After an hour's hard walking, the path grew wider and wider, the hedges lower, and before long both disappeared and Jane found she was standing at the top of a shallow valley, looking across to the little hill. It was becoming dark and a cold breeze had blown up from the valley which, in the gloom of the evening and with its scattered rocks, looked most uninviting. Nor was there yet any sign of a village or indeed of any human beings at all, in fact the countryside was growing visibly more wild and frightening. However, having decided to reach the top of the hill, Jane could think of nothing better to do. It was still true that if there were any villages then she would most easily see them from there.

Accordingly she set off, jumping over the stones and little rocks and walking round the larger ones, until all at once she thought she heard voices. She stopped and listened. They had come from the left, but had been very faint.

'Hullooooo,' shouted Jane, 'is there anybody there?' No one answered.

'I'm *sure* I heard voices,' thought Jane, and climbing onto a nearby boulder she was about to shout again into the gloomy valley when she saw a slowly moving figure coming towards her.

It was a little girl of about her own age. As she walked she looked at the ground and put one foot carefully in front of the other in the way Jane herself often did when she was pretending to walk on a tightrope.

'Hullo,' Jane called excitedly.

The little girl looked up, waved, and then looked down again. As she came nearer, Jane was interested to see that she was wearing the same jeans as she was. Also she had the same short hair, which now hung over her face as she walked on her tightrope. Not until she was quite close, and Jane had again said 'hullo,' did she look up. And then Jane saw the most remarkable sight. She found that she was looking at herself.

The little girl was not just rather like her, or reminded her of her, or could have been her sister—she was *exactly* like her. She had the same nose, the same eyes and mouth and teeth; she had a mole where Jane had a mole and a tiny mark on her throat where Jane had a mark. She *was* Jane.

Jane stared at her, and she looked back at Jane, though without nearly as much interest. She had one eye with a speck in it like Jane did, and her parting was on the left.

'Who are you?' said Jane at last.

'Jane Charrington,' said the little girl.

'But you *can't* be,' said Jane, 'I'm Jane Charrington. At least, you may be as well. It must be a coincidence. But we look exactly alike.'

'How do you do,' said the other Jane, smiling kindly. Jane took her hand and shook it. It fitted exactly, and they gave, she noticed, exactly the same number of shakes.

'I know,' said Jane, 'you're my identical twin. Are you an orphan? Have you never seen our mother?'

'I've never seen my mother,' said the other Jane.

'But you *must*,' said Jane, 'how did you get here? I never knew I had a sister. You must have been stolen away from hospital and Mummy doesn't even know about you.'

'Well, I don't know about that,' said the other Jane, 'after all, there are quite a lot of us.' And now Jane saw that they were being joined by other figures emerging from behind the rocks and arriving, in fact, from all directions. And all of them were wearing jeans and shirts, all of them had short brown hair and brown eyes and moles and marks on their throat. All of them were Janes.

'This is Jane Charrington,' said the first Jane as they came up, and each one said, 'How do you do? I'm Jane Charrington.' And for a while the air was full of Jane Charrington, Jane Charrington, how do you do, I'm Jane Charrington, Charrington, Charrington, Charrington.'

'But you *can't* be,' shouted Jane tearfully, 'we can't be. We can't all be the same person.' Suddenly she began to feel very frightened and strange. She wanted to cry, and then run to Mrs Deal or her mother.

'Do you know Mrs Deal?' she said, 'do you know Curl Castle?'

'Well, *she* knows Mrs Deal,' said one of the Janes pointing to another Jane, 'but of course I'm very good at English.'

'So am I,' said Jane; 'yes, that's true.'

'But I'm very bad at maths,' said yet another Jane.

'So am I,' said Jane.

'I like fish fingers,' 'I tell myself stories in bed,' 'I can swim,' 'I want to go to school.' All the Janes were speaking at once (and there now seemed to be about three hundred of them), and the noise grew so loud that Jane, the real Jane, suddenly felt she would go mad if they didn't stop.

'IT'S ALL TRUE,' she shouted, 'I'M LIKE THAT TOO.'

At once there was complete silence. Jane had a strong feeling that no one liked her. At last the first Jane said quietly 'You can't be. No one is *all* the Jane Charringtons. I *only* walk on a tightrope and Jane over there is the *only* Jane who tells herself stories.'

'And I'm *only* bad at maths,' said another Jane.

'And I wouldn't *dream* of pretending I knew what Jane meant when she said Curl Castle,' said another, 'I only talk about Mrs Deal and her dusting.'

And suddenly, in the middle of a muttering chorus of 'I *only* . . . I wouldn't . . . I'm the Jane who . . .' one of the Janes pushed through and gave her a violent push on the place where she had once broken her arm.

'Ow,' cried Jane, jumping back, 'that's my sore place. That's where I broke my arm.'

At once the Jane who had pinched her shouted, 'SHE'S SAYING SHE HAD *MY* BROKEN ARM. SHE'S PRETENDING SHE'S *ALL THE JANES. WE MUST KILL HER.*

'I'm not, I'm not,' cried Jane, 'I'm Jane Charrington of Curl Castle. I'm *not* pretending.'

But the crowd of Janes just seemed to become angrier. They began to mutter louder and louder, to crowd closer and hold out their hands, their little hands so exactly like hers; and all at once Jane found that she had turned round and was running as fast as she could away from them towards the hill.

It was now much darker. The rocks appeared suddenly out of the shadows and had to be jumped or dodged. But though Jane could hear all the other Janes running along behind, she realized that probably only one of them would be able to run as fast as her. And in fact, when she looked hurriedly back, she saw that none of them were yet gaining.

But although they could not run any faster, they certainly knew the way better. Three, four, five times she tripped and each time they drew closer. Suddenly, quite close, she saw a Jane rushing towards her from the left, and when she swerved to the right, another Jane appeared yelling and waving a stone which she at once threw at Jane with all her might.

Jane tripped again, and then again. Loud cries of triumph came from all sides. She scrambled up and ran panting on, but now she heard the sound of feet close behind and stones began to whizz past as the awful pack of little girls threw and shouted and threw again.

Just as she was about to give up in despair, Jane saw in front of her a flight of stairs. They rose straight out of the ground, and without thinking she rushed up them.

Twenty stairs. But as she reached the top, another twenty appeared before her. And as she ran up them, another twenty. From the ground, as she climbed, there came a great roar of rage.

Looking back, Jane saw that, as fast as she climbed, the stairs disappeared behind her. Now, gathered in the last evening light, a vast circle of little girls looked up to where she stood on the staircase in the air above them. They were jumping and shouting and, suddenly feeling that they were not, in fact, really like her at all, Jane called down, 'Shut up. You are all just dreams. I am the real Jane Charrington. Not you.'

Then, ignoring the yells and shouts, she began to climb the staircase as it appeared before her, turning back every now and again to make sure it was disappearing behind, and had not suddenly shot down to earth to allow her terrible pursuers to start their chase again.

Jane climbed as fast as she could because she hoped that the stairs would soon reach somewhere. But the higher she climbed, the emptier seemed the evening sky, and the dizzier she grew. The valley was just a vague dot in the gloom and soon it had disappeared altogether. Then all at once Jane stumbled and had she not seized the stairs would have fallen to a hideous death on the rocks below. Luckily just after this the stairs became a moving staircase and she was able to sit down and let herself be carried swiftly higher.

As she rose, it grew much lighter because the sun had still not set at that enormous height, and in its light Jane saw that at last the stairs seemed to have some object in their climb. They were approaching a vast cloud, miles long, which hovered pinkly above them. They drew rapidly closer. Soon they had plunged into its thick, damp folds. But still the stairs went on; indeed they seemed to move even faster and for so long that Jane became quite wet and expected any second to pop out of the top of the cloud.

At last they stopped. At the same time, the cloud became a little thinner and Jane saw that she had arrived at the walls of some large though, because of the cloud, dim building. Its walls were made of steel and were entirely smooth except for a small door against which the top of the stairs now rested. As she walked towards this, it slid silently open and Jane quickly stepped through. The door at once shut itself behind her.

She was in a short, brightly lit tunnel, with curved steel walls which reflected her in the oddest shapes, like looking into a spoon. Jane followed this to its end and there, where it divided, found a notice saying 'Visitors This Way'. Several times the tunnel divided and each time there was a similar notice, until eventually she came to another sliding door saying 'Visitors' Lift'. The door, as she had expected, opened as she came to it and shut behind her.

The lift was very small, with a small red stool in its corner. One wall was covered with 994 buttons—each numbered—and the 995th button had an arrow pointing at it saying 'Visitors' Button'.

She pressed it and immediately the lift shot upwards with a purring sound. Each time they passed a floor there was a little ping. In four minutes, nineteen seconds the lift stopped at the 995th floor and Jane stepped out into a large, round room.

Opposite her, in a curved steel chair, was a tall, elderly man with thick grey hair, bright brown eyes and very fuzzy eyebrows. He was wearing a white silk dressing-gown and purple pyjamas.

'Welcome, my dear,' he said in a deep, kindly voice. 'You must be tired and hungry. Come and sit down.' He led her over to a smaller steel chair opposite his own, and went on, 'Now before I satisfy your curiosity, I shall order some food. What would you like to eat?'

Jane found that she was not in the least shy of the kind man. After thinking a moment, she said 'Could I have some fried eggs, fried bread and bacon and a glass of Lucozade, please.'

The man pressed a button on his chair and speaking into mid-air, repeated her order. 'Won't be long,' he said, smiling at her.

The round room had no windows and only one door. There was a thick, woolly rug on the floor. In front of the man a large desk stuck out of the wall, and this was covered with buttons, dials, telephones, switches, levers, and, in the middle, a round television screen. After looking carefully at everything, Jane said 'Perhaps if it's not rude to ask, you could begin to satisfy my curiosity *before* my supper arrives.' But as she spoke there came a soft ping and a little table rose up in front of her laden with food.

'Of course,' said the man, 'now you have a good meal and I'll explain while you eat.'

'You have come,' he began, 'to what you would call the capital of the Land of Dreams.

'Here we make dreams and send them out to everyone who sleeps. When you've finished eating I'll take you round and show you how it works. I am the Dream Master. Once, when dreams were made by hand, I was very busy, solving problems, inventing dreams for prophets, priests and so on, but now that everything is done by electric brains and computers, I don't really have quite enough to do.'

'I see,' said Jane, who didn't exactly see. 'Do you mean that everyone in the world who dreams, has their dream made here?'

'Everyone,' said the Dream Master, 'we are a very large organization.'

'And those people I saw on my way here,' said Jane, 'were they people dreaming, or am I really asleep and is all this my dream?'

'Oh, you're awake all right,' said the Dream Master, 'the people you saw were dreaming. As I remember you passed through part of the Hopeful Country, where people dream of what they hope will happen. Except when you went into a Nightmare Valley and had a small nightmare.'

'But where *are* we?' said Jane, who was becoming more and more puzzled. 'Do people who fall asleep come a long way and have their dreams here? If so, what happens to their bodies?'

'It's difficult to explain,' said the Dream Master, 'in fact I wouldn't worry about it. You see the Land of Dreams or Dream Land, is everywhere, but people can only see it and enter it when asleep. To find it when awake, as you have done, is much more complicated and very rarely happens. Now look,' the Dream Master pressed a switch on the desk and at once the steel wall of the room grew paler and paler until it had become like glass.

Jane, who had finished her supper, stood and looked. They were at the top of a very tall tower. Below them, sticking out from its bottom like the spokes of an enormous wheel, nine long steel buildings stretched into the distance. The cloud through which Jane had arrived was all around the Dream capital, but seemed to be kept back as though by an invisible wall.

'Each of those buildings is thirty miles long,' said the Dream Master pointing down, 'each one makes and sends out a certain sort of dream. That one, for instance, is the Dream-of-the-Future factory, that one Nightmares, that one Dreams of Food and Love. Often, of course, people's dreams are very mixed. Then each factory sends part of the dream to this tower and it is made up and sent from here.'

Jane looked down at the strange scene. She didn't really understand it at all, but she had noticed that ever since she had arrived in Dream Land nothing had surprised her in the least. Mr and Mrs Forth, even the appearance of all the other Janes had seemed quite normal. And so, although what the Dream Master was saying was most mysterious, she found that she was quite ready to believe it without understanding it. However, because it always seemed rude to say nothing when people explained things, she tried to think of an intelligent question.

'What happens if two people dream the same dream?' she asked.

'Exactly the same dream is very rare,' said the Dream Master, 'though it sometimes happens to twins, and people very much in love. As a matter of fact I believe you met two people on your way here who both have the same dream every night. Now I'll show you round.'

They walked together over to the lift and soon found themselves walking down a long steel corridor. It was rather like a hospital, with shut doors on either side, each with a green light above it. From time to time men in white dressing-gowns and green pyjamas came out of the doors carrying notebooks or armfuls of steel tins. When they saw the Dream Master they bowed low and waited till he and Jane had passed.

'The steel tins you see those men carrying hold dreams which have been dreamed and are going to be put into storage. We keep all dreams, of course, forever.'

'Could you show me some of my old dreams?' asked Jane.

'Easily,' said the Dream Master, 'though you'll find your own old dreams don't often interest you anymore. But it's rather fun looking at really old dreams. Some of the Biblical ones are tremendous. I watched Potipher and Joseph again only the other day. And of course Jacob dreamt a great deal. I'll show you some.'

He did. He showed her lots of dreams all over the world (except those of people she knew, which wasn't allowed). He showed her how dreams were made and let her make some. He showed her the old equipment-coloured powder, spinning dream wheels, crystal globes— which had been used before the electric brains, lasers and other modern machinery had been put into the Dream capital. But at last he said that he had work to do and that they must return to the tower.

When they were once more sitting opposite each other in the round room, there was a short silence. Then slowly he leant forward and took both her hands in his. She saw that his kind brown eyes were very serious and that he had bent his thick eyebrows into a grave frown.

'Before you go, my child,' he said, 'I shall give you some words of warning and advice. You must listen very carefully.

'Visitors to Dream Land are very rare. Though many people have dreams, very few people have the vision to dream and stay awake. You are one of them. The last visitor we had of your age was a little girl nearly two hundred years ago. She . . . but no, I won't tell you what happened to her. I think you may one day find out.'

'But, and this is the point, if you are to return to your home you must never, never while you are here, fall asleep. Not for an instant, not for a single second, however tired you are, however clever the temptations. You must not doze or even nod your head. If you do, you will be lost.

'But cheer up,' went on the Dream Master, smiling. Jane, who had certainly been rather frightened and had suddenly begun to wish she had never left Curl Castle or Mrs Deal and never opened the Book, poor Jane tried to smile back. 'I'm sure you'll be all right,' said the Dream Master, 'you are a brave girl and as long as you keep your head there's no need to worry. Good luck. And now I'm afraid you must be on your way.'

'Which way?' said Jane, looking nervously round the steel room.

'Well, I suppose I am the easiest way of all,' said the Dream Master. He walked over to the wall and leant against it.

'Goodbye,' he said.

'Goodbye,' said Jane, and then, as she watched, she saw that the Dream Master was slowly changing. Gradually a space appeared in his middle. This grew and grew and at the same time his arms and the edges of his body began to form themselves into the rocky outline of a cavern door.

As she hesitated the rocky door, or gap, suddenly spoke in the Dream Master's voice, 'Don't be afraid,' it or he boomed, 'step through me. Good luck.'

Without giving herself time to be afraid, Jane took a last look round, then stepped through and began to feel her way forward.

7. More Adventures in Dreamland

THE Dream-Master-door led, by way of a short passage, to another even smaller opening. As Jane groped towards it, she heard growing ever louder the sound of wind and distant thunder. A few moments later she had stepped through, and at once was almost blown flat by a great gust of cold wind.

She was standing on a stony path which, in the frequent flashes of lightning, she could see twisted away down the side of a high mountain. All round her a terrible storm was raging. Swollen black clouds sped before the continual gusts of wind, thunder rumbled and echoed and, most exciting of all, each time the lightning flicked and zipped across the sky, Jane saw quite clearly a whole wild country, with ravines and mountains and waterfalls stretched below her, and steep, craggy peaks rising above her. But when, during an especially bright flash, she turned to see the tunnel from which she had just stepped, she could see nothing. In its place was just a gulf, where the mountainside plunged into blackness.

Jane was by now quite cold and was about to hurry off down the mountainside to find some shelter, when she noticed that the lightning had begun to behave in the most curious way. Instead of darting all over the place like ordinary lightning, it now all seemed to flash down at a place about two miles below her on the side of the mountain. And rather rapidly the flashes were coming nearer. Jane watched in amazement as the lightning jumped up the mountainside towards her. It was not until it struck a huge rock only twenty yards away, turning it instantly to dust and filling the air with a cloud of yellow smoke, that she realized the lightning might strike her. Turning round, she began to run as fast as she could up the little path.

The mountain was very steep and the wind now full in her face. Fast as she ran, Jane could hear the lightning gaining. Each time it struck, there was a noise like a bomb; and often it tore great chunks out of the mountainside and started little avalanches, which added their roar to the rumbling grumble of the thunder.

She was about to collapse and allow herself to be turned into a puff of yellow smoke ('it will be a million times worse than the worst electric shock,' she said to herself), when she saw ahead a glimmer of light coming from a long, thin crevice in the side of the mountain. She leapt towards it, and at the same time, with the most terrible CRASH, the lightning seemed to land right on top of her head.

It must, of course, have struck just behind her, because instead of an electric shock the force of the explosion hurled her into the air, luckily straight through the crevice. There was a moment's dizzy whirling and then Jane landed on something very soft.

It was a large bed. Sitting up, Jane saw that it stuck out from one side of a wide, ill-lit cave. Sitting in the middle on a stool was an elderly lady in a long black cloak. She smiled at Jane and said in a somewhat croaking voice, 'How very kind of you to come and keep an old lady company on a stormy night.'

'I'm Jane Charrington,' said Jane, crawling off the bed and coming across to shake hands, 'how do you do?'

The old lady held out a thin, bony hand, with very long, curved finger-nails, and smiled at her. 'How do you do?' she croaked, 'I'm sure there is no need to tell you, but I am a witch. Please don't be alarmed.'

Looking quickly round, Jane saw that there was indeed no need to be told. Hanging on one wall were several long black cloaks, all with a pointed black hat, a broomstick and a fat black cat hanging beside them. From the ceiling dangled bunches of bats, and a great many string bags which Jane could see were full of skulls, herbs and odd-shaped lumps which were obviously pieces of newt, toad-stool, dried blood, etc. In front of the witch an enormous black cauldron gently bubbled over a log fire; by her side, as large as an Alsatian, crouched a huge toad, its skin glistening in the light of the candles.

'I'm very sorry to interrupt you,' said Jane, feeling rather timid despite the witch's assurances, 'but the lightning suddenly began to behave in a very odd manner.'

'I'm afraid that was my fault, my dear,' said the witch, 'I felt so much in need of company that I decided to tempt you here with the light-ning. Please forgive me.'

'Oh, it's quite all right,' said Jane, 'I'm very glad. It's very nice here.' She still, however, felt rather nervous and turning round went and sat carefully on the edge of the bed again.

'Nice,' croaked the witch. 'but boring. So boring, boring, boring. Can you imagine what it's like being able to do exactly what you want? Soon you don't want anything. I long ago learnt everything a witch should know, except the one spell it seems impossible to discover, how to un-learn. Here I sit, year after year, producing storms and plagues and rainbows and everything else out of terrible boredom. All the time bored, bored, bored.'

'But can you do *anything*?' asked Jane.

'Anything,' said the witch, 'everything except stop being a witch. Would you like me to show you? Ask me.'

'Well, let me think,' said Jane, suddenly finding she could think of nothing at all. Then, seeing the gloomy gleaming eyes of the toad on her, she said, 'Could you turn your toad into a daffodil?'

'Certainly,' said the witch. She dipped one curved finger-nail into the cauldron, scattered some drops on the toad, muttered, and at once it blinked, quivered all over and then turned into a three-foot-high daf-fodil growing out of the rug.

'There you are,' croaked the witch. 'Quite simple. You may pick it if you wish.'

'Can you turn it back again?' asked Jane, feeling that it might be cruel to pick the toad-daffodil.

'Indeed I can,' said the witch, and muttering to herself she waved her bony fingers over the daffodil, which to Jane's pleasure immediately became a toad again. 'As a matter of fact it's quite useful,' the witch went on, leaning over and sniffing at the cauldron, 'this mixture is getting rather weak and could do with some toad! In you go.' The toad, how-ever, did not move, but just squatted looking at the witch with an expression in its bulging eyes that Jane thought was unhappy. The witch looked at it crossly and pointed one curved finger-nail at the caul-dron. '*In you go,*' she said sharply.

At this command, the toad gave a little sigh, looked sadly at Jane, and then sprang into the air and landed heavily in the cauldron, sink-ing at once out of sight.

'Oh, *poor* toad,' cried Jane, jumping off the bed and running to the cauldron, 'poor, poor toad. Please bring him back.'

'It's a painless death,' said the witch, 'the mixture acts as an instant anaesthetic and the heat cooks him in about eight seconds.'

'Oh but can't you bring him back?' said Jane.

'It's not a question of can or can't,' said the witch in a rather irritable voice, 'it's a question of having to keep on undoing things I've just done. I hate going backwards. However, I suppose I did offer to show you what I could do, so'—poking a long finger-nail into the steam hovering over the cauldron and then hooking it up as though pulling out a minnow on the end of a line—'out you come,' she said in her commanding voice. And at once the toad floated up out of the cauldron and landed gently beside her chair again. He looked at Jane again; this time, she thought, with gratitude.

'Oh thank you,' said Jane, 'how clever you are.'

'Hardly clever,' croaked the witch, though she gave a pleased and crooked smile, 'I don't think it would be possible to imagine a simpler spell.'

'Could you just do one more thing?' said Jane hesitantly, 'one more tiny thing?'

'Very well,' said the witch, 'on one condition, I won't go backwards again.'

'I was wondering if you could just send him out onto the mountain to live happily ever afterwards,' said Jane.

'That doesn't require a spell at all,' said the witch, 'you seem so keen on him I thought you'd probably want him to become a Prince and me to send you both out onto the mountain to live happily ever afterwards. However, no doubt you are right. I'm obviously not going to get rid of him any other way. Off you go, toad.' At the wave of her hand, the toad didn't wait for an instant. With five huge rubbery jumps he covered the distance to the entrance, and with the sixth was gone.

The witch looked after him in silence, and then suddenly said, '*Happily* ever afterwards. He'll hardly be happy all alone. We need more toads.' She raised her arms, muttered rapidly to herself, and clapped her hands.

Immediately the cave was full of toads. Green toads, grey toads, black toads, pink toads. Little toads and huge toads. Croaking, clacking, jumping, squelching, swelling, roaring, stinking toads; popping up from all over the place, and then at once bounding towards the end of the cave and out of it with their elastic legs stretched straight behind them. After five minutes when at least ten thousand toads, or so it seemed, had passed before Jane's amazed eyes, the witch clapped her hands and all was quiet again.

'You see,' she said, 'witches can be as kind and thoughtful as anyone else. It's only boredom makes us spiteful.'

'What shall we do now?' said Jane.

'Ah indeed!' said the witch, 'you see what I mean, once everything becomes possible, you don't want anything. After all, you can only want what you don't have, and now we have everything. We could talk, I suppose. Or you could talk and I could listen.'

There was a short pause, while Jane found she could think of nothing.

'Or I could talk,' said the witch, 'and you could listen. That, I confess, is the way round I prefer.'

'Or we could both talk and neither listen, or both listen and talk at the same time or taking it in turns,' said Jane. She suddenly felt rather reckless and bottled up. The witch looked at her with an odd expression.

'I think you need a sleep, my dear,' she said, 'however, for the moment I think I'll talk and you can listen.'

'It was interesting,' she began in a new, deep, monotonous voice which Jane felt could go on forever, 'that the first spells you made me do were turning something into something else. People, when they first discover magic, always turn things into other things. Now . . .' and then the witch stopped. 'I know what we'll do,' she said briskly.

'What?' said Jane.

'We'll play the transformation game,' said the witch, 'I haven't played it for over a hundred years. It's very simple. The idea is that whatever your opponent turns into, you turn into something to beat it. For example, if I turned into a pin, you'd turn into a pin-cushion. If you turned into a fire, I'd turn into water, then you'd turn into a cow to drink me. I'd turn into a lion and so on. Now what would you do if I turned into butter?'

'Turn into a butter knife,' said Jane.

'Quite good,' said the witch. 'Of course you could have melted me. Right. Are you ready?'

'But I can't turn into anything,' said Jane. 'How do I do it?'

'Ah yes, very simple,' said the witch. She dipped a nail into the cauldron, scattered some drips over Jane and muttered to herself. 'Now all you have to do,' she said, 'is to think hard about what you'd like to be. You'll find that whatever it is, you will still be able to think and therefore turn yourself back. Of course, think is all you will be able to do which whatever you are can't. I mean, if I became soup, and you turned yourself into a spoon, you wouldn't be able to walk. You'd just be a thinking spoon. Unless, of course, you had turned yourself into a spoon with legs. Do you understand?'

'I think so,' said Jane. 'I should hope so,' said the witch. 'It is extremely simple. Now practise. Turn into something.'

Jane thought for a minute, and then found herself thinking of a box of matches. The next moment, there she was—squat, square, small and handy, a box of matches on the floor. In a very odd way, like having eaten a lot, she felt the matches inside her. From far above came the witch's voice, 'Well done,' it said, 'turn back.'

Because the witch had spoken, Jane thought of the witch. In an instant she was standing opposite and looking exactly like her, with long dark cloak, curved finger nails and pointed hat.

'No, *no*,' said the witch irritably, 'not into me. Turn into yourself.'

Jane thought hard about herself, and, after a confused moment when she felt herself turning into a mirror, returned with relief to her usual shape.

'Good,' said the witch. 'Very quick. Now, let us begin the transformation game. The rules are that if you can't think what to turn into after fifteen seconds, you lose ten points. I will begin.'

'Please start with something easy,' said Jane.

'Of course, I will,' answered a high voice at her feet. Looking down Jane saw a cat. That was certainly easy; she thought hard about dogs, and immediately shot down onto four furry legs and heard herself growling. But almost at once she felt something tighten round her neck; the witch had turned into a collar and lead. Leads reminded her of holding leads, so Jane imagined herself a hand and found she was holding the lead with all of her turned, as it were, into hand. The witch turned into warts. Quickly Jane thought herself a snail—Mrs Deal's cure for warts—and began to crawl over the hand. Then she felt something pecking at her, as the witch became a bird. Jane thought of her father's gun and at once felt herself seized. The witch had become a cowboy.

Jane became a sheriff. 'Well done,' said the cowboy, immediately becoming a troop of Indians, whooping and shouting. Jane, remembering an old film she'd seen on television, at once thought of a prairie fire. The witch became a rainstorm. And when the cave was half full of water, Jane first became a plug and then, feeling she was too small, a very large, thirsty cow. The witch turned into a lion. Jane a mouse. The witch a cat. Jane a dog. The witch a kennel. Jane an axe. The witch . . .

But at this moment Jane realized that the transformation could quite easily go on for ever. So when the witch turned into a grindstone and began spinning towards her, she decided to do nothing but just let the witch win.

After a moment the grindstone stopped spinning, and became the witch again. She waved her hands over the axe and made it Jane again. 'Ten points to me, I'm afraid,' she croaked with pleasure. 'Of course a grindstone is always difficult. As a matter of fact oil and water beat a grindstone, also a blacksmith and strangely enough, spit. If you'd become spit, I would then become a mouth, you could become a dentist or a gum shield, me the dentist's female assistant or a boxing glove, you . . .'

'Excuse me interrupting,' said Jane timidly, 'but though the grindstone was far too clever for me, I also remembered that I had a train to catch.'

'A train to catch?' said the witch 'well, you had certainly better go at once. Now, where was I? Yes—I'm a boxing glove or the dentist's assistant, you become a referee or a disease, I become a hospital or . . .'

'I really *must* go,' said Jane, 'thank you so much.' But the witch took no notice of her at all.

'. . . a hot water bottle or a toothmug,' she was saying, 'you would of course become a pin or a clumsy boy, I become a puncture outfit or a pin cushion or a cane.' Jane tip-toed to the door of the cave, then turned and waved goodbye. 'Thank you, witch,'—she said under her breath in case the witch should hear and whisk her back. But there was no danger of that. The witch had her back to the door and was speaking as fast and as loudly as her croaking voice would allow.

'. . . I would become boredom or death or a railway time-table or a mattress,' she was shouting, 'you'd become possibility or a new-born baby or a cancellation or a house-on-fire. I . . .'

Very quickly and very quietly Jane stepped through the crevice and out onto the mountainside.

There was, however, no mountainside left. Nor, getting used to the sudden changes in Dream Land, was Jane particularly surprised. She found that she was standing in warm sunlight outside a small railway station. Hedges and fields stretched on every side and from the distance came the sound of church bells.

Walking up to the station, Jane went through the door marked 'booking office'. The hall was empty, though on it's far side, where an iron gate led to the platform, she could see the ticket collector asleep in his green ticket-collector's box. The little booking office window was open and just inside it someone had left an untidy heap of green tickets and a note saying 'Please take one'.

Jane did this and then walked over and prodded the ticket collector, whose spindly legs were blocking the way to the platform. At once he sprang to his feet, touched his cap and said, ' 'Oi be mighty zory Miss— oi do indeed. But a body git a mite dozzy these tiddly zummer arternoons.' Jane found she could scarcely understand what he said.

'What time is the next train and where is it going to?' she said briskly.

The ticket collector scratched his head, took a straw from his hair and put it in his mouth, then pulled a huge silver watch from his breast pocket, clicked it open, stared at it, clicked it shut, put the straw back in his hair and said, 'The zee-zide and market train do be due in foive minutes, miss.'

Somewhat impatient with this performance and still not certain what it meant, Jane let him punch several holes in her ticket, thanked him and hurried out onto the small platform. Neat notices on the other side showed that the station was called 'Job's Mill', and this curious name was also picked out in pansies on a little bank some way down the platform.

Jane did not have long to wait for the train. After a few minutes there came a gentle tooting and in a moment the engine appeared.

It was quite small, with a high funnel. Attached to the engine were four gaily painted carriages, which were quite bursting with people. Some sat on the roof, some clung to the doors or bulged out of windows; as the train came nearer many of them jumped down. And when the train actually stopped, snorting and steaming and blowing its whistle, it appeared to explode. Doors and windows were flung open and such a torrent of people poured out that Jane hurriedly climbed onto the little bank to avoid being squashed.

Jostling and pushing, they rushed past her. The men with hats, beards or side whiskers; the women with long sweeping skirts, bonnets and ringlets. All of them were carrying baskets of fruit, strings of onions, bundles of flapping chickens and every sort of thing from their farms. One giant of a man, with an apple-red face and knicker-bocker breeches, even had a calf flung across his broad shoulders.

The ticket collector tried for a moment to stem this crowd, Jane heard him cry 'Good gentle folk!', but then the man with the calf reached out and neatly tucked him under one huge arm and he was born away feebly shouting and waving his ticket puncher in the air. In a few minutes the station was quite empty.

Jane climbed thankfully into the last of the carriages and took a corner seat in one of the compartments. It was surprisingly tidy, with pretty curtains. Before long a man with a top hat came down the platform shutting doors, and a moment later the train started to move.

Jigadi-dig, jigadi-dig—the puffing of the engine was very peaceful as they slowly joggled through the pretty countryside. The sun had made the compartment almost too warm, and the soft seats covered in dark purple velvet were almost too comfortable. Jane began to feel sleepier and sleepier, and though she still remembered the Dream Master's stern warning about not sleeping, she couldn't remember if he had said anything about dozing. After all, she thought, she hadn't been to bed for two or three days, and though there was obviously something about Dream Land which made people need less sleep, they, or rather she, couldn't be expected to have no rest at all.

She was just about to stretch herself out on the seat, where she would no doubt have fallen at once into a deep and fatal sleep, when the train gave a loud whistle and stopped so suddenly that she was flung to the floor. At the same time, Jane heard the sound of shouts and cheering. She scrambled crossly to her feet and looked out of the window.

Just ahead was another little station, but this one was packed from end to end and on both platforms with a jumping, yelling crowd; all waving their arms, hats, shrimping nets and buckets and spades. The train moved slowly into it and stopped. At once all the people began to scramble in.

In seconds all the seats were taken. It made no difference, because they immediately began to sit on each other's knees. No one seemed to object. A huge woman stood in front of Jane, turned round, and then calmly sat down, completely enveloping her in petticoats, knickers and skirts.

Jane began to struggle violently. But the woman, who was extremely heavy, paid not the slightest attention; and at last, nearly suffocating, Jane wriggled out from beneath her large legs and down onto the floor of the compartment.

Even here she was little better off. Everywhere was legs, with an occasional walking stick or spade; and as Jane crawled towards the door of the corridor these kicked and poked her and often prevented her progress altogether. But at last she reached the door, forced it open, and fell exhausted through it into the corridor, which for some reason was quite empty.

Almost at once the train started again and Jane, ignoring the hubbub from the compartments behind her, opened the window and looked out at the slowly passing scenery. It was very peaceful: little cottages, small square fields with white and brown cows in them and, once, a slow, sleepy river. Jane leant lower and lower out of the window, the warm air ruffling her hair, and was about to fall into a doze when she heard a loud splitting noise coming from the end of the corridor to her right.

She looked sharply round and saw that a large crack had appeared in the floor of the corridor. As she watched, it grew swiftly longer and wider, running up both sides and then beginning to travel across the curved ceiling.

'Stop!' cried Jane, 'look out!' But even as she shouted, the crack grew into a gap and with a splintering of wood and clang of metal the whole back of the train fell neatly away onto the track.

She looked wildly round for a communication cord, could not find one, and began to bang on the door of the compartment behind her. But as she did so, there came another splitting sound and a crack appeared at her very feet. Appeared, and at once began to grow. Jane turned and ran farther up the corridor. She stopped once to look back; but before she could do so a loud splitting noise at her heels sounded the appearance of another crack. The train was crumbling away under her feet.

She reached the next carriage, but had no time to stand and stare. Already the floor at her feet was falling away and bouncing onto the lines. Jane rushed up to the next carriage, and the next and the next. This was the last, and reaching its end she flung open the door and climbed up onto the roof by a ladder she found conveniently bolted to the side of the train. Then she jumped straight onto the coal at the back of the old fashioned engine.

It was as well she did so, because when she looked back the last and final carriage had disappeared too.

The train was now moving very fast indeed. Jane climbed carefully down off the coal and into the engine driver's cabin. Perhaps, she thought, if I pull enough levers I may be able to stop it. But, before she could touch so much as a knob, she heard behind her a familiar and terrifying noise. It was the loud sound of tearing metal, followed by the rattle of coal falling onto the railway lines.

As quickly as she could, Jane pulled herself out of the little door at the side of the driver's cabin onto a narrow platform which ran beside the engine. Then, buffeted by the wind and nearly boiled by the boiler, she pulled herself forward, hearing behind her the crashes and clangs as the engine crumbled away.

At last she had reached the very front of the engine and was sitting in between the buffers. Her legs dangled over the railway lines as they shot underneath her. And behind her . . . Jane looked back, and saw that behind her was nothing. Only the two front wheels of the train remained with Jane on top of them, and these now began to go slower and slower until eventually they stopped. And when they had done so, they simply faded quietly away, leaving Jane sitting comfortably on a wooden sleeper.

The front two wheels had stopped at the top of a low cliff which looked down onto a narrow shore of pebbles and endless grey sea. Quite close to where the line ended, Jane saw some steep white steps cut into the cliff side and a notice saying 'BEACH'. She hurried over to the steps and started down them.

'BEACH' was a rather exaggerated name for what she found at the bottom. The strip of pebbles was even narrower than it had looked from the top, and there was no sand at all. To her left, where the shore stretched quite straight until it reached the horizon, she could see nothing. And, though to her right it quite soon curved out of sight round the edge of the cliff, she felt that it was just as empty. The same was true of the sea. Flat and calm as a bowl of soup, it seemed to go on for ever, without waves or ships or sign of land, hardly licking the pebbles at its edge.

And yet Jane had a strange feeling that somehow she would cross it. Several times already in Dream Land she had felt she was on a special journey, and that was why she had felt no hesitation, for instance, about getting onto the train, and why the sudden appearance of the steps in the air, or the crevice leading to the witch's cave, had not surprised her. And so now she not only felt sure she must cross the sea, but was quite certain that some method or other would soon arrive to let her do so.

And indeed no sooner had she thought this than she heard a curious lolloping crunch coming from her right, and looking round saw a familiar figure bounding towards her. It was the witch's toad.

'I had to come and thank you,' panted the toad, landing heavily at her feet, 'for making the witch let me go.'

'Oh, not at all,' said Jane, 'I was very pleased to be able to do it. How are you?'

'Quite well, quite comfortable,' answered the toad in his rather deep voice, 'too many of us of course. It was a typically extravagant gesture; kindly meant no doubt, but far too extravagant.

'But how are *you*? Can I help in any way?'

'Well there is one thing,' said Jane, 'I very much want to get to the other side of this sea.'

'I think I can help,' said the toad, sounding pleased. 'I cannot take you all the way because it is too far. But I can certainly start you off. The water is delightfully warm.'

Jane waded out until the water came up to her waist. Then, on the toad's instructions, placed her arms tightly round his wrinkled neck and floated out behind him while with vigorous kicks of his long strong legs he started to swim through the water.

They swam for hours. At first the gentle sound of the sea washing past them, the soothing warmth of the water, filled Jane with the same longing to sleep she had felt on the train. But the toad, feeling her fingers loosen round his neck said, 'I shouldn't go to sleep, my dear,' and told her the story of his life with the witch. He had been with her a hundred years. ('A hundred years!' said Jane, 'and she was going to turn you into that spell mixture. How cruel!' 'A hundred years isn't much when you are thousands of years old like she is,' said the toad.) The story of his life was so interesting that she had no difficulty at all in listening, and she was still wide awake when, as evening fell, they swam to a small, bare rock poking up out of the grey sea.

'Here we are,' said the toad. 'Now, I am going to take you down quite deep into the sea to meet a new friend of mine. He will, I think, be able to help you further. But while we dive, I must ask you to hold your breath. It will take no more than a minute—but that is quite difficult.

'Ready?' said the toad.

Jane nodded nervously.

'One, two three—go!' cried the toad. And as she took an enormous breath, he stood on his head and with Jane clinging tightly to his neck plunged under the water.

Down, down, down, down—just as she was about to explode, Jane felt the toad shoot swiftly upwards, a dazzling light sparkled round her and a high, piercing voice said, 'Well, well, well—what a charming surprise!'

Panting, ears popping, Jane opened her eyes and saw—

But no. Perhaps it is best not to tell what she saw. To describe all Jane's adventures underneath and on top of that huge, grey and dangerous sea—to tell how she saw a man cut off his arm and roast it, how she was allowed to borrow a mermaid's tail, of the land of the giant but kindly jelly fish, of how she was captured and escaped from an atomic submarine—to tell all these and many others would take a book longer than this one is already. It is only possible to hurry on to her final adventure in Dream Land, the one which led to her escape, for that in the end is what became necessary, from that strange and mysterious place.

Jane's last adventure took place early one morning nearly three weeks after the toad had carried her to the rock. She was standing on the deck of a small pirate ship when all at once from out of the mist there came rushing the most enormous wave she had ever seen.

There was not even time to sound the alarm. With a terrible roar the wave crashed upon the ship, breaking it at once into hundreds of pieces. But Jane was caught by one of the whirlpools which all really large waves have spinning inside them, and in a moment was carried to the top. She was swept several miles until at last the wave crashed into a cliff, dumping Jane, wet and battered but unhurt in some soft bushes at its top.

She was near the entrance to a wide, grass road which soon disappeared over the top of a gentle slope. On either side as far as Jane could see, rose a forest of giant lilies.

The grass had obviously been recently mown, so Jane set off up the slope. She had not walked far, when she heard the tinkling of a great many little bells. Moments later, there appeared over the top of the hill a curious procession.

First came running about twenty young black boys in white cloaks and turbans, then twelve black boys carrying a large litter covered in orange and green cushions finally more black boys.

When they reached Jane, they bowed low, the bells on their turbans tinkling, and pointed smiling to the litter, When she had climbed rather embarrassed into the cushions, they picked her up, turned round, and trotted away up the slope again.

From the top, Jane saw that the grass road first went down for a little way and then rose steeply up quite a high hill. And at the top of the hill, gleaming like sugar in the morning sunshine, was a large white palace. Big, onion-shaped lumps bulged all over its roof, two towers rose from its middle, and from all sides broad marble steps led down to the hundreds of fountains that surrounded it.

They soon reached the marble steps and ran up them. Then the little black boys lowered the litter, at the same time the two bronze doors in front of which they'd stopped slid silently open and there appeared a tall, white-robed man with a long, thin beard. He took two steps towards Jane, and bowed low.

'Welcome, brave girl,' he said, 'your travels and torments are over. Welcome to your just reward. This palace is yours. Here you will find rest and comfort, playmates and sweetmeats, plums and pomegranates, and sweet, sweet, sweet sleep.'

Jane stepped between the doors and saw stretching ahead a long, high, marble hall with pillars on either side. From invisible windows a dim light filtered through.

'I am your Vizier,' said the man, 'ask and it shall be done.'

'How do you mean this is mine?' said Jane, who already found the Vizier a little tiresome. 'Has someone given it to me? Who?'

'That I cannot yet say,' said the Vizier. 'All mysteries will be resolved later. Now we must refresh you,' and clapping his hands he beckoned a group of young black girls in white tunics and politely bowed Jane into their hands.

Jane, who was too tired even to think, went with them without protesting. All she wanted to do was to get back to Curl Castle and go to bed. She couldn't really understand why she hadn't gone days ago. In fact several times during the past three weeks she had been about to pull the piece of paper out of her jeans and quietly disappear only each time something like the huge wave or a particularly strange new monster had arrived to prevent her. These had also prevented her from dozing off, though she had often nearly done so. Now, however, she determined to return home as soon as she could; although she thought that first she might just find out a little more about the palace.

The young girls brought her to a chamber with a bath in it as big as a swimming pool. The moment she stepped into it Jane was thankful that she had waited at least till then.

The water in the pool was a deep purple, scented and warm. As she sat in it, Jane found her tiredness growing less and less, all the aches and bruises from her adventures were soothed away, and even her cuts closed up and healed before her eyes.

So relaxed did she feel, that when the little girls took away her jeans and her shirt and dressed her instead in a long pink silk dressing-gown, she did not call them back.

When she was ready, the girls lead her to the Vizier again, who bowed and said, 'Now Mistress, we have prepared a little entertainment for you. A few sweet meats. Some music.' He clapped his hands and a dozen black boys appeared with an enormous black silk cushion the size of a sofa. When Jane had settled herself in it, they caught the tassels at its edge and carried her from the hall.

After a great many stairs, passages, corners, rooms and steps they arrived eventually at a small chamber which must have been nearly at the top of one of the tall towers. Through its wide, richly curtained windows Jane could see the forest of lilies stretching to the sparkling sea. The windows had no glass and, faint as a whisper, the delicate scent of the lilies was wafted in on a gentle breeze.

The chamber had thick carpets, tapestries on the walls and brightly coloured cushions everywhere. But in the middle of one wall a far larger heap of cushions formed a rough bed. Onto this the black boys carefully laid Jane and her giant cushion. All but four of them then left (backwards), and these four picked up guitars and very softly began to pluck them.

As soon as she heard the lovely notes, Jane felt a great drowsiness come over her. Snuggling down, she let herself relax deep into the cushions. As she had realized before, something about Dream Land made sleep less necessary, but even so she hadn't so much as dozed for three weeks. She sank deeper into the cushions, and heard at the same time the voice of the Vizier by her ear. 'You wish to sleep, Mistress? Then sleep, sleep, sleep.'

And then, as her eyes were closing, she seemed to hear another voice: *'If you are to return to your home you must never, never while you are here, fall asleep. Not for an instant, not for a single second however tired you are, however clever the temptations.'*

Immediately Jane pushed herself up and said in a loud voice, 'I will not go to sleep. Vizier.'

'Yes, Mistress?' said the Vizier bowing low.

'Stop that music,' said Jane, 'and bring me my jeans.'

'Your old clothes?' said the Vizier, waving his hands at the boys who at once stopped playing. 'Why do you want your old clothes? Have a sweetmeat. A pineapple?'

'I *want* my clothes, that's all,' said Jane. Suddenly she felt she was about to cry. 'I want my jeans.'

'Ah,' said the Vizier, 'you want the little message in the pocket?'

'Yes,' said Jane.

'But we have had it copied out for you on parchment,' said the Vizier. 'Bring the Mistress her parchment' he called, and immediately a black boy came running with a scroll in one hand.

Jane took it, unrolled it, read it. It was the spell! Without even bothering to say goodbye, she held it up and read in a slow, clear voice:

'Turn again, oh Book please turn,

Now through your pages I return.'

Then shut her eyes.

Nothing happened. When she opened her eyes, she was still among the cushions. There was the Vizier, still bowing low. All that had changed was that one of the black boys had brought in a small, iron brazier, from which was rising a thin stream of pale blue smoke.

Jane said the words again, and then again. Still nothing happened. She leant back into the cushions and felt a hot tear run down her cheek. Very gently, the Vizier took the parchment from her hand. 'Do not worry, Mistress,' he said, 'do not cry. Just sleep.' As he spoke, the music began again, softly, soothingly.

And all at once, Jane didn't worry. After all, why not stay in this comfortable palace? She could make friends with the little black girls, go riding in the lily forest. She could sleep. Perhaps later she would find some way of returning.

But, as her eyes were closing, a curious thing happened. The scented blue smoke from the brazier, which was now drifting all over the room, suddenly reminded her of someone. It was of her father. It had the same smell as the stuff he put on his hair. And immediately, thinking of him, she remembered her mother, Mrs Deal, Curl Castle. It seemed the most important thing in the world to go home.

With a great effort, she pushed herself up out of the cushions.

'I command you to get my clothes,' she said, 'at once.'

For a moment the Vizier looked coldly at her with his piercing black eyes. Then 'Very well,' he said, and turning round left the room.

He returned carrying her shirt and her jeans. Jane took them and eagerly searched the pockets. The paper was there. She opened it and, though the words were smudged by all the sea water, it had been tightly folded enough to protect them.

'Turn again, oh Book now turn,
Back through your pages I return.'
said Jane.

And at once she felt herself sinking through the cushions and a great cloud seemed to sweep through the room.

She found herself sitting on the cover of the Book in the old library. Through the open windows came the sound of birds and the clinking of someone doing something in the garden.

Jane took off the pink dressing-gown and put on her jeans and shirt. Then she climbed the book shelves and hurried back to the lived-in part of the Castle.

At her bedroom she paused just long enough to write a note— 'PLEASE DO NOT WAKE SIGNED JANE'—pin it to her door, then undressed and slipped into bed. She fell asleep almost at once.

8. The Land of the Lilies

JANE was woken up, however, very much earlier than she had hoped. Mrs Deal, without any floods to distract her, had noticed her absence almost at once. At first she had not been very worried. It was understood that when Lord and Lady Charrington were away, Jane should always be allowed to go and stay with her friends, provided she told Mrs Deal first.

But after ten days, when no postcard or telephone message arrived, she decided to ring some of the friends up herself, taking the numbers from Lady Charrington's leather telephone book. As friend after friend said—no they *hadn't* seen Jane, Mrs Deal became more and more worried. She hurried into one of Lord Charrington's studies and dug out a large heap of his very old private telephone books, some dating back to before the First World War. Mrs Deal spent two days slowly telephoning her way through them. Sometimes getting rather odd replies, since many of the people in the books had died or moved.

That very morning she had decided that if no message arrived from Jane by lunch time, she would telegram Lord and Lady Charrington in New York and call out the police and the fire brigade. Her feelings when she found Jane's note, therefore, were rather mixed. First she felt relieved, then surprised and curious, and finally, when she remembered her hours, in fact days, of telephoning, she felt angry.

She hurried into the bedroom, pulled back the curtains and then shook the little girl with a bony hand.

'The death of me,' said Mrs Deal. 'You'll be the death of me. Now where have you been, Lady Jane? You know full well your mother said you must always tell me when you go. I'll have a tale to tell her when she comes home.'

Jane sat up blinking. She felt dizzy and had a headache. 'I went to see some friends, Mrs Deal,' she said in a small, I'm-sorry voice, 'I meant to write, but I was so busy there wasn't time to let you know.' In a way this was true.

'Friends indeed!' said Mrs Deal, 'I've telephoned all your friends. I've telephoned all the friends the Earl and Countess have ever had; and some of the old Earl's *friends'* friends too. Now what have you been up to?'

Jane thought. It was no good telling Mrs Deal about the Book. She wouldn't believe a word. 'She'd think I'm mad,' thought Jane.

'I've been staying with Kate, Sophie, Frances and Algy Behrens,' she said.

Now the Behrenses were the one family who didn't have a telephone. They lived in a boat on the Paddington Canal in London.

'I see,' said Mrs Deal. She patted her grey hair and made a vague dusting motion with her hand.

'Please, Mrs Deal,' said Jane, falling weakly back, 'I don't feel very well.' It was true. Not only was her head aching, but she felt very hot and rather sick.

And then Mrs Deal, who really loved Jane and was very pleased to see her back, and who in any case was now thinking it was very foolish of her to forget the Behrenses who had no telephone, Mrs Deal bent forward and gave her a soft dry kiss on the forehead.

'Well, never you mind,' she said, 'next time you send me a postcard or you'll have me grey before my time. Now just you lie there and we'll take your temperature.'

Jane's temperature was 102, so Mrs Deal called the doctor. He said that she had caught a feverish chill and must stay in bed. This she did for four days, sleeping most of the time, and having delicious invalid food like fish rolled up and cooked in milk, chicken broth and large white grapes from the Curl Castle greenhouses.

After a week she had completely recovered, except that Mrs Deal, although it was still what Jane considered summer, made her wrap up when she went outside.

She decided that she would not, for a while at least, go inside the Book again. Partly because the last adventures, though she had enjoyed them, had been almost too exciting. And partly because Mrs Deal had told her that her father and mother were expected back in a fortnight. Jane longed to see them both again and was determined not to be roaming about somewhere in the Book when they returned, also she knew that, if she weren't at home when they arrived, it would be far harder to convince them that she'd been staying with the Behrenses than it had been Mrs Deal.

However, there were a lot of things to do at Curl. All the servants had their children back again, and Jane played with the ones she liked. The one she liked best was called Simon, the son of the head gardener, a boy about her own age with very black hair and dark brown eyes. Mrs Deal said he was 'a bundle of charms', and although Jane knew this to be untrue, since he sometimes teased her, fought her and made her cry, she much preferred playing with him to anyone else.

But one night, about a week after her return, and after a particularly long, hot day playing in the wood, Jane found she couldn't get to sleep. This was something which quite often happened to her. The night too was hot, with no wind, and even taking off her pyjamas and lying very still under just a sheet, always meant to make you cool, made no difference. She told herself stories, tried to think of nothing, even—completely use-less—counted sheep.

When the clock in the stables struck twelve with deep, melodious chimes, she decided to go down to the kitchen and get herself a glass of milk and some fruit.

The Castle felt full of sleep when she stepped in her dressing-gown out into the corridor. But even so, like all old houses, it gave continual creaks and made sudden noises as though the furniture, the walls and the floors were moving and stirring in the middle of strange dreams. Jane's bare feet made no sound on the thick carpets and her room was dimly lit by a faint moon shining through the windows.

When she reached the balcony running round the main hall (the same one Mrs Deal had been carried through by the piano during the flood), she stopped to look down. It was a little lighter here because of the many windows, and the chests and sofas threw shadows which, for a moment, Jane could imagine concealed monsters or burglars.

She was not on the whole a frightened girl, though anyone, whatever their age, can be frightened in the dark; but at that moment the ghosts of Curl Castle made her wish she was safe in bed again. It was true they nor-mally stayed in their own separate bits—the little girl, for instance, around the old library, the monk in the bowling alley—and it was true that none of them had been seen for years. All the same, she looked closely round the moonlit hall and, especially after some particularly loud creaks, it was some time before she was quite sure nothing was there.

Through the hall, then into a short, uncarpeted stone passage, some steps, and finally another stone passage which led to the kitchen. It was while she was feeling her way down this that Jane suddenly heard a very definite loud noise. It was not a creak or a crack such as the sleeping furniture made but a clink, and almost at once it was repeated, as if someone, *or something* thought Jane, had knocked a cup over in a saucer. A little farther, on tip-toe, and she saw that a dim, flickering light was coming from the kitchen door.

Jane crept gradually closer. Now she could hear distinct sounds of careful movement. Her heart beating, she reached the door and slowly, slowly looked inside. What she saw for a moment stopped her breathing.

It was the little girl!

About Jane's size and wearing a long white dress, she was standing near the stove with a long candle in one hand. Her long dark hair was held back by a ribbon. With her other hand she was heaping various things onto a plate: an orange, some pieces of bread and, nearby, a glass of milk. It was seeing these, exactly the sort of thing she had planned to get for herself, that made Jane all at once feel quite unafraid. Perhaps, in fact, it wasn't *the* little girl at all, but just one of the servants' children dressed in a rather peculiar night dress.

So stepping firmly into the doorway she said in a loud voice, 'What do you think you are doing here, please?'

At once the little girl gave a tremendous jump and knocked the orange onto the floor. Then turning round she ran and stood with her back to the sink, at the same time her appearance began to alter. Very slowly she became transparent. When Jane could see the draining board quite clearly through her stomach, the windowsill through her chest, and the taps through her right shoulder, the little girl raised her arms and said in a slow, ghostly voice, 'Wooo, wooo.'

'You don't frighten me,' said Jane, though she did feel a bit nervous, and began to walk towards the sink.

'Wooooo, wooooo, *wooooo*,' went the little girl, pointing her small, transparent hands at Jane.

'You still don't frighten me,' said Jane, 'it's you who are frightened, otherwise you wouldn't go "woooo" like that,' and she continued to walk towards what, it was now obvious, was the ghost.

'Why aren't you frightened?' the little girl said, beginning to turn solid again. 'Nearly everyone else I've done that to has either fainted or else run away as fast as they could.'

'I'm just not,' said Jane, stopping by the table, 'but why do you do it? Do you want to frighten people?'

'Well, it stops them asking questions,' said the little girl, coming towards Jane. 'When I first came back here people would try and catch me and if I told them where I came from they didn't believe me. So I use the transparent trick which—well, which someone taught me.'

'Where *do* you come from, if you don't mind me asking?' said Jane.

'In a sort of way I come from a book,' said the little girl slowly.

'You mean the Book in the old library?' said Jane.

'Ah, you know about it?' answered the little girl. 'I wondered if it was you. I knew someone had found it by the footprints in the dust. But I must say I'm surprised to see you still here.'

'How do you mean?' said Jane.

'Oh, doesn't matter,' said the little girl, 'you'll find out.'

'But do you mean you *live* in the Book?' said Jane. 'Does that mean all the other people in it can come out and roam about Curl Castle?'

'Oh no,' said the little girl, 'but it's a long story; I can't explain now.'

Jane wondered if the little girl could answer any of her questions. She said, 'Well, why did you come here tonight?'

'Oh, all my friends have gone away for a week,' said the little girl. 'Also I was due to come. I hadn't realized it would be night.'

There was a small silence while Jane wondered what to say next, but found that she could only think of the questions the little girl wouldn't answer. Then suddenly the little girl said, 'You wouldn't like to come and stay with me, would you? We could have great fun and I could show you all my things. I might be able to teach you how to go transparent.'

Jane thought. There was Simon; then there were her mother and father, but they weren't coming back for a week. 'All right,' she said. 'But I can't stay more than six days.'

'Then let's go now,' said the little girl, 'if we're quick we'll just be in time for supper and then you can go to bed. I left about tea time.'

'First I must dress,' said Jane, 'and I *must* leave a note for Mrs Deal, or else she'll explode.'

They went upstairs together. Jane dressed rapidly in her jeans and a clean shirt and placed a sharp penknife in a back pocket. She wrote a quick note to Mrs Deal saying 'Gone to stay with Kate, Soph, Frances and Algy Behrens again. They may take me to Guernsey so don't bother to write. Back in six days. Love, Jane.' Then they set off through the long silent corridors for the old library.

During the walk, the little girl, whose name she discovered was Clarissa, didn't talk very much, so Jane told her about the great flood and how she'd blown open the tunnel.

'I remember that tunnel being dug,' said Clarissa.

'Do you?' said Jane, 'but surely that must have been hundreds of years ago—do you mean that . . .'

'Well, don't let's talk about it now,' said Clarissa, hastily interrupting her, 'we must hurry or it will be dark at home. Let's run.'

'Yes, all right,' said Jane, and they began to jog along, the candle flickering. She longed to ask Clarissa a great many questions. She was probably the only ghost she'd ever meet. If Clarissa *was* a ghost—she seemed far too solid.

Once they were both in the library, Clarissa put the candle, now burnt quite low, onto the chair and lifting open the Book slowly began to turn its pages.

Jane watched closely. She had noticed that each time she returned to the Book all the pictures had been different. So it had always seemed impossible to return to the same place again. After a while, she asked Clarissa about this.

'Well yes, the pictures do sort of change,' said Clarissa, 'but not as much as it seems. Once you've been in one place then somewhere in the Book there'll always be a bit of that place again. For instance, I think,' she stopped turning the pages and looked closely at the picture, 'yes, I recognize this part. It's not too far from my home. Now come and stand beside me and hold my hand. I'll say the words.'

With heart beating, Jane stepped up beside her and felt for her hand. At the same time she looked down to see where it was they were going. But before she could take in more than a general picture of paleness, which might have been water and might have been cloud, Clarissa had stepped off the Book and blown out the candle. 'It may come in useful,' she said, 'I'll leave the matches too.' Then she stepped back, took Jane's hand and said quietly:

> 'Shut eyes, do not look,
> Close your pages on me Book.'

Once again, familiar now, Jane felt herself begin to sink down into the softening paper.

In the moonlit greyness of the old library, the heavy cover of the Book rose slowly up and without a sound closed firmly on the two little girls.

They were standing on the shores of what, until Clarissa told her it was a very large lake, Jane thought must be the sea. It was early evening, and in the fading light she could see that behind and stretching away on either side was a field of giant plants. Among the dense mass of forty-foot grasses, there were huge daisies and house sized buttercups swaying in the wind. In the distance, skyscraper thistles and nettles rose still higher and even the crumbling grains of soil were, close-to, as large as Jane herself.

'Where are we?' she said.

'Quite near where I live,' said Clarissa, 'around here is a land of insects, but on the lake live the Lily people. But we must get home quickly. It's never very safe and even as late as this there's always a chance of hunter ants. But now look, try and get four pieces of grass about this long,' and she stretched her arms about two feet apart.

Jane found that the shorter blades of grass were no harder to cut than thick cardboard, and had soon sliced off four lengths with her penknife.

'You see, the lake is very salty,' said Clarissa, 'it's a salt lake, a sort of sea inside the land. This means it has a sort of skin on it like boiled milk. In some places you can even walk on it in shoes, but its better to have these pieces of grass.' She had meanwhile been tying the lengths of grass to both their feet with some leather straps she produced from her pocket. When they were both ready, she tucked her long dress up round her middle and then led the way to the edge of the lake.

Jane at once found out what she meant by a sort of skin. When she looked closely at the water, she could see it had a thick, almost oily appearance, and when she put a finger on the surface it dented down like pressing a sheet. If she pushed harder, the surface broke, but even then the water felt quite thick, her finger, when she pulled it out, tasted of salt and as it dried, little speckles of salt appeared on it.

'Now look,' said Clarissa, 'it's very easy. You sort of slide out on your grass, and then push one foot and then the other to move along. Like this.' Jane saw her walk carefully to the edge put one length of grass onto the surface and then push off with the other. In a moment she was gliding gracefully upon the top of the water, calling Jane to follow.

And it was in fact as easy as it looked. Jane found that, nervous as she had been that she would simply sink straight to the bottom, her first foot was firmly supported. She pushed off with the second one and at once glided forward, rising with the heave of a long, gentle wave. To move forward she did just what she did when roller skating, which was shove with first one foot and then the other.

When Clarissa was sure Jane could do it, she said, 'Now we must go straight out for about half an hour. And don't worry if you fall over. It's impossible to sink and you'll just get wet and salty.'

They skated steadily in the direction of the setting sun. The thick yet slippery surface of the water moved slowly up and down in swelling waves and the speed gained sliding down into the valleys carried them almost up the other side so that a single push sent them over the crest. Unlike ordinary waves, these ones never broke or splashed.

Just as it was starting to grow really dark, Clarissa swooped closer to her and called out, 'Now we must go to the left a little. It's not far.' They turned left and after ten minutes, Clarissa called again. 'There you are. That's Lilytown.'

Peering ahead, Jane could just see numbers of small, black islands rising out of the sea. 'What are they?' she called. But Clarissa, obviously excited to be coming home again, had sped off to the right. Pushing hard with her feet, Jane raced after her.

Clarissa stopped at one of the islands. Jane swished up beside her, and found that it was not really an island at all. It was a vast lily leaf.

It was round and enormous, about the size of a tennis court; its edge was turned up so that all round it ran a low wall. And in its middle, Jane could see the outline of a small cottage with a little shed standing near it.

'This is *my* lily leaf,' said Clarissa proudly, 'and that,' she pointed 'is my house. Now you must come in at once, you must be exhausted.'

They climbed easily over the rim of the leaf, took off their grass water-skis and walked up to the house. Jane felt the ground, or rather leaf, of the lily, sink a little at each step like walking on a firm, new mattress.

Clarissa's cottage had one large room downstairs, with a larder, and two small bedrooms and a bathroom upstairs. The downstairs room had comfortable armchairs round an iron cooking stove, a table, four little windows with gay curtains and had soft rush matting on the floor. While Jane looked around, Clarissa piled logs into the stove, lit several oil lamps and soon had every thing warm and cheerful.

'It's lovely,' said Jane, 'it's so snug and sweet. I think it's lovely.'

'Yes, it is nice,' said Clarissa, 'but I'll show you round properly tomorrow.'

'Why are the chairs stuck to the floor?' asked Jane, who had tried to move one.

'Well, we sometimes have terrible storms,' said Clarissa, 'and then everything rocks and rocks and slides about. That's why my ornaments have to have little holes to sit in as well. But let's have some supper now and then go to bed.'

The two little girls prepared some bread, something like honey, some milk and some fruit, and when they had eaten it, excited and interested as she was, Jane found that she was in fact feeling very sleepy. After all, she told herself, it must be nearly four o'clock in the morning at Curl Castle. So Clarissa showed her to her room (which was very small, with a sloping ceiling, one window and a small bed covered in a blue and yellow eiderdown). They kissed each other goodnight, and in a few minutes she had fallen asleep.

Jane woke late, to find the sun streaming in through the little window. A cuckoo clock hanging opposite her showed it was already half past ten. And then, as she slowly stretched and yawned and thought about where she was, Jane noticed something rather strange. The whole room was gently rocking: the curtains, the oil lamp hanging from the ceiling, the dressing-gown on the back of the door which Clarissa had lent her, were all swinging together from side to side.

Jumping out of bed, Jane quickly dressed and ran down the stairs to the main room, staggering several times as the house lurched. Clarissa was already up and bustling about, and when she saw Jane, smiled happily.

'Did you sleep well?' she said. 'Have some breakfast then we'll go out. It's a lovely day.'

'Why is the house moving about?' said Jane, clinging tightly to the back of a chair. 'Is it a storm?'

'Oh no,' said Clarissa, 'It's often like this. There's a bit of a swell. But it's perfectly safe. The lily leaves have strong roots and never get swept away. Also the house is tightly pegged. You'd soon know if it was a real storm. I've been in some where it was almost like being upside down.'

Reassured, Jane sat down and had a delicious breakfast of hot milk, honey, and some rather curious eggs with very soft shells. Then, when she had washed and Clarissa had tied her own long hair back with a ribbon, the two girls went out onto the leaf.

It was indeed a lovely day. The sun shone bright and hot, a breeze blew towards the distant shore and all round them was the thick, oily sea, not sparkling, as at home, but gleaming in the sun. It was heaving in long, large swellings which were repeated, Jane saw, in long, large swellings moving across the green lily leaf at their feet. And behind them were the other lily leaves—Jane thought about two hundred. They all seemed much the same size as Clarissa's, and on each was a little house. Some had been joined together to hold larger houses. Floating everywhere between the leaves were large white blooms, themselves as big as cottages—the lily flowers.

Pointing excitedly, Clarissa showed Jane where her friends lived: 'That's Rupert's house, and that's Marius's,' she said, 'that's Sofka's and that's Inigo's and Aaron's and Luke's and Tino's, and that big house on two leaves is Petronella's shop. And you see that small, very pretty house there? That's Sophie Partridge's. Oh dear, if only you could have come earlier what fun we'd have had. You see all the Lily people go away at this time of the year for a long holiday.'

'I'd like to see it all, even if there's no one there,' said Jane, who longed to try sliding on the water again.

'Yes, all right,' said Clarissa, 'but first I must let Fly out.' And running over to the shed beside the house, she threw open its double doors.

To Jane's amazement there stepped slowly out, stopping once or twice to rub its nose briskly with two long and hairy front legs, the most enormous fly she had ever seen.

'Out you come,' said Clarissa, in the sort of voice Jane had heard girls use at pony club, 'steady now, mind your wings.'

The fly was somewhat larger than a large horse. Its body consisted of a series of overlapping, dark blue plates and long hairs; on each side of its back two sets of transparent wings were already quivering, and every few seconds there shot from its jaws a tongue like a thick tube, with a flat fleshy end. This made a loud squelching noise as it hit the leaf. Clarissa looked fondly at this monster for a moment, then stepping close she gave it a friendly slap and said, 'Off you go, Fly.'

At once, with a whirring of wings, the giant fly shot thirty feet into the air, hovered buzzing above them for a moment, and then sped zig-zagging away in the direction of the shore.

'He's a bit surprising at first,' said Clarissa, laughing at Jane's amazed expression, 'but you'll soon get used to him. I'll take you for a ride when he gets back from feeding. It's rather fun.'

Jane did not feel so sure of this, however she followed Clarissa across the gently undulating lily and, when they had both strapped on their grass skis, they climbed over the rim and set off across the lake.

For nearly two hours Clarissa took her round Lily town, telling her about the people and what she did with them. About how the pale, honey-tasting nectar came from the lily flowers, and how they had races on the water beetles.

It was all very interesting, but what Jane enjoyed most was the skat-ing or skiing. She found that the bigger the long, slow waves, the more fun it was. Soon, like Clarissa, she had learnt to wait for a large one, chase after it, and then balancing easily on its rounded top allow it to carry her swiftly forward. She practised swooping along the shallow troughs; practised turning, jumping, whizzing along on one leg. By lunch time, though exhausted, she felt quite sorry when Clarissa came up to her and said, 'I think we'd better go back. I left some spider's legs in the oven and we don't want them to spoil.'

The two girls had a good lunch (the spider's legs were rather tough, but Clarissa had made a delicious gravy to go with them) and then sat comfortably back in the soft chairs and ate some fudge.

It was very peaceful in the little cottage. The sun streamed in through the windows, the lily gently rocked, and a kettle gently steamed on the black stove. Jane felt that the moment had come to ask all the questions which Clarissa had not answered the day before, so she sat up and said in a careful voice: 'Clarissa, would you mind telling me about how you came here, and all about the Book and that sort of thing? You needn't if you don't want to,' she went on quickly, seeing Clarissa look rather worried and fidgety, 'but then I could tell you about my adventures.'

Clarissa thought for a moment. 'All right,' she said, 'I suppose you're sort of one of us. It's not that I mind telling, because it doesn't matter. It's just, well, I don't know . . .' she stopped. 'Well, it all began one winter when my mother and father had to go to London for the season, leaving me in Curl Castle with my brothers and sisters.' And settling back, she began to tell her story.

It was a very long story. It took three hours, because often Jane stopped her to ask questions, and because Clarissa, once started, told every single tiny thing that had happened.

Like Jane, Clarissa had found the Book because she was lonely. Her brothers and sisters had all been much older than she was, and in trying to find something to do, away from their loud, teasing games, she had accidentally stumbled across the old library. Like Jane she had found a piece of paper with the same strange words on it, and had at once begun to go adventuring.

Unlike Jane, however, she had discovered for herself quite quickly how to return to the same part of the Book, and this had made it much more fun. Because when she made friends she was always able to go back and see them again and have more adventures with them. Also in those days the servants as well as being very much more frightened of their masters and mistresses, always did what their masters' and mistresses' children told them, and Clarissa was able to do more or less what she liked. She began to spend weeks at a time in the Book. By the end of the winter, it seemed almost as unreal to return to Curl Castle as it had been at first to leave it.

Then, one day in the early spring, she had entered a land quite different from all the others she had been in before. From her description of it, Jane was at once certain that it was the Land of Dreams. She was about to say she had been there too, when for some reason she decided not to. And in a few moments it turned out this was very lucky. Clarissa had also seen the Dream Master, had liked him and still remembered his advice.

'He told me,' said Clarissa, 'that on no account was I to go to sleep. Well now, I know you haven't been there yet. But I know you will one day and that is the only reason I can tell you all this.'

'Yes,' said Jane in a vague voice, 'go on.'

'Well when he tells you about going to sleep,' said Clarissa, 'of course you can do what you like. But I can tell you it doesn't matter if you do go to sleep.' She looked rather anxiously at Jane, so Jane said brightly 'Oh, I'm sure I will go to sleep. I'm *always* going to sleep.' Clarissa smiled and went rapidly on. She too had found the grey sea, and she too, after many adventures, had ended up at the Palace surrounded by the forest of giant lilies. ('Perhaps that's why you like living on water lilies so much,' said Jane.) Like Jane she had been tempted and tempted with music and fans and slaves and incense and deep, soft, scented cushions. And suddenly she just couldn't be bothered any more and had, as she put it, sort of drifted off into a wonderful, long, endless sleep.

She had slept, she thought, for about 180 years. When she awoke she had been given a parchment with the Book's words and told politely she must go. So she had returned to Curl Castle, and of course it had quite changed. Her mother and father and all her brothers and sisters had long since died, and because the Castle looked very different and because people asked such irritating questions, she used to walk about transparent, a trick she had learnt on an earlier adventure. She also found that she was only able to return to Curl Castle three times a year. Though this made adventures in the Book much more dangerous, she had decided to live in the Book forever. She had tried various places until at last she'd found the Land of the Lilies.

When she had finished, the two girls sat in silence for a while. Although Clarissa wasn't in the least unhappy, or even lonely, Jane felt sorry for her. It must be sad to have no mother or father or proper home.

'Look, Clarissa,' she said at last, 'would you like to come home with me? I know Mummy and Daddy would love you and we could play together and have adventures in the Book.'

'It's very very kind of you,' said Clarissa, 'but you see I don't really want to. It's all changed so much since I was there, and now this is my home. You wait till you have slept in the Palace for 180 years. You'll understand then.'

'But do you mean you'll never get married?' said Jane, 'never have children? Will you always be a little girl and never ever grow up?'

At once Clarissa sat up. 'I hate that word!' For the first time she looked upset, with an expression on her pretty face half angry and half frightened. 'Who wants to grow up anyway? Grown-ups die, they get tired, they're never excited; they don't understand. I want to be like this for ever and ever and ever.'

But though Clarissa looked defiantly ahead and spoke in a brave, loud voice, Jane saw two small tears, and then two more roll down her pink cheeks. She hurried over and put her arms round her.

'Don't cry, Clarissa,' she said, 'don't cry.'

'It's not that I'm sad,' said Clarissa, starting to smile, 'it's just that word. It always makes me cry without making me sad.'

'Tell me about the other people,' said Jane, 'the other non-Book people. Who are they?'

'Oh, mostly quite young,' said Clarissa, 'though there are one or two older ones. There's a very nice boy who writes poems. He says he can fly. But I don't often see them. You just sort of hear about them and sometimes see them.'

'But how do they get in,' said Jane, 'they can't all have Books. And they can't all use Curl Castle.'

'Oh they have maps,' said Clarissa vaguely, 'thoughts and mirrors and special walks. Some have books.' She didn't seem very interested, and kept on looking towards the windows, through which Jane could see the sky was already getting darker as evening began to fall.

Though she felt sorry for Clarissa, she also felt rather envious. In a way it would be nice not to go back to Curl Castle, or only go back when she wanted, when her parents were there.

'I suppose you're a sort of relation of mine,' she went on to Clarissa, 'are you a Charrington?'

'Yes,' said Clarissa.

Jane was beginning to work out what sort of relation, how many great-greats, etc., when Clarissa suddenly jumped out of her chair and ran to one of the windows. As she did so, the cottage which Jane had dimly noticed seemed to be swaying more than usual, gave a great lurch so that Clarissa was thrown quite roughly against the wall and Jane nearly fell out of her chair.

'I thought so,' said Clarissa, 'we're going to have a storm. They blow up in a moment at this time of the year. Here take this and come and help me.' She handed Jane an enormous spanner and together they hurried out onto the lily leaf.

It was very different from the sunny calm of the morning. A strong wind, blowing straight into their faces as they came from the cottage, was sweeping a cover of dark cloud low across the sky. Rising waves, which in some places had broken sluggishly over the rim of the lily, were beginning to lift them up and down, up and down, so that one moment they were hidden in a small, watery valley, and the next were on top of a rolling grey hill and able to look across the waters to where all the other lily houses were also bobbing up and down.

'Tighten all the bolts round the house,' shouted Clarissa above the wind. She pointed to a corner of the cottage and Jane saw that along the walls, where they rested on the leaf, large, six-sided bolts stuck up every two feet, holding it down. It was becoming difficult to stand, but by crawling on hands and knees she managed to pull the bolts as tight as she could with the large spanner.

When she had worked her way round to the front of the cottage again, she saw that Clarissa had opened the door of the shed and, clinging to it, was now anxiously scanning the sky. In one hand she held a long length of what looked like white, nylon rope; in the other a small wooden whistle which, when she blew it, gave a loud, piercing squeak.

As Jane pushed her way towards the shed, Clarissa suddenly shouted, 'There he is!' and pointed excitedly into the air. Following her finger, Jane at last made out a tiny black object corning slowly towards them from the direction of the shore.

It was Fly. As they watched, though continually blown back and buffeted by the wind, he came gradually nearer. After about five minutes, he was hovering more or less above them.

Clarissa now stepped forward and with a quick movement threw the rope high into the air, holding fast to one end. Immediately, before it could be blown away by the wind, Fly plunged down and caught it nimbly in his mouth.

'Quick—help me!' shouted Clarissa. And as the rope tightened, Jane seized the end too, and they began to pull him in, hand over hand like pulling in a large kite. Soon he had landed and quickly they hustled him into his shed and closed the doors.

Now, on hands and knees, they struggled back to the cottage through what, even in the short time they had been out, had already turned into a real gale. Gigantic waves were beginning to break over the rim and the wind was making a curious and terrifying howling noise. But after five minutes they were safe inside and Clarissa was bolting and then double bolting the stout wooden doors.

Both girls were soaked to the skin from the water breaking across the leaf, and already the salt was making their clothes stiff and white.

'First we must change,' said Clarissa, 'and then make everything sort of ship-shape.'

Already it was impossible to stand without holding on to something. Every few moments the floor became first uphill and then downhill, and though the chairs and tables were firmly pegged to the floor, cushions and table-cloths slid off, and ornaments were falling out of their holes.

When they had changed, Clarissa locked wooden shutters over all the windows and lit storm lanterns. Jane put all the ornaments in a special cupboard, which had cotton-wool compartments, and coiled up the white rope. ('It's really from one of the giant spiders on the shore,' called Clarissa, 'very strong.') Before long the little, rocking room was quite tidy, with everything that could move carefully put away. The last thing Clarissa did was to unpeg a bit of the rug in the middle of the floor and roll it back. Jane saw that it covered a round trap-door with sunk-in bolts. These Clarissa tightened with a large box spanner.

'What's that?' Jane called.

'It leads to the lily stem,' Clarissa shouted back. 'I was going to take you down but we'll have to wait till the storm is over. It's rather exciting. It has steps going round and round and leads right down to the bottom of the lake where the roots are, and there are little bow windows you can look out of. But it might be dangerous just now, even though the stem is very strong and elastic indeed.' Then holding onto the mantelpiece, a table and the wall, she worked her way round until she could pull herself into the chair next to Jane. 'What shall we talk about?' she shouted.

So began one of the strangest nights Jane had ever spent. Outside the storm raged louder and louder with a fierce roaring noise. Every few moments the heaving, salty water crashed against the windows, and in the wind and buffeting the little house creaked and groaned like an old ship. It was almost impossible to hear each other speak. And in fact Jane had shouted back, 'What shall we *shout* about you mean,' though in fact she didn't want to talk or even think about anything at all.

It wasn't exactly that she felt sick. But often the lily almost stood on end and she had to cling to the chair to prevent herself falling out, and then the whole room would tilt up the other way, leaving her stomach quivering somewhere on the ceiling or so it felt. When this happened there came a deep thrumming from under the floor, which Clarissa explained was the lily stem vibrating as it stretched. And all the time the storm lanterns swung to and fro, so that mad shadows shot up and down the wall. Jane didn't quite feel sick, but she was glad that they had decided it was too rough to make any supper.

At about 10 o'clock they decided to go to bed. There was no sign of the storm ending, indeed the crashing and roaring and switch-backing seemed worse than ever, and even Clarissa, who was more used to it, was exhausted with clinging to her chair. So holding tight to banisters and door, they pulled themselves upstairs. Clarissa showed Jane how to strap herself into bed with the storm straps and then slithered out of the door and disappeared to her own room.

Although it was like being on a very soft, very violent see-saw, Jane almost immediately fell asleep.

9. The Ants

WHEN she woke up in the morning, the storm was nearly over. The cottage still rocked, and there was still the sound of a high wind, but no longer the terrible tossing of the night, or the crash as heavy salt water thundered against the window panes.

Jane had woken once before at about two o'clock. She seemed to have heard some loud noise, like the twanging of a huge harp string or a deep bell, but after listening for a while she had decided it must have been the storm and had gone to sleep again.

She now lay warm and snug, watching the gentle swaying of the curtains and the sun coming through the cracks in the shutters. 'I wonder what they are doing at Curl Castle,' she thought, and was just about to slip into a daydream about Mrs Deal and Simon and her mother and father, when the door flew open and Clarissa rushed in.

'Oh Jane,' she said, 'come quickly. The most terrible thing has happened. I don't know what we're going to do. Quickly, come downstairs,' and breathlessly she shot out of the room, 'I'm going to look for a gun,' she shouted back.

Jane pulled herself out of bed and scrambled into the clothes Clarissa had lent her the night before. What on earth could it be? A gun? Perhaps a dangerous crab had been swept onto the leaf by the storm and was about to attack them.

When she came downstairs she found Clarissa kneeling by one of the cupboards holding an old flint-lock gun in her hands. 'It's old, but I think it still fires,' she said, as Jane came in.

'But what's happened?' said Jane, 'what is it? Are we in deadly danger?'

'Look,' said Clarissa. She went to the door and Jane followed her out onto the leaf. It was a lovely sunny day, with a brisk breeze. The leaf was dry again though covered with bits of wood and weed. But this was not what Clarissa was pointing at so dramatically. Following her finger, Jane looked. And at once she realized. *The leaf had moved.*

Gone were the other lilies. Gone the distant shore. Instead, they were in a wide passage between two islands, or in an enormous river. The current was very fast, carrying them between the steep mountains which rose up on either side.

'You see?' said Clarissa, 'the storm must have broken the lily stem.'

'Yes, and I think I heard it,' said Jane.

'Did you?' said Clarissa. 'But do you realize where it has swept us? To where the ants live. At least I think so.'

'Ants' said Jane. 'Why does that matter?'

'Come and have breakfast,' said Clarissa, 'and I'll explain. But we must keep a watch on the shore.'

While they prepared a large and delicious breakfast of soft-shelled beetle eggs, lily honey and toast, and while they ate it, she told Jane about the ants.

They were supposed to live in giant ant heaps at the far end of the lake. 'Supposed to', because none of the Lily folk now alive had ever ventured there; but there were stories of earlier expeditions which had set out to explore and never returned. The ants were hunters who lived entirely off flesh, and during the day they sped in their millions through the tall grasses of the lake shore killing and eating. One thing about them was unusual. They never hunted at night. Indeed they were supposed to go into a sort of trance as soon as the sun fell and not come out of it again till sunrise. If you were captured, Clarissa said, this was the only time you could escape; provided you were still alive, or not had a leg or two snipped off.

'But are you sure this is the right end of the lake?' asked Jane.

'Not really,' said Clarissa, 'but the storm blew from the west and the ants are said to live in the east.'

'Anyway,' said Jane, 'this river or passage has very wide-apart banks. Perhaps we'll never get nearer to them.'

It was true that the banks were far away; nearly a mile on either side. And they remained at this comforting distance all the morning as the two girls worked on the cottage. First they cleared away all the weed and debris from the storm. They also tied a plank to the back of the leaf with some spider-web rope, so that they could steer the leaf well away from the banks and give the ants no chance to spring aboard.

Throughout the morning they had both kept looking at the banks and both had agreed they were as far apart as ever. Gradually, however, though she still said this, Jane felt that somehow they were not as far apart as before. Inch by inch they seemed to be closing in. Then she would look again, and they did in fact look just as far away.

But now there could be no doubt about it. They were nearer. She could see tall grasses instead of a blur and rocks stood out clearly.

'Clarissa,' said Jane, standing up, 'the awful thing is I mean I think the awful thing is . . .' She pointed out of the window.

'I know,' said Clarissa, 'I thought so too, but I didn't like to say anything.'

They ran out onto the leaf and what they saw was even more alarming. The river, or passage, had begun to twist. They were at that moment swinging round a long left bend and the lily, as a result, was being slowly swept towards the right-hand bank. They seized the plank and managed to steer gradually back to the middle again.

Once round the corner, they saw ahead another bend, and then another. Each time they had to strain on the plank to force the lily back into the centre. Each time, though it was difficult to be sure, the banks seemed a little closer.

It was after about ten bends that they passed a little clearing in the tall grasses on the left. Jane was staring idly at this when all at once the grasses parted and a huge insect ran swiftly across the space. As large as a horse, it had six legs, long, low-hanging jaws, bulging black eyes and two bodies joined like a wasp.

'Look, Clarissa,' she shouted. But it had gone. The next instant another appeared. And then five more. At least thirty had crossed the clearing by the time it had slipped out of sight behind them.

'The ants,' whispered Clarissa. 'Oh Jane, whatever are we to do?'

Soon they realized that they were surrounded by ants. The banks were now not more than fifty yards apart and drawing closer. Having seen the ants once, they could more easily see them again. A flash of fierce dark eyes staring motionless out of the grass, a sudden swirl of stems as the large bodies brushed through them; a glimpse of a shiny back catching the sun. The ants were quite silent, easily keeping up with the swiftly flowing current and the little cottage.

Or rather the once swiftly flowing current. Because Jane now noticed that quite suddenly the current had begun to slow down. The lily became harder and harder to steer. Soon the waters stopped moving altogether and then, sluggishly, the lily began very gently to drift towards the left-hand bank, spinning as it drifted.

'What shall we *do*?' said Clarissa for the second time. 'We'll be eaten alive.'

'We must escape at once,' said Jane. 'Will Fly carry two?'

'I think so,' said Clarissa, 'Yes, I'm sure he will for a little way. He's very strong.'

'Quick then,' said Jane, 'we've only a few minutes. You get Fly.'

As Clarissa unbarred the hut and began to coax the startled fly out onto the leaf, Jane dashed into the cottage and fetched the spider's-web rope from the wall. Then she hurried out and joined Clarissa.

The fly was now standing quietly, though Jane could see that its stubby transparent wings were quivering in the sunlight. Clarissa helped her up onto its broad back, and was just holding out a hand to be pulled up herself, when she suddenly said, 'I must just get the gun,' and rushed off into the cottage.

The lily had now drifted to within ten feet of the shore, where it seemed for the moment to have stopped. But everything the girls had done had been watched intently by hundreds of hungry eyes along the bank. And gradually there could just be heard a very high, sinister whistling, more like a vibration than a noise. And now, suddenly, Jane saw the grass swish aside. For an instant she saw one of the huge insects gathered back on its six hairy legs. Then it sprang out over the water towards the lily.

There was a fearful lurch as its forelegs crashed onto the leaf. It nearly slipped off, but then digging into the soft fibre with the cruel pincers which were its feet, it pulled itself dripping out of the water. The fly, with Jane clinging to it, backed trembling away. At the same time Clarissa came running from the cottage with her gun.

She saw the ant. Screamed. Fired a wild shot, which missed by many feet, and then, as she turned to run to Jane, was seized and lifted from the ground by one snap of the long jaws.

'Help, Jane! Help!' she cried.

But Jane could do nothing. The fly had been terrified at the appearance of the ant. At the sound of the gun it had become uncontrollable. With a leap and a whirring of its powerful wings it had shot into the air, and now Jane stared down in agony a hundred feet above the terrible scene below.

She saw Clarissa struggling, heard her call. Saw the ant shake its head and fix her more firmly between its jaws. Then watched while it sprang off the leaf, land some way out in the water, swim to shore and disappear into the darkness of the tall, waving grasses.

'Don't worry, Clarissa,' she shouted down as loudly as she could, 'I'll rescue you.' There came no answering shout.

It took Jane some time to learn how to control the fly. The sections on its back were covered in coarse, short hairs, which made sitting quite comfortable and holding-on easy. After several experiments such as saying 'Go *down*, Fly, *down*,' she found that all she needed to do was to pull the hair on its left to make it go left, on the right to make it go right, to pull the hair on the middle of its back to make it go up, and push down to make it go down. Soon she was skimming just above the feathery tops of the grasses more or less where she had seen Clarissa disappear.

For a long time she saw nothing. The grass forest seemed deserted, even the smallest insects having been devoured by the hordes of hunter ants. But suddenly she saw some way ahead, as she flew back along the shore, a waving movement in the grass. She forced Fly lower, till the grass tops brushed his legs, and saw, now here, now there, the unmistakable forms of giant ants rushing along below.

It was a long line, which must have held some two thousand ants, and Jane raced back and forth from end to end of it. Once or twice she thought she caught a glimpse of an ant with something white in its mouth, but she couldn't be sure.

It had been about the middle of the afternoon when the ant had attacked. It was getting on for early evening when Jane noticed that the line of ants had turned away from the shore and begun to climb up towards the mountains. Before long she saw ahead a wide clearing, filled with large tea-cosy shaped hillocks nearly as high as the grass. The clearing, and the surface of the hillocks were swarming with ants and she could hear the same sinister whistling she had heard before. Soon the line of ants entered the clearing and poured in a black stream towards the nearest hillock. In a few minutes they had all disappeared inside it.

Jane at once decided what she had to do. First, return to the lily and rest Fly. He had now been in the air for some two hours and was obviously getting tired. Then she would get some equipment and return to rescue Clarissa.

She therefore fixed the position of the clearing firmly in her mind (luckily it was on a line between two mountain peaks on either side of the river), then, pulling Fly's hair, turned him round and headed back the way she had come.

For half an hour they flew down above the waving tops of the grass jungle. The unpleasant whistling soon died away behind them and the only sound was the gentle humming of the fly's wings and the swish of air past Jane's ears. Gradually, as they drew closer, the strip of water grew wider and wider, glinting in the evening sun. They were directly above it, and Jane was about to turn Fly left in search of the lily, when she saw to her surprise that it was already there, floating on the water below her. She pressed Fly's back and they plummeted down.

Fly was quite wobbly with exhaustion and Jane quickly bundled him into his hut, where she was interested to see him instantly shoot out his long tongue and begin to suck greedily from a bucket in the corner. Then she hurried out and, carefully avoiding the ugly gash which the ant had left with its pincers, ran into the cottage to fetch the emergency anchor that Clarissa had shown her hanging in one of the cupboards. She found it, attached its rope to the peg and threw it over board. A moment later she felt a comforting jerk as it caught on the bottom. For some reason the current in the river was flowing in the opposite direction, carrying the lily back to the lake. Now, firmly anchored, she would only have to fly straight up the mountainside again to return to the clearing. Jane hurried back into the cottage again.

First she collected a bag of things for Clarissa: bandages, some ointment, and a bottle of lily milk. Then a bag of things for the rescue: thirty-six reels of white cotton, which she found in the store room, some matches, her penknife, and a hurricane lamp full of oil. She also put into her pocket the wooden whistle with which Clarissa had called Fly in the storm. Next she had a quick meal and washed her face and hands to refresh herself.

Fly also looked much better when she carried all the things out to his hut. He trembled his wings at her in a way she decided was affectionate, and didn't seem to mind in the least when she tied all her bundles into the thick hair on his back.

It took them half an hour of straight flying to reach the clearing again. As Jane brought the fly quietly in to land on the branches of one of the bushes at the edge, the sun finally went down behind the mountains and darkness fell.

The first thing Jane noticed, was the silence. The whistling had stopped. Nor, as her eyes grew used to the darkness, could she see any movement which might have been an ant. But this did not mean very much. They could easily just be asleep. Clarissa had said they were only supposed to go into a trance at night. Jane knew that she would only find out if this were true when she actually tried to enter the ant hill itself. But before doing this she decided to wait until she was quite sure there were no ants and until the moon rose to give light.

She waited on the branch for several hours. Eventually, at about half past twelve, a large moon rose high into the sky above her head. The huge hillocks cast long black shadows and in a ghostly way it seemed almost as light as day.

Jane decided she could put it off no longer. She crept back along the branch and up onto Fly's back. Then tugging gently she urged him into the air and they soared out, hovered for a moment and then came lightly down onto the ant hill nearest the riverside edge of the clearing.

Its top was quite broad, made of dried earth and long stalks of dead grass. To one of these she tied Fly with a thin piece of spider's rope. Not to stop him escaping if, say, an ant attacked him, but because she hoped that it would keep him there till she came back. *If* she came back.

She took the two bags and slung them over her shoulder, lit the hurricane lamp and with a last longing look down at the empty, silent, moon-lit clearing, walked slowly towards a large black hole in the centre of the hill top.

Holding up the lamp, she could see that the hole led very gradually down into the hill. An unpleasant, warm breeze, smelling slightly of rotten meat came from it; but that was all. No sound. Nothing to see.

Slowly, heart beating, she took a few steps, then stopped to listen. A few more steps. Another stop. And now, already out of sight of the entrance, the tunnel forked. Putting down the lamp, Jane took the first of her reels of cotton, tied one end firmly to a stick of grass and then started walking slowly on again, unreeling the cotton behind her.

The tunnel slope became steeper, the smell of rotten meat stronger, and now the divisions, forks and side turnings became more and more numerous. Jane had just taken a left turn and was holding her lantern high above her head, when she saw her first ant.

It was standing ten feet away, leaning against the side of the tunnel and staring at her fiercely, its large, black eyes glinting in the light.

Yet it did not move. And as she came slowly closer, clutching her penknife, it was plain that it had no interest in her at all. Even when she was right under its huge, hideous jaws, and reached out a hand to poke one of its hairy legs, it remained quite still. Jane's lamp hissed in the silence.

At once she felt better. So it was true about the trance. Now, it was safe to search for Clarissa as fast as she could, safe, that is, till dawn. Taking out another cotton reel, she hurried rapidly on.

As she drew near the centre of the ant hill, the tunnels became more like hundreds of huge rooms joined together. In some she found giant ant eggs, lying row upon row guarded by sleeping ants. In others were whole jumbles of ants, in black motionless piles. And in some, the most disgusting, were heaps of dead grass hoppers, flies and moths. It was these that smelt so strongly, but though it revolted her Jane always looked carefully into them, terrified of finding the body of her friend.

But of Clarissa there was no sign. And slowly Jane began to despair. Perhaps she had already been eaten alive. Or perhaps she had already struggled free, taking, like Jane, advantage of the ants' trance and was even now running through the grasses to the river. And how, Jane wondered, could she ever find anything in this vast heap? She had now been searching for several hours. The tunnels and rooms became more and more confusing. Several times she found herself in places which already had cotton along their walls and had to wind herself back to save thread. And in fact the cotton reels were beginning to run low. She longed to escape from the hot, dark walls, the army of motionless, frightening ants, the smell.

It was at this moment that she found her first real clue that Clarissa was, or had been, in the ant hill. She was stumbling down yet another dark, uneven tunnel, when her foot kicked against something. Looking down, she saw Clarissa's gun lying by the wall. She picked it up excitedly. It seemed very unlikely that an ant would have brought it back without Clarissa; but quite possible that Clarissa would have clung to it for as long as she could.

Now Jane began to search harder than ever. She looked into every crevice, every little room and tunnel, always, when she had gone some way from the gun, returning to it and setting out in a new direction. Even so she nearly missed Clarissa.

She had searched a large chamber in which all the ants had tumbled over, and was just about to leave it, when she noticed in the farthest corner one huge ant still upright. It was frozen in a guarding position. She clambered towards it, and coming close held her lamp high. There, lying between the thick hairy legs, was Clarissa's body.

She was bound to the neck in tight strands of what seemed like nylon. Her face was white, her eyes closed, but putting her cheek very close, Jane could feel a faint breath. She was alive! Swiftly Jane took out a penknife and cut through the white strands. As they fell away, she saw that poor Clarissa's arms and legs were all blue and swollen and felt very cold. But at once she began to massage them and move them about.

After about five minutes, Clarissa gave a low moan. Then, as Jane continued to massage, she heard her murmur, 'Where am I? What is it? Oh my arms, my legs.'

'It's me,' said Jane, 'Jane.' Clarissa's eyes opened, then shut, then opened and fixed on Jane. 'Jane,' she said weakly.

At once Jane lifted up her head and shoulders and propped them against her chest. Then she took the bottle of lily milk out of the bag and put it to Clarissa's mouth. 'You must drink this,' she said.

A lot was spilt, but soon Clarissa was drinking it hungrily, in huge gulps. Then Jane began to massage her again, bending the numb legs and rubbing the cold arms. At last, 'Now try and stand,' she said.

'I can't,' said Clarissa.

'You must,' said Jane. 'We've got to escape.' Very slowly, she dragged Clarissa to her feet, held her swaying, while Clarissa weakly tried to move her legs.

And then, faint and terrifying, they heard a noise. It was a high, wavering, piercing whistle, a vibration which seemed to come from the very heart of the ant hill. The ants were waking up.

Immediately Jane dragged Clarissa to the entrance of the chamber and out into the tunnel.

'Please, Clarissa,' she said urgently, 'please try and walk.'

'I am trying,' said Clarissa. 'I am, I am.' She was so weak that Jane realized it would be impossible to follow the cotton back up to the top of the ant hill. They would have to go down, and even that was hard enough. At every step Clarissa's legs gave way and Jane really had to carry her.

Now she could hear and feel the ant hill coming alive all round them. The whistling spread from room to room, down the winding tunnels, seeming to penetrate the walls themselves. And as they stumbled down, the hurricane lamp sending its swaying light ahead, Jane could see movements in the chambers on either side of them. Ants stretching, ants standing up and clashing their jaws, ants getting ready for another day's hunting.

She felt herself tiring. Twice Clarissa fell down and had to be dragged to her feet again. Jane was beginning to feel that they would never escape, that any minute an ant would spring out and seize them, when suddenly she saw a gleam of light ahead. Another three stumbling steps and there in front of them was a wide entrance.

'Quick Clarissa,' she said, 'look, we can escape. Quick.' With a last effort she heaved her friend along, Clarissa's legs managed a few more steps, and the next moment they were out in the early morning sun, blinking in front of the ant hill.

But still not safe. All round them stretched the bare earth, the air was filled with a whistling that was now deafening, and as Jane watched an ant ran from the entrance of a nearby hill, seemed to sniff the air and then ran back. It was at this moment that Clarissa began to sink to her knees. 'I can't go on,' she whispered. 'Jane, say the words of the Book and escape. Leave me behind.'

And suddenly Jane remembered Fly. As Clarissa lay fainting at her feet, Jane began to rummage frenziedly in one of the bags. In a moment she had found the whistle, in a moment blown it, and then blown it again and again.

Could he hear above the ants? Would he break the grass? Jane blew again. And then, looking up, she saw the fly hovering high above them. She waved. Blew the whistle. Fly saw her, buzzed down, hesitated, buzzed down farther, and eventually landed lightly beside them. Jane dragged Clarissa across the ground and somehow pushed and heaved her onto his back. Then she scrambled up herself, pulled at the stiff hairs, and very slowly they began to rise into the air.

Below them an ant dashed out of the ant hill. Stood looking left and right, and then dashed back.

There is really very little more to tell. They flew by easy stages back to the lily leaf and Jane, after putting ointment on Clarissa's bruises and washing the worst of the earth off her, put her straight to bed. Then she had a bath and went to bed herself.

She slept all that day and the following night, waking the next morning completely refreshed but very hungry. Clarissa too, though still stiff and bruised, was well enough to get up and together they made an enormous breakfast. Then, Clarissa doing the easy things, they began to tidy the cottage.

Jane stayed two more days. They mended the rip in the leaf, went for rides on Fly, and making a sail out of some sheets started to get the lily back to Lilytown. But at the end of the second day Jane decided that the time had come to return to Curl Castle. She had now been away six nights and she didn't want to get back after her father and mother.

Clarissa was miserable when she heard. 'Oh please don't go,' she said, 'please. You've saved my life and we have had such fun. I want you to meet my friends and come down the lily stem and go fishing and show you how to become transparent. Please stay, please, please, *please*.'

But Jane explained that, though she'd love to, she simply had to get back.

'But its not like going away for ever,' she said. 'You come and see me next time you're due to come through the Book and I'll come and see you again very soon.'

'And anyway soon you'll go into the long sleep and then in the end we can be together for ever,' said Clarissa. But Jane pretended not to hear this and hurried into the cottage to get her jeans and her shirt and have a last look round.

Because in fact she too was sorry to go. She loved the little house, with its curtains and sweet furniture, and she had grown fond of Fly, but most of all she loved Clarissa, with her dark hair and the gay way she liked doing things. And yet at the same time there was something sad about her, something that worried Jane and made her want to protect her.

When she came out onto the leaf she put her arm round her and kissed her. 'Goodbye,' she said, 'good bye.' And then seeing that Clarissa was unable to speak, but could only brush two large tears away from her eyes, she squeezed her very tightly and said, 'Don't worry, I'll come again soon. I'll see you *very* soon. I promise. Goodbye.'

'Goodbye Jane,' whispered Clarissa, 'goodbye.'

And very quickly Jane said the words of the Book, because she knew that otherwise she'd cry too.

10. The End of Lord and Lady Charrington

IT WAS pitch dark when Jane stepped out of the Book in the old library. However she soon found the matches and candle which Clarissa had left on the chair, and, having lit them, quickly climbed up the shelves and down the iron pegs on the other side.

Once she had reached the bedroom she wrote a note for Mrs Deal—'Have got back, love Jane'—brushed her teeth and climbed into bed. In a moment she was asleep.

She was woken by the familiar bony hands and Mrs Deal's voice at its most brisk. 'So the wanderer returns! Whatever next! Now up you get and have a good wash and then down to your father and mother. They arrived back late last night. But don't you worry. I said you were with the Behrenses and would be back this morning, keeping my fingers crossed.'

Jane leapt out of bed, pulled on her dressing gown and raced out of the room. Mummy and Daddy! She threw open their door and with a great leap sprang into the middle of the big, pink bed.

'Mummy!' she cried.

'Darling!' cried Lady Charrington, holding out her long arms.

'Well, well,' said Lord Charrington, putting down his newspaper, and taking off his glasses and then putting them on again. He put his big arms round her and pulled her against his silk pyjamas.

What had she been doing? How were the Behrenses ('very well' said Jane); did she know that their friend Sabrina had had a baby boy and was going to call it Benjamin, so nice for Jenny to have a brother . . .

nestling between their pillows Jane talked and listened for half an hour. Then she said, 'And what was America like? Was it fabulous?'

At this there came a little silence. Or rather her mother became silent. Her father began to smile and make little chuffing noises which Jane knew meant he was about to say something interesting and, to him, exciting.

'Your father has something to tell you,' said Lady Charrington in a mournful voice. 'Yes,' said her father, 'yes. Now, Jane dear, in America they lead a very different sort of life to the one we lead here.'

Lord Charrington had been extremely impressed by America. He had been a great many times before, but somehow this time had been different. Although he was an Earl, for the first time they treated him as though he weren't one. And he had found that this meant they treated him exactly as they had treated him before. This is not as complicated as it sounds. It happened because in a hotel one day he gave his name by mistake as Mr Charrington instead of Lord Charrington, and yet they still said 'This way, sir' and treated him with all the respect he was used to. Although the fact that he was obviously very rich may have had something to do with it, this had impressed Lord Charrington. After that he had called himself Mr Charrington all over the place. And still they had treated him with respect. Lord Charinngton had decided that it was the respect due to him as a HUMAN BEING. As well as this he had read certain books which had impressed him; the result was that Lord Charrington had decided to drop his title and be known, as soon as certain papers had been signed in London, as Mr Charrington. It was this that he tried to explain to Jane as shortly as he could.

'And I have decided we shall live as ordinary people as well,' he said, one arm round his daughter, the other waving in front of them. 'We shall give up this huge castle and live in an ordinary council house by the sea.' He made a little shape like a box in the air. 'I have already ordered one at Aldeburgh in Suffolk in the name of Mr and Mrs Charrington. I shall keep the Observatory of course. That will be my job. I shall be Mr Charrington the Scientist. The rest of the Castle I have been dividing up: the middle is for the National Trust, the South Wing is for a Mental Hospital, the East Wing is for an Old People's Home, the West Wing is to be a Youth Hostel and the North Wing is going to be a Holiday Camp. The roof will be bowling alleys, skating rinks, dance floors and swimming pools. Now, what do you think of it?'

Jane found she could think of nothing at all. 'Can I take all my things to the council house?' she said.

'We may all take anything we like,' said Lord Charrington, 'your mother has—ahem—already begun to make a little list.'

'When do we go?' said Jane.

'As soon as possible,' said Lord Charrington, 'next week.'

At this, Lady Charrington gave a low moan. Seeing that she looked rather sad, Jane put her arms round her.

'Oh, poor Mummy,' she said, 'don't you want to move?'

'Your father knows best,' said Lady Charrington. But she gave a little sigh. She *enjoyed* being a Countess. She liked being called M'Lady, she liked the sound of shopkeepers on the telephone saying, 'Yes Lady Charrington, certainly M'Lady.' Mrs Charrington seemed somehow—well, less *interesting*.

'Well, now, up we get,' said Lord Charrington. He ran his hands through his thick grey hair so that his bald patch became covered and jumped out of bed. He was a big, thudding man, and the fact that he was about to turn into Mr Charrington had filled him even fuller of energy than usual. 'We have a great deal to do. Come on, darling. Come on, Jane. You must go and sort out your toys. Just remember, though, a council house is very small.' And again he made a small square in the air, as though they were going to live in a matchbox.

The next week was extremely busy. Jane went carefully through all her possessions and decided that she really needed them all. Lady Charrington not only went through her possessions but through much of the Castle and came to the same conclusion. Jane would pass her in the corridors, her tall thin frame looking rather odd on a vacuum cleaner, with one of the under-butlers running beside her with a list, while she said, 'and *that*, and *that*, and *that*, and *that*.' Lord Charrington, although he had said they could all take what they wanted, at first tried to make them take a little less. 'Remember, darling,' he said, 'we shall only have four rooms in our new house.' But in the end, partly because he was himself finding it very difficult not to take things like all his guns and all his fishing rods, he let them do as they wanted. He said that perhaps they should learn gradually how to be Mr and Mrs and not in one jump. He began to talk vaguely about buying two or even three council houses.

But the most important reason for his not minding was that he was still in a great state of excitement about becoming Mr Charrington. He put several announcements in *The Times* and in all the local papers; he had ten thousand sheets of new writing paper printed with *Mr Christopher Charrington* at the top; and he went round telling everybody to call him Mr Charrington now and even Christopher or Chris if they liked, although the papers in London had not yet been signed.

Lady Charrington took quite the opposite point of view. 'I shall call myself Lady Charrington until the last possible *minute*,' she said.

The result of all their searches was that a continual stream of servants poured from the Castle carrying chairs, tables, pictures, books, carpets, curtains and everything else one can imagine. And a fleet of enormous furniture vans soon stretched all the way from the front door to the Lodge.

Jane enjoyed all this very much. She didn't mind what her parents were called: Lord and Lady Charrington, Mr and Mrs Charrington, or even Mr and Mrs Sausage. What she did mind was that somehow she must get the Book packed away and taken to their new house.

Her chance came the night before they were to leave. Lord Charrington had decided to speak to all the servants in one of the Great Halls. He had arranged that when they left all the servants would be taken on by the various organizations which were to move in. All, that is, except Mrs Deal. She was to accompany the Charringtons into their new council houses. But he wanted to tell them this. He also wanted to thank them all, since many of them had worked for the Charrington family all their lives, he wanted to speak about his new life, about the new England and why it didn't need titles, and also, for the hundredth time, explain how he had decided to be like them, a plain mister.

Jane found that she was sitting at the back of the hall next to her friend Simon. After her father had been speaking for a little while, she leant forward and whispered in Simon's ear. 'Follow me,' and quietly slipped out into the passage.

In a moment, Simon had joined her. 'What is it then?' he whispered.

'I'll tell you in a minute,' Jane whispered back, 'but we've got to hurry.' She ran to the store room and fetched a long coil of rope which she had seen there that afternoon, also a torch, and then went and collected two vacuum cleaners.

It took Jane a little while to persuade Simon that the old library wasn't haunted, but eventually, ashamed of seeming a coward in front of a girl, he agreed to go in. Once inside, they tied the rope firmly round the Book, passed the rest of it through a large ring in the library door and tied it fast. Lastly they tried to get the Book through the window.

It was extremely heavy, but by resting it on a chair and then both heaving at once they managed to get it first onto the sill and then sent it toppling out. At once the rope tightened and they heard the Book bumping against the outside wall of the tower.

Now they slowly lowered it hand over hand, until, when the rope went suddenly slack, they knew the Book had landed.

Immediately they hurried out of the library, onto their cleaners and roared back again. Ten minutes later they had carried the Book to the Land-Rover in which Jane and her parents were to travel, hidden it under some rugs, and were sitting in the back of the hall in time to hear Lord Charrington cry—

'. . . and so, from this moment on, I want all of you to put Lord Charrington from your minds. Let me be plain Mister Charrington. Mr Christopher Charrington, an ordinary scientist, like yourselves.' After a few embarrassed cheers and some hand-clapping, the hall emptied. Jane was sent early to bed as they were to start next morning at six o'clock.

The day dawned fine and sunny. From the start, all was hustle and confusion, with forgotten things being remembered and Jane's mother wandering about as though in a dream. But all too soon, it seemed, they were ready to go.

Mrs Deal, who was crying, had been comforted with a little gin and put into the back of the Land-Rover warmly wrapped in rugs, among piles of luggage. Lord and Lady Charrington, or rather Mr Charrington and Lady Charrington, and Jane climbed into the front. There were waves from the servants gathered at the windows and then they were off.

A little way down the drive, where it rose over a lump, Lady Charrington said, 'Stop a moment, Christopher, let's just look back.'

Lord Charrington stopped the car and they all looked.

Curl Castle rose huge, magnificent and beautiful in the golden early sun. Its windows flashed, the creepers waved upon its high walls. There was the long roof where Jane and Mrs Deal had sheltered from the waters when the dam burst. There were the windows to the nursery and Jane's bedroom. Rising high to the left of the castle was the observatory. Far to the right, the tower of the old library, where so many adventures had begun and ended. And round about were the woods and fields where Jane had played so often.

And all at once Jane felt very sad. This had been her home. Only now did she properly realize that they were leaving it for ever. In a small voice, she said, 'Daddy, we can go back sometimes, can't we?'

'Of course, said her father, 'of course. But naturally on visiting days. And then we'll be like ordinary people. We'll pay our 10p like everyone else. Unless, of course, we go to the Mental Hospital, in which case we'll have to prove that we are mad.'

But Jane's mother put her arm round her daughter's shoulders and kissed her. 'You can go back whenever you like, darling,' she said, 'you can spend all your holidays there and as much time as you like. We may well take a flat there.' She kissed her again and Jane kissed her back. At the same time she slipped her hand under a rug near her in the back. Beneath it she felt the hard, comforting corner of the Book.

'And I've got you, Book,' she whispered to herself. 'I can go to you whenever I like.'

'Ready?' called Lord Charrington, 'well, off we go then.' With a loud poop of the horn, the Land-Rover shot forward, and in a few moments Curl Castle had disappeared behind them, hidden by a clump of trees.

Jane's Adventures on the Island of Peeg

For Jenny and Benjamin

1. Settling in at Alderburgh

WHEN Mr and Mrs Charrington, their daughter Jane and their help, Mrs Deal, first arrived at Aldeburgh, two difficult decisions had to be taken immediately.

The first concerned their house. Mr Charrington had chosen No 2 in a row of thirty-five brand new empty council houses which had been built at the back of Aldeburgh. But when they arrived in their Land-Rover, followed by forty large furniture vans containing very nearly everything from their former home, Curl Castle, they realized at once they would need either a great deal less furniture or else something a great deal larger to live in.

Mr Charrington was a large, decisive man. He liked nothing better than a firm decision. He put Mrs Charrington, Jane and Mrs Deal in the Wentworth Hotel, made the furniture vans park outside the Golf Club, and hurried off to find the Chairman of the Aldeburgh Rural District Council.

Fortunately, the Housing Committee of the District Council was having a meeting that very morning. Mr Charrington spoke to them persuasively and decisively for ten minutes and they soon agreed that, though they could not sell council houses, if he gave them enough money to build two council houses, they would let him rent one council house for 999 years. If he gave them enough to build four council houses, they would rent him two council houses, and so on.

Mr Charrington returned with beaming face to the Wentworth Hotel.

'My darling,' he said to his wife, 'I have rented No 1 and No 3 for 999 years!'

'Rented? Oh dear,' said Mrs Charrington, who had been taught that it was always better to buy houses. 'Do you think that's wise? What happens when they no longer belong to us? What then?'

'999 years,' said Mr Charrington a bit impatiently. '999 years, darling.'

'Yes, but you know how time flies,' said Mrs Charrington. 'Still, I suppose it's better than nothing.'

For the rest of the morning the men worked hard, and by lunchtime Nos 1, 2 and 3 council houses were full of furniture and only four of the furniture vans were empty. Mr Charrington hurried back to the Housing Committee and rented Nos 4 and 5 for 999 years. By the end of the week all the furniture vans were empty and Mr Charrington had rented all the council houses for 999 years at a cost of £172,500.

The second decision was about Jane's school. Mr Charrington had originally decided that she should go to a State school.

'You will agree, my darling,' he said, 'that in our new position—plain Mr and Mrs, a single servant, living in a council house—'

'Houses,' said Mrs Charrington.

'Houses—you will agree that Jane should go to the sort of school any other boy and girl in her sort of position goes to.'

Mrs Charrington did not agree. She did not, in fact, think there *was* anyone in Jane's position. After some discussion, they reached a compromise. Jane was to be sent to a school in the north-west of Scotland, which advertised itself as being ready to take anyone—'of whatever colour, creed or background'.

The fees at Peeg School were £600 a year and there were, therefore, very few of the sort of girls Mr Charrington had meant. And there were other things that might have stopped him sending Jane there had he known of them. The head mistress, Miss Boyle, though very fair and not unkind, was extremely strict. She believed in physical fitness and beating in 'extreme cases'. Football, hiking and tossing the caber were all compulsory. About twice a year there would be 'an extreme case' and some frightened little girl would have her bottom smacked with Miss Boyle's slipper.

Also, Peeg School was in a very wild and remote place. Peeg House was very large, with pinnacles and pointed windows. It had first been the home of Lord Kinross, Laird of Peeg, and then a hotel. It stood all alone in the middle of a small island called the Isle of Peeg. It was, in

fact, not quite an island at all because it was joined to the shore by a narrow strip of land, or causeway.

The Isle of Peeg was a mile long and three-quarters of a mile wide. The school was in the middle, in a small valley. All round it the heather-covered ground rose gently up and stretched away to the low cliffs which faced the sea. Behind the school and towards the front of the island there was quite a steep hill, which rose high enough to be called Mount Peeg, and from its top you could see the whole island and across to the mainland of Scotland. Halfway up the island and two hundred yards out from the shore there was a large, rock in the sea called Little Peeg.

The weather on Peeg was extremely wet; everywhere you went you could hear the trickling sound of water, and had to be careful to avoid bogs and marshes. Even at the top of Mount Peeg there was a small pool with reeds and moss. In winter there were terrible storms; you could see from the school the plumes of spray where the waves dashed above the cliffs. Even in summer, when the girls would pick the velvet moss bulging up onto the tops of the rocks or scream at the black slugs, there were sudden rain storms. But for most of the time, winter and summer, it was not so much rain as mist, a perpetual muslin of mist in which you only had to stand for ten minutes to be soaking wet, and which trailed gloomily over the heather, or came drifting down into the valley to lie for days in patches and pockets and hang caught in the damp needles of the pine trees growing at the lower end of the burn.

Jane did not really enjoy her first term. She hated the school smells of floor polish and cooking cabbage. She kept very quiet and was careful to be very good. She made one friend—a girl called Jemima Garing. It was not till the third week of her second term that she began to behave more like her real self. And it was in the third week, also, that two things happened, quite independently of Jane's behaviour, which were to start what *The Sunday Times* was later to describe as 'one of the most extraordinary adventures of our time'.

2. The First Explosion

A FAVOURITE game for naughty girls at Peeg School was shooting butter pats at the dining-room ceiling. You stuck your knife blade into the gap underneath the table top, pulled down the handle with a butter pat balanced on it, and let go. With a faint, vibrating brrrrr the butter soared into the air and sometimes stuck to the ceiling.

It was this that Jane was trying to do one dreary October day in the third week of term. Three times the butter sprang into the air and three times another yellow blob appeared on the ceiling. All round the dining-room the girls chattered and talked at high tea, doing their best to eat boiled cabbage. But all the little girls at the same table as Jane giggled nervously and kept on looking to see if the prefect was watching. 'Do be careful,' they whispered, 'don't get caught.'

Jane smiled. 'One more,' she said boldly.

As before, the small round pat shot from the knife handle. But this time, instead of rising into the air, it went forward. It skimmed over the head of the prefect, sped like a tiny flying saucer across five tables and then, before Jane's horrified eyes, fell out of sight at the far end of the dining-room.

For three minutes nothing happened. Jane began to eat her cabbage very fast and interestedly. Then, suddenly, there came the tinkle of the Staff bell which was only rung at the end of tea or for very important announcements. Out of the corner of her eye, Jane saw the thick figure of Miss Boyle standing at the end of the Staff table, bell in hand.

'Girls,' cried Miss Boyle, 'a butter pat has just landed on the table in front of my plate.'

There was dead silence. Everyone was far too frightened of Miss Boyle to dare even to smile.

'Who did it?' said Miss Boyle. 'I am waiting. Come on. The girl who launched this projectile please stand forward immediately.'

Jane stopped breathing. She imagined for a second that she *was* the cabbage, or even a worm inside the cabbage, boiled and dead, quite beyond the reach of head mistresses and slippers. Everyone in the large, dim-lit dining-room stared at their plates.

'Unless the culprit stands forth immediately,' said Miss Boyle, her bell giving a tiny tinkle of emphasis, 'the entire school will be kept in tomorrow. No one will go to the Glenelg Highland Games.'

At this dreadful threat, dreadful at least to the Scots girls at Peeg School, a murmur broke out. Jane felt herself turning into one huge blush. Clenching her teeth, she very slowly stood up.

'*I* threw the butter, Miss Boyle.'

Like sixty torches, all the heads turned towards her, including Miss Boyle's. 'Who's that?' she called.

'It's Jane Charrington, 1st Form, Miss Boyle,' called the prefect officiously.

'I will see Jane Charrington later,' said Miss Boyle. 'School may resume high tea.'

After tea, all the girls disappeared to their various evening duties. The 1st Form had an hour's free time in their common-room and then had to go to bed. The moment they were all together, they crowded round Jane. 'It's bound to be an Extreme Case.' 'The Boil will beat you black and blue.' 'Poor Jane.' They were all very sympathetic.

But after half an hour Miss Boyle had still not called her. Bath-time came; bed-time; it was not until nearly lights-out and Jane was sitting up in bed in her nightie that there came the slap slap slap of slippered feet running down the corridor.

'Jane Charrington to see the Boil!'

It was not, after all, so terrible. The walk along the dark, polish-smelling corridors was terrifying. So was the wait outside Miss Boyle's study.

But once inside, Jane suddenly felt quite calm and confident. Miss Boyle stood facing her, legs as usual wide apart. Her heavy, lined face was serious. In her hand she held the large blue *Report Book* in which was entered details of all the school punishments.

'Come in and sit down,' she said. 'I will be brisk and to the point. I always like to get to the point and I would like all my girls to do the same. Now—why did you throw the butter?'

'I don't know, Miss Boyle,' said Jane.

'You don't know,' said Miss Boyle. She walked over to the chair by the fire and pointed to one opposite. When they were both sitting down, she took off her spectacles and leant forward. 'I see from the *Report Book* that this is the first time you have seriously misbehaved. Now, at one jump, you become an Extreme Case. Because, make no mistake,' said Miss Boyle, 'this is an Extreme Case. Do you know why?'

Jane wondered whether to say yes or no. She decided the best thing to do was to mumble. 'Mmmmm,' she said.

'An ambiguous answer, Jane,' said Miss Boyle, 'that is to say an answer which could mean two things—yes or no. I shall explain why throwing butter is an Extreme Case.'

Then Miss Boyle began one of her famous talkings-to. She spoke in her firm voice for thirty-five minutes. Quite soon Jane stopped listening and began planning. She was quite sure this was not the sort of school her mother and father meant her to go to. It was difficult to describe it to them in a letter, so the best thing would be to run away to Aldeburgh and tell them. She would do this tomorrow. Once or twice Miss Boyle interrupted Jane's thoughts by asking questions.

'What do you suppose would happen if everyone in the dining-room threw butter?' she said at one moment.

Caught off guard Jane began, 'Why, I think it would—' But suddenly noticing the stout leather slippers, which in the evenings replaced her brogues, sticking out below Miss Boyle's long tweed skirt, she ended humbly, '—it would be terrible.'

'Terrible,' agreed Miss Boyle, imagining it.

In the end, however, she grew quite kind. 'It was brave of you to stand up in the dining-room,' she said. 'You have an excellent record. You come of rich and distinguished parents. In fact, *very* rich and *very* distinguished. Yes. In the circumstances, although an Extreme Case, I have decided not to exact the usual penalty. Instead, out of the whole school, you alone will miss the Glenelg Highland Games. You will stay here and write out two thousand times "I must not throw butter at Miss Boyle".'

Walking back down the darkened corridors, in which only a few Seniors lounged about, Jane thought that what was really wrong with Miss Boyle was that she was out of date. This alone would make Mr Charrington take her away. She didn't mind missing the Games at all, except that a large moon rocket was going to be launched during them and this she had wanted to see. She was quite determined not to do any lines.

All this she explained to Jemima when she got back to the dormitory. Everyone else was asleep and the two little girls whispered together excitedly. Jemima said she was very lucky not to be beaten and really quite lucky to miss the Highland Games, though she agreed it was sad to miss the rocket. But when she heard about Jane running away, she became very serious. She begged her not to and said she would certainly be caught, and then Miss Boyle would really beat her into tiny pieces and possibly expel her. Jane said she thought this most unlikely, but agreed to think about it. Secretly, however, she decided that by the same time next day she would be far from Scotland.

By the time the early morning bell went at six o'clock it was real Peeg weather. Thick fog covered the island and a strong, cold wind blew straight from the mainland (coming in the first place from Siberia, as the Geography Mistress had explained) and moaned through the pines and round the goal posts on the lacrosse fields. But the Glenelg Games took place whatever the weather. Indeed, Miss Boyle had said, while teaching the senior girls how to 'flight' a caber with the wind, that the worse the weather the better. 'The Highland Games are a test of skill,' she said, 'not mere brute strength.'

The whole school hurried through breakfast and then out onto the gravel sweep in front of the front door. Four buses were to take them, the teachers and all the domestic staff, to Glenelg, forty miles away.

Only Jane and old Macmillan were left behind. Jane to do her lines, Macmillan because he was ninety-two and had to look after his boiler. 'He will also keep an eye on you,' said Miss Boyle.

Ten minutes later Jane was standing at the window of the 1st Form classroom, watching the buses disappear. She heard a door banging down one of the gloomy corridors. She began to feel very small and alone, and quite unlike even leaving the classroom, much less running away from school.

She felt even more alone a quarter of an hour later when old Macmillan stumped in and said he was off. 'I havenny missed one of the Heeland Games fey eighty years,' he said, 'and ame noo changing me customes noo.'

Shortly after, he left in a small black car covered in dents. Now Jane was the only person on the Island of Peeg. And suddenly she began to feel rather frightened. As the wind rattled the windows and the fog wrapped itself closer and closer around the house, she remembered the ghost stories they used to tell each other after lights-out in the dormitory. How one girl had felt a cold hand on her neck down by the changing-rooms one night; about the unearthly screeching heard coming from the music rooms. On tiptoe, Jane moved to the door and very quietly turned the key in the lock. Obviously she couldn't run away today. She would stay quietly in the 1st Form classroom and not move an inch.

She was just beginning to feel calmer and safer when her eye was caught by the handle of the door. It was moving.

Someone—or something—was turning it very slowly, trying to get in. Jane was rooted to the spot. She said afterwards that her hair had stood completely on end and she had felt her heart stop beating. And when the door was suddenly shaken and a strange, high, quavery voice wailed 'Whooooooooo,' she had almost fainted.

There was dead silence. The wind moaned in the chimney. Then the door shook violently again, 'Whooooooooo.' As though sleep-walking, Jane began to move very quietly towards the door. Once more it rattled, once more the eerie voice cried 'Whooooooooo.' Then, shaking with fear, Jane turned the key, pulled the door open, and stared into the long corridor outside.

Standing there, her long fair hair rather wild, her face tear-stained, stood Jemima Garing.

'Jemima!'

'Jane!'

The two little girls flung their arms round each other and kissed and hugged and excitedly explained. Jemima had decided that if Jane was going to run away then she would run away too. She had slipped off the bus after her name had been checked and hidden round by the kitchens. Then, walking through the empty school looking for Jane, she had become more and more frightened. The locked 1st Form classroom and the silence had been the last straw. Especially the silence.

'Why didn't you *answer?*' said Jemima.

'I was rooted to the spot,' said Jane.

She did not say, however, that she had decided not to run away. Jemima was a sweet and gentle girl who, though sometimes surprisingly daring, was usually more timid than Jane. That was one reason Jane liked her. She had been very impressed by Jemima slipping off the bus and then walking all through the empty school, and she didn't want to admit that she had been too frightened even to leave the classroom, much less run away.

In any case, now that Jemima was with her, she decided they could, after all, run away.

'First,' said Jane, 'we must go to the kitchen and collect enough food for our journey. Then get a map, mackintoshes, warm clothes, torches, etcetera.'

Giggling and shouting, they hurried down to the kitchens. Jane's plan was to borrow two bicycles and go to the nearest railway station at Blair, thirty-five miles away. This would take them a day. They would catch the first train to Aldeburgh and, with all the changes, this would take them another day. To last them for two days they packed a loaf of bread, a pound of butter, four pints of milk, twenty-four slices of ham and some bars of chocolate. Jane thought that the larder seemed extraordinarily empty for so large a school; but then she remembered that it was Saturday, the day when the food arrived from the mainland, and that Miss Boyle, among other ideas about food, was always determined there should be no waste.

They soon finished packing and then dressed themselves warmly in jeans, sweaters, thick socks and gumboots. They were hurrying along to Miss Boyle's study to see what money they could borrow when Jemima, who was a little way behind, suddenly called out, 'I think I can hear a car coming up the drive.'

It was true. Leaning out of the window, they could hear the muffled sound of an engine coming through the fog. It seemed to be moving very slowly and every few seconds blew its horn. Before long they could see headlights and then the vague outline of its shape.

It was a Land-Rover. And as it came slowly closer, it became more and more familiar. It had a streak of white paint on the bonnet, which Jane recognized; there was a dent in one of the back mudguards which she remembered; and when it stopped and Jane could see that its number was LLJ560F, there could no longer be any doubt.

'It's Mummy and Daddy,' she shouted. 'It's our Land-Rover.' And followed by Jemima she ran down the corridor to the main stairs.

They arrived at the front door as the big knocker was banged twice.

Jane undid the bolts, turned the heavy handle and pulled it open.

There, standing in the fog, a huge tartan scarf wrapped several times round her throat, stood Mrs Deal.

'Well, what a piece of luck,' said Mrs Deal. 'Fancy you opening the door yourself, Miss Jane. I was quite prepared for a man or a stranger.'

'What are you doing here, Mrs Deal?' said Jane, amazed. 'I thought it was Mummy and Daddy. I didn't know you could drive.'

'There's a lot you don't know about me,' said Mrs Deal. 'Indeed I can drive. Now let's get in out of the wind.'

The wind was now so strong that it was quite difficult to get the door shut. When they had done so, Mrs Deal took off her large leather gloves and unwrapped the long scarf. She was quite a small woman, with bright eyes, greying hair tied into a bun on the back of her head from which the hair was always getting loose, and a passion for dusting and cleaning.

Looking at this short, neat figure, which she had now learnt could drive, Jane suddenly found herself thinking how much warmer and easier and cheaper it would be to run away in the Land-Rover.

'And who's your friend?' said Mrs Deal.

'Jemima Garing,' said Jane absently. Somehow they must get Mrs Deal on their side or else trick her into taking them to the station.

'Pleased to meet you,' said Mrs Deal, holding out her thin hand. 'But it seems so quiet and empty. Where are all the other girls? At prep?'

'No, all the other girls have escaped,' said Jane without thinking. 'I mean,' she said hurriedly, 'have gone to the Glenelg Highland Games. You see, there are a lot of rather terrible things about this school which Mummy and Daddy don't know. The thing is, Mrs Deal, could you help us? You see . . .'

But before she could finish, a strange and terrifying thing happened. There was suddenly, quite close, the most tremendous explosion. For an instant the hall was lit by a dazzling flash. And then a moment later all the windows blew inwards with a crash, scattering the floor with glass. The lights went out, there came another, fainter explosion, and then silence, except for the wild flapping of the long curtains and the sound of the storm outside.

The three of them stood trembling. At last Jemima whispered, 'What was it?'

'It might be blasting in the quarry,' said Jane. 'You know, Jemima, opposite the causeway.'

But Mrs Deal raised her arm and said in a deep, odd voice, 'Russians!'

'How do you mean?' said Jane.

'It was the bomb,' said Mrs Deal. 'I knew they'd come. It was in the *Sunday Mirror* last Sunday. That was a minor tactical bomb.'

'Oh, I'm frightened,' Jemima suddenly cried. She ran to Mrs Deal and seized her arm. 'What shall we do?'

'We must cover ourselves in brown paper at once,' said Mrs Deal, looking round the dark, windy hall.

'Oh, don't be silly,' said Jane, whom Jemima always made feel brave. 'Why should the Russians bomb Peeg? It was probably the dynamite in the quarry blowing up. It happened last term only not so bad. Come on, we must go and look.'

She took hold of Jemima and pulled her to the door. Reluctantly, Mrs Deal followed them both out onto the drive.

It was blowing a real storm. The fog came now thick, now thin, as the wind whirled it along; the rain was lashing down in a way not even Miss Boyle would have dared call Scotch mist, and the blown pines sounded like a heavy sea.

'Quick,' said Jane, running to the Land-Rover. 'We must go and see what's happened.'

'A minor tactical bomb,' repeated Mrs Deal, remembering the *Sunday Mirror*. 'Blast area half a mile.' But she let herself be shoved into the driving seat and soon, with windscreen-wipers swishing, they were moving slowly through the fog towards the causeway.

'At least your poor parents will be safe,' said Mrs Deal after a while.

'Why?' said Jane.

'That's why I came up here,' said Mrs Deal. 'Your father thought I would soften the blow. He kindly lent me the Land-Rover to take a holiday and visit my brother in Peeblesshire, but mainly so that I could tell you that he and your mother have had to go suddenly to America for three months. They were very upset—but now, of course, it turns out for the best.'

'I see,' said Jane. She was sad that her mother and father had gone to America again, but they would be back soon. In fact, once she and Jemima had escaped she could fly out and join them. Except that she had no money. Also, if the council houses were shut up, where could she and Jemima stay? Jane suddenly decided that the best thing would be to take Mrs Deal into their confidence.

'Mrs Deal,' she said, 'I think I must confess something to you.'

'What is it, Miss Jane?' said Mrs Deal, slowing the car almost to a walking pace and peering into the fog which had suddenly grown very thick. 'Have you been misbehaving?'

Then Jane explained about Peeg School: about tossing of the caber, about Extreme Cases and being beaten with Miss Boyle's slipper and all the other things she was sure her mother and father would have objected to. She told Mrs Deal about the butter and how she had decided to run away, and how she hoped Mrs Deal would help them. 'Please, Mrs Deal,' she ended, 'I know Mummy and Daddy wouldn't want me to stay here.'

To her surprise, Mrs Deal seemed scarcely interested. 'Well, I can't say about all that, Miss Jane,' she said. 'That's not my province. You'll have to speak to Mr and Mrs Charrington. At the moment we must *all* try to escape. If it's the Russians on the move, which seems more and more likely every minute to me, there's no knowing where it will end. We'll make first for my brother Frank in Peeblesshire and then let him decide.'

They had now nearly reached the end of the drive. But as Mrs Deal slowly drove nearer the sea, the most extraordinary sight became clear through the fog. The waves were high and fierce, filling the air with noise. But instead of breaking against the causeway and crashing over it as usual in a storm, they now careered in uninterrupted lines between the mainland and Peeg. A jagged break in the road showed what had happened. The explosion had blown the middle of the causeway to smithereens. They were cut off.

The two little girls and Mrs Deal stared into the fog in silence. But as they stared, Jane began to notice something even stranger. The length of the causeway had hardly been a hundred yards. Valerie McClaughlan of the 6th, who could toss a caber as far as a man, had easily been able to throw a stone from shore to shore. But now even her great arm would scarcely have landed one half-way. It was almost impossible to see across to the mainland. Jane rubbed her eyes and peered out. Perhaps it was a trick of the explosion or the fog. And yet . . . Jane stared and calculated. And then suddenly—there was proof!

'Look!' cried Jane. 'Look Jemima, look Mrs Deal.' Turning excitedly, she pointed to the left.

At that moment, as can happen in those parts of Scotland, the fog lifted entirely. Following Jane's finger, they looked across the rough, grey sea and saw a tiny island, more like a rock, peeping round the end of the headland. It was Little Peeg, and normally it couldn't be seen at all, *normally it was only half-way up the island*.

'Do you see?' said Jane. 'It's Little Peeg. And see how far we are from the shore. We're floating. We're floating away to sea.'

As they watched, the little stub of rock came fully into view; a gap widened as they gradually floated past it; and then, as suddenly as it had cleared, the fog flowed round them again and everything was hidden.

'Now,' said Mrs Deal in a trembling voice, 'none of us can run away, even if we wanted to. No one can escape. We're trapped.'

3. They Nearly Die of Thirst

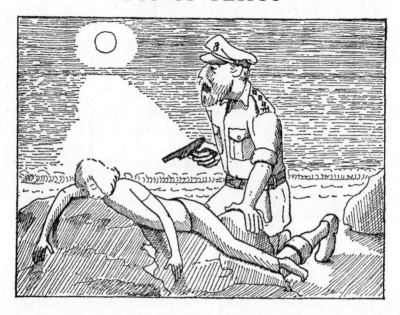

THOUGH it was not long before they found out, part of what had happened was fairly simple. The storm had not yet reached Glenelg and the moon rocket had therefore been launched as planned. Unfortunately it had gone off course. Rising slowly to the roaring of its motors and the oohs and aahs of fifty thousand people watching, it had suddenly started to turn to its left. The launch control officer had immediately pressed his destruction button. But a fault in transmission had delayed the explosion until the exact moment that the rocket had crashed onto the causeway between Peeg and the mainland.

As to how Peeg floated, they were also in fact to find out that quite soon. But, naturally, it was this that surprised them most of all.

'But are you *sure* it's floating?' said Jemima, as they drove back to school through the fog. 'How could a huge island made of rocks and earth float. It must weigh a million tons.'

All the windows on the side of the school near the causeway had been broken by the explosion. The glass, paper and dust and general mess had completely cheered up Mrs Deal.

'Come on, girls,' she said, 'you've discussed the island quite enough. I'm sure there is some quite simple explanation which we will hear on the wireless. There's so much work to do here I hardly know where to begin. Now, Jane, show me where the dusters are kept.'

They worked all morning to repair the damage caused by the explosion. The electricity, of course, had been cut off with the causeway. Jane found five dozen candles but, not knowing how long it might be before they were rescued, she and Jemima decided to use them as little as possible. In the semi-darkness of the storm, they swept and straightened, led by a reanimated Mrs Deal who had obviously decided to forget the Russians and who sometimes actually sang with pleasure, until, except for the smashed glass, you would hardly have known anything had happened.

But the broken panes caused a lot of trouble. In the end they decided to live on the far side of the school, looking out over the lacrosse fields, where the windows weren't broken. They chose Miss Boyle's study for their sitting-room and soon had a large fire blazing in the grate. Mrs Deal was given Miss Boyle's bedroom, and Jane and Jemima chose a small, comfortable room nearby.

Lunch-time brought a shock. While the two girls finished moving their clothes from the 1st Form dormitory to their new room, Mrs Deal went down to the kitchen to prepare the meal. Almost at once she came back.

'Jane, Jane,' she said, hurrying into their bedroom, 'where's the food? I've never seen such a larder in my life. It's a disgrace.'

Following her down, they found that the larder, as Jane had noticed when they were preparing their picnic, was almost empty. On its long, cool, marble shelves, under its seventeen wire-gauze covers, there were only four tins of sardines, four pints of milk, a loaf of bread, one dozen eggs and some sliced ham.

'We're not going to keep body and soul together on *that* for very long,' said Mrs Deal.

'There's our picnic,' said Jane.

'Picnic, indeed,' said Mrs Deal. 'What else? I'm not blaming you, Miss Jane.' Indeed, Jane had begun to feel rather guilty. 'But this is no way to run a school. Perhaps there are two larders? Or a store of tins?'

Jane said she didn't know, but suggested they all searched later. They made a good lunch, sitting in the warm kitchen of ham and fried bread and fried eggs—two each, which Jane thought rather extravagant of Mrs Deal, considering the desperate straits they were in.

When it was over, Jane said, 'Now I think we should all take pieces of paper and go round the school and make lists of things that might be useful in our emergency.'

'I have a lot to do, Miss Jane,' said Mrs Deal. 'The least we can do is to keep the school tidy and clean during our visit here.'

'But we must know what we've got,' said Jane. 'Fishing-nets or food or even gunpowder. It's like that time we were trapped on the roof of

Curl Castle in the flood. We might easily need gunpowder again. Isn't it like it, Mrs Deal?'

'It's a good deal safer than that, I'm glad to say,' said Mrs Deal, beginning to bustle with the dishes.

'I don't see it's all that safer,' said Jane. 'Supposing we started to sink. Think of that.'

'Islands don't sink,' said Mrs Deal firmly, clattering and clinking knives and glasses.

'Islands don't normally float,' said Jane crossly. 'I would have thought once they started floating they could start sinking.'

Jemima stood up and said, 'You don't really think that, do you, Jane? We won't drown, will we?'

'We could easily drown,' said Jane. 'That's why we must look for life-belts and boats and gunpowder for making signals, etcetera. Actually, I think we are sinking a bit. I felt a definite lurch just then.'

'Oh no,' cried Jemima, 'oh no. I'm so bad at swimming.'

Mrs Deal left the sink and came up to the table. 'That's enough of that, Miss Jane,' she said. Then, putting her arm round Jemima, she said. 'Don't you worry. There's going to be no sinking on this island while I'm on it. You depend on the Royal Navy. My husband was in the Navy and I know what I'm talking about. They'll find we've gone in the morning and come and take us off directly. And I shouldn't wonder if we didn't bump into one of the other islands before we drift much far-ther. Don't you worry, we'll be off here by tomorrow night. Now you two run off and make your lists. We'll meet again for an early supper at seven and then off to bed.'

Despite their fear of ghosts, and even though the storm made it dark enough to use torches, Jane and Jemima decided to search separately.

In fact, Jane found that she was no longer frightened as she hurried down the dark corridor on the top floor. When Peeg House had been a school it had seemed forbidding and haunted. Now, however, they were setting out to sea. They were in the middle of a storm which she could hear drumming on the roof and roaring through the pines. The school was their only protection. It was their only supply of food and weapons, more like a ship in which they had been wrecked, and as she searched Jane pretended she was Robinson Crusoe looking for things to help them in the dangers ahead.

Unfortunately, a school is not the ideal thing to be wrecked in. The two girls found very few things they thought could be of much use. Jane found twenty bars of chocolate in the girls' lockers. The Games Mistress had a large transistor wireless and a small fishing rod. In the Geography Mistress' desk she found twenty-four compasses. In Miss

Boyle's bedroom cupboard she found three and a half bottles of gin, which would be useful for medical purposes.

Jemima had written down: one shed full of coal, one pile of peat outside back door, one large birthday cake in Latin Mistress' room.

But the person who had done worst was Mrs Deal. Instead of a list, she had just gathered all the brooms, dusters, tins of polish, etc., she could find. When they returned to the kitchen they found her holding a candle by her collection, counting.

'That makes ten brooms, five mops, sixteen dusters, two vacuum cleaners (which we won't be able to use, of course), eight tins of Mansion House and six dustpans and brushes.' Mrs Deal turned to Jane. 'At least there's no shortage of essential cleaning materials,' she said.

'Honestly, Mrs Deal,' said Jane crossly, 'don't you realize this is an an emergency? For one thing Jemima and I have found hardly any more food, so we've only enough for a few more days. We may have to try and get the butter off the dining-room ceiling. Here, take your compass. You may need it.'

Mrs Deal put the compass absently into her apron pocket. 'We've plenty for our purpose, Miss Jane,' she said. 'I'll make a nice ham omelet tonight, and we can start off with sardines on toast.'

'What do you mean?' said Jane. 'We must have rationing. We may not be rescued for days. Or weeks.'

'Or months,' said Jemima in a small voice.

'If I thought *that* I'd jump right out of that window this minute,' said Mrs Deal.

Since they were on the ground floor, Jane didn't think this meant Mrs Deal was taking the situation very seriously. Nor was she able to persuade her that they should just have half a sardine each for their supper. But when they had finished it, something happened which did convince Mrs Deal that things might become more dangerous than she had supposed.

They were sitting round the fire in Miss Boyle's study. Mrs Deal was sipping a tumbler of medicinal gin to settle her stomach. Jane and Jemima were testing their compasses. All at once the clock on the mantelpiece struck nine and Jemima suggested they listen to the news to see if there was anything about them. Mrs Deal turned on the Games Mistress' wireless and in a minute they heard the calm voice of the announcer.

'. . . extraordinary tragedy this morning. The moon-probe rocket, whose flight was to be a highlight of the Glenelg Highland Games, went off course. It headed south-west and its landing on the little Island of Peeg unfortunately seems to have coincided with the functioning of the faulty destruct mechanism. As a result, the Island of Peeg has been totally destroyed. The Island of Peeg was the site of Peeg Girls' School, nearly all of whom were fortunately at the Games. The head mistress, Miss Boyle, has stated that she believes only two girls were on the island, and it is feared that they must have perished with it. Their names have been withheld until the next of kin have been informed. The Minister of Aviation has promised a full inquiry into the misfiring of the rocket.'

After this momentous news, Jemima switched off the wireless. 'They think we're dead,' she said.

'That certainly means they won't come and look for us,' said Jane. 'Days may pass before we are rescued. Or, as Jemima said, months. Then a little ship will pull up on our rocky shore and find our poor pathetic skeletons, bleached and burnt by the sun, huddled round the remnants of our last fire. Only the faltering sentences in our log will tell the sad tale of courage and suffering to a waiting world.'

Mrs Deal, who had been nervously patting her bun and sipping her gin, looked up sharply. 'That will do, Miss Jane. Certainly the situation is a little more serious now and we will have to go carefully with the food. But I've no doubt that some good ship of the Royal Navy will soon find us. We must trust to Providence and to the Royal Navy and not make matters worse by thinking gloomy thoughts.' Her own face, however, became gloomier and gloomier, even though she quickly had another tumbler of medicinal gin. And when she went to bed soon afterwards, forgetting to tell the two girls to go to bed as well, Jane knew she must be quite worried.

She herself was very excited and soon managed to cheer up Jemima. They sat far into the night, talking and planning. They decided they would have to hunt for food on the island. They wrote out messages to put in bottles and throw into the sea. They agreed they would like to be rescued, but not for a week at least.

However, when at last they got into bed and said goodnight, Jane did begin to wonder if it would be as enjoyable as she and Jemima imagined. Listening to the storm rage round the house in the darkness, she suddenly realized that the island must actually be moving. But to where? To what? Perhaps her joke was true, and if they hit an iceberg or were struck by a typhoon or cyclone or hurricane they might actually sink. Lying on her back, listening to the rain on the window, she thought she heard a new noise, deeper and more menacing, like distant lions roaring in a jungle. It was in fact the sea, raised into great waves by the storm, dashing itself against the rocks and beaches all round the island. And as it washed against the cliffs, as the fierce wind swept on and on, the Island of Peeg moved slowly but steadily into the night, farther and farther out upon the wide Atlantic.

They awoke next day to find the storm blowing harder than ever. When Mrs Deal went out to see if she could find some vegetables to make a soup, she returned almost at once, wet, breathless, her bun of hair unwound and wild. 'Nearly blew me inside out,' she said.

However, there was a lot to do indoors. After a breakfast of two sardines, one glass of milk, a slice of bread, a slice of the Latin Mistress' birthday cake and two slices of ham each, Jane and Jemima went out to light the boiler. Mrs Deal took a bucket and mop up to the hall and said she would have another really hard look for food.

The boiler took all morning. It was a large iron one, like an old-fashioned train engine. Jane and Jemima made a tiny fire at the opening and then, once this was lit, they added more and more coal to it, gradually building it farther and farther back under the boiler. After two hours they had quite a good fire going and were having to feed coal onto it with long-handled shovels. Hands began to move on dials attached to various pipes. Steam hissed out of minute cracks. Thermometers rose. The boiler-room grew hotter and hotter and, by the time Mrs Deal called them for lunch, their fire had grown to a furnace and its cheerful roaring filled the cellar.

For lunch they had two more sardines each (the last), two slices of ham, a glass of milk, another slice of the Latin Mistress' birthday cake and a bar of chocolate each. Mrs Deal had failed to find any more food.

During the afternoon time began to drag. They all felt hungry, though no one mentioned it. The continuous noise of the storm began to wear them down. Every time they looked out of a window all they saw was whirling mist and streaming rain. Even feeding the boiler, which ate a tremendous lot of coal, seemed less exciting.

For supper they had two slices of ham, two bars of chocolate, one piece of bread and butter and a glass of milk. To save candles, they ate by the light of the ones on the Latin Mistress' cake. Luckily she was, or was about to be, forty-nine.

After supper they were quite definitely hungry. Mrs Deal wrote a long letter to her brother Frank, to be put in a bottle when the weather improved. Quite early they all had baths and then went to bed, not forgetting to turn down the boiler first.

Jane was woken early, after a night filled with dreams about huge meals, by a really painful pang of hunger. She lay still for a while, her eyes shut, trying to get back into the last dream, which had been something about being found in a storm by some gypsies who immediately gave her plate after plate of pheasant, rabbit and onion stew and mugs of hot, sweet tea.

But when she opened her eyes, food was forgotten. For there at last was the sun. Sun, pouring through the curtains and shining on the wall; sun, making the birds sing and the air smell fresh. Jane raced out of bed, woke Jemima, and together, when they had dressed, they ran down to Mrs Deal's room. She too seemed excited that the storm had gone. Soon all three were hurrying out of the front door, eager to see whatever they would see.

'If we're near a passing ship or one of the West Highland islands,' said Mrs Deal, her confidence restored, 'we can light a bonfire. I may even,' she added grimly, 'take to the water.' Mrs Deal was a very good swimmer.

The walk from the school up to where they could see the sea round the side of Mount Peeg, though it only took a quarter of an hour, was steep and boggy. But the tough, springy heather, the sponges of moss, the light, mild air, the freshness, the wetness, the excitement, made them laugh and run and forget how hungry they were. Larks rose towards the sun. Partridges whirred up and glided away down the hillside.

'We could try and catch some trout in the burn,' said Jane happily.

'And there's gulls' eggs,' said Jemima.

As they neared the curve of the hillside they began to run. Even Mrs Deal urged her thin legs to a lively pace.

The sight was incredible. Gone was the islet of Little Peeg. Gone the grey lumps of big Peeg's neighbours—Eigg and Muck. Instead, a vast expanse of blue ocean, a prairie of endless waves, whipped at their tops by the brisk wind into fluffy ridges and covered in enormous rafts of foamy bubbles.

'It's lovely,' said Jane. 'It's like a miracle.'

'Look at the waves. Look at the gulls,' cried Jemima. 'It's so exciting.'

'It's terrible,' said Mrs Deal. 'Really, Miss Jane, this is a serious situation. How we are going to inform your father and Lady, that is Mrs, Charrington, I have no idea. Now we must immediately get round the side of this hill and see if we can see what's happened to the islands and the mainland. We must pray they are not too far behind us, or I shall have to prepare myself for several hours in the water.'

But another ten minutes hard walking, by which time they could see over the school and the fir wood, back to where the rest of Scotland should have been, brought no comfort. There was no sign of land or ship. Only the blue Atlantic stretching to the horizon, its great flatness dancing in the sun.

Mrs Deal at last resigned herself.

'Well, there's nothing more we can do,' she said, 'except as I said before, put our trust in Almighty Providence and the sharp eyes of the British Navy.'

'It is rather odd that a huge, big island should be blown along so fast,' said Jemima. 'Yet it's always seemed quite real. I mean real heather and rocks and earth and things.'

'It's rather odd that it should float at all,' said Jane, 'leaving out its speed of floating. It's definitely an odd island. We'll have to study it later. But I'm ravenously hungry. Let's go and have some breakfast.'

Reminded of their hunger, they all hurried back to the school. Breakfast consisted of a glass of milk each (the last of the milk), one bar of chocolate each, two slices of ham, two slices of bread and butter (the last of the bread and the butter) and a slice of birthday cake.

After breakfast they set out to get food. Jane fetched the fishing rod from the Games Mistress' room, where Jemima found a tin full of hooks and a float in her dressing-table, and then they started together for the burn.

The two girls walked to a spot known as the Deep Pool. If you lay on the large rock above it and kept quite still, you would soon see the dark, submarine-shaped trout dart beneath the surface or hang in the water, their tails just waving, where the bubbles from the waterfall were thickest.

But now the burn was very full from all the rain. Jemima, who seemed to know about fishing, said, 'We'll be lucky if we catch anything today. My brother says the fish can't see when the water's muddy like that. Let's get some worms.'

They turned up the large, flat stones on the bank and soon had a good collection of fat and thin worms. Jemima put a piece of one of these on her hook, stood on the bank and flicked her line into the burn just by the waterfall.

Jane sat on a rock and watched. She was rather surprised at Jemima's skill, and also a bit jealous. But when, after ten minutes there was still no bite, she began to worry again about what they would eat. But suddenly, when she was also beginning to get rather bored, the float bobbed under the water twice and then shot across the pool.

Immediately Jemima shouted, 'Come and help me.'

By the time Jane reached her, a huge trout (nine inches they measured afterwards) was leaping and spinning on the end of her line. Jemima seized it in her hand and with a quick yank pulled the hook out of its mouth. Then she threw the trout onto the grass behind her.

'Oh, the poor thing,' said Jane.

'You're really meant to hit them on the head,' said Jemima, 'but I never can. They soon die. My brother says they can't really feel. Look out, I'm going to cast.'

Jemima now began to catch trout much faster. She caught two more and then let Jane have a turn. But Jane twice caught her hook in the grass, and once in her finger, and when she did get it in the burn somehow all the trout took no notice of it. So Jemima took it again, and after two hours six brown trout were scattered in the grass, and they decided it was enough to take back to the school to eat.

Nor had Mrs Deal been idle. Behind the boiler house she had found Mr Macmillan's garden. The old Scotsman had grown a mass of uninteresting but useful vegetables, and the kitchen table was piled high with potatoes, turnips and swedes. These Mrs Deal cooked and heaped around the grilled trout. For pudding, she fried the last slices of the Latin Mistress' cake.

For the first time since the island had floated away they felt really full. Mrs Deal said she thought she had the strength to start on some mopping and dusting. The two girls hurried out into the sun and spent the afternoon getting food. Jemima caught four more trout, and Jane, climbing dangerously on the cliffs, collected twenty-four gulls' eggs.

They went to bed that night, after an enormous ham omelet, with the larder full, full themselves, and all much happier. Mrs Deal said she had a strange feeling the Royal Navy would arrive the next day.

So began four of the calmest weeks they were to know on the Island of Peeg. Each morning the sun reached a little higher in the sky as they slowly drifted, or were blown, farther south. In fact, their speed was not all that slow. Pieces of wood thrown into the sea were soon left behind. Jane and Jemima thought it must be something to do with currents, but they couldn't really understand it and decided it was just another odd thing about the island.

For the first two weeks, although there was no rain, it was quite often cloudy. But during the third week it began to get hotter and hotter. At night they took off blanket after blanket until they were lying naked under a single sheet. During the day the two girls just wore knickers, while Mrs Deal, odd but practical, took to wearing an old bathing dress she'd found in one of Miss Boyle's cupboards.

There was a great deal of work to do. All their food had to be caught. Gulls' eggs and trout were what they mainly ate, but Mrs Deal also made nettle soup and vegetable tea. Jane made a snare out of some fishing line and managed to catch one of the island's few rabbits. Sad though it was, Mrs Deal resolutely killed this while the two girls were out. 'Needs must,' she said, 'and the devil take the hindermost.'

Every morning and every evening water had to be hand-pumped up to the roof. The boiler had to be raked out and stoked. Wood had to be collected for a bonfire in case the never-arriving Royal Navy should suddenly arrive. Mrs Deal herself, apart from cooking, had decided to spring-clean the entire school from top to bottom. 'I shall hand it over in a better state than I found it, if it's the last thing I do,' she said. And as it grew hotter and Mrs Deal worked harder and faster and longer, Jane thought it probably would be the last thing she did.

They began to swim every day. And it was when they first did this, from the school's favourite swimming beach, that they noticed a curious thing. The beach was much smaller. This meant, as a terrified Jemima immediately pointed out, that Peeg had sunk. But by putting a stick in the pebbles at the highest point the waves reached, they found that the island didn't seem to be sinking any more.

They found a huge heap of old bottles in a shed by Mr Macmillan's garden. They threw three of these a day into the sea with messages in them. The messages, except for the one which had Mrs Deal's letter to her brother, all said:

From the Island of Peeg, Scotland

The Island of Peeg was not sunk by the moon rocket, but is floating rapidly south. Jane Charrington, Jemima Garing and Mrs Deal are alive and well on it. Will the finder of this message please contact the British Government or the Royal Navy at once. Reward of £500. Signed Jane Charrington, Jemima Garing, Alice Deal.

It was Jemima who first noticed that all was not well. She came back one morning from her fishing and said, 'You know I think the burn is getting smaller.'

After lunch (scrambled gulls' eggs, parsnips, spring water) she took Jane to see. There was no doubt about it. You could see the marks on the rocks showing how the level of the water had fallen at least six inches. The water was also much warmer. Nor did the level in the burn fall slowly. By the end of the same afternoon it had fallen another inch. The next morning Jemima caught two trout—there were very few left now—with her hands in a tiny pool which had become cut off from the main stream of the burn. By the next day that pool, and others, had completely dried up.

And it was now they began to notice how dry the whole of Peeg had become. No longer was there the endless trickle of water, the glistening rocks. The moss was drying and turning brown. Only the tough pines seemed unaffected by the blazing sun which all day long poured its heat upon them.

Mrs Deal, strong as she was, could only work for an hour before having a dip in the sea. And the two girls simply spent every minute of the day in the water, except when they were looking for food.

But matters didn't grow serious until four nights after Jemima had discovered that the burn was drying up. It had been a particularly hot day, the air quivering so hard it looked as though the sun had already succeeded in setting the island on fire. When they went to bed, Jane fell asleep almost at once, exhausted by long hours in the warm sea.

She was woken at about one o'clock in the morning by a low rumbling. At first she thought sleepily it might be thunder, but she soon realized that it came from somewhere inside the school. She woke Jemima and they went out into the corridor to listen.

'I think it's an earthquake,' whispered Jemima.

'Nothing's shaking,' said Jane.

'Perhaps it's a terrible sea monster crawled out of the sea,' said Jemima.

'Nonsense,' said Jane, beginning to feel quite brave. 'We must go and look.'

They put on some clothes and then set off hand in hand down the corridor. All round them the house was silent and warm, dimly lit by the large moon; the lines of dormitory beds, still neatly made as the girls had left them on the morning of the Glenelg Highland Games, had teddies and dolls by their pillows. The sea was gently swelling and murmuring in the distance. Jane began to feel less brave.

As they drew closer, the rumbling became more of a jumping clank. At first they thought it was in the kitchen, but when they slowly and nervously peered round the door, it was as usual; hot from the stoves, and the floor, by Jemima's torch, covered in scuttling cockroaches. The noise, however, was now very loud; not only the sound of straining, banging metal, but loud hisses.

'I know what it is,' said Jane. 'Quick. The back door.'

As they came out into the backyard, she saw at once that she had been right. Against the darkness of the outhouses they could see a great cloud of steam gushing from the door next to the coal cellar. From the door, too, came a deafening thumping and clanging, a whistling, roaring, trembling din which seemed to shake the ground they stood on.

It was the boiler. Crawling on their hands and knees to avoid the billows of boiling steam, the two girls reached the door and looked in.

The most extraordinary sight met their eyes. The boiler itself was red hot all over (they found afterwards that Jemima, whose turn it had been to stoke it, had left the damper jammed open with a shovel). Each nut and bolt on it glowed fiercely in the dark, and its curving iron sides were in places almost white with the heat from the furnace roaring underneath. But the noise they had heard came from the huge hot-water cylinder above the boiler. The ever-increasing heat of the fire had made the water in the cylinder boil; then the pressure of steam had blown out the safety valves and started the cylinder jumping. Now, to the sound of furious but muffled bubbling from inside, the vast iron object, encased in white plaster, was leaping up and down on its supports, shaking off great white chunks, loosing piercing jets of steam from safety valves and other vents, and looking every second as though it would wrench itself away from its pipes and its platform and come crashing down onto the red-hot boiler beneath.

They crawled backwards and then ran to the kitchen. 'You turn on all the hot taps, then come and help me get the fire extinguishers,' shouted Jane.

The fire extinguishers were scattered about the school. Jane collected one from the hall and another from outside the geography-room. On the way back she met Jemima.

'It's extraordinary,' Jemima said. 'I've turned on all the hot taps in the kitchen and the pantry and all that comes out is steam.'

'She'll blow up soon,' said Jane, remembering a film she'd seen where boilers were called 'she'. 'Here, take this extinguisher.'

They ran back and were soon crouched before the boiler. By the glow, Jane read the instructions: 'Strike knob sharply with both hands. Then direct nozzle at fire.'

Jemima leant over the cylinder and banged her hands on the knob. Jane shielded her face and directed the nozzle at the boiler.

For a moment nothing happened. Then it jerked in her arms, there was a gentle whoosh, and a great cloud of white foam shot from the nozzle.

'Come on,' shouted Jane. 'It's fun.'

Six times they had to run back to fetch a new extinguisher. But at last

the fire was out, the cylinder stopped leaping and the boiler-room, though several feet deep in white foam, seemed safe to leave. Wearily the two girls returned to the school. As they trudged through the kitchen they could hear steam still gushing from the hot taps. Without even bothering to wash off the dirt and extinguisher foam they got into bed and immediately fell asleep.

But it was Mrs Deal who discovered the true meaning of the boiler incident. When they came down to breakfast she was sitting gloomily in front of a dozen gulls' eggs.

'I don't know what you girls were doing last night,' she said. 'I won't speak of the mess in the boiler-room. You must have gone mad. A week's work there would be a conservative estimate. But you've run the tank dry and there's no water in the well.'

'No water?' said Jane.

'No water,' said Mrs Deal. 'I shall have to do the scrubbing with sea water. It's almost unheard of.'

Jane and Jemima explained how the boiler had nearly blown up, and Mrs Deal then agreed that they had done very well.

After a somewhat drying breakfast of salty flat-fish Jemima had caught in the sea and some thick scrambled gulls' eggs, the two girls set off with buckets to get water from the burn.

The burn was dry.

'But it can't be,' said Jane. 'Surely it wasn't dry yesterday.'

'I didn't go yesterday,' said Jemima.

'Let's walk down,' said Jane, 'there's bound to be some water left in one of the pools.'

But it was the same down the whole of the winding, tumbling course. The smooth rocks, the thickly scattered stones were white in the sun and almost too hot to touch; already, between them, the mud was starting to crack. Even worse, as they walked slowly towards the sea, was the smell of dead trout. There were few of these left from Jemima's fishing but, as the burn had dried, those that remained had floundered down to the deeper pools. When these evaporated, the trout had died.

The two girls stared horrified at this unpleasant scene. At last Jane said, 'We must get back to Mrs Deal. We must plan. This is a real emergency.'

'Well at least we won't starve,' said Jemima. 'There's plenty of gulls' eggs still and I can catch fish in the sea.'

'Yes, but being thirsty is quite different,' said Jane. 'You say "starving" but you don't say "thirsting", you say "dying of thirst"; it's much more serious. You can only live a few days without water.'

Mrs Deal either rose to occasions or sank beneath them. Now she chose to sink. When Jane and Jemima told her about the burn, she sat abruptly down.

'Well, that's that then,' she said. 'The End. It's been a long life and a gloomy one, but I won't say I shan't be sorry to go. I *shall* be sorry to go. Until our time comes we'd best keep on as normal. You two girls go and make your beds while I make a start on the boiler-room.'

After lunch, which was already difficult to eat, Jane and Jemima decided to go and look for water. They took umbrellas to shield them from the fierce sun, but even with these they were soon forced to turn back. The heat was so great that they felt they were being dried in front of a fire. The peaty earth of Peeg was cracked and baked, the heather and grass shrivelled brown. 'We'll go out at night when it's cooler,' said Jane.

They spent the rest of the afternoon lying exhausted in Miss Boyle's hot armchairs, listening to the wireless. Apart from a lot of crackles, they could only get faint African music and, since Jane had noticed from her compass that they had never stopped moving south, she decided that they had probably reached the Equator.

For supper Mrs Deal gave them bowls of raw gulls' eggs as the most liquid thing they had. But their throats were beginning to swell and they could only swallow a few mouthfuls.

It grew dark, as Jane said, with tropical suddenness, but hardly any cooler. When the two girls went out to look for water it was still like walking in a large, uneven oven.

Their search for water was no more successful than during the day. They walked slowly up the side of Mount Peeg to the springs which had supplied the burn, but they were all dry. Then they walked out to the low, forty-foot cliffs at the front of the island. The tiny streams that had once oozed and trickled from hundreds of places had all disappeared.

They even climbed down to the beach. Here it was Jemima who noticed something rather odd. She threw an old piece of driftwood into the calm water, but instead of slowly being left behind by the island, as would have happened before, it just floated there, unmoving.

'Even the current has stopped carrying us,' whispered Jemima.

They arrived back at the school exhausted. 'We're getting weaker,' said Jane, as they stood panting in the kitchen.

'Look, even the cockroaches are thirsty,' said Jemima. In their search for moisture they seemed to have lost all fear: the moonlit floor was alive with the crunchy beetles.

Jane spent a restless night. Several times she dreamt she was on fire and was then blissfully put out by a huge hose spouting water. Twice she was woken by what she thought was a gentle rain pattering on the window, only to find it was Jemima snoring.

The next two days were a nightmare. They all felt too thirsty to eat, and so weak that it was a long time before they managed to get out of bed. Each day the sun blazed its way across the huge steely sky and not a breath of wind moved on the Atlantic. They lay about, dozed, occasionally talked with swollen lips, fanned each other; afterwards, those two days were all jumbled and confused in Jane's mind.

Towards the evening of the fourth day without water Jemima grew feverish. Hot as they all were, it was plain that she had grown hotter. Her cheeks were flushed and there was a black rim to her lips. She suddenly burst into tears and fell on her bed calling for her mother.

'Mummy, Mummy,' she cried, 'why have you left me?' Then she fell into a sort of daze, lying with her eyes open, muttering and crying.

Mrs Deal put her to bed and then sat soothing and fanning her. 'Poor child,' she said, 'it's no more than we can expect.'

Night fell. Jane lay listening to Jemima's muttering and the swish-swish of Mrs Deal's magazine fanning. She tossed and dozed, woke up and heard Jemima again; dozed and tossed. Her tongue was swelling. She thought she was back at Curl Castle, swimming in the river. She felt she was flying in a cool wind over endless fields of snow. She was in a garden at night. Suddenly it began to rain. Huge, cool drops as big as pigeons' eggs falling and bursting in her mouth. All at once she woke up again. Jemima was still muttering. By the pale light of the moon she saw that Mrs Deal had fallen back against the wall and was asleep.

And then, deep within her, like a secret, angry determination to do something, even though she had been told not to, she felt she must fight for them all. If they went on lying there another day they would all be dead. There must be a way out.

She put her legs on the floor and stood up, weakly. She walked down the corridor slowly so as to save her strength.

Outside it was very hot and very quiet. The moon was high in the cloudless sky, making the landscape of Peeg soft and sinister with its pale light. Jane walked away from the school, up the hill towards the front of the island.

The dead grass rustled as she walked. But this was the only noise. Even the ocean had fallen silent as though waiting for them to die. It stretched away all round the island, miles and miles of wrinkled, moonlit water, peaceful at Jane's feet. She walked a little way along the cliff-top and then climbed down a steep pathway which led to a narrow beach.

Here the silence was even stranger. The water hardly lapped the rocks. Jane suddenly felt how frightening it was to be floating in such deep water. What lay underneath, down in those dark cold fathoms below them?

Suddenly, she heard a noise, loud in the silence. It came from her left, a faint chink. Jane felt gooseflesh in spite of the heat. Very slowly she turned her head.

From about thirty yards away, a man was creeping towards her. Though he was bending forward, Jane saw he was quite tall. The moon caught his white hair.

As she stared he stopped and stood up. 'Don't move,' he said. 'I have a gun.'

Jane tried to speak. Her dry tongue filled her mouth, her cracked lips were open.

'Advance and be recognized,' said the man. 'I don't wish to shoot, but there's a war on.'

Jane suddenly felt she was going to be sick. The sea tilted towards her and then sank back. She raised her arms, took one weak step forward and then, with a low, hoarse cry, fainted onto the stones.

4. The Mystery of Peeg Explained

WHEN Jane fell, the tall man continued to move slowly and warily towards her, his revolver still pointed at her body. But once he was sure she was really unconscious, he put the gun back in his pocket and lifted her gently onto his huge shoulders. He turned and crunched back up the shingle until he reached some large slabs of rock which were leaning upright against each other. Moving round these the man stopped at the side of a particularly large one which was half embedded in the cliff. Reaching forward and bending down he felt round the edges of this until suddenly there was a faint click and the rock swung slowly open. The moonlight was just strong enough to show steep stone steps going up and into the cliff. The man stepped calmly through, Jane still hanging over his shoulder, and the rock door shut behind them.

Back at Peeg School, the heat seemed to be growing greater not lessening as it did sometimes towards morning. Mrs Deal had woken at three o'clock. She saw almost at once that Jane had gone but was too weak even to mind. 'Soon we shall all be gone,' she thought to herself. 'Oh, lads, you come too late; oh, Admiral, where are your long boats now?' She felt her mind becoming feverish as Jemima's had been. Now that she was going to die she thought more and more about the Navy, in which Mr Deal had served until his own end so long ago. 'Lower away, bosun,' said the voice in her head; 'Mr Mate, get a tackle on that body there. Pipe it aboard, Sir, pipe it aboard.' Jemima had fallen asleep. Her lips were quite black. Mrs Deal lifted her magazine and weakly tried to fan her burning forehead. 'Captain's compliments, Mr Mate. The funeral is to be with full Naval honours—burial at sea.'

Someone was pouring water gently between Jane's lips. She knew it wasn't a dream because it was too real and cool; at the same time she didn't open her eyes because she feared that if she did it would stop, as it had so often before when it had really been a dream.

A voice said, 'That will do, Sergeant. It says in the manual, "Dehydration must be treated with care. Six to eight ounces of fluid every ten minutes."'

'Very good, sir.' The water stopped. Jane opened her eyes. A thick grey beard waved just in front of her face. 'That's better, that be a sight better,' said the beard. 'She's coming round, sir.'

The beard moved and Jane saw that it belonged to a short, bald man of about sixty, dressed in shorts, khaki shirt and a peaked cap. His face and hands, she noticed, were quite amazingly white.

She was lying on a sofa in a long, low room, lit by electric lights with faded shades and with photographs in frames on the walls, some tables with magazines on them and several armchairs. In one of these sat the man she had seen creeping towards her along the beach.

'Can I have some more water, please?' she asked him.

'I'm sorry, young lady,' he said in a deep but brisk voice, 'the manual's instructions are quite clear. Six to eight ounces every ten minutes. You can have some more in six minutes.

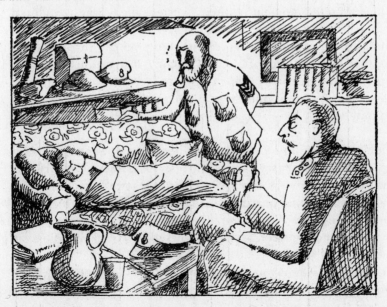

'Meanwhile, let me introduce us. This is Sergeant Cobbin, I am Captain Thomson. Both of the 7th Hussars, seconded for the duration to Project Peeg.'

'I'm Jane Charrington,' said Jane, her voice still very weak.

'How do you do,' said Captain Thomson. He stood up—and Jane noticed how incredibly white his skin was too—and came over to her sofa. 'I'm afraid I'll have to interrogate you properly later, as you probably realize. But now tell me, are you alone?'

'Alone!' cried Jane, remembering with a guilty rush the reason for her journey. 'Oh, how could I have forgotten? No—quick, you must rush to Peeg School at once with water. Jemima may be dead. You must save Mrs Deal and Jemima.'

But Captain Thomson bent his tall frame swiftly forward over her and then turned hurriedly to the Sergeant. 'Jemima? Mrs Deal? These sound like code names. Has there been infiltration? Mrs Deal Platoon? Battalion Jemima?'

'I doubt it, sir,' said Sergeant Cobbin in his comforting Suffolk voice. 'They sound real enough names to me. No doubt the young lady's companions.'

'At all events a situation to be investigated,' said Captain Thomson, marching swiftly about the room. 'Get the jerry cans, Sergeant. And you, Miss Jane, I must warn you, if Mrs Deal Platoon gives trouble— then short shrift. Short shrift. You may have one glass of water every ten minutes.' Captain Thomson then strode from the room, beckoning Sergeant Cobbin to follow him.

Jane waited a moment till their footsteps died away, then hurried to the jug and poured herself some water; one, two, three, *four* glasses. So wonderful did it feel, cooling and soothing her dry throat, her swollen lips, that she quite ignored the Captain's instructions. Luckily these were for people actually dying of thirst, and although she finished the entire jug it did her no harm at all. She pulled herself back to the sofa and immediately fell into a deep sleep.

Jane slept for six hours. She missed the return of Sergeant Cobbin and Captain Thomson carrying the unconscious bodies of her friends. Mrs Deal had still been conscious when they had found her, but at the sight of Sergeant Cobbin's beard she had risen shakily to her feet and with a loud cry 'The Navy!' had fainted into his arms. She missed the careful forcing of water between Jemima's cracked and blackened lips, the gentle bathing of her forehead. By the time Jane awoke it was morning (though no daylight entered what Captain Thomson had called the ante-room) and she already felt much better.

That was the strange thing about thirst. Although they had nearly died of it in four days, once they could drink again they recovered almost at once. By that same evening Jemima was sitting up and talking, and Jane and Mrs Deal felt almost normal.

They were all three sitting talking in the ante-room when the two soldiers came in to join them.

Captain Thomson said, 'Ladies, I feel we should have a conference. We have avoided asking you disturbing questions after your terrible experience, but, as you can imagine, the Sergeant and myself are simply burning with curiosity to know about the progress of the war. We also need to know how you got involved in Project Peeg, though it is evident you got involved by mistake. Now, Sergeant, you ask the big question.'

'Well, it's the war,' said Sergeant Cobbin, tugging at his beard and showing, for him, signs of excitement. 'You be the first real news we've had for twenty-eight years.'

'Twenty-eight years?' said Jane, amazed. 'What war are you talking about?'

'Why, The War,' said Sergeant Cobbin. 'The War. The *War* that started in 1939.'

'Good heavens,' cried Captain Thomson, springing impatiently to his feet. 'The War! The War! The War!'

So Jane and Jemima and Mrs Deal began to learn the extraordinary story of the two old soldiers. It would take too long to tell it in their own words, but made much shorter, it was this.

At the very beginning of the Second World War, Winston Churchill had decided that the Island of Peeg would be one of his secret weapons. The idea was simple but amazing. It had long been known that Peeg was a volcanic island; what few knew was that it was one of those rare volcanic islands which, while ordinary granite, earth and heather on the surface, consisted inside almost entirely of soft pumice stone. *And, of course, pure pumice stone floats.*

One of the few people who knew about Peeg was Winston Churchill, who had often explored those parts when a boy. He also knew that at the far end of the island the sea had scooped an immense cavern out of the soft pumice stone, the entrance to which was out of sight below the water.

Churchill's plan was to enlarge the cavern and fill it with an enormous amount of high explosive. Large buoyancy tanks would be attached all round the island, an engine-room would be built at the back by the causeway and the causeway itself would be mined with explosive. Then, at a suitable moment, the causeway would be blown up. The island, Churchill hoped, would be jolted free of the mainland, float out to sea and could be slowly steered to some position where its destruction would most harm the enemy. If it did not float away, then all that would have been done was to destroy the causeway, the Island of Peeg would remain as an excellent storeplace of high explosive, invaluable for resistance if Great Britain lost the war.

All but the last part of the experiment was carried out. For two years an army of fifty workers, sworn to secrecy, toiled on the island. The huge cavern was made even larger and eight million tons of TNT stored in it. Vast buoyancy tanks were attached at regular intervals round the island some forty feet below the level of the sea. An engine-room was built about seventy yards from the causeway. In 1942 Captain Thomson and Sergeant Cobbin, then aged 35 and 37, were moved into their quarters, which had been hollowed out of the pumice stone three-quarters of the way up the cavern. Captain Thomson, as well as an excellent soldier, was an amateur geologist who knew a lot about rocks; Sergeant Cobbin was an engineer who had also had lessons in explosives.

Two days after they moved in, the workers moved out. Unfortunately the train which was carrying them south was hit by a large bomb and everyone in it was killed. This much was known to Captain Thomson and Sergeant Cobbin. But the day after that their wireless, the only link they were allowed with the mainland, was irreparably destroyed by a fall of rock. Their instructions had been very strict—on no account were they to contact anyone. They would be called on when they were needed. And for thirty years no one had called on them.

For thirty years Captain Thomson and Sergeant Cobbin had waited to serve their country. Then the moon rocket at Glenelg had crashed onto the causeway and—proving Churchill right—set Peeg upon her course. To Captain Thomson and Sergeant Cobbin—who still thought the war was going on—it seemed as though their task had at last begun.

To persuade them that the war was, in fact, over was the first thing that Mrs Deal and the two girls tried, gently, to prove to them. It was extremely difficult, and for a long time Captain Thomson and Sergeant Cobbin refused to believe it. In the end Jane remembered that there were a lot of old newspapers in the 5th Form common room used in Current Affairs classes. These, though they didn't mention the war at all, being only one or two years old, did finally convince them. Indeed, it was just because they didn't mention the war at all that they were so convincing.

'And you say it ended in *1945*?' said Captain Thomson. 'Twenty-seven years ago?' It had been a great shock to them both.

'I can't rightly get used to the idea,' said Sergeant Cobbin. 'You say we won? Well, that's good. That's what we hoped. But there were we thinking them Germans had overrun the country and that stout resistance was going on in the ditches and the hedges as Winston had foretold.'

'No doubt,' said Captain Thomson sadly, 'no doubt in the excitement of victory, they just forgot Project Peeg.'

'Oh surely not,' said Jane. 'I'm sure you weren't forgotten.'

'I expect a flying bomb hit some Government building and destroyed everything about you,' said Mrs Deal, little knowing how accurate she was.

Captain Thamson brightened. 'That's true,' he said. 'And in that case perhaps there's some honour in having stuck to our post through the years.'

'Indeed there is,' said Mrs Deal; 'a great deal of honour. You have stood by your post, through thick and thin, at great personal inconvenience, in a way which adds glory and lustre to the great name of the British Navy.'

'Army, ma'am, Army,' said Captain Thomson.

'Army, Navy, Air Force—all men at arms,' said Mrs Deal, looking quite flushed. 'What does it matter? We're afloat now. To me you'll always represent the *spirit* of the British Navy in the glorious *uniform* of the British Army.'

'Hurrah!' cried Jemima from her sofa.

'Sergeant—salute!' cried Captain Thomson. And as he and Sergeant Cobbin leapt to attention and saluted, Jemima and Jane shouted hurrah and Mrs Deal, overcome with emotion, sprang to her feet and saluted too.

However, apart from a few moments like these, they all had a great deal to ask each other.

'But what did you eat?' said Jane.

'Well, we had a special arrangement with a shop in Dunlaig,' said Captain Thomson. 'They were to leave certain supplies at the end of the causeway every week. We collected at night. They weren't told who it was for and were paid by the Government. If a bomb did destroy our records in London, no one remembered to stop that. Also we have two and a half years' supply of tinned food stored here. There's plenty of water of course. Two hundred thousand gallons of fuel oil for the engines.'

'Supplies of drink are running low, sir,' put in Sergeant Cobbin.

'Perfectly true, Sergeant,' said Captain Thomson, 'perfectly true. We're down to a crate or two of rum as I remember.'

'We've got one bottle of medicinal gin left you can have,' said Jane.

'Very good of you,' said Captain Thomson, bowing politely to her.

'I must say,' said Mrs Deal, 'I feel I would have *felt* the war had ended. Did you not feel it in your bones?'

'My *bones*?' said Captain Thomson thoughtfully, 'bones? Can't say I did.'

'You see, ma'am, our instructions on that point were very strict,' said Sergeant Cobbin. 'We were only to come out at night, talk to no one, see no one. All orders were to come over the wireless. Unfortunately, as the Captain told you, a chunk of old rock fell on that shortly after we moved in. But I reckoned how as we didn't answer or send any signals they'd have guessed about that and got any orders to us by other means.'

'And you must remember,' said Captain Thomson, 'that in the event of defeat we were to be more secret than ever.'

'But thirty-three years!' said Mrs Deal. 'Well, that's a lot of time for a war—thirty-three years.'

'Not at all,' said Captain Thomson. 'If you'll excuse me contradicting you, ma'am, there was the Peloponnesian War—at 431 BC to 404 BC very nearly twenty-nine years. The Wars of the Roses—1444 to 1484. The Crusades. It can all be gleaned from my encyclopedia of famous painters.'

'There's the Thirty Years War and the Hundred Years War,' said Jemima, whose best subject was history.

'We were ready to stop here till we died,' said Sergeant Cobbin in a comfortable voice.

'Brave men!' said Mrs Deal, flushing again.

Jane wanted to know what they had done all the time and if they hadn't been bored.

This amused Captain Thomson a great deal. 'Bored?' he said in his deep, quick voice. 'Oh no, oh dear me no. This is a Military Establishment, run on Military lines. Of course the Sergeant and I have relaxed discipline a little. That's inevitable in the circumstances. But besides Parades, Orders, Mess Nights, weapon training, we've had a great deal of work to do.' And then he began to describe what he and Sergeant Cobbin had done over the years.

They had decided that the more of the island that blew up the more effective it would be as a bomb. They had therefore dug long tunnels through the pumice stone, which now reached to every part of the island. At regular intervals off these tunnels they had dug little rooms; each room was packed with high explosive.

'Isn't it very dangerous?' said Jane.

'Very,' said Captain Thomson. 'Luckily I don't smoke, and Sergeant Cobbin only likes an occasional pipe. A dust explosion is our main worry.'

'Dust?' said Mrs Deal. 'You have problems with your dusting?'

'Now that we are getting older, the dusting certainly becomes no easier,' said Captain Thomson.

'I think I may be able to help,' said Mrs Deal. 'Let me see, we have ten brooms, five mops, six dustpans and brushes and sixteen dusters. Yes, I've no doubt I can help with the cleaning.'

'If you'll excuse me asking,' said Jane, 'how old are you both?'

'Not at all,' said Captain Thomson. 'I am sixty-five. Sergeant Cobbin is sixty-two.'

He went on to explain how there had been the Buoyancy Tanks to inspect and the engines to keep well oiled. 'We started these after Peeg was launched,' said Captain Thomson. 'Unfortunately, the explosion bent the propeller shaft and made steering difficult, but we headed South because I had an instinct that's where they'd want us. Then, two days ago, something went wrong with the engine and we stopped.'

There had been many other things to do. Captain Thomson had collected many interesting rocks and fossils and was writing a book about them. He was also interested in Art and had been studying an *Encyclopedia of 2000 Famous Painters*. 'Know the thing off by heart,' he said. There had been clothes to mend, a task, Jane noticed, which they cannot have found very easy; both their uniforms were covered with large, odd-shaped patches, clumsily stitched. They had enlarged their rooms, adding another bedroom, a shooting range, a map room and building a staircase from the Blow-up room to the cliff. And Sergeant Cobbin had frequently studied the aeroplane they had been given. This was in special collapsible form and was an idea of Winston Churchill's so that when the island was exploded they could fly away to safety. Unfortunately there was not room to make it in the ante-room. On warm nights they had gone out onto the narrow beach and while Sergeant Cobbin had smoked a pipe, Captain Thomson had done some fishing; often they had just sat and looked at the lights twinkling on the shore and wondered how the war was going and when the time would come for them to be of use.

'No war,' said Sergeant Cobbin sadly. 'That's going to take a while to get accustomed to.'

'We'll get used to it,' said Captain Thomson briskly. 'Military discipline, Sergeant. We've got used to a good many things together.

'But in answer to your question, Miss Charrington. We were never bored. We kept busy. That may not be the secret of happiness, but it's the secret of not being bored.'

Everyone was silent. Jane still had several questions to ask, but it was now quite late in the evening of the second day of their rescue. Jane and Mrs Deal and particularly Jemima still felt weak; and the two old soldiers were obviously still worried, despite Captain Thomson's briskness, by there being no war. So after a quick supper from the store of tins, consisting of dried egg and powdered potato, they all went to bed. Before she went to sleep on her sofa, Jane thought how nice it was knowing that there were men there to look after them and protect them and take charge if things went wrong.

Next morning when they woke up even Jemima felt well. Captain Thomson asked them to stay as long as they liked in what he called 'the Mess' (though it was in fact, as Jane pointed out, exceptionally tidy). However, they decided they would sleep in the school and just have meals with the soldiers.

'It's not that we haven't enjoyed sleeping here,' Jemima said, 'but it is rather strange sleeping underground.'

'That's just what I wanted to ask,' said Jane. 'Didn't you long to see the sun sometimes?'

'Well, I did miss the sun at first, that's certainly true—did I not, sir?' said Sergeant Cobbin.

'You did,' said Captain Thomson. 'For the first five years you did. The Sergeant really wanted to be an airman,' he went on, turning to Mrs Deal. 'That's why he spent so much time checking over the aeroplane Special Kit.'

'Fancy,' said Mrs Deal. 'I'd have said the Sergeant had more of a Naval aspect with that beard. The air? Well, naturally he'd miss it in that case—and all that goes with it.'

'Whereas the Captain here,' said Sergeant Cobbin in his calm way, 'never minded a jot, did you sir? Never so much as noticed one way or the other.'

'I wouldn't say I never *noticed*,' said Captain Thomson rather irritably. 'I'd have been a buffoon not to notice. I put up with it, that's all. And we must now learn to get used to daylight again, Sergeant. Now the war's over we must start to adapt to a surface life.

'Nevertheless, madam,' he said to Mrs Deal. 'I think we won't come with you. You will have noticed that our skins are a little pale. We must take it slowly.'

'There is that tunnel, sir, we dug, what was it? 1950 or thereabouts. Comes out in the boiler-room,' said Sergeant Cobbin.

'So there is. Well, we may come and meet you. But lunch here, in the Mess, one o'clock sharp.'

It was wonderful to get out into the air again. Although not exactly fresh—indeed it felt hotter than ever—it was refreshing to see the sparkling waves and be able to run and jump as much as they wanted to again.

They were just about to go down past Mount Peeg to the school when Jemima, turning to see how far behind Mrs Deal had got, noticed a strange dark line, far away, stretching the length of the horizon. 'What's that?' she said.

'I think it must be a storm,' said Jane after a moment. 'We'd better be quick and do what we've got to do before it reaches us.'

Quite what it was they had to do none of them knew. There was something depressing about the school, stifling in the heat. Cockroaches lay on their backs dead of thirst; also two rats. And their bedrooms reminded them how nearly they, too, had died. Mrs Deal only had one task, which was to collect the brooms and mops and dusters.

On their way back to lunch Jane said, 'Let's sleep in the Mess after all, Mrs Deal. Captain Thomson and Sergeant Cobbin are so nice. Also it was so cool there.'

'A good idea, Miss Jane,' said Mrs Deal. 'I felt quite rude refusing. I'll say we've changed our minds.'

When they could see the sea again, Jane pointed to the horizon. 'It definitely is a storm,' she said, 'and it's getting nearer.' The thin black line had now grown until it was a thick band along the horizon. Already it was a little menacing.

Captain Thomson and Sergeant Cobbin were delighted they were going to sleep in the Mess.

'Guests at Project Peeg after all these years, Sergeant,' said Captain Thomson. 'The two young ladies can have the map room and I'll give up *my* room to Mrs Deal.'

'I shall give up *my* room to Mrs Deal,' said Sergeant Cobbin.

'Sergeant,' said Captain Thomson, a flush spreading on his large white cheeks, 'I said *my* room.'

'And I said my room,' said Sergeant Cobbin obstinately.

'Gentlemen, gentlemen,' said Mrs Deal with great pleasure. 'Not on my account, pray.'

The two men glared angrily at each other. Jane noticed that they had both put on new uniforms since the morning, ones that were almost unpatched.

'A compromise would be turn and turn about,' said Captain Thomson. 'The good lady could have my room one night and your room the next night.'

'That's ridiculous,' said Jane. 'Think how inconvenient for poor Mrs Deal.'

'Why don't we sleep in Captain Thomson's room and Mrs Deal in the map room,' said Jemima.

'Yes,' said Mrs Deal, 'I should be delighted with the map room.'

'If that's what you wish that's what I wish,' said Captain Thomson gallantly. 'Certainly that solves the problem. I shall sleep in the firing range.'

'Oh come, sir,' said Sergeant Cobbin, 'that's the most uncomfortable place in the island. There's room enough for both in my room. Join me.'

'Well, that's very generous of you, Sergeant,' said the Captain. 'I shall.'

After lunch Mrs Deal and the two girls hurried back to the school to collect sheets and clothes and things like the wireless, the gin and the compasses. If possible it was hotter than ever; but it was a quite different heat from the days before. The air was completely still and seemed to be pressing on the island. The storm clouds reached half-way up the sky; they seemed like a lid rolling up to close over the world, and Jane thought she could hear the first faint rumblings of thunder.

Once at the school, they bustled about their tasks. They packed their clothes and Jane put the wireless and all the compasses by her case and a book of Miss Boyle's called *The Second World War* which she thought would interest the two soldiers. Mrs Deal made a bundle of clean sheets and also tied the mops and brooms together.

While they were all busy it grew gradually darker. The air became heavier and hotter, until Mrs Deal and Jane, who was in the kitchen helping her, were actually dripping wet.

'Oh please, can't we stop?' said Jane. 'I want to swim. Why must we clean the ovens *now*?'

'We're almost done, Miss Jane,' panted Mrs Deal. 'I'd never forgive myself if these lovely hot plates got rusty. We've been put in charge of this lovely old building and we must not betray our trust.'

Though this was hardly an accurate account of how they came to be at Peeg School, Jane felt too hot to argue. She leant against the sink and watched Mrs Deal rush the wire brush up and down the long copper range. Was that thunder in the distance?

'There,' said Mrs Deal at last. 'You can't leave these things a minute in the tropics.'

This time it was unmistakably thunder. Much closer, it rolled towards the school. There was a faint sighing of wind and the hot air in the kitchen moved. Then everything was still again.

'We'll collect our things and get back before the rain,' said Mrs Deal. But neither of them moved. It was as though they were waiting for something and for no particular reason Jane began to feel nervous.

Mrs Deal suddenly said, 'Is that Miss Jemima?'

Jane listened, but then there was the sound of clattering on the kitchen stairs and a moment later Jemima raced through the door.

'Quick—you must come to the 4th Form dorm. There's the most terrific storm I've ever seen. I'm sure it's terribly dangerous.'

The view from the dormitory window was indeed strange and terrifying. The black clouds had now swept up directly over the school. Yet these were not like English storm clouds, not black lumps moving solidly like angry elephants across the sky. The clouds above Peeg were writhing and boiling as though enormous winds were twisting through them. But there was no noise. After that single grumble of thunder the storm had advanced silently. The hot air hung over the island as heavily as it had the night they had nearly died of thirst.

'The calm before the storm,' whispered Jane.

For four minutes this hot calm continued. Then, like a bull breathing out before it charges, a single gust of hot wind swept over them and was gone. They saw the pines down by the burn bend and straighten. A second gust. Stillness again.

And suddenly, with a steady rumbling as thunder trundled from one end of the sky to the other, with a dazzling flicker of lightning, the storm was upon them.

It struck first with a furious blast of wind. The two girls and Mrs Deal were nearly blown over, but with a great effort they just managed to shut the windows. It grew swiftly dark and they would have seen nothing except that the lightning flashed so often that it was as bright as a moonlit night. Then with a roar the most tremendous rain storm crashed onto the school. They heard it rattling on the roof, and the windows streamed so much that when they looked out the lightning and the wildly moving trees were bent and distorted.

How long they watched Jane didn't know. Twice pine trees were struck by lightning, flared for a moment, and were then doused when the rain swept furiously over the island again. Sometimes for a few seconds there would be silence and they would think the storm was moving away. Then the wind would roar and they would hear the answering roar as great waves swept against the little island's cliffs.

Jane was just beginning to think what fun it would be to run out with no clothes on as she had in summer storms at Curl Castle, when she realized something very odd was happening to the window. She could feel, as though a giant's hand was on the other side, the glass pressing harder and harder against her face. Looking up, she saw the catch beginning to give way.

'Quick,' she shouted. 'The window's opening. Push.'

All three of them leant against the window. But the giant was too strong. For a moment they held it shut, then suddenly, contemptuously, the wind thrust it open, there was a crash as the glass panes smashed against the walls, and Jemima, Jane and Mrs Deal were literally blown off their feet by the hurricane that swept in.

Now it was impossible to hear anything but the storm. Jane saw Jemima's mouth moving as she tried to shout something. Bedspreads were lifted off the beds and flung against the walls. But by crawling along the floor and then pulling themselves up by the radiator they were able to look out of the edges of the window again.

They could see the pines thrashing and bending; the burn, overflowing its banks, rushing over the lacrosse fields; below them old Macmillan's potting shed had begun to lose its roof and the large slates were leaping off as though they were tiddlywinks. But it was over the hill, rising from the sea like the giant itself, that they saw what Jane thought was the most terrifying thing she had ever seen in her life. It was a thick black column reaching up into the seething clouds. All round it, darting from its very centre, lightning flashed and forked. And as it moved towards them it didn't roar as the wind had done, but howled and screamed like some furious demon determined to kill. A whirlwind— heart of the storm.

Swiftly it moved closer. As it advanced, it bent and swayed.

'It could lift a house,' thought Jane.

But still they watched. Thunder crashed repeatedly, and sometimes spirals of lightning spun down the black column and flashed into the sea. It was not till Jane saw a clump of large firs snatched effortlessly from the ground that she realized they were in danger. The whirlwind was now moving across the island; and it was heading straight for the school.

'Quick,' she shouted to the others. 'We must escape.' But her voice was drowned by the shrieking of the wind. And looking at Mrs Deal and Jemima, Jane thought that even if they had heard they wouldn't have moved. They stared dreamily out into the lightning and watched the whirlwind move towards them with happy smiles. Jane seized their hands and pulled.

Out in the corridor, however, they recovered at once. The school shook and shuddered, its old bricks already beginning to feel the fury of the whirlwind. Leaping over the puddles, they ran towards the kitchen.

'Boiler-room,' Jane had screamed, but Jemima and Mrs Deal had already realized that that was their only hope.

In the kitchen, Mrs Deal paused for an instant to gather an armful of brushes and mops, then they wrenched open the back door.

The courtyard was in chaos, and the wind was so strong that several times they were blown onto their faces.

But it was one of these gusts which saved them. Suddenly, in a heap, they were blown right across the yard and against the boiler-room door. Jane pushed it open and they almost fell down the four steps.

The whirlwind must now have been almost upon the school. Its scream was deafening. Yet above it, Jane could hear a rending, crashing noise, and looking up she could see that the tiles of the boiler-room were already lifting.

Frantically they began to search, digging with their fingers round the flagstones. A patch of tiles was plucked off one end of the boiler-room roof. 'We're doomed,' thought Jane; 'doomed to a terrible death.'

And then the flagstone on which Jemima was kneeling tilted up, tipping her over. A chink of light appeared. The flagstone was pushed back and the grey head of Captain Thomson rose up through the hole.

The moment he saw them, he beckoned them towards him, and dropped out of sight. They ran over and scrambled down one by one. Captain Thomson rose up on Sergeant Cobbin's shoulders again and pulled the heavy flagstone back over the tunnel. Almost as he did so there was a deafening, splintering crash and the boiler-room finally broke into pieces and disappeared into the whirling sky.

For a few moments they stood in silence looking at each other. At last Jane said, 'We would have been killed.'

'How did you guess?' said Jemima.

'We didn't notice for quite a time,' said Captain Thomson. 'Then Sergeant Cobbin thought he'd take a turn on the beach. He said there was a big storm blowing, so we thought we'd come and have a look.'

'Captain,' said Mrs Deal.

'Yes, ma'am?' said Captain Thomson.

But Mrs Deal could say no more. Suddenly, with a low moan and a clatter of brushes and brooms and mops, she flung up her arms and fainted upon the floor of the tunnel.

'Shock,' said Captain Thomson decisively. 'Nothing serious, but needs a good rest. Come, Sergeant.'

Tenderly the two old men lifted Mrs Deal in their arms and with slow steps they all set off towards the Mess. Jane and Jemima walked at the back carrying the cleaning things.

5. Life on the Island of Peeg

MRS DEAL had almost recovered after a good night's rest, but the two soldiers insisted that she stay in bed, with bundles of old war-time magazines and jugs of hot lemon squash. Jane and Jemima would have been rather bored cooped up in the Mess, but Sergeant Cobbin suggested that this might be a good time for their tour.

The entrance from the beach split almost at once into two forks. If you took the right hand fork you found yourself on a long sloping ramp which went all round the cavern gradually rising in spirals to its top. Half-way up the ramp a round opening showed where the main tunnel began; and three-quarters of the way up was the stout wooden door which led into the Mess.

The Mess itself consisted of two corridors with rooms leading off them. You can see how the various rooms fitted by looking at the plan on page 166. The Blow-up room contained the complicated mechanism for blowing up the island. Over the years, however, it had become gradually filled with Captain Thomson's rocks. These had even overflowed onto the staircase, which led from the Blow-up room up onto the cliffs. The opening here was concealed among a small outcrop of boulders.

After they had thoroughly explored all the rooms Sergeant Cobbin said it was time to see inside the island. He and Captain Thomson normally used two old bicycles, but he had soon made a box with wheels, just large enough to hold them both and which he could tow behind his bicycle.

After lunch he wheeled this into the tunnel opening and pressed a switch in the wall. They saw that the tunnel sloped steeply down and then bent to the left, so that all they could see was the electric light shining round the corner. They climbed into the box, Sergeant Cobbin swung his leg over the saddle and they were off.

Although the Island of Peeg was only a mile long and three-quarters of a mile wide, Sergeant Cobbin and Captain Thomson had dug more than twenty miles of tunnels. These crossed and re-crossed it in all directions, none of them straight and all going up and down like country lanes in Wiltshire. As they rode along Sergeant Cobbin explained that the tunnels twisted because they had had to follow the soft veins of pumice stone running through the rock.

Every twenty yards or so there was an opening in the wall and after a while, when Sergeant Cobbin had stopped to turn off the electric light in one section of the tunnel and turn it on in the next, Jane asked him what these openings were.

'Come with me,' said the Sergeant, 'I'll show you.'

They walked down a short passage, Sergeant Cobbin pushed open a door, turned on the light, and they were in a low square room the size of a bathroom. It was packed from floor to ceiling with wooden boxes on each of which was written 'EXPLOSIVE—HIGHLY DANGEROUS.'

'TNT and dynamite,' said Sergeant Cobbin. 'The whole island's a bomb. You could do a tidy bit of damage with this island. Or you *could* have done,' he added sadly, no doubt remembering again that the war had ended.

'But isn't it very dangerous?' said Jemima. 'I thought you could blow up high explosive by sneezing.'

'Oh no—no fear of that,' laughed Sergeant Cobbin. 'But of course explosive is dangerous stuff. If you could get behind those boxes to the back you'd find the ventilation tunnel. That's a narrow pipe cut through the pumice stone which carries fresh warm air to all the explosive rooms so that they stay dry and at the same temperature. I put a metal vent at the opening to control the flow. Some of the store-rooms you can see the pipes, on account it comes out at the open bit between the boxes.'

'How wide is it?' asked Jane, immediately thinking it would be rather fun to crawl down it, or even be blown down it like the change in the old-fashioned shop called Ing Ltd on the High Street in Aldeburgh.

'I'd say between eleven inches and one and half feet,' said Sergeant Cobbin. 'That'd be about it—eleven inches to one and a half feet.'

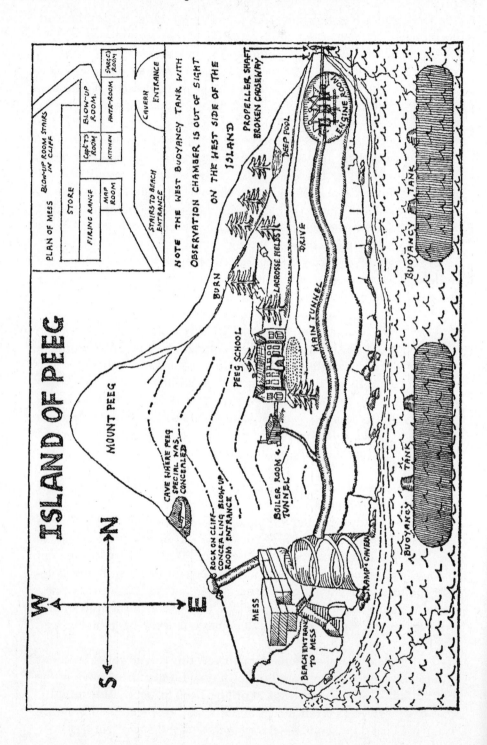

ISLAND OF PEEG

MOUNT PEEG

N

W

S

E

CAVE WHERE PEEG
SPECIAL WAS
CONCEALED

ROCK ON CLIFF
CONCEALING BLOW-UP
ROOM ENTRANCE

PEEG SCHOOL

BURN

LACROSSE FIELDS

BOILER ROOM &
TUNNEL

MESS

BEACH ENTRANCE
TO MESS

RAMP & CAVERN

MAIN TUNNEL

DRIVE

DEEP POOL

PROPELLER SHAFT

BROKEN CAUSEWAY

ENGINE ROOM

BUOYANCY TANK

BUOYANCY TANK

BUOYANCY TANK

PLAN OF MESS

BLOW-UP ROOM STAIRS
IN CLIFF

STORE

FIRING RANGE

MAP ROOM

CAPT'S ROOM

BLOW-UP ROOM

KITCHEN

ANTE-ROOM

STAIRS(?) ROOM

STAIRS TO BEACH
ENTRANCE

CAVERN ENTRANCE

NOTE THE WEST BUOYANCY TANK WITH
OBSERVATION CHAMBER IS OUT OF SIGHT
ON THE WEST SIDE OF THE ISLAND

'And do you mean you dug all these tunnels and the little tunnels and put in the electric light all by yourself?' said Jemima.

'Well, it weren't *all* that difficult,' said Sergeant Cobbin modestly. 'The pumice is very soft. But then you might think two or three miles of new tunnel every year weren't too much. That's about what we managed. But, as you says, there was the ventilation tunnel to dig, your electrics to put in, your explosives to move, then we lost a lot of time with the Captain going after his rocks and his fossils . . . oh there was a fair old bit of work, I can tell you. And of course the Captain and I didn't get any younger, as you can imagine.'

'I think it's marvellous,' said Jemima.

'So do I,' said Jane.

'Well, thank you,' said Sergeant Cobbin. 'Thank you kindly. But you haven't seen the best yet. Now I'll really show you something.'

They hurried after him out of the explosive room and climbed into the box again. Before they set off, Sergeant Cobbin said, 'I was going to take you to the West Buoyancy Tank, but I think we'll leave it till another day. There's no knowing how that old iron is standing up to the storm and we don't want an accident. The buoyancy tanks are frightening enough at the best of times. But make sure you remind me to take you later, and there's the Observation Chamber you must have a run round in.'

After half an hour the tunnel came to an end at a wall of grey rock. In the middle of it was a door. 'Now just wait till you see this,' said Sergeant Cobbin. He pushed open the door, turned several light switches, and stood aside.

They were standing on the topmost of about six steel catwalks which went round and across a fairly large, well-lit cavern. Steel ladders and steps ran up and down between the catwalks. And filling the cavern, thrusting spokes and wheels and boilers and pipes and gleaming brass knobs and dials and levers up among the ladders and steps and catwalks was an immense amount of machinery.

Sergeant Cobbin stood and beamed at it. 'Twin cam-shaft interlocking rotary units,' he said. 'Runs on diesel oil and crude slick same as the *Queen Mary*. Each unit develops eight thousand horse power, turns the screw at eleven thousand revs a minute. What do you think of her?'

Jane looked. She felt rather disappointed, though quite what she had expected she wasn't sure.

'It's very clean,' she said at last.

Jemima, more sensibly, said, 'What does that big wheel over there do?'

At once Sergeant Cobbin stumped towards it, 'That turns the rotary pump and brings the fuel forward for burning,' he said. 'Follow me round and I'll run through her with you.'

He took them over the whole polished mountain of the engine. He explained each dial and valve, every pipe and every nozzle. In one corner a sort of baby engine, attached to the main one by wires and tubes, was actually running, to supply, Sergeant Cobbin said, dried warm air to the ventilation tunnels and to make electricity.

'How fast can the island go?' said Jemima.

'And why couldn't you just drive us home?' asked Jane.

'Ah, there's the pity of it,' said Sergeant Cobbin. 'In all the years I tended these engines I never had an opportunity to run them. Then just when my chance came, when I'd had them going a week or two and was getting to know them nicely, they packed it in. Also that explosion bent the propeller shaft. But I am working on that too. If you'd like to come down I'll explain how it's going.'

But the two girls, who were already exhausted with explaining, hastily said thank you but they really ought to get back to supper or Mrs Deal would be worried. Sergeant Cobbin was obviously sad to leave his engines, but at the idea of Mrs Deal getting worried he agreed they must go and five minutes later they were bumping along the tunnels again.

So began the last happy weeks on the Island of Peeg. Day after day the wind blew them on, veering now east, now west, but on the whole south down the middle of the Atlantic. Captain Thomson, who had once learnt navigation, plotted their course with pins on a battered map of the world which hung in the map room. And each week they watched themselves slide farther and farther down it, passing Africa on the right (as you looked at the map) and South America on the left. Jemima once said she smelt spices, but Captain Thomson said she couldn't have because they were six hundred miles from the nearest land.

They went up onto the surface again the day after seeing round the tunnels. The two old soldiers, though they still seemed reluctant to face daylight, said the sea outside was choppy but not rough.

When they climbed up the steep stairs from the Blow-up room which led out onto the top of the cliff, Mrs Deal stood and faced the sea, breathing deeply.

'How those two good men endured being cooped up for thirty years I'll never understand,' she said. 'My lungs feel like a bag on a vacuum cleaner. I must get on to dusting that Mess directly.'

Certainly it was wonderful to be out in the air again. The sky was grey, the wind fresh, but the storm had gone, though it had left many signs of its passage. Shingle and even quite big rocks had been flung up from the beach onto the cliff. But it was Jemima who first discovered the most amazing thing the storm had done.

Mrs Deal and Jane were walking rather slowly arguing about whether or not to bring school books back so that Mrs Deal could go on teaching them. 'Out of the question,' said Jane impertinently, though she could see Mrs Deal meant it.

Suddenly they heard shouting from the brow of the hill where Jemima had run ahead. She was jumping and shouting and pointing. When they came up to her they saw why.

The school had disappeared. The giant hand of the hurricane had picked it up and put it down—where? Perhaps it was still being carried above the waves and would soon be dumped in Africa, giving someone quite a surprise. But now, in front of them, of those high brick walls, those pointed gables and tall chimneys, not a trace remained.

Or rather they found, as they ran (even Mrs Deal) down the hill towards the school, that there were a few traces. Here some bricks, there a beam of wood or a metal girder accidentally dropped by the hurricane as it had gone screaming and whirling across the island. But even when they were standing exactly where the school had been there was not much more. The boiler-house had gone and so had the boiler. The cellars had been scooped out as though by a spoon. Only the bare bricks of the foundations remained.

'What a mercy I remembered the brushes and mops,' said Mrs Deal. 'Everything else has gone—the spare polish along with it.'

'The compasses too,' said Jemima.

'The Land-Rover!' cried Mrs Deal suddenly. 'Oh glory me I'll never forgive myself—your father's favourite Land-Rover.'

'Everything,' murmured Jane to herself, thinking with pleasure of the school books scattered across the ocean. '*Everything*,' she repeated and then, thinking of all the dormitories and the gym mats and the butter pats on the ceiling and Miss Boyle's brogues and the desks and the inkwells and maps and rulers and rubbers, all of this gone forever, suddenly Jane felt very gay and began to run about shouting at the top of her voice, 'EVERYTHING'S GONE! EVERYTHING'S GONE! EVERYTHING'S GONE!'

On the way back to the Mess Mrs Deal moaned and lamented the loss of the Land-Rover. She interrupted this only once, to say gravely to Jane, 'Now Miss Jane, I meant what I said about lessons. Mr and Mrs Charrington would never forgive me if I didn't arrange something.'

'You've just been saying they'll never forgive you anyway so I don't see why you bother,' said Jane crossly.

'That will do,' said Mrs Deal. 'I shall speak to the Captain about it directly.'

By the next day the rough weather had completely disappeared, and once more the sun shone all the time, the warm seas sparkled, and slowly they drifted south, over the Equator and on and on and on, feeling, as Jane said, that no human eye had ever gazed on those waters before.

At first Captain Thomson and Sergeant Cobbin refused to go out at all, except in the evening, when they would mooch uneasily about on the beach in the shade of the cliff. But then one day Mrs Deal said what she really liked were brown men, that is, she thought a nice tan was most becoming. Preferably, she said, on a sailor, though actually, she added, she was really getting fonder and fonder of the Army.

This simple remark had an immediate effect on the two soldiers. The very next afternoon Jane discovered Captain Thomson stretched out behind a rock dressed only in his shorts with a flannel over his face. A day or two later, walking along the cliff, Jemima thought she saw a large white bird on the top of Mount Peeg. But climbing carefully towards it she had realized quite quickly that it was Sergeant Cobbin with no clothes on at all.

After thirty years away from the sun it was hardly surprising they both got badly sun burnt and Mrs Deal had to rub tinned margarine all over them.

'You should be ashamed of yourselves,' she said. 'Two great grown men like you.' Sergeant Cobbin and Captain Thomson did look rather ashamed and after that were more careful. By the end of a fortnight Sergeant Cobbin had turned a lovely golden peach colour. Captain Thomson, to his irritation, only went a rusty red and became covered in freckles.

Mrs Deal led a life which was in fact little different from the one she'd led in Aldeburgh. Every day she marked out some extensive stretch of tunnel and carefully swept it down and dusted it out. She cooked all the meals and explained to Jane and Jemima that, though of course they weren't born when the war was on, they could probably understand what pleasure it gave her to use her old war-time recipes again. The two girls did understand, but they rather wished Mrs Deal realized that if you hadn't been in the war there was considerably less pleasure in *eating* the old recipes. Pilchards on toast, whale-steak pie, dried-egg scrambled egg, carrot tart—luckily they still managed to catch quite a lot of fresh fish which made things better.

She also had to pay quite a lot of attention to the old soldiers. Captain

Thomson and Sergeant Cobbin wanted her to inspect everything that they did, probably, Jane thought, because they had been starved of a woman's gentle touch for so long.

'I wonder if I might trouble you for your advice, madam?' Captain Thomson would ask. 'I am sure, like most women, you have green fingers.'

Sergeant Cobbin built an even larger trailer to fix to the back of his bicycle and would trundle her off to see his engine room; journeys from which he would return red and panting, while Mrs Deal would say, 'Next time, Sergeant, I shall insist you let *me* tow *you*.'

'A man's as young as he feels, Mrs Deal,' the Sergeant would gasp.

Despite their age, Mrs Deal's attention stimulated the two soldiers to a great deal of work. Captain Thomson rediscovered an interest in gardening. Every morning and evening, to avoid the heat of the day, he would dig Mr Macmillan's vegetable patch. The hurricane had plucked every plant by the roots, but Captain Thomson found several packets of seeds in the store room and soon the hot sun and frequent watering produced crop after crop of huge lettuces, potatoes, carrots, peas and tomatoes. He also found flower seeds and before the month was up was arriving with bunches of enormous geraniums, marigolds and Michaelmas daisies every morning. These he courteously presented to Mrs Deal with a brisk bow, somewhat to Sergeant Cobbin's irritation.

In the afternoons the Captain arranged his fossils and rocks and wrote out neat cards saying what they were and where he had found them. He also studied his *Encyclopedia of 2000 Famous Painters*.

The interest and praise of Mrs Deal produced a friendly rivalry between the two soldiers. (Or fairly friendly. Jane sometimes noticed quite a glint in Captain Thomson's eye as he staggered in with another basket of vast new potatoes or a bouquet of gigantic chrysanthemums. And when Sergeant Cobbin asked Mrs Deal if she'd like to come and see how the propeller shaft was doing, he made sure Captain Thomson was listening.)

Of the two, Jane thought what Sergeant Cobbin did was more interesting. First of all there was the aeroplane. Sergeant Cobbin produced this from the store room a few days after the hurricane. It was contained in seven large crates marked 'Peeg Special' and they all helped him drag these up the Blow-up room stairs to the cliff-top. Next the plan of the aeroplane was pinned to the side of the largest crate.

'First, Box A,' said Sergeant Cobbin looking at the plan. Box A contained dozens of six-foot wooden struts and coils of thin, tough wire. The struts had to be joined together by glue and screws to form the framework of the Peeg Special. This took Sergeant Cobbin a week.

Next came Box B, which contained the wings. Box C held the wheels and tail.

As he worked, watched by the two little girls, and sometimes by a gracious Mrs Deal, Sergeant Cobbin told them about his life as a boy in Suffolk.

Gradually the plane grew before their eyes and soon only Boxes F and G remained. Box F contained the engine and Sergeant Cobbin had to test this before fitting it in. He knocked long steel rods all round it and then tied the engine to them with wire. 'That'll keep her from flying away,' he said.

All one hot afternoon the island shook to the sound of bellowing engine. Every so often Sergeant Cobbin stopped it and tinkered with his screwdriver. Eventually, when it was almost impossible to stand behind the propeller for the rush of air, and when you could see the rods straining from the ground, he decided it was perfectly tuned and carefully bolted it into the front of the Peeg Special.

Box G contained the skin of the plane. It also contained various small things like gloves and cushions for the cabin and a tin of paint with which Sergeant Cobbin wrote 'Peeg' on the side behind the propeller.

The cabin had three seats and a space for luggage, but it was very small. Sergeant Cobbin explained that the Peeg Special had two fuel tanks which could hold enough to fly about sixteen hundred miles. Top speed was 220 miles per hour, which Sergeant Cobbin thought quite fast. Jane and Jemima hadn't the heart to tell him how much faster planes went now than they had done in the war.

The afternoon it was finished Sergeant Cobbin said he would try and fly the plane the next day. The two girls spent the morning walking very slowly along the cliff-top picking up stones and rocks. Captain Thomson, who had been a trifle stand-offish while the plane was being built, now came generously forward to help pull it into line, pump up its tyres and generally assist with all the other little things that were so necessary. Mrs Deal put the final stitches in a parachute she had been making secretly all this time as a surprise.

After a light lunch, Sergeant Cobbin put on his helmet and goggles. ('Fancy me knowing an airman now!' cried Mrs Deal.) Then he had a few words with Captain Thomson, shook them all by the hand and walked slowly over to the Peeg Special, which looked very frail and rickety standing beside the empty boxes. Captain Thomson followed him and Mrs Deal and Jane and Jemima hurried a little way up the side of Mount Peeg to get a good view of the flight.

They saw Captain Thomson pour can after can of petrol into the tank, while Sergeant Cobbin fussed about, tightening screws and test-

ing struts. Then the two old soldiers shook hands, talked a moment, shook hands and suddenly, bending forward, embraced each other. Sergeant Cobbin climbed briskly into the cockpit and pulled his goggles over his eyes. Captain Thomson strode round to the nose and stood with his large hands resting on the propeller.

'Right, sir,' they heard Sergeant Cobbin shout.

Captain Thomson raised himself on his toes and with a downward heave pulled on the propeller. It spun down, the engine coughed, the propeller stopped. Again Captain Thomson heaved. Again it spun and coughed, stopped. Captain Thomson put his hands to his back and slowly straightened. He raised his hands for the third time, paused, and this time pulled so hard he stumbled forward and nearly fell.

The engine coughed, coughed again—and with a roar and puffs of smoke the propeller began to spin. Captain Thomson just had time to run out of the way and the Peeg Special was bumping along the grass. Faster and faster, bump bump bump; but not nearly fast enough to take off Jane thought. It looked as though it might crash over the edge where the cliff fell into the sea. 'Please don't let it' Jane whispered. Sparks were coming from the exhaust pipes. And suddenly—it was flying! An extra bump seemed to bounce it into the air, and then it was turning away over the sea and climbing higher and higher into the blue sky.

They all jumped and waved. Even Captain Thomson was leaping about and waving an oily rag in his hand. When Sergeant Cobbin came flying past low over the ground, he took off his goggles and shook them in the air. Three times he circled and then, bumpily but safely, landed on the cliff-top.

After that he flew nearly every day, and they all took turns going up in the little cabin. At night they helped him push the Peeg Special into a large shallow cave in the side of Mount Peeg, just in case there was another hurricane. They shut up the mouth of the cave with some old sheep hurdles stuffed with dead heather and bracken. So dry and dead was the whole surface of the island by now that this made the cave mouth look just like a part of the hillside, and it was difficult to recognize even when you were quite close.

The other thing which Sergeant Cobbin worked at was not quite as interesting. This was his engine room and in particular his mending of the bent propeller shaft. Every afternoon he rode slowly off into the tunnels with tools or, occasionally, with Mrs Deal in the box behind. Jane and Jemima sometimes went too, more to hear about his life in Suffolk than to watch him work, which was rather boring even though Sergeant Cobbin explained exactly what he was doing all the time.

'Actually,' Jane said to Mrs Deal after one of these visits, 'it's *because* of all the explaining that it is boring.'

'The Sergeant is a very clever man,' said Mrs Deal. 'So indeed is the Captain. I've quite come round to the Army.'

'So I've noticed,' said Jane.

One morning, nearly a month after the hurricane, Sergeant Cobbin said at breakfast that the propeller shaft was now straight.

'She's ready when you are,' he said to Captain Thomson.

Captain Thomson made some calculations and eventually said that though it was in fact about four hundred miles behind them their quickest course was to aim for South Africa. Sergeant Cobbin, almost speechless with excitement, started the engine, the Island of Peeg slowly swung round, course was set and slowly, very slowly they began to move north towards the Cape of Good Hope.

So the days passed. Mrs Deal carried out her promise, and made sure they had lessons. But as she was busy keeping the Mess clean, sweeping the tunnels and cooking the meals, she had to leave the teaching to the two soldiers. On Monday Sergeant Cobbin taught them shooting on the rifle range. On Tuesday he taught them how to fly an aeroplane (not actually flying, but sitting in the cockpit and being taught how to fly). On Wednesday morning they had drill; in the afternoon Captain Thomson taught them Art Appreciation, which was mostly dates and influences. On Thursday they had, in the morning, Platoon tactics (fire and movement) and Judging Distance; on Thursday afternoon they did the Bren Gun, the two-inch mortar or the Hand Grenade. Friday was Geology. On Wednesday and Thursday lessons took two hours, but the rest of the time they were only an hour so it wasn't too bad.

Despite much searching from the cliff-tops Jemima and Jane never saw any sea monsters. Porpoises they saw, sometimes a great many, rolling past like grey balls, now on top, now underneath the sparkling waves. Also flying fish, which would suddenly skip out of the water and skim across it, occasionally landing on the shingle. The two girls, who had soon discovered they weren't good to eat, would hurry down and throw them back.

Nor did they see a single ship. Nothing stood out on the great flatness which surrounded them. Two or three times they did see aeroplanes, miles up and impossible to hear, pulling the white thread of their vapour trails across the sky. But, as Jane remarked, even though Peeg was a mile long and three-quarters of a mile wide, from that great height it can only have appeared as a speck upon the limitless ocean.

So the days passed, and so no doubt they would have continued to pass for the month or so that Captain Thomson had estimated it would take them to reach Cape Town, when one day something happened which Jane was to remember with terror ever after and which introduced a whole new element of danger into their peaceful and happy lives.

6. How Jane and Sergeant Cobbin Nearly Drown

IT WAS, as usual, a fine day. The Island of Peeg (or the good ship Peeg, as Mrs Deal had taken to calling it since the island had begun to move under its own power again) had been thrusting steadily north for about two weeks, when Jane suddenly remembered the Observation Chamber. It was at breakfast.

'Sergeant Cobbin,' Jane said, 'do you remember you asked us to remind you to remember to take us to see the Observation Chamber?'

'I do,' said Sergeant Cobbin slowly, pouring some condensed milk over his porridge.

'I'm reminding you now,' said Jane.

'Well, let me get some breakfast inside of me,' said Sergeant Cobbin, 'and we'll have a go.'

When they had eaten, the two girls helped Mrs Deal wash up in what she now called the galley. (The two soldiers had at first been quite offended at her nautical terms and Captain Thomson had even said, 'We used to call that the cook-house, Madam.' But Mrs Deal had soon won them round.)

When the galley was ship-shape, Sergeant Cobbin wheeled his bicycle down the sloping ramp, the two girls climbed into the box and they set off.

After twenty minutes and several hundred yards of tunnel, he turned into a narrow tunnel on the left. It seemed to Jane as they bumped on, that it was getting colder.

All at once the bicycle stopped. Sergeant Cobbin climbed off his saddle. 'Here we are,' he said. 'West Buoyancy Tank.'

They were in front of a small iron door set in the rock. On this, just visible in the dim blue light from a bulb in the roof, was a faded notice: DANGER.'

'We'll be about thirty-five feet below sea level here,' said Sergeant Cobbin in his slow Suffolk voice. He tapped the walls of the tunnel. 'You get a fair amount of seepage.'

Jane and Jemima reached out their hands and found that the walls were, in fact, dripping wet.

'Is it quite safe?' Jemima said.

'Oh you're safe enough *here*,' said Sergeant Cobbin. 'It's in the Buoyancy Tank I always feel a bit nervous.'

He was standing with his ear pressed to the iron door; now he raised his fist and knocked twice. They heard the door ring with a hollow, empty sound.

'No water behind that then,' said Sergeant Cobbin. 'So far so good.'

He drew back the bolt and putting his shoulder to the door pushed it slowly open. Then he reached inside and turned on a switch.

Jane saw narrow stone steps cut in a thin cleft down through the rock. Another blue bulb shed a feeble light. Sergeant Cobbin walked down the steps and stopped at another iron door at the bottom. Once more he listened, and again raised his fist and brought it down with a heavy thud on the door.

And then they heard one of the strangest sounds they had ever heard in their lives. From behind the door there came, in answer to Sergeant Cobbin's knock, a long, low, echoing note, as though an immense gong had been struck in the depths of a mine. It reverberated and echoed for about half a minute, and during it they heard grow a second sound, a hushed whispering rushing sound like wind in pines or the sea through a fog.

Twice more Sergeant Cobbin thumped his fist and twice more the gong echoed and whatever it was hissed and whispered; then he said, 'Well, that do sound empty enough. In we go then.'

'I don't want to,' said Jemima suddenly.

'What's that?' said Sergeant Cobbin.

'I'm frightened,' said Jemima tearfully. 'Don't let's, Jane.'

'Oh don't you worry,' said Sergeant Cobbin in a kind voice. 'I've been laying it on a bit. There's nothing to be afraid of. Come on now, Jemima, be a brave girl.'

'I think it's dangerous,' said Jemima.

'What about you, Jane?' said Sergeant Cobbin, beginning to look rather disappointed.

'I don't know,' said Jane slowly. 'Well—yes I think I'll come. But I don't see why Jemima should if she doesn't want to.'

'No one must come if they don't want to,' said Sergeant Cobbin. 'Now Jemima my dear, you go and sit comfortably in the box behind my bike. We'll only be gone about twenty minutes, less than that I dare-say.'

Watching her walk slowly up the steps Jane suddenly felt that it was really Jemima who was being brave. She had admitted being afraid; but Jane, who was also afraid, wanted to impress Sergeant Cobbin and didn't dare say she was frightened. She almost called out and chased after Jemima, but Sergeant Cobbin had already pushed the second door open and was saying, 'Come on, Jane,' so she stepped through.

They were standing quarter-way up the inside of what looked like the largest airship in the world. Peering down its dark curving side Jane could hardly see the bottom below her, despite the lights strung out along the ceiling far above. And it was quite impossible to see the ends. It smelt dank and unpleasant.

'Well, she seems to be holding firm enough,' said Sergeant Cobbin, 'though there do look to be a bit of water down there at the bottom.' His voice was echoed by a hollow booming, followed by the rustling sound, this time much louder.

Sergeant Cobbin said, 'This here, the West Buoyancy tank, is much the biggest of the tanks, by reason the engineers found this side of the island has a lot of granite.' (Boom boom went the buoyancy tank—*boooooooooom*.) 'It's a 100 yards long and 150 feet high. The steel plates are an inch thick and it be pinnacled to the island every ten yards with five-inch-thick steel bars driven five feet into the rock.'

Comforted by his Suffolk voice, Jane began to feel better. 'That sounds safe enough,' she said.

'Yes,' said Sergeant Cobbin. 'Oh they're strong all right. But there's been the explosion that set Peeg off and there's been the hurry-cane. And don't you forget these tanks have been underwater thirty years. That's a long time. Listen.' Putting down his foot, he scuffled at the side of the tank. At once there came the slithering sighing sound Jane had heard before. 'Rust,' said Sergeant Cobbin. 'There's a good quarter inch of it all over the sides and we don't know how much outside. I wouldn't gladly spend a night in one of these, not when that were rough, that I wouldn't.'

'Is it safe to go on now?' said Jane anxiously. 'Perhaps we'd better get back to the Mess.'

'Well you wanted to see the Observation Chamber,' said Sergeant Cobbin. 'She's lasted thirty years, I reckon she'll last another half an hour. We'll get along to the Chamber now. You'll be safe enough there.'

Jane found that the side sloped quite gently and was easy to walk down. Each footstep echoed and boomed, sending cascades of rust ahead of it. Quite soon she reached Sergeant Cobbin who was standing near the bottom looking at a long pool of water.

'Bit more than when I was here last,' he said. 'Must be a small leak somewhere.' He turned left and set off up the tank. 'I'll show you the Observation Chamber,' he said, 'then we'd best be getting back.'

Jane hurried after him. Strong as the lights had seemed from the entrance, the top of the tank was so far above them that it was quite gloomy at the bottom. She didn't want to get left behind by Sergeant Cobbin.

After about five minutes of echoing walk, the rust rather like sand under their feet, they reached the end. Here the tank came to a blunt point, about four feet across with a round door, firmly bolted, in its middle. Sergeant Cobbin undid this, to reveal a short tunnel with a further round door at its end. He crawled through, opened the further door and continued into the Observation Chamber. Then, when Jane followed him, he crawled back, locked both doors and joined her again.

But Jane noticed none of this. The sight that met her eyes from the Observation Chamber was so wonderful, so extraordinary, that she could think of nothing else.

They were in a round glass bubble held motionless in the middle of the sea. To their left Jane could see through the clear water the great bulk of the island, the rocky, jagged side of it, stretching forward and backward, up and down. But down only about sixty feet, where suddenly, frighteningly, it ended in jagged points hanging above the immense blue depths of the ocean. Looking down through the glass floor of the Observation Chamber into these depths, at the ragged chunks of rock at the bottom of Peeg, Jane suddenly got the strange feeling that she was standing on her head looking up between her feet at the sky and that the ragged points at the bottom of the island were mountain peaks. Except that, instead of the sky being pale, the blue of the deep water was dark, and the deeper she looked the darker it became until finally her gaze became lost in a deep, dark, blue blackness. It was with relief she looked at the surface. This was about forty feet above them, and she could see the sun sparkling and rippling, broken into dazzling fragments by the waves. But she found that it was actually impossible to see through this surface. There was no sign of the island above the sea; only an endless, shifting, undulating mirror through which, or into which, thousands of lights were shining. Behind the Observation Chamber bulged the West Buoyancy Tank like a vast, rust-coloured cigar. Jane could see on her left where it was fastened into the rock by a safe-looking rod.

And everywhere, below, above, on all sides, darting, lazing, sinking, rising, were thousands of fish. Little gold fish twinkling round the glass sides of the Observation Chamber like specks of dust; larger, rainbow-coloured fish swimming in shoals and diving down into the rocky holes and crevices beneath Peeg; and here were one or two quite big grey fish which swam steadily and purposefully through the water and then suddenly sped forward and slowed down again for no visible but obviously sensible reason.

'Well, what do you think of it, eh?' said Sergeant Cobbin.

'It's marvellous,' said Jane. 'It's the most marvellous, wonderful, extraordinary, marvellous sight I've seen.'

'Well, it is interesting,' agreed Sergeant Cobbin in a gratified voice. 'I don't know why we don't come down more often. Of course the water wasn't so clear in Scotland. You didn't get quite what you might call such a fishy effect.'

'What's that?' said Jane, pointing to a largish drum at the side of the Observation Chamber. A thin cable was wound round it, the end of which disappeared back into the buoyancy tank.

'Well, it's like this,' said Sergeant Cobbin. 'When you want to go on an Observation trip you pull this lever and that breaks the connexion between you and the tank. Then you release the drum and the cable pays out to a distance of a mile and a half. You stay joined to the tank so's you can wind yourself back. Now, you see that little old engine slung underneath us there? That can take her round a bit to see what's going on.'

'Can we go on a trip now?' said Jane eagerly. 'Let's drive off now.'

'Well, not now,' said Sergeant Cobbin. 'We ain't tried her out for more'n a year. I'll test her out tomorrow and then we'll see.'

'Oh, go *on*,' said Jane.

'No, miss,' said Sergeant Cobbin. 'Captain Thomson wouldn't allow it and I agree with him.'

One of the large grey fish swam up to the curving side of the Observation Chamber and seemed to be looking in. Jane felt she could have touched it. She felt she was actually in the water itself. And this feeling was even stronger when she looked down. There seemed no reason why she didn't just sink down into the dark blue depths. She pointed down and said, 'How deep do you think it is, Sergeant Cobbin?'

'Oh that'll be several miles,' said Sergeant Cobbin. 'Terrible pressure down there. If we was to sink we'd be crushed to powder.'

'Hardly powder,' said Jane. 'We'd be too wet. Something more like jam or very flat seaweed.' As she spoke. she saw a small rock fall away from the side of Peeg, and sink swiftly into the blue. Down, down, down it sank until now she saw it, now she didn't, thought she glimpsed it again and then it did finally disappear.

'They do say as how even rocks get crushed down there,' said Sergeant Cobbin.

'Nonsense,' said Jane, but she was impressed all the same.

For twenty-five minutes they stood and watched the marvels of the sea. Then Sergeant Cobbin said they'd best be getting back. He was just about to unbolt the steel port-hole which led to the tube into the buoyancy tank when Jane said, 'Listen—what's that?'

Sergeant Cobbin cocked his head and listened. 'I don't hear nothing,' he said after a minute.

'Yes,' said Jane. 'It's gone now, but I definitely heard it, a sort of thrumming sound. Ssssh. Listen.'

They listened and in a moment they heard it quite clearly, not thrumming so much as throbbing, a thud thud thud that gradually grew louder, until the Observation Chamber began to shake and the fishes shot off in droves to hide among the rocks.

'It's a boat!' shouted Sergeant Cobbin. 'That's the sound of her engines.'

'They sound like very big engines,' shouted Jane. 'Perhaps it's the *Queen Elizabeth*.' And indeed the throbbing had now grown into a continuous dull shuddering roar.

'There she is!' cried Sergeant Cobbin suddenly pointing.

And there she was coming towards the Observation Chamber directly up the line of the West Buoyancy Tank and not ten, no not five feet above it. The noise became deafening. For an instant Jane thought there was going to be a collision. The Observation Chamber, in fact the whole tank, leapt and shuddered. The ship was now right above them, her great, swiftly-flowing bulk shutting out the sun. Then Jane saw an explosion of bubbles, felt the Observation Chamber pressed down, glimpsed whirling propellers, and then it was already past and the ship was speeding away, the roar growing fainter. But before she could say anything, the Observation Chamber gave a sudden lurch. Jane looked out towards the side of Peeg and saw what was certainly, she realized, one of the most frightening sights of her life.

The West Buoyancy Tank had in fact been very much more weakened by the hurricane than Sergeant Cobbin had realized; also thirty years of salt water had eaten deep into the unprotected steel. Some of it was less than one-tenth of an inch thick. The sudden vibration of the boat passing so closely overhead was the final straw. As Jane looked, the long bar which joined their end of the tank to the island suddenly snapped. This threw additional strain on all the other bars along the side of the tank. In a moment they had broken loose too and at once, liberated from its bonds, the huge tank burst to the surface like an old whale.

Worse was to follow. Jane and Sergeant Cobbin had only time to see that the Island of Peeg, no longer supported by the West Buoyancy Tank, was sinking over onto its side, when further disaster struck.

Some of the bars had not broken or been wrenched out of the rock, but had instead pulled great pieces of rusty steel plate out of the side of the tank. Into these gaping holes the sea water rushed. The buoyancy tank began to settle lower and lower until the Observation Chamber was three-quarters under water again. Suddenly, as the far end of the tank began to sink, the Observation Chamber was lifted into the air, paused there, and then, with the speed of a slowly descending lift, the whole tank and Observation Chamber slid downwards and in a moment had disappeared beneath the waves.

When the West Buoyancy Tank ripped itself loose from the island, the settling of Peeg flung Jemima against the iron door. She guessed immediately what had happened because even through the inch-thick metal, securely bolted, she could hear the muffled sucking and gurgling as the sea poured up the passage and surged against the door.

'Oh Jane, my darling Jane,' whispered Jemima. 'Oh please God make them all right.' And seizing the light off the front of Sergeant Cobbin's bicycle she set off up the passage. As she walked, trying desperately to remember the way among the dark winding tunnels, tears poured down her cheeks and fell onto the rocky floor.

At about the same time, Mrs Deal was busy preparing supper in the galley, helped by Captain Thomson who had just arrived with some huge onions.

'They'll do fine,' Mrs Deal was saying, 'if I can get the peel off them without crying my eyes out.'

Gallant Captain Thomson was about to peel them himself, when the galley gave the most tremendous lurch and they both staggered sideways into the wall.

'Ahoy there! Ahoy there!' cried Mrs Deal with surprise. 'Where's my sea legs gone to then? It must be gale force nine out there again.

Another hurricane, I shouldn't wonder.'

Captain Thomson however, having regained his balance, was looking at the light. 'Notice how it hangs,' he said. 'We've tilted towards the west. Now that can't be heavy seas. We've struck something—yet what? There's not a jot of land on the charts for the next six hundred miles.'

'A beasty perhaps?' said Mrs Deal. 'Oh dear.'

'We must investigate at once,' said Capain Thomson. 'Quick—the Blow-up room stairs.'

They hurried through to the Blow-up room and up the stairs to the cliff-top. Here two extraordinary sights met their eyes.

Though it was plain they had hit nothing—the sea was as flat and calm and empty as always—it was also plain that the island had tilted. The flat grassy stretch at the top of the cliff was definitely sloping gently downhill. And when they looked down at the beach it had grown about five feet wider.

After they had looked at this strange sight for a moment, Captain Thomson said slowly, 'It can mean only one thing. The West Buoyancy Tank has either sunk or broken to the surface. Quick, Mrs Deal, we must hurry to see if the girls and Sergeant Cobbin are all right.'

But instead of following him, Mrs Deal just stood pointing out to sea.

'Look!' she said dramatically. 'Look yonder, Captain Thomson. There she blows!'

Startled, Captain Thomson stopped and looked, and for a moment he too thought Mrs Deal had seen a whale.

About three hundred yards out from the shore the surface of the water was being violently agitated. Vast bubbles appeared and burst. The waves churned and spouted. Suddenly, from the middle of the disturbance, a vast black hump rose swiftly up, and then went on rising, higher and larger and longer.

It was a submarine. But it must have been one of the largest submarines in the world. It was black all over and its bulging metallic smoothness was interrupted only by the conning tower which stuck out like the turret of a small castle. On top of the conning tower was what looked like a large dome of glass.

They stared at it in amazement and then Mrs Deal turned to Captain Thomson and grasped his hand. 'It's the Navy,' she whispered, trembling. 'At last.'

Captain Thomson looked at the submarine with a slightly peevish expression on his face.

'It certainly doesn't look like the Navy to me,' he said. 'No distinguishing marks whatsoever. No fleet marks, no convoy marks, no flotilla, line of battle or harbour or squadron or station marks what-so-*ever*.'

By now several men had appeared under the glass dome and seemed to be scanning the island with telescopes. A long pole also appeared and as they watched a flag was pulled to its top and unfurled in the gentle breeze. It was white with a large red tulip in the middle.

'HMS *Tulip*,' said Mrs Deal.

'No doubt some wog flag of convenience,' said Captain Thomson crossly.

At that moment there came the crackling of a loudspeaker across the water and a voice boomed, '*Tulip* to Island, *Tulip* to Island. Identify yourself. Identify yourself.'

'Good heavens,' cried Captain Thomson. 'What am I doing here? The girls and Sergeant Cobbin.' He immediately ran off along the cliff, shouting over his shoulder, 'They may be floating. Get that ship to send a boat. Must hurry.'

'Hullo there,' boomed the loudspeaker. 'Who are you? Answer please. *Tulip* to Island.'

Mrs Deal cupped her hands round her mouth and shouted as loud as she could, 'Ahoy! HMS *Peeg* here. Ahoy! Come ashore. HMS *Peeg* here.'

Then hurried back along the cliff towards the Mess thinking, as she afterwards admitted, less about Jane and Jemima and Sergeant Cobbin, than about the impression she would make on the Royal Navy and how she must spruce up a bit.

There was still a lot of air trapped in the West Buoyancy Tank and this meant that at first it sank quite slowly. Jane and Sergeant Cobbin could look up and see the bottom of the island disappearing above them. It was rather like looking down on a very ragged range of minia-ture mountains from a rising balloon. But all the time, with a sinister gurgling and rumbling, huge footballs of air bubbled out of the Buoyancy Tank and went wobbling up to the surface. They began to sink faster. The bottom of the island became a blur far above them; sud-denly there was an extra explosion of escaping bubbles and then silence. Jane's stomach jumped, and then the tank seemed to settle to its task, plunging swiftly downwards into the limitless depths of the sea.

'What shall we do?' said Jane.

'I'm thinking,' said Sergeant Cobbin.

Everything had happened so quickly that Jane felt she could think of nothing. She guessed Sergeant Cobbin found the same. Yet, despite the appalling danger they were in, it was almost peaceful. Soon it was pitch dark. The only sign that they were sinking was that it began to grow very cold.

Jane wondered what dying would be like. Suddenly the glass of the Observation Chamber would break. Water would pour in and they would drown, all their past lives passing before them—Curl Castle, the Book, the time the valley had flooded . . . Or perhaps the pressure would kill them. Would it be very quick, like being smacked flat between a giant's two huge wet hands? Or very slow, like being wound round by a snake, tighter and tighter, round and round . . .

Round and round! Suddenly Jane realized what they must do. 'Quick, Sergeant Cobbin,' she cried. 'The cable. You must unwind the cable.'

'Good girl, Miss,' said Sergeant Cobbin. 'Me brains was addled.'

She felt him brush past her, there was a click as he separated them from the buoyancy tank, and then a whirring noise as the cable drum began to spin.

Immediately the Observation Chamber started to shoot up. Jane felt her stomach left behind. So fast did the drum spin that there was a smell of burning oil.

It began to grow lighter and warmer. The sea was now a deep, black blue, now swimming-pool blue, now pale and watery. They could see fish again, seeming to swirl down as they sped up, and now, far above them and to the right, Jane could see the long black smudge of the island's underneath, floating there, waiting, as they rushed towards it.

'Come and stand by me,' said Sergeant Cobbin.

Jane stood beside him and they watched the spinning drum. It was obvious the cable would end before they reached the surface.

It did so. There was a violent jerk, then they continued to rush upwards.

'Cable must have broke,' said Sergeant Cobbin. 'Shows there's some good comes out of everything rusting away.'

'I suppose it means that the tank is more than one and a half miles down,' said Jane.

'And still sinking,' said Sergeant Cobbin.

Now that it was all over, Jane found that the idea of the giant Buoyancy Tank plunging down through the inky, freezing sea was terrifying. She was trembling.

The next moment they burst out into the sunlight and the Observation Chamber began to bob and rock on the waves.

Although it had seemed like hours, the whole thing could scarcely have taken ten minutes. But the Island of Peeg had already moved some way and they now floated about two hundred yards behind it.

'We won't catch her by swimming,' said Sergeant Cobbin, a note of pride for his engines in his voice. 'I'll get the motor to work.'

It started after four tries and soon they had climbed out onto the shore. They noticed at once that the island had tilted about four feet over to the old west side. 'You can see the angle by that green line along the causeway,' said Sergeant Cobbin.

Jane and Sergeant Cobbin then set off for the Mess. When they reached the place where the school had been Jane said, 'Let's go by the boiler-room tunnel, Sergeant Cobbin. It'll feel so safe underground.' She still found it hard to realize they were all right again, at the same time, so quickly had it all happened, it was difficult to realize they had been in any danger at all.

They were walking back along the tunnel when all at once Sergeant Cobbin switched off the lights in the section they were in and whispered, 'Hush, Miss. Listen a moment.'

In a moment Jane heard a noise she knew well, a quiet crying, with a little catch and hiccough at the end of each cry—Jemima's crying. At the same time they saw coming up the tunnel from their left the faint wavery beam of Sergeant Cobbin's torch.

'It's Jemima!' shouted Jane. 'Turn on the lights. Jemima! Jemima! Where are you?'

There was Jemima, standing amazed in the light of the tunnel. When she saw them she rushed forward and flung herself into Jane's arms.

'I thought you'd drowned,' she cried. 'I heard those engines and then the sea and—oh Sergeant Cobbin, Jane, I'm so pleased to see you.

Oh oh oh.' And once again Jemima burst into tears, but this time tears of joy.

At the Mess they found considerable confusion. Mrs Deal had changed into her best clothes—tweed coat with long tartan scarf, a two-piece jersey wool dress, petal hat and leather boots. Though smart, these must have been extremely hot. Nevertheless, Mrs Deal was engaged in a major dusting.

'Now girls, now Sergeant Cobbin,' she said the moment she saw them, 'there's not an instant to lose. Into your best clothes and then help me get this place ship-shape and Bristol fashion.'

'We've had the most terrible time,' said Jane dramatically.

'They've been saved from a watery grave,' said Jemima. 'No doubt you have,' said Mrs Deal, whirling her duster over the ante-room notice board. 'Now out of those clothes and into something respectable. And it's your blues for you, Sergeant. We're hosts to the Senior Service.'

'But you don't understand,' said Jane. 'We're lucky to be alive.'

'We're *all* lucky to be alive,' said Mrs Deal. 'Or unlucky, depending on how you look at it.'

'The lass is right,' said Sergeant Cobbin. 'We had a narrow squeak right enough, and it were her that saved us.'

'See—it's true,' said Jane. 'It was like this. I'll explain,' and before Mrs Deal could interrupt again she described everything that had happened as fast as she could but without leaving anything out.

Mrs Deal, though of course she listened, appeared no more than mildly interested. She continued to dust and tidy feverishly and Jane had to follow her about as she rushed from room to room. When Jane finished with '. . . and so here we are,' Mrs Deal said, still dusting, 'Well, that certainly does sound very foolhardy. Very sensible of Miss Jemima not to venture into such a dangerous object.'

'But now,' went on Mrs Deal, 'I've something really exciting to tell you.' She stopped dusting and, after calling Sergeant Cobbin and Jemima in to listen, said in a ringing voice, 'The Navy has at last arrived!'

'Where? What? When?' cried Jane and Jemima and Sergeant Cobbin together.

'Yes, the Royal Navy,' said Mrs Deal again. 'One of Her Majesty's Warships of the Submarine class is at present stationed just below the cliff—HMS *Tulip*. I have extended an invitation to the crew to come aboard, though I'm not sure whether they heard me. No doubt, however, they will be sending a landing party. That is why we must clear decks at once. Duster and brooms are in the galley.'

But the two girls and Sergeant Cobbin were already running for the Blow-up room stairs and the cliff-top.

There, as Mrs Deal had said, floated the giant submarine. At last they had been discovered. This meant, Jane thought, that they would be rescued. Suddenly she felt rather sad.

Sergeant Cobbin, who may have been feeling the same, was looking very suspicious. 'I don't like it,' he was muttering. 'No proper markings, and that be far too big for a submarine in my opinion. You say the war is over. But who else don't know it? That great thing could lie about not knowing it for a devil of a time. Must have been the thing that passed over the West Buoyancy Tank and sank her. I wondered why she were so low above us. May have been on purpose.'

But Sergeant Cobbin's speculations were cut short by Jemima. 'Look,' she said suddenly, 'there's Captain Thomson. Something's happened.'

Coming along the cliff was a sad sight. Head bowed, feet dragging, Captain Thomson was slowly returning to the Mess. Every now and then he stopped and clasped his head in his hands or brushed them across his eyes.

'I know what it is,' said Jemima. 'He thinks you're dead.'

'So he do,' said Sergeant Cobbin. 'Poor fellow. We'll put him out of his misery.' He cupped his hands and shouted, 'Captain Thomson. Captain Thomson, sir. We're safe and sound.'

But Captain Thomson didn't hear them. He continued to drag his way slowly and miserably along the cliff, head bowed.

So Jane and Jemima ran towards him, shouting. And suddenly he did hear. He stopped in amazement, looked up, and then flung his arms wide and ran towards them. He picked the two girls up and whirled them round. 'Safe!' he cried. 'Safe!' But when Sergeant Cobbin came hurrying up, Captain Thomson could no longer contain himself, and Jane saw tears pouring down his cheeks as he seized his old friend in his big arms. All he could say was, 'I thought you'd gone, Sergeant. I thought you'd gone.'

After a while he felt better, and looking at them all, he said, 'But what happened? What in the blazes happened? I saw the tank had gone. You can see for yourself the island's tilted. I thought you'd be at the bottom of the sea.'

Now Sergeant Cobbin and Jane had a really interested listener. Indeed, so interested did they all get, with Sergeant Cobbin explaining about Jane's brilliant idea, and Captain Thomson saying, 'Good gracious and what happened then?' and praising Jemima for her good sense, that none of them noticed that a large boat, laden with sailors, had set off from the submarine *Tulip* and was speeding towards the shore.

7. Mr Tulip

THE first sign they had that there were visitors ashore was a voice booming through a loudspeaker from the beach.

'Parlez vous Français?' it boomed, 'Sprechen sie Deutsch? Parlare Italiano? Do you speak English? Habla usted Español? . . .'

It went on for some time, speaking languages which none of them had ever heard before.

But even odder than all the languages was the effect it had on the two soldiers. With a cry of 'Cover!' Captain Thomson flung himself on to his stomach and began to crawl rapidly towards the Mess, with Sergeant Cobbin close behind.

'They're mad,' said Jemima. 'They think they're Germans who don't know the war has ended.'

'I know,' said Jane. 'Isn't it pathetic?' To the two soldiers she shouted, 'They are friends.'

'Come on, Jemima,' she went on, 'let's wave.' The two girls walked to the edge of the cliff and waved down to the fifteen or twenty men on the beach. Several of them waved back.

'They're waving to us,' shouted Jemima.

Captain Thomson and Sergeant Cobbin stopped crawling and turned their heads as though listening. Jane wondered if they expected to hear gunfire. After a moment they stood up and came towards the girls.

'You can't be too careful,' said Captain Thomson as he came up. 'We may *not* be in a time of war, or then again we may.' He stared belligerently down at the beach. 'Come, Sergeant. We're outnumbered and out-gunned. We must parley. Stay here, girls and keep your heads down.'

The two girls, however, followed the soldiers down the cliff path, and hid behind one of the large rocks that littered the beach. They saw Captain Thomson and Sergeant Cobbin march grimly up to the men, halt, salute, and then heard Captain Thomson speak in a clipped, official voice.

'May I ask who you are, sir, and by what right you land on the Island of Peeg?'

'I am Commander Hautboyes,' said the tall man with the loudspeaker in a slight accent. 'I am of the vessel *Tulip*. And you, sir?'

'Captain Thomson of the 7th Hussars, Sergeant Cobbin of the 7th Hussars,' said Captain Thomson. 'Commanding Project—that is the Island of Peeg. What do you want? Water? Fresh fruit? What's your business in these waters?'

Commander Hautboyes did not answer at once, and Jane noticed a small white ear-plug in his ear to which he seemed to be listening. Like all the other men, he was dressed in a spotless white uniform with a peaked hat. The only difference was that he had four red tulips stitched onto his cuffs, whereas his men only had one.

After a pause, Commander Hautboyes said, 'I am instructed to invite you to dinner tonight. My Captain would be delighted if you would condescend to honour his table at eight o'clock this evening.'

'Well, I don't know,' said Captain Thomson slowly. 'I'd like to know a bit about you. What flag do you sail under? I know the war is apparently and officially over, but I daresay, well—y'know, pockets of resistance and so on, what I'm driving at to speak plainly is are your intentions peaceable?'

'One moment, mon Capitaine,' Commander Hautboyes spoke rapidly into the mouthpiece of the loudspeaker, but instead of any noise coming out, he must have flicked some switch which put him in touch with the submarine, because once more he listened intently, holding the small white ear-plug with his hand.

At last he said, 'Mon Capitaine, I am instructed to tell you that all your questions will be answered this evening. But may I assure you that our intentions are entirely peaceable. A boat will be here at eight o'clock less ten minutes.'

Captain Thomson and Sergeant Cobbin saluted. Commander Hautboyes shouted a few orders, the sailors climbed into the boat, and soon they were chugging back to the looming bulk of the submarine.

'We had no choice,' said Captain Thomson. 'Superior force. Come, Sergeant, we must adjourn to the Mess and discuss tactics. We have only two hours to prepare a plan of action.' They at once set off for the

Mess, talking earnestly. Jane and Jemima followed behind more slowly, eagerly discussing what the dinner would be like and how exciting it was to be going to see a submarine.

At first, however, it looked as though no one but the two soldiers would go. Despite the two children's desperate entreaties, and Mrs Deal's refusal even to consider not going, Captain Thomson was firm.

However, it was Sergeant Cobbin who changed his mind. Reading, in preparation for the dinner, through a manual on *Infantry Tactics*, he came upon a section called 'When Dealing with Superior Force'. This said that the most important single rule was never to divide your forces. When this was pointed out to him, Captain Thomson immediately saw its sense.

'Hadn't occurred to me,' he said. 'But of course, the Manual's right, as always. While we were at dinner Commander Hautboyes or some other of those dagos could sneak in and take you all. No—we stick together. Get dressed, girls—no time to lose.'

Captain Thomson and Sergeant Cobbin's best uniforms had only been worn on Christmas days for thirty years. Fortunately they had been well surrounded by moth balls and Mrs Deal said, that though they would both smell strongly they would look smart enough.

'You two girls are the problem,' she said, turning to them next. 'No doubt the Captain of HMS *Tulip* will be an Admiral at the least. We certainly can't have you both dining at the table of a belted Admiral in jeans and shirt.'

Fortunately Mrs Deal was a quick worker with a needle. After some thought, she took two of Captain Thomson's summer shirts, rapidly cut and stitched them to fit the girls like short party dresses, and then cut some strips from a length of green mosquito netting and sewed them to the cuffs.

They had only just finished dressing, when Captain Thomson clanked impatiently into the ante-room and said it was already eight o'clock and they must get down to the beach. He and Sergeant Cobbin were in thick blue uniforms with huge metal epaulettes and spurs at their ankles. The weather was still very hot, though they were south of South Africa, and Jane felt they must both have been boiling, as indeed was Mrs Deal who, after taking off her coat and long tartan scarf, had now put them on again, together with her close-fitting hat of brightly coloured felt petals.

'Forward,' said Captain Thomson. 'We are outnumbered and out-armed. But we are British. We shall take no weapons except my ceremonial sword. Guile and cunning shall be our watchwords. Sergeant—the Manual.'

'How you do go on, Captain,' said Mrs Deal. 'As though we'd any-thing to fear from our good ship *Tulip* of Her Majesty's Royal Navy.'

They hurried down to the beach and then crunched along the nar-row strip of shingle towards a boat already bobbing close to the shore. Sergeant Cobbin's and Captain Thomson's spurs jingled and clinked loudly on the stones.

It was a smaller boat than before with room for about six in comfort-able seats at the back. Commander Hautboyes stood politely waiting for them as they came up.

When he saw Mrs Deal and the girls he bowed towards them. 'I had no idea . . .' he said. 'Les demoiselles . . .'

'Allow me,' said Captain Thomson. 'Mrs Deal—Commander Hautboyes. Miss Jemima Garing, Miss Jane Charrington—Commander Hautboyes.'

'Enchanté, enchanté,' said Commander Hautboyes, bowing to each in turn. 'Enchanté.'

A few moments later, having climbed or been helped aboard, they were roaring out over the calm sea towards the still bulk of the submarine.

'I could do with this breeze, sir,' said Sergeant Cobbin, holding his hot red face into the wind.

'What?' shouted Captain Thomson.

'I said, "I could do with this breeze, sir",' shouted Sergeant Cobbin. But Captain Thomson shook his head to show he couldn't hear. Mrs Deal sat bolt upright with her eyes shut.

The boat swung round in a fast, small circle and then came gently to rest against the high, bulging side of the submarine.

A little above them, one of the steel plates had slid silently open and a platform moved out above the motor boat. Two sailors hurried out, secured the boat and lowered some steps.

It took several minutes to get them all aboard. Jane and Jemima skipped up easily enough and so did Sergeant Cobbin, only more slowly. But Captain Thomson kept on getting his sword caught in his legs or the steps and eventually had to hold it out behind him like a tail. Mrs Deal was still affected by the buffetings of the journey. Keeping her eyes shut, she more or less abandoned herself to the strong arms of the Navy and was almost carried up. Once inside, however, she soon recovered and they all set off after Commander Hautboyes.

At first sight, the submarine seemed rather boring. It seemed to be all steel corridors with a few doors and iron ladders leading off them. There was a low humming all the time, a great many pipes, and every now and then they would pass one of the white-suited sailors, who would salute Commander Hautboyes.

Mrs Deal, walking close behind the Commander, would graciously incline her head each time this happened. After a while they came to a lift. This carried them swiftly down until they must have been nearly at the bottom of the submarine.

'Madame, demoiselles, messieurs—the stateroom,' said Commander Hautboyes.

The lift doors opened. They stepped out. The doors closed behind them.

They were standing in a room which was so grand that for a mad moment Jane thought they had been magically carried to Buckingham Palace. The walls were lined with elegant white panels and hung with huge mirrors and pictures with little lights above them. On the floor was a thick white carpet decorated with scarlet tulips, and scattered upon this were sofas and chairs, a harpsichord, and tables covered with china objects and large expensive-looking books. Opposite the lift wall there were four huge windows with long scarlet curtains. The doors of the lift itself were so cunningly disguised to resemble panels that they were quite difficult to find. Round the room, in huge vases, there were dozens of sweetly smelling bright red tulips.

'Well I never,' said Mrs Deal.

'No expense spared here,' said Sergeant Cobbin, treading the thick carpet appreciatively.

Captain Thomson, whose expression, at the sight of the pictures in their curly golden frames, had become sharp and knowledgeable, now clanked up to one of them and, pretending not to read the large gold label underneath it, said, 'Good lord—a Zoffany. Born 1734. Studied in Italy. Influenced by Hogarth. Died 1810. And what's this?' He moved on to the next picture and, after a quick downward glance, said, 'Let me see—I'd say a Fragonard. Am I right? Yes. Jean Honoré Fragonard. Goodness me, a Fragonard in a submarine. Born 1732. Studied under F. Boucher and also C. Van Loo. Influenced by Tiepolo. Died 1806. This is the most extraordinary submarine I've ever seen.'

'Didn't know as how you'd ever seen a submarine,' said Sergeant Cobbin.

'What I meant, Sergeant,' said Captain Thomson, 'is that if I had I imagine this *would* have been the most extraordinary of them all.'

'Oh, I don't agree,' said Mrs Deal. 'It's no more than what you'd expect from the Navy. They've always done the best by their men. My husband used to say, "when the Navy says welfare, they *mean* welfare!"'

'If you'll pardon me, Mrs Deal,' Captain Thomson said stiffly, 'welfare is one thing; this—this—well, I can find no words to describe it. This magnificence—extravagance—is something quite different.'

'Do you think so?' said Mrs Deal, taking one of the huge scarlet curtain tassels in her hand. 'It's no more than what I'd expect in the Lord High Admiral's quarters.'

It looked for a moment as if an argument might start. But at that moment there came the sound of a door opening and shutting from just beside them and a high voice cried:

'How perfectly delightful. Cavalry. Gentlemen—welcome to the *Tulip*.'

Standing in the door they saw a short, fat man with carefully brushed but rather thin fair hair. He was wearing a white uniform with little red tulips embroidered neatly all over it. He had a fat white face and fat red lips and as he came closer Jane saw that he was really quite old; about forty.

'My dear friends,' he said, 'so rude of me. The sight of that familiar uniform quite drove the formalities out of my silly head. Let me introduce myself—Mr Tulip.'

He held his hand out, but before anyone could answer, Mrs Deal, already secretly worried by the white uniforms, burst out '*Mister* Tulip? Did you say *Mister* Tulip? Do you mean—er I mean excuse me, sir—but aren't you an Admiral? Are you not an officer in Her Majesty's Navy?'

Mr Tulip looked at her in astonishment, then suddenly screamed with laughter. '*Tee*-hee-hee-hee, Oh hee-tee-tee-tee.'

'Alas no, Madame,' he said at last when he had recovered. 'A charming idea. One day perhaps—as a midshipman. But at the moment I cultivate my garden.'

'Your garden?' said Mrs Deal, looking wilder and wilder. 'Which garden?'

'An expression, dear,' said Mr Tulip. 'Now let us become acquainted.'

At this, Captain Thomson made a great hurrumping noise in his throat and introduced them. His face was rather red and hot and he seemed embarrassed by Mr Tulip. However, he relaxed a bit when Mr Tulip said, '7th Hussars and—don't tell me Captain—3rd Regiment. What a regiment! What a record! What men!'

'You know them, sir?' cried Captain Thomson eagerly. 'Hear that, Sergeant. We—myself and Sergeant Cobbin—would be most interested to hear any news . . .'

'Intimately,' said Mr Tulip. 'But let's tell each other everything over dinner. For the moment we'll ask Gorgeous to get us all a drink.'

He walked over to the wall and lightly pulled a long crimson cord. Almost at once, one of the panels in the wall swung open and a large, red-faced young sailor stepped through.

'Come here, you luscious gooseberry,' said Mr Tulip. 'Now, Mrs Deal, what would you like?'

Mrs Deal, who was still trying to get over the shock of discovering

that Mr Tulip wasn't an admiral in the Navy, made a little speech she
had plainly prepared before. 'I should be proud, sir,' she said, 'to par-
take of some grog.'

'And Miss Garing and Miss Charrington? What would you like?' Jane
and Jemima had Coca-Cola, the two soldiers had whisky. Mr Tulip said
he'd have mineral water with a slice of lemon in it.

The young sailor saluted and walked rather slowly towards the door.
At once Mr Tulip made a run towards him shouting. 'Be off, you
baboon—be off! Hurry you clod—hopping ox, or is it a taste of Lily
Lash you want, you muscly morsel?'

The sailor galloped out of the room and Mr Tulip came back to them
helpless with laughter. 'Oh dear,' he said when he'd got his breath. 'Oh
dear. Some of them are no more than boys really. I joke and play with
them. I'm a brother to them really. A father, too. A mixture between
brother, father, mother, sister and nanny. Ah me.' He sighed, and then
turned to Jane. 'What do you think of my little place?' he said.

'I'd hardly call it little,' said Jane, who was finding Mr Tulip more
and more surprising. 'I think it's huge and very grand.'

'What I would venture to ask, sir,' said Sergeant Cobbin, who was almost
bursting with admiration, 'what is the exact size of your craft, sir?'

'Fourteen thousand, three hundred and twenty tons, six hundred
feet long, seventy feet deep, forty-five foot beam,' said Mr Tulip briskly.
'Now—let's have dinner.'

As they followed him, Captain Thomson said, 'Fine collection of pictures, Mr Tulip.'

'Thank you, dear,' said Mr Tulip.

'I thought I noticed a fine Guardi,' said Captain Thomson. 'Born
1698, studied under his father Domenico Guardi, died 1760.'

'1699, dear,' said Mr Tulip.

'Also studied under Pittoni,' intoned Captain Thomson. Then he
said, 'I beg your pardon?'

'1699,' said Mr Tulip. 'Guardi was born in 1699 not 1698.'

'1698,' said Captain Thomson stiffly.

'Oh no, definitely 1699,' said Tulip, seeming to lose interest.

Captain Thomson stopped and went very red. '1698,' he said loudly.

Mr Tulip looked at him and then gave a light laugh. 'As you will,
Captain,' he said, 'as you will. Mrs Deal, you lead.'

This moment of embarrassment was quickly smoothed over by Mr
Tulip himself. He spent the first twenty minutes talking entirely about
the 7th Hussars. He found several officers whom he and Captain
Thomson both knew, and the old soldier's eyes almost filled with tears
as he heard about friends he had not seen for thirty years. Mr Tulip

seemed to know nearly as many, if not more Hussars who were ser-
geants, corporals and even privates, and so was able to give Sergeant
Cobbin a lot of news as well.

The dining-room was as grand as the stateroom. It was panelled in
long, ornamental mirrors, with occasionally a marble statue in an alcove.
Twisted silver candle-sticks had tall candles burning in them. When everyone had finished their soup and a delicious mousse of hot salmon, and
were well into large helping of tender beef and Yorkshire pudding, which
made them all realize how tired they had been getting of fish and wartime
tins, Mr Tulip said, 'Now I'm sure we are all simply dying to know all
about each other. You must wonder how I have this submarine; I am certainly very intrigued by the way your charming little island moves
through the water at nearly two knots an hour against the current. But let
me tell you my tale first. It is a humble story, quickly and simply told.'

Humble it certainly was not, though Jane agreed that Mr Tulip told
it quickly enough. He had been brought up and educated in England,
and had always had a deep love of the sea (here Mrs Deal, who had
drunk several large goblets of various coloured wines and begun to
look very sleepy, gave a loud, sympathetic sigh). Unfortunately his
father had compelled him to earn his living in the family nickel mines
in Australia. Just after his father had died, gold and oil had been discovered in the mines and he had been able to retire at a young age with
two hundred million pounds. Since then he had sailed the oceans in his
submarine, doing good wherever he was able and providing a home for
sea-loving youngsters of every nationality, race and colour.

'And there you are,' he finished, spreading his podgy hands; 'a poor
tale, but my own.'

'Two hundred million is a fair whack,' observed Sergeant Cobbin, no
doubt emboldened by the wine. 'You'd do better to call it a rich tale but
your own.'

'Tee-hee-hee,' laughed Mr Tulip. 'A hit, Sergeant, a palpable bit.
Poor in incident, almost a dull life is what I meant.'

'Why do all the sailors carry guns?' said Jane.

For a moment Mr Tulip looked at her without saying anything. Jane
felt he was irritated by her. Then he smiled and shrugged his shoulders, 'Well, sweetie, you know how it is. The world's not always a very
nice place and suddenly popping up as we do out of the sea we *have*
found ourselves in some rather ticklish spots. And then, as the good
Captain will tell you, dear, there's nothing like a little arms drill and
weapon training to make a youngster brisk and lively.'

'They didn't seem all that young to me,' said Jane. 'Some were
proper old men.'

'Everyone benefits from arms drill and weapon training, dear,' said Mr Tulip shortly.

Feeling he really was rather irritated, Jane didn't go on, and after a moment, all chins and smiles again, Mr Tulip begged Captain Thomson to tell him about the island.

Captain Thomson cleared his throat and finished his glass of brandy. Mr Tulip politely filled it for him again.

'Well,' said Captain Thomson, 'there's no point in beating about the bush. You'd find out for yourself soon enough and if, as I understand, the war is now finally over—and I take it this is so, is it, sir?' He looked inquiringly at Mr Tulip.

'The war?' said Mr Tulip.

'The 1939 war,' said Sergeant Cobbin.

'Yes, dear,' said Mr Tulip, looking mystified.

'In that case, Project Peeg need no longer remain a National Secret,' said Captain Thomson.

Then he told Mr Tulip the whole story. As he said later, not only could Mr Tulip have found it out, or the most important part which was the explosive, himself, but he felt he could trust a man who had obviously been on close and friendly terms with the 7th Hussars.

Mr Tulip was an excellent listener. He looked steadily at Captain Thomson all the time, occasionally lifting his hands in silent admiration or amazement. Only once did he interrupt and that was when Captain Thomson was describing the amount of explosive packed into Peeg.

'Eight million tons!' he'd cried. 'Are you sure? Why, that's more powerful than an atomic bomb. It approaches a hydrogen bomb.'

'The figure is quite correct,' said Captain Thomson. 'No question about that. We checked the entire complement every three months. I signed it over to Sergeant Cobbin one quarter, he'd sign it back to me the next. Helped to pass the time.'

At the end of Captain Thomson's account, which took about half an hour and during which Mrs Deal fell into a deep and rather obvious sleep, Mr Tulip raised his hands, looked round at them all and said, 'My dears—I'm simply stunned. Such courage! Such resource! And you, Captain, and you, Sergeant—steadfast at your post these thirty years. And the adventures since! To think I might have inadvertently caused the destruction of Jane and the good Sergeant here. This is the raw meat of life. You make me feel a schoolboy.'

'Come, sir, come, Tulip,' said Captain Thomson gruffly and modestly, his face red. 'Only a soldier's duty. A soldier stands by his post, that's all.'

'Well, I think it's *heroic*. Really I do,' said Mr Tulip. Then leaning forward he said in a serious voice, 'But tell me, Captain. Isn't it possible that all that explosive might have—er gone bad in some way over the years? Got wet or damp or damaged, not be able to explode?'

'Not a chance of that, Mr Tulip, sir,' said Sergeant Cobbin, lolling comfortably back in his chair. 'We've a fool-proof ventilation and drying system, running on a subsidiary turbine.' Briefly, though in full detail, he outlined the system of pipes and vents. Mr Tulip was soon convinced.

'Fancy,' he said, 'a hydrogen bomb not three hundred yards away from us. Extraordinary.'

They talked a little more about this and that and then Mr Tulip suggested they stay the night with him. 'Mrs Deal has had a busy day, as one can see,' he said. 'I have some comfortable guest rooms. Pray stay.'

They all agreed, particularly Jane and Sergeant Cobbin who had been exhausted by their plunge in the Observation Chamber, which had happened only that morning, though it seemed like days ago.

Indeed, Jane and Jemima were so tired that when they were shown into the room they were to share, they didn't even bother to wash, but just undressed and got straight into bed without any clothes on. They both fell asleep almost at once.

They were woken at nine-thirty by a small wizened Chinaman wheeling in a trolley with two trays of breakfast.

They each had cornflakes and cream, a dainty rose-patterned teapot, a jug of milk, toast and butter and marmalade and two boiled eggs.

'Gosh, aren't the boiled eggs wonderful,' said Jemima.

'And the butter!' said Jane. 'It's completely fresh.'

'What do you think of Mr Tulip?' said Jemima.

'I think he's rather nice,' said Jane slowly. 'He's rather like an actor Mummy and Daddy know who used to come and stay at Curl Castle. He called everyone darling or dear too.'

Chattering away through breakfast and while they shared a bath (the water was hot and salty, but the shower had a notice saying 'Fresh Water'), they agreed that Mr Tulip was nice, but that there was something a bit sinister about the submarine.

'He was definitely cross when I asked him about the guns,' said Jane.

'Yes, and I think Captain Thomson suspects him of something,' said Jemima.

'I think Captain Thomson is just embarrassed to be called darling,' said Jane. 'He's frightened of emotion.'

When they were dressed, the Chinaman appeared and politely took them to the stateroom. The others were already there.

'Ah, my dear Miss Charrington, my dear Miss Garing.' Mr Tulip came towards them with open arms. He was wearing lavender-coloured shorts and a wide straw hat. 'I have asked some of the mischievous imps in the galley to prepare us a little picnic. A *fête champêtre*.'

He led them to a different door, and having shown them through into a new, rather wide corridor, said, 'Now this is another little device I'm rather proud of. A moving corridor. Don't be alarmed.'

He raised his foot and lightly tapped a small knob on the floor. Immediately they began to move—and quite fast. Jane and Jemima seized each other and Captain Thomson's sword, sticking awkwardly against the wall, made a fearful rattling until he hastily pulled it away.

'Oops! Oops!' cried Mrs Deal.

'Steady, darling,' said Mr Tulip, and gripped her arm.

After a few moments of swift progress, the corridor as abruptly slowed and then stopped. They were below five steps leading up to the bridge.

This was about thirty feet long, rather pointed at one end and broader at the other. At the pointed end were a lot of instruments—a spoked wheel, binnacles, rows of levers and dials—in front of these were two large comfortable leather chairs. At the broad end there was an awning, with deck chairs and tables.

The bridge was in an empty steel chamber the same shape as itself and somewhere, Jane supposed, at the bottom of the submarine. When they were all aboard, Mr Tulip hurried over to the instruments and pulled several levers. Immediately they saw the roof of the chamber slide swiftly back and at the same time the whole bridge shot upwards. A moment later it reached the top of the submarine and they burst out into the sunshine.

They were high above the sea, about forty feet up; in front and behind stretched the submarine.

It was so surprising that for a moment no one could speak. Then Jemima, who had been looking anxiously about, said, 'But Mr Tulip, where's Peeg?'

Only then did Jane realize that the sea around them was completely empty and she wondered, for a cold moment of fear, whether Mr Tulip was as kind as he seemed, and whether perhaps he hadn't carried them away during the night.

But Mr Tulip laughed kindly and putting his arm round Jemima led her over to a screen among his instruments. Pressing a switch he lit up a band of light sweeping across it which revealed various bright blobs.

'There's Peeg, dear,' he said, pointing to the largest of these. 'Fifteen miles away. The good Sergeant's engines haven't faltered.'

Though it was nice to be in the fresh air, it was very hot. There was no wind and the sun beat down from almost overhead. Mrs Deal, whose jersey dress had been comfortable enough in the air-conditioned submarine, began to look very hot. So indeed did the two soldiers. They all three now hurried under the awning and fell panting into the deck chairs.

'Don't worry, darlings,' called Mr Tulip. 'It will be better when we start.' He pulled some more levers and gradually the huge ship (somehow it seemed too big to be called a submarine) began to glide forward.

Soon they were moving quite fast, with the water churning and whirling far out at the back. Captain Thomson went and stood by the rail and looked over the edge. Mrs Deal spread in the breeze and abandoned herself to its blowing. Sergeant Cobbin came and joined the two girls beside Mr Tulip.

'They didn't have nuclear power in your day, Sergeant,' Mr Tulip shouted.

'What's that?' called Sergeant Cobbin.

Jane went over and stood by Captain Thomson, and together they watched the sea split aside as the submarine sped through it.

'Must be doing twenty-five knots,' cried Captain Thomson.

'What are knots?' shouted Jane.

'It's how you measure how fast you are going at sea,' Captain Thomson shouted back. Jane nodded sensibly and looked down at the rushing, green, foam-covered water and quite soon, after half an hour, they were rapidly overtaking Peeg.

They arrived at the beach where the Mess entrance was at eleven-thirty. Mr Tulip lowered the bridge down into the submarine until they were level with the sea. A panel slid open in the side of the submarine, a short walk, and they stepped out into a motor launch. Two sailors came with them to carry one of the picnic hampers.

Mr Tulip was very excited by the Mess. He rushed from room to room peering at the faded notices on the notice board and running his fat fingers delightedly over the covers in the ante-room.

'But this is a little *gem*, darling,' he kept calling to a rather embarrassed Captain Thomson. 'A jewel. It's authentic to the last *detail*. And so *comfortable*, Captain. And don't I detect,' Mr Tulip turned a roguish eye on Mrs Deal, at the same time indicating a vase of wilting flowers, 'a woman's gentle hand? How they must have relished your soothing presence, dear, after those harsh years alone.'

'Indeed we did,' said Sergeant Cobbin. 'A right change she made and no mistake.'

Mrs Deal tut-tutted modestly and went off to change out of her jersey dress. Mr Tulip now asked if he could be shown the tunnels and the three men set off.

One thing had rather surprised Jane and Jemima. When Captain Thomson had shown Mr Tulip round the Mess he had carefully avoided the Blow-up room. Mr Tulip's sharp brown eyes had noticed it had been left out and immediately asked where the door led to. 'A broom cupboard,' Captain Thomson had said, and hurried him on.

There was probably a reason for this which they would be told, but it did make them wonder.

'What do *you* think of Mr Tulip?' Jemima asked Mrs Deal, who was already dusting.

'Now don't you bother me with your questions,' said Mrs Deal, flipping and flicking. 'I've never seen dust settle as it does in this place. He's a proper gentleman.'

'Yes, but do you like him?' said Jemima.

'You can never tell with a fat face,' said Mrs Deal. 'A fat cheek smiles whether it will or nay.'

'You see, we were wondering why Captain Thomson didn't show . . .' began Jane, when Mrs Deal arrived near her with a positive whirring of duster and mop.

'How can I get into the corners if you two great lumps are forever filling them? Move over, child.'

Realizing they'd get no sense out of her, the two girls went through the Blow-up room and up the stairs to the cliff. Here an amazing scene was taking place. A large white awning decorated with red tulips had been set upon the grass. Under it was a round table laid for six, with silver and glass and a gleaming white cloth. Dozens of sailors were bustling about with buckets of ice, champagne bottles, bowls of fruit, and unloading hampers filled with pastries, jars of caviar and paté and other delicacies. Two motor launches skimmed continually to and from the submarine, bringing more food and drink; also chairs, a swinging sofa, and iron stoves which were immediately lit and then concealed within brightly striped tents from which the most wonderful smells soon began to waft.

When at last Jane and Jemima dragged themselves away and went down to the Mess again, the two soldiers and Mr Tulip had returned and were in the kitchen.

'I've never seen explosive in better condition,' Mr Tulip was saying as they came in. 'My dear Sergeant, you've done a magnificent job. If you ever need employment come to me. Every stick of dynamite as dry as a bone. Every block of TNT firm and solid. Now, Captain—I have a *tiny* suggestion. I could use that explosive. For, well for—' Mr Tulip looked for an instant rather flustered. 'For various philanthropic and charitable purposes,' he went on quickly. 'For scientific surveys and slum clearance. For swamp destruction and famine relief schemes—you can imagine, darlings. What I propose is that I *buy* your explosive.'

'*What?*' said Captain Thomson.

'Oh don't let price worry you,' said Mr Tulip airily but swiftly. 'No,

no, dear—as I said I'm wealthy, ducky. Two hundred and fifty thousands? Pounds? Well, why not a round figure? Say half a million, dear.
Oh darling—what am I *quibbling* about? A million. A cool million.'

At last a purple Captain Thomson managed to speak. 'Mr Tulip, sir! Mr
Tulip, sir!' he burst out. 'This island is the property of His Majesty's
Government. Your philanthropic plans have allowed you to become carried away. There can be no question of a sale. Sergeant Cobbin and myself
hold it on trust. We have signed for it. The explosive must be returned to
the proper authorities as soon as possible—every stick and box intact.'

'Yes yes yes yes,' said Mr Tulip very rapidly indeed. 'Quite so, quite so,
quite so. I was forgetting it didn't belong to you. I completely forgot. Silly
me. Oh, ducky, what a mistake. Of course you are quite right. Let's go and
have lunch.' And Mr Tulip set off at a great rate for the beach staircase.
Jane was about to say why didn't they go by the Blow-up room because it
was quicker, indeed she actually said, 'I say . . .' when she saw Captain
Thomson shaking his head at her fiercely with his fingers on his lips.

This little unpleasantness—because in fact it was plain that Mr Tulip
had been irritated by Captain Thomson's brisk refusal to sell the explosive—was soon forgotten over lunch. They laughed and talked and drank
far into the afternoon. Grouse and snails and sauces on things they had
never dreamt existed flowed from the little tents all round. Sherbert
(and some champagne) for the girls; lots of champagne and other
wines, and brandy for the grown-ups. When they had finished, Captain
Thomson and Sergeant Cobbin sang several very long songs. Then Mr
Tulip had the table cleared, climbed onto it and, to music from a

gramophone which the Chinese steward had sensibly brought, showed them how to tap dance.

'Oh dear,' said Mr Tulip, patting his stomach and climbing down at the end of the record. 'So good for one. No one does it now of course, but when I was young it was all the rage.'

At about six-thirty, when they were sitting under the awning having tea and watching the sun go down, Mr Tulip suddenly said, 'Darlings— I have a suggestion. I haven't enjoyed myself so much for years. Why don't you all come and stay with me aboard the *Tulip*? I'll take you back to Cape Town and we can go on enjoying each other's company. I'll put Commander Hautboyes in charge of Peeg with a party of sailors and he can bring it back behind us.'

They all looked down at their cups and saucers. No one spoke. Then Captain Thomson said, 'That's a kind and generous offer, Mr Tulip.'

'Oh come, darling,' Mr Tulip suddenly interrupted. 'Call me Edward. Call me Eddie. All of you.'

'Er yes,' said Captain Thomson. 'Mine's Anthony. Tony. As I was saying —er, Edward, Eddie—that's a very generous offer. But on behalf of Sergeant Cobbin and myself I must reluctantly refuse. We cannot abandon our post on Peeg until we hand her over personally to the Royal Navy.'

Only Mrs Deal looked disappointed. The submarine, though not exactly a ship and certainly not in the Royal Navy, was as near as she had been to either for a long time. She had been looking forward to a week or two on the ocean wave. However she said, 'My place is by the Captain's side, Mr Tulip.'

'Eddie,' said Mr Tulip.

'Mr Eddie,' said Mrs Deal. 'And I must insist that Miss Jemima and Miss Jane stay with me. Their parents would wish it.'

Jane and Jemima were secretly delighted by this. Though they had enjoyed their little green room and the huge meals, it had all been too strange and grand. Also they wanted to go on doing all the things they had done on Peeg before.

'Yes,' said Jane, 'I think we ought to stay with Mrs Deal really.'

'Very well. I see what you mean. It does you credit,' said Mr Tulip, looking suddenly rather weary and also cross. He got up and shouted to the Chinese steward, 'Hoo—get the boat ready.'

'Er—Eddie,' said Captain Thomson awkwardly, 'there is one thing you could do. If you could radio Cape Town and inform the authorities of our presence; tell them Project Peeg is intact and ask them to inform the parents of these two girls. That would be very civil.'

'And my brother in Peeblesshire,' said Mrs Deal. 'I'll give you his name and address.'

'Not a chance, dear,' said Mr Tulip, looking more cheerful. 'Wireless is totally out of order. Of course I'll do it as soon as I can. Hoo—hurry up with that boat.'

They said goodbye and thanked him for his lunch. But Mr Tulip still seemed quite disgruntled and left after a few brisk words. Down in the Mess, Mrs Deal, still affected by the delicious lunch, said she thought it was due to the frustration of his charitable purposes.

'Burning as he must be with the desire to do good,' she said, 'it would naturally irritate to have the chance removed.'

'It's an odd charity that requires all that explosive,' said Sergeant Cobbin.

'Not at all,' said Mrs Deal. 'He works in a big way, clearing slums and such like. This is none of your small charity—your flags and the like.'

'Maybe,' said Sergeant Cobbin.

'Oh I've no doubt the fellow's genuine, Sergeant,' said Captain Thomson. 'I don't think that Major Gribble of the 7th would know a bad 'un. No—he's a bit embarrassing sometimes, but a man can behave as he wishes on his own ship I suppose. But he's been civil to us, very civil.'

'He's a regular gentleman,' said Mrs Deal. 'Not precisely *in* the Royal Navy, but you can tell the sea is in his blood. He runs that craft to the manner born, a perfect amateur seaman.'

'It's a nice bit of engineering,' said Sergeant Cobbin.

'Trim,' said Mrs Deal, 'very trim I'd call it.'

'Fourteen thousand, three hundred and twenty tons,' recited Sergeant Cobbin, 'six hundred feet long, seventy feet deep, forty-five foot beam.'

'Why didn't you show him the Blow-up room?' Jane asked Captain Thomson.

'Yes—well, I thought we ought to keep something up our sleeves,' said Captain Thomson. 'One never knows. But I'm sure he's above board.'

They had a light supper of dried-egg omelet and condensed milk pudding and then retired early to bed.

8. The Other Side
of Mr Tulip

THE next day began how once so many days had begun on Peeg.

Mrs Deal planned the largest dust she had ever undertaken; nothing less than the entire island. Or rather those parts that could be dusted: all the rooms in the Mess, the tunnels, each explosive chamber and the engine room.

For the first part of the morning Captain Thomson gave Jane and Jemima a lesson called 'How to give a lecture.' This only lasted till ten o'clock, and the two girls then went for a walk along the cliff to see if they could find any gulls' eggs.

'Don't go near the Peeg Special,' said Captain Thomson, to whom suspicion, a strong part of his character, had returned during the night. 'They may be watching from the *Tulip* and I'd like to keep something else up our sleeves.'

He himself worked in his garden. There was a lot of weeding and watering to do and also, although the rivalry between him and Sergeant Cobbin had grown much less recently, he still liked to surprise Mrs Deal with a giant turnip from time to time, or a basket of tomatoes.

Sergeant Cobbin went to his engine room. 'There's always some-thing needs doing to an engine,' he said, as he bicycled away down the tunnel.

They gathered in the kitchen again at one o'clock for lunch.

'It's good to be back at work,' said Sergeant Cobbin.

'Not a moment too soon,' said Mrs Deal. 'The dirt and dust in the shooting range! You wouldn't believe it.'

'Some of those weeds had grown two inches,' Captain Thomson said.

'Another day and me tappits would have clogged,' said Sergeant Cobbin.

Jane and Jemima were pleased too, though their lessons were hardly work. Certainly Miss Boyle would not have thought so. But there was something comforting and safe about everyone settling down to their tasks again. However, this peaceful start was interrupted in the middle of lunch. They had just finished their baked beans and sardines when there came the sound of running footsteps outside the kitchen door. It burst open and in rushed Mr Tulip.

'Darlings! Eating—how awful of me. But I have news. This morning there was a flicker of life from our wireless. Before it went dead again. I learnt two things. South Africa is a tiny bit dangerous at the moment—the British base has closed. But a large Naval fleet is going to visit Australia just after Christmas. Now, *mes enfants*—I have a plan. Let us attach Peeg to *Tulip*. The nuclear engines are very powerful. I should be able to tow you to Australia much sooner than you'd have reached the Cape at the rate you're going now. You, my dear, remain in charge; not so much as a *crumb* of explosive is to be moved; but you get there earlier.'

Captain Thomson thought for a moment and asked Sergeant Cobbin what he thought. Mrs Deal said the presence of the Navy was in the plan's favour. Quite quickly they all decided the idea was a good one and Captain Thomson gave a little speech of thanks.

'Don't mention it, dear,' Mr Tulip interrupted half-way through. 'Now if you'll excuse me, I'll set the boys to work this very moment.'

When they came onto the cliff-top after lunch, the whole of Peeg seemed covered in men. Among them, quite frantic with excitement, jumped, spun, sped fat Mr. Tulip, calling everyone Luscious, Gorgeous, Scrumptious, or getting very red and angry and threatening them all, from Commander Hautboyes downwards, with a taste of Lily Lash.

What they were doing was to hammer eight thick steel girders deep into the rock of the island. These would then be joined to the *Tulip* with steel ropes. It was very hard work. The girders bent and had to be replaced, the drills broke, the heavy machine for hammering in the girders had to be dragged to and fro. By evening the work was still not done and it continued all night by the light of powerful lamps.

Not until lunch the next day did eight long sagging steel wires hang between Peeg and the submarine *Tulip*. To one of them a telephone cable had been attached, running into the Mess.

They all gathered on the cliff-top to see the submarine start towing. At first nothing much happened, except that the sea at the back end of *Tulip* seethed and bubbled and the long drooping wire ropes tightened. But very gradually, they noticed tiny ripples spreading back from the rocks sticking up out of the sea off the beach. These grew gradually larger. Then they noticed a faint breeze blowing onto their faces off the sea. After four hours they were moving at five knots, and the submarine very slowly began to pull round to the right until, after turning the island round nearly a half circle, it set off straight again, headed for Australia.

So the Island of Peeg began her last voyage. The first two weeks were very peaceful. Work on the island continued as usual. Mrs Deal completed clearing the Mess and began on the tunnels. At night if a wind got up they could hear the cables humming and throbbing. By day, sea gulls used to sit on them. Mr Tulip seemed very busy and preoccupied; nevertheless he asked them to several meals and showed them some films. But he always politely refused their own invitations saying that he had too much to do (Jane and Jemima had decided that he was frightened of Mrs Deal's cooking). Then at the end of a fortnight two rather strange things happened.

The first took place on one of those days they were having lunch on the *Tulip*. Jane had a bad cold and a temperature so Mrs Deal said she must spend the day in bed. Jemima had gone for a long walk in the morning to see if she could find some flowers for Jane's room. This is not so surprising as it sounds, for Peeg had started to change from the desert it had become on their journey south. The weather had been getting colder and twice recently there had been a little rain.

Lunch with Mr Tulip was rather boring, at least for Jemima. He produced several bottles of what he said was a special wine which she of course didn't drink. But the others had quite a lot. Even Mrs Deal said, 'Well, if you *insist*, Mr Tulip' (they had all long ago given up trying to call him Eddie or even Edward).

After lunch they were all talking so much that Jemima slipped out of the dining-room. She suddenly thought she would explore the submarine. She and Jane had discussed only the day before how odd it was that they had never looked at any part of it without Mr Tulip or Commander Hautboyes being there to show it to them. No one seemed to have noticed that she had left the dining-room, so it seemed an ideal opportunity to escape. Jemima slipped through another door and in a moment was off down a long steel corridor.

For over an hour she wandered down one corridor after another, up and down steel ladders and lifts. She saw the kitchens, a billiards room, and the little cabins with six bunks each where the crew slept. Normally she would have been too nervous to do this sort of thing without Jane, but in fact it wasn't at all difficult. She started off imagining what she would say if anyone stopped her, but the sailors stepped politely aside to let her pass and one of them saluted her. Also Jemima was rather pleased that she would have something to tell Jane.

At last however, she thought she'd seen enough. Her legs were tired and she felt it must be getting late. She was about to ask the way back to the stateroom when she saw a steel door with a notice on it saying 'No Admittance'. At once, her heart beating, she gave it a tiny push. To her horror it immediately and easily swung open.

Jemima knew that Jane would have gone in. How exciting to be able to go back and tell Jane that that was what she had done. Hoping that a sailor might appear and say, 'Hey—you can't go in there,' Jemima very slowly walked towards the open door.

No sailor came. She was standing in an enormous chamber, larger even than the stateroom. It was as wide as the submarine and must have been about forty feet high. Down both sides, tilted at a slight angle, there was a row of large rockets. Each rocket had 'US Air Force' printed on it, and each pointed nose which she could just see high above her in the semi-darkness, rested against a round bolted trap in the side of the submarine.

What were they? Perhaps, thought Jemima nervously, they were atomic rockets. She walked slowly up the large dim chamber, the twenty-four rockets (twelve in each row) standing in silent ranks as she passed. Why should Mr Tulip want twenty-four atomic rockets? Perhaps they were something to do with weather and he only planned to fire them up into the clouds to see how hot they were or wet or something. But somehow they looked more frightening than this, too sharp and fat and long.

At the far end of the chamber there were two large panels in the wall covered with dials and knobs and other instruments. She was examining these, when she heard a dull clang and then the sound of echoing voices.

Coming towards her from the steel door she saw Mr Tulip and a tall, elderly man in white overalls she had never seen before. Luckily they were talking so hard they did not notice her and she was able to hide behind the tail fins of the nearest rocket.

'Well I still haven't decided, ducky,' Mr Tulip was saying. 'I've alerted all those who might be concerned. But you know the problems, Dr Interdenze, as well as I do, don't you dear?'

'Certainly, sir,' said Dr Interdenze, in a strong German accent.

'We could certainly equip these suggestive objects,' Mr Tulip said, waving a fat hand vaguely at the rockets.

'I haf worked out plans for them, sir,' said Dr Interdenze.

They began to talk about things Jemima simply could not follow. Crouching down among the tail fins of her rocket she noticed that though Mr Tulip scattered his conversation with his usual darlings and lusciouses and made his usual silly jokes he was in fact rather quicker and brisker. He asked a lot of short questions. Dr Interdenze was very polite; indeed, he seemed rather frightened of Mr Tulip.

Perhaps it was this that kept Jemima hiding. She did not quite know why she had hidden in the first place and she had meant to come out and surprise Mr Tulip after a few minutes. But now she decided to try and creep away without being seen. Somehow she had left it too late; also there was something a bit different about Mr Tulip, something a bit frightening.

Very carefully, she slipped along to the next rocket. They went on talking. She tip-toed to the next and then the next and soon was quite near the door. She could see Mr Tulip and Dr Interdenze standing with their backs to her looking at the panels. The next moment she was in the corridor again.

One of the sailors took her back to the stateroom where she found Commander Hautboyes who told her that the others had gone back to Peeg some time ago. He didn't seem very interested in what she had been doing and at once had her put on a boat and taken back to the island.

Jemima arrived in the Mess just as Sergeant Cobbin and Captain Thomson were about to set off on some expedition.

'Stop!' she cried, 'I've found out something very odd.' As fast but as carefully as she could she told them everything. Everyone listened in complete silence. Jane, whose bed had been put in the ante-room so that she could be near the telephone, got out of it and came and stood nearer so that she could hear.

'Goodness, how *brave*,' she said to Jemima when she'd finished. 'I wouldn't have dared. Weren't you scared stiff?'

'Well, I was a bit,' said Jemima, feeling very pleased and proud. 'But I was quite safe. I'm sure Mr Tulip would never hurt me. They're probably weather rockets.'

'Well, I think you're very brave,' said Jane putting her arm round Jemima's shoulders.

'You've done very well,' said Captain Thomson in a grave voice. 'This is very interesting. The rockets *may*, as you say, be weather rockets, but they may not. You say Tulip said he had alerted all those who might be concerned? Now that may mean weather stations, but it may not. Certainly, if the submarine is a weather ship, why didn't he tell us? And if he can alert people it shows his wireless is really working. Forewarned is forearmed. Sergeant, go and see that the Peeg Special is loaded with petrol. See that it is well hidden. I will go and check the mechanisms in the Blow-up room. Mrs Deal, Jemima, stay with me, Jane get back to bed. We must all get fighting fit.'

The change in the two soldiers was considerable. That evening they both changed into what Captain Thomson called patrol kit, which consisted of big loose jackets painted various autumn colours, tight trousers, things like large stockings on their heads, and covered their faces in boot polish. They disappeared dressed like this after dinner and didn't get back until everyone else had long been asleep. Before they had set out, Captain Thomson had started to read a small pamphlet called *In Enemy Territory*.

The second strange thing occurred at the beginning of the third week. It was a grey, blustery day with low clouds. Sergeant Cobbin, Captain Thomson, Jane and Jemima were standing on the cliff-top watching the Tulip plough through heavy seas: the long cables connecting her to the island hummed and vibrated and were often buried by large waves.

Captain Thomson suddenly said, 'It's been getting cold very quickly. What direction have we been heading, Sergeant?'

'I ain't certain,' said Sergeant Cobbin, 'But I'd reckon we'd have been going south.'

'That's what I feel,' said Captain Thomson. 'Yet Australia is more south-east surely. Something odd here.'

'I can check easy enough,' said Sergeant Cobbin. 'I'll just go and have a look at the old compass in me engine room.'

In half an hour he was back, red, panting and dramatic. 'It's gone!' he said, pointing towards the engine room.

'Gone?' said Captain Thomson. 'How do you mean gone? What's gone?'

'Me compass has bin took,' said Sergeant Cobbin, sounding very Suffolk. 'Someone's bin and unscrewed it from the old binnacle and took it.'

'I see,' said Captain Thomson slowly. 'Someone—presumably under Mr Tulip's orders—has taken our compass. Things get stranger and stranger. We must plan our strategy and our tactics. Sergeant Cobbin—O group tonight at eight-thirty. Things are coming to a head.'

But for some days nothing new happened. It got colder and wetter, and in the evenings they lit the iron stove in the ante-room and took hot water bottles to bed with them. The more it rained the more Peeg changed. Shoots of heather appeared and a lot of moss, which had seemed completely dead, suddenly came alive. A thin trickle of water ran down the middle of the burn again. Several times Sergeant Cobbin and Captain Thomson got up in the middle of the night, put on their patrol kit, covered their faces in boot polish and disappeared until morning. Jane and Jemima couldn't imagine what they were doing, and when they got back at breakfast time the two soldiers were too tired to be asked questions.

Then, suddenly, at the beginning of the second month they found out the whole terrible truth.

It was one of the first fairly calm days that they'd had for a week. In the morning Mr Tulip rang them up and asked them if they'd like to come over for a game of ping-pong before tea. They had done this quite often before Jemima's discovery, and the soldiers had both enjoyed it. Captain Thomson said that, though circumstances were different now that was all the more reason for going. On no account should they rouse Mr Tulip's suspicions.

Mr Tulip himself was, as usual now, too busy to play. But a number of other officers at once challenged Captain Thomson and Sergeant Cobbin to a match. Normally the others sat and watched the men play about seventy games. Sometimes Jane and Jemima were allowed one game at the very end. This time, however, Jane whispered quietly to Jemima, 'Say I've gone for a walk if anybody asks, and quietly slipped out of the sports room while everyone was settling down.

Captain Thomson had been reading *In Enemy Territory* aloud to them all in the evenings. Jane walked slowly and innocently, whistling and smiling. 'Keep your eyes open,' Captain Thomson had said. 'But don't ask questions.'

For a while she saw nothing. The submarine hummed and quivered as it plunged on through the sea. Sailors bustled about their business, receiving huge innocent smiles whenever they passed Jane.

She was about to turn back when she turned a corner and saw, half-way down a short stretch of corridor, two Tulip sailors with rifles over their shoulders standing guard by a door.

This was certainly unusual. Jane sauntered up to them and forgetting Captain Thomson's orders, said, 'Could you tell me, please, what happens in there?'

'Clear off,' said the sailor roughly. 'Mr Tulip's orders. No one's allowed round here.'

This too was unusual. Normally the sailors were very polite, and Mr Tulip was always saying that he wanted them to look on the whole submarine as their home. However, feeling very cunning, Jane just walked slowly away, saying vaguely how interesting.

'Get a move on,' shouted the sailor. 'All right, all right—keep your hair on,' said Jane crossly, hurrying round the corner.

Once out of sight, however, she slowed down again. This was clearly extremely suspicious. Even the rockets hadn't been guarded. Quite obviously she must get into the room behind that door—but how? There were no windows and no other doors, just the bare steel walls and the usual bundle of pipes and wires running along under the ceiling.

It was the sight of the pipes and wires which gave her an idea. They ran everywhere all over the submarine, and every so often, where they disappeared into a bulkhead or steel wall, there would be a small square door high up with 'Inspection Point' written on it. Jane ran down to the end of the corridor—a short one—and there sure enough she found one, with steel rungs set in the wall. With a quick look round to see that no one was coming, she climbed the rungs and pushed at the door.

It opened onto a long, low place like a deep, narrow cupboard. Jane crawled quickly in and pulled the little door shut behind her.

She could only lie on her stomach. By the light of a faint, pale blue bulb she saw a maze of pipes and wires, which ran into a lot of boxes with dials and knobs on. But far more exciting than this was the faint but definite sound of voices; a burring she could hear above the humming of the submarine. Jane wriggled to the end of the inspection point and saw at the corner a ring of light round two pipes disappearing into the room on the other side. Lying flat, she put her eye to the crack.

She saw a small bit of a round table. Sitting at it, in full view, were Commander Hautboyes; on his right she saw half of a tall thin man she did not recognize, and to the left she could just see the hands of Mr Tulip, with his large red ring on a fat forefinger. Everything else was cut off by the edge of the hole, but she could tell by the murmur of voices that several more people were sitting there. She found that by putting her ear to the crack she could hear quite well.

'. . . I would like,' said the tall thin man.

She heard Mr Tulip say distinctly, 'I'm sure you would, dear—wouldn't we all?' Then she saw him smack one plump hand firmly on the table.

'Darlings,' he said. 'To business. I've called you here today to tell you something really rather thrilling. Interdenze and myself have finally completed our plans for the Island of Peeg.'

With a jump of excitement, Jane realized she must be going to find out what some of the mysterious happenings meant. She pressed her ear to the little opening.

'As you know,' went on Mr Tulip, 'this innocent island is loaded with some eight million tons of TNT and other explosive. The equivalent of two or three hydrogen bombs. My plan is very simple. In a month's time we will have towed Peeg to the Ross Ice Shelf. Now Interdenze, dear, before I go on, just give a very brief resume of what would happen if we were to explode the island beside the Ross Ice Shelf.'

Jane heard a scraping of chairs and a clearing of throats. Then the thin man said. 'An explosion of this magnitude would subject four or five square miles to searing heat and devastating disturbance. First an immense tidal wave, some hundred miles long and one hundred feet high would sweep out over the ocean. It would reach Tasmania in three days at a height of approximately forty feet. The coastal regions would be devastated. Loss of life and property would be catastrophic.

'The second result of exploding Peeg is more interesting. A vast area of the Ross Ice Shelf will be detached. Millions of tons of ice, in the form of huge icebergs will be carried first north-west by the prevailing currents and then, when they meet the Roaring Forties, back onto Australia. Our computers estimate that over a period of two years the temperature along the whole of Southern Australia will drop 30° Fahrenheit. It is true to say that Australia will be crippled.'

'Vivid, darling,' said Mr Tulip. 'Now, gentlemen—when we have placed the Island of Peeg against the Ice Shelf, the submarine *Tulip* will immediately proceed to the Indian Ocean. I shall instruct the Australian Government to drop five hundred million pounds sterling—or say twelve thousand million dollars—in the form of gold bullion into the ocean at a particular place. I shall warn them that all ships must be cleared round the area to a distance of one thousand miles for one week while we recover the gold and make our escape. I shall warn them that if the area is entered, which our radar can easily detect, I shall explode the island. They will hardly wish to blow it up themselves, but if so much as an Australian mosquito lands on it, I shall immediately explode it. The instruments to detect entry and to explode are at this moment being secretly installed on Peeg.'

A voice said, 'Can the Australian Government afford five hundred million pounds?'

'They can't afford not to afford it, darling,' said Mr Tulip. 'They will borrow it.'

'Suppose they send a rocket into the Indian Ocean and destroy us,' someone else said.

'Destroying *Tulip* will automatically set off the exploding mechanism,' said Mr Tulip. 'What will we do with the Peeg party?' said a third invisible voice.

'Ah me,' said Tulip, spreading his hands. 'You know how tender-hearted I am, dear? I've grown quite fond of the two little girls. I shall offer them positions in the organization. I am afraid they will refuse. We will have to leave them on their island.'

Soon after this they left. Jane heard them all pushing back their chairs and peering through the crack saw bits of them moving about and then disappear. She found she was trembling, and felt a mixture of excitement, fear and importance. Her chin ached where it had been pressing against the pipe. She must quickly tell Captain Thomson. They must stop Mr Tulip. But how? What could they do against so many tough men with rockets and guns and a huge submarine?

She crawled back down to the door and down into the corridor. When she got back to the others they had finished playing ping-pong and were standing about talking. Mr Tulip was there too, beaming and bouncing, his usual talkative self.

'And how's this little darling?' he said, trying to ruffle her hair.

Jane moved sharply away, causing Captain Thomson to frown fiercely at her.

'Quite well, Mr Tulip,' she said. She felt frightened of him and thought he must somehow be able to tell that she had overheard him just by her expression.

Jemima noticed at once that something was wrong and coming beside her said:

'What's happened?'

'Nothing,' Jane whispered. 'Sssh. I'll tell you later.'

'Darlings—we must see more of each other. I've neglected you in the last few days. Come to supper—tomorrow, Captain?'

'Splendid,' said Captain Thomson heartily. 'Excellent. We'd love that. Very good of you.'

Soon afterwards they left, Jane managing to avoid Mr Tulip's kiss. It was foggy and quite cold out on the sea, but not rough. At first they could not see Peeg at all, but just the black dripping cables disappearing ahead of them.

The moment they arrived in the Mess, Captain Thomson turned to Jane, his big kind face red and cross. 'Now, Jane, I'm most displeased,' he said. 'I've told you how important it is not to arouse Mr Tulip's suspicions. You must let Mr Tulip pinch you and ruffle your hair. He's the pinching sort. He even pinches me and Sergeant Cobbin.'

'But don't you see,' said Jemima. 'Something's happened.'

'What?' said Captain Thomson.

Jane paused, feeling very dramatic. Then she said, 'I know what Mr Tulip is going to do.'

She couldn't remember all the details, like the name of the ice shelf, but she remembered quite enough to convince them of the really terrible danger. No one spoke, except Mrs Deal, who cried at regular intervals, 'No!' and 'I can't believe it!'

When she'd finished, Jemima, who was still holding her arm, said, 'Goodness—weren't you terrified? You see—I knew you'd be just as brave.'

'And him a Naval man, or at least a man of the sea,' said Mrs Deal. 'I can hardly credit it.'

'I'm afraid it's true,' said Captain Thomson, who was looking extremely grim. 'Not that Mr Tulip wishes to kill us. I imagine that he supposes the Australians will be willing to pay up and that after an uncomfortable time we will be rescued. But that this is his plan I have no doubt. There have been other indications. Not only the rockets Jemima discovered, but other signs—have there not, Sergeant Cobbin?'

There was no answer. 'Sergeant Cobbin?' said Captain Thomson sharply. 'Where's Sergeant Cobbin?'

'He's gone!' cried Mrs Deal. 'Oh mercy me. They're snatching us up one by one. We'll be taken in our beds. Come here, Jane, Jemima.'

However in a few minutes Sergeant Cobbin came through the door. 'She's right,' he said. 'Just bin taking a look down the old tunnel. Someone's fixed a length of new wire right along the roof. They'd hidden it well, but I see'd it soon enough.'

'Now,' said Captain Thomson, 'we are dealing with a dangerous man. He is certainly rather mad. No one but a madman could contemplate such a deed. Luckily Sergeant Cobbin and I have worked out various plans for various situations. I think plan D would fill the bill, don't you, Sergeant?'

'She'd fit it a treat,' said Sergeant Cobbin.

'Will we have to put boot polish on our faces?' said Jane, giggling.

Captain Thomson looked at her rather coldly, then went on. 'The details of the plan are not quite worked out. We'll do that tonight, Sergeant.'

That night, before they went to sleep, the two girls talked and talked, discussing Mr Tulip, trying to think of their own plan.

'We could all get into the Peeg Special—fly away,' said Jemima.

'But would it hold us all?' said Jane. And where would we fly to. And how far? And anyway, I expect he'd shoot us down with one of his guns.'

'Well, what?' said Jemima.

'We could tip the boxes of explosive one by one secretly into the sea at night,' said Jane.

'Eight million tons?' said Jemima, 'it would take ages.'

'Yes, I suppose so—weeks, anyway.'

'Years,' said Jemima.

In the end they couldn't think what was to be done. 'We must just hope plan D is good,' said Jane.

'He was awfully cross when you said boot polish,' said Jemima. 'I know,' said Jane, 'but honestly—I mean it makes them both look so silly and they never get it all off. I'd have thought seeing boot polish behind their ears would be enough to make Mr Tulip suspicious. He must think they're mad if you ask me.'

The next morning after breakfast Captain Thomson gathered every-one in the ante-room to explain plan D.

It was simple but brilliant. That very day they would ask Mr Tulip to supper. He never came over with more than two or three sailors and these just used to sit and gossip in the kitchen with Mrs Deal. Halfway through supper in the ante-room, Sergeant Cobbin would leave the table on some pretext, go through to the kitchen—picking up a machine gun on the way—and hold up the sailors. Mrs Deal would tie them up. And they would then have Mr Tulip in their power and be able to dictate terms.

There seemed only one drawback. 'We have asked Mr Tulip to sup-per at least nine times,' said Jane, 'and he's always refused.'

'Oh don't worry about that,' said Captain Thomson confidently. 'I wasn't Mess secretary for nothing in the good old days you know. I'll turn on the charm.'

After lunch Captain Thomson settled himself at the telephone. Quite soon he was engaged in a rather difficult conversation.

'Mr Tulip? Ah—Thomson here . . . Very well thank you. And you? . . . Good . . . Look, there's been a bit of a chin-wag here about coming over for supper tonight. We feel you should come here, sir. We'd like to invite you to supper. Just a snack. Dress informal.'

There was a silence while Captain Thomson listened. Then he said, 'No, no, Mr Tulip. We'll take no excuse. We insist. It's our turn, old fellow.'

Again Mr Tulip must have refused. Again Captain Thomson insisted. Again and again and again Mr Tulip refused. Captain

Thomson began to look rather red, he begged and pleaded; after a while he charmed.

'Look—er—Edward—er—Eddie—think nothing of it, old man. My dear chap—it's humble fare, I know, but for you—er—Eddie—dear chap . . .' He asked Mr Tulip to tea. He asked him to come and have a sandwich He asked him to come and have drinks. A drink.

In the end he became quite desperate. 'Look here, Tulip,' he said. 'It's a question of hospitality. As an English gentleman you'll understand I really don't feel we can come to you again—we won't come to you again until you've come to us. It's a matter of etiquette, an Englishman's honour.'

In the end Mr Tulip agreed to come and have a drink with them that evening provided they all then had dinner on the submarine. Captain Thomson mopped his forehead, exhausted but triumphant.

'You see,' he said to Jane and Jemima, 'I knew I'd persuade him.'

'Force him, you mean,' said Jane. 'Don't you think he'll suspect something?'

'Oh, good gracious no,' said Captain Thomson. 'He understands. He may be a villain, but he's a gentleman. That is, he knows how gentlemen behave.'

Captain Thomson was right. Prompt at six o'clock Mr Tulip appeared at the Mess. He was wearing a clean white uniform sparingly embroidered with scarlet tulips, and carried a light malacca cane with a tulip made of some large red stone on its top. A ruby, he explained to Jemima, a bit of foolishness he'd had made for him in Bombay.

They had spent all afternoon rehearsing what to do. The first drink was to be served from rather a small jug. When it ran out, Captain Thomson was to ask Sergeant Cobbin to get some more. On the way he would collect his machine gun from the cupboard outside the kitchen. While he kept the sailors covered with the gun, Mrs Deal would tie them up. They would be gagged and left with Mrs Deal, to whom Sergeant Cobbin would give his gun. Sergeant Cobbin would then return to the ante-room and blow his nose twice if everything was all right. This would be a signal for Captain Thomson to go to a drawer and say, 'I think these would interest you, Mr Tulip,' producing two more guns, one of which he would toss to Sergeant Cobbin. They would then discuss terms with Mr Tulip. If more than four sailors appeared or if Mr Tulip showed any signs of being suspicious, then the whole of plan D was to be immediately abandoned.

But in fact only two sailors appeared and Mr Tulip was gaiety and politeness itself. He smiled and giggled—he told amusing stories about

Gorgeous being rude to Commander Hautboyes, and Luscious being rude to someone they hadn't met called Herr Interdenze (Jane and Jemima exchanged a quick look). He laughed and laughed, and was eventually almost weeping with laughter, with his fat, round, white hand on Captain Thomson's stiff bony knee, and crying out, 'Oh, my dear! My dear—you simply wouldn't *believe* the goings on.'

There had been some trouble over the drink. All they had left were two bottles of rum, but Mrs Deal had cleverly made a punch by mixing this with lemonade crystals, sugar and hot water. It tasted, Jane and Jemima thought, delicious, very sweet, boiling hot and very strong.

They had been talking happily about this and that for about quarter of an hour when Captain Thomson said in a casual voice, 'Oh, Sergeant, the jug's empty. Go and get some more, will you?'

'Not on my account, darling,' said Mr Tulip hurriedly. 'I have ample, ample.' He held up his glass, which was indeed still almost full.

'Nonsense nonsense,' said Captain Thomson. 'Nonsense—er Eddie. Drink up, sir. Off you go, Sergeant.'

'Right you are, sir,' said Sergeant Cobbin. They heard him clump off towards the kitchen.

A silence fell. Jane's heart was beating and she tried hard to hear the sound of a struggle in the kitchen. Even Captain Thomson seemed under strain. He was brick red and kept on pulling his moustache. Someone must speak, thought Jane.

'Did you sleep well last night, Mr Tulip?' she said at last.

'Well, I had a rather restless night, darling,' said Mr Tulip. 'A touch restless. And you?'

'Very restless,' said Jane. Then thinking this might sound suspicious, she added quickly, 'very restless at first, then very calm.'

Captain Thomson cleared his throat. 'Where were we?' he said loudly. 'What was I saying?'

'Nothing, darling,' said Mr Tulip.

Captain Thomson pulled his moustache. 'It's been restless weather —er Edward—Eddie. Normal for these latitudes, I suppose?'

'My dear, I haven't the faintest idea,' said Mr Tulip. 'I don't even know what latitude we're in. I leave all that to my navigators.'

There was another silence. Jane could hardly bear it. Captain Thomson said suddenly, 'Where the hell's Cobbin?'

And then the door opened and in came Sergeant Cobbin. He was smiling and carrying a jug. He put it down and pulling out his hand-kerchief blew his nose twice, very loudly. Captain Thomson tried to fill Mr Tulip's glass. When he was waved politely away he said, 'I've got something here I think would interest you, Tulip.'

He walked over to the table and stood for a moment with his back to them. Then he opened a drawer, picked something up and whirling round pointed the gun at Mr Tulip's chest.

'It's this,' he said. 'Right, Tulip, I'm afraid the game's up. Raise your hands above your head and stand up. I shall not hesitate to shoot.'

Behind him, Sergeant Cobbin had taken the second gun and moved to where he could keep it pointing at Mr Tulip.

Mr Tulip said, 'Careful, dear—those old weapons, terribly dicey.'

'I mean it, Tulip,' said Captain Thomson.

But Mr Tulip did not move. He seemed quite unconcerned. He looked calmly at the two soldiers, and then said rather coldly, 'Look darling—you don't think I didn't know about this, do you? I'm not a ninny, you know.' Suddenly he raised his head and turning it to the door, he cried out in a high, sing-song voice, 'Haut*boyes*! *Haut*boyes— HAUT—BOYES!'

Immediately the ante-room appeared to be full of sailors. Led by Commander Hautboyes they poured in, ten, fifteen, twenty of them, heavily armed and very tall and strong. Before Captain Thomson and Sergeant Cobbin could move they were seized and thrown to the floor. Jane saw a huge sailor seize Jemima, and was then seized herself.

'I shall see them in the stateroom in an hour,' said Mr Tulip. 'Don't be too rough with the girlies.' He bowed to Captain Thomson and Sergeant Cobbin, almost buried by struggling sailors. 'Thanks for a delicious drink, darlings,' he said, and then daintily tripped out of the door.

They had been waiting in the stateroom for a quarter of an hour. Captain Thomson and Sergeant Cobbin were tightly bound at the wrists; Jane and Jemima and Mrs Deal were free. Two sailors with rifles stood guard. No one spoke, though now and again a quiet sob came from Jemima who was sitting very frightened on Mrs Deal's lap.

At last the door into the dining-room opened and Mr Tulip appeared, somehow rather in the same way as when they'd first met him. He sat down at the table and beckoned them over. The two guards followed them and stood behind the two soldiers when they sat down.

'Well I'm sorry it's happened like this, darlings 'said Mr Tulip. 'I hate unpleasantness—but you left me with no choice really, did you?'

'How did you find out we'd found out?' said Jane.

'My dear—the first thing I did was to have the Mess bugged,' said Mr Tulip. 'If that's not a vulgar way of putting it. Little microphones in every room, Captain. They've developed a lot since your day. I've heard everything. I heard when Jemima found the rockets. I heard about your little prank, Jane. I could have taken you all then, but I was interested in what you'd do.

'Now—I've a lot to do. I shall make you this offer. I can give you all positions in my organization. You two girls I would take under my wing. I would like you to think of me as a father. What do you say?'

'I can answer for us all,' said Captain. 'I don't know what your organization is or what it does, but the answer is NO.'

'I feared you'd say that,' said Mr Tulip. 'Well—the alternative I'm afraid may be unpleasant, though I certainly hope not. It all depends how sensible the Australian Government is.'

'You are quite obviously mad,' said Captain Thomson. 'Do you suppose the Australian Government will do anything but ignore your mad messages?'

'Darling,' said Mr Tulip, 'you don't actually know a great deal about me, do you? Because I have a—well, slightly theatrical way of talking you imagine I'm only acting, don't you? A lot of people have underestimated me for much the same reason. Let me explain a few things to you in about thirty seconds.

'I am the head of an extremely powerful organization called Pilut,' he began, and suddenly, though he looked no different, Jane felt frightened of him. He seemed cold and hard and somehow dangerous. His light jokes, his affected way of talking, instead of being rather foolish, now appeared as disguises for someone very clever and very scheming.

'My name,' Mr Tulip went on, 'is in fact Pilut. I am a Hungarian of ancient family born and brought up in England.'

'I thought you said your family owned a nickel mine in Australia,' said Jane.

'So I did, darling,' said Mr Tulip rather sarcastically. 'What makes you thing that Hungarians can't own nickel mines in Australia?'

Jane didn't answer and after a moment Mr Tulip went on. 'In the last ten years Pilut has been partially or largely responsible for the Cuban Revolution, the race riots in America and the Arab-Israeli wars. Also robberies and forgeries too numerous to mention. None of this, of course, our good soldiers will understand. It all happened while they were, somewhat ridiculously I can't help feeling, cooped up inside Peeg waiting for a war which had ended ten or fifteen years before.'

Captain Thomson did not answer this insult, but Jane saw Sergeant Cobbin clench his large fists.

'Pilut has been responsible for a great deal of lucrative crime and national disturbance. Our name is kept hidden by governments seeking to destroy us. But they also pay us. Last year, for instance, Pilut made a profit of three million pounds.' Mr Tulip was silent. And looking at him Jane was suddenly reminded of a film she had seen.

'I think you're just making it up,' she said all at once. 'It's too child-ish. It's just like a James Bond film I saw once.'

The effect of this was quite extraordinary. Staring at her, Mr Tulip slowly stood up. He grew whiter and whiter and began to tremble. For ten seconds he was unable to speak and then suddenly leaning across at her he screamed at the top of his voice, 'DO YOU THINK IAN COULD HAVE WRITTEN HIS BOOKS WITHOUT ME?'

Jane didn't answer.

'DO YOU?' screamed Mr Tulip.

Jane was too terrified even to look at him. But Mr Tulip was now striding up and down the stateroom in a frenzy of rage, jumping up and down, trembling.

'Of course he couldn't,' he cried. 'I *made* Fleming. My existence, which he discovered by nefarious means, inspired him. It was through his villains that he came to his hero. But to go unrecognized for what Ian stole from me is the least of my worries. A humble Pilut—yes, hum-ble not rich. I claw my way to the top. I sell my soul, my body, my life to achieve power and what—still I am payed like a tradesman. I shall be recognized. The world must cringe . . . how dare they . . . Pilut . . . my childhood . . .'

They watched in amazement as Mr Tulip became more and more disjointed and incoherent. From a scream his voice fell until, choked with tears, they could barely hear what he was muttering. Eventually he managed to calm himself down and came slowly back to the table, look-ing suddenly very tired.

Captain Thomson said, 'What will you do with five hundred million pounds?'

'I haven't decided, dear,' said Mr Tulip wearily. 'I shall equip twenty or thirty more Tulips. Those rockets Jemima discovered are empty, I shall buy atomic warheads for them. I shall attain the status of a great power without possessing a country or territory of any sort. Nothing but an immensely powerful navy. It is an interesting idea.'

He stared at his plump fingers and became lost in thought. After a long silence, Captain Thomson stood up and cleared his throat. He said that he personally felt sorry for Mr Tulip. It was plain that he was deranged. Nevertheless, if even one tenth of what he had said was true, he was plainly also a dangerous blackguard. He, Captain Thomson would do his best to see he was brought to justice for his crimes. He said a great many other things too. Then Mrs Deal got up and said that, though she hadn't fully followed the discussion, she thought she felt sorry for Mr Tulip too; nevertheless she had come to the conclusion as well that, though apparently not technically in the Royal Navy, he was still a disgrace to the traditions of the sea.

Mr Tulip didn't answer, but just stared at his fingers. He looked gloomy, his fat mouth sucked into a tiny bud. Jane was reminded of his expression when he'd once lost at ping-pong. That reminded her of the time they'd first seen him and how he'd tap danced on the table, and refused to go swimming and all the lunches they'd eaten in the dining-room. She realized she'd grown very fond of him, even of his absurd way of talking and his jokes.

'We liked you so much, Mr Tulip,' she said. 'At least I liked you. Please don't try and blow up the ice, please be nice like you used to be. I don't want not to like you. Please, Mr Tulip.'

'Please, Mr Tulip,' said Jemima.

Mr Tulip looked up at them and stared without speaking. He looked very sad. At last he spoke.

'You don't understand, my dear, what it's like for people like me—if there is anyone else like me. There are things we can't control even if we wanted to.' He stood up and walked slowly to the door. Then without looking back he said, 'Take them away.'

They were each locked up in separate explosive storerooms on the Island. The sailors were not too gentle. Jane was thrown onto the beach and then dragged along by her hands. She heard Jemima cry out somewhere to her left and when Sergeant Cobbin who was close enough to see in the semi-darkness, shouted at the sailors, she saw one of them hit him on the side of his head with his fist.

It was hard and uncomfortable in the storeroom. They had turned the light off and there was just one blanket. Jane felt frightened and lonely. She didn't know where the others were. She suddenly longed for her mother and father to come and get her. Trying not to cry, she wrapped the blanket round her and lay down against one of the long wooden boxes and at last went off to sleep.

9. The Last Explosion

FOR a week the Island of Peeg continued to move steadily south-east towards the Ross Ice Shelf. The weather grew worse and at night, huddled in her blanket, Jane thought she could hear the sea pounding upon the rocks.

She never saw any of the others. Three times a day rather plain meals were brought to her on a tray. Every morning a guard would take her for an exercise walk on the cliff; three times along and back.

There were several guards, who took it in turn. Most were not very nice, one in particular being surly and silent. But one was younger and quite nice. He told her that Mr Tulip had helped him escape from a prison in America. He was so grateful that he'd joined the Pilut organization. He said the life was exciting and the pay good, but that he missed his mother.

'You're lucky,' he told Jane. 'Them two soldiers there is tied up and Sergeant Cobbin can't smoke, which he hates.'

'Is Jemima all right?' Jane asked.

'She's better than she was,' said the sailor. 'She don't cry near so much.'

'How's Mrs Deal?' said Jane.

'Weepy,' said the sailor, 'weepy at first. But she's completely changed since we gave her a duster.'

Twice Commander Hautboyes came in and asked her if she'd changed her mind and would like to join the Pilut organization. She said no. Her nice guard said that the others were visited by Mr Tulip.

'He really admires that Captain,' he said. 'He'd sure like to get him in our team.'

Jane wondered why Mr Tulip didn't visit her. 'He fears my persuasive tongue,' she thought.

It grew colder. She had to wear a coat for exercise, and at the end of the week there was half an inch of snow. The Island of Peeg shone under the grey skies and looked as it used to look in the winter term.

'Three more weeks and they say we'll be at the ice shelf,' said the nice guard. 'Then the fun begins.'

Jane had of course thought of escaping the moment she was thrown into the storeroom. But it did not take her long to see that she had no chance at all. The storeroom was hollowed out of the solid pumice stone and filled from floor to ceiling with heavy wooden boxes of explosive. There was only a small passage between the boxes, stretching from the door to the wall and here Jane had to sit on a small chair or lie on her blanket. After the first night, the light was left on all the time, coming from a feeble bulb in the middle of the ceiling.

Many times during those first, long, boring days she got up and minutely searched the rock face. She looked all over the ceiling to see if there were any cracks or holes she could enlarge. There was nothing.

It was the cold weather made Jane think of escaping again. Though snow fell every day now, it never grew any colder in the storeroom. She still only needed one blanket and wore exactly the same clothes as when she'd come in. It was, she realized, the ventilation. She suddenly remembered Sergeant Cobbin telling them about the fat tubes which carried dry air at the right temperature to every single explosive store. Immediately she began to look for her tube.

By climbing up the wooden boxes, she found that there was a small gap between the top ones and where the ceiling curved in its middle. She pushed her way down the gap, her back scraping against the rocky ceiling, until she reached the wall. She found that the boxes had not been packed quite tight against the wall. There was a gap of as much as ten inches, often more than a foot, between the wall and the boxes. By wriggling and pushing with first her tummy and then her knees and feet against the boxes and her back to the wall, Jane began to force a way down.

By evening she had reached the floor on the far side of the boxes and found, about a foot above it, the metal grills which led to her ventilation tube. She could put her hands through them and feel the warm air streaming through. She couldn't quite remember how wide

Sergeant Cobbin had said the tubes were, but she seemed to remember they were quite big.

She struggled up again and went back to wait in front of the door for her supper. Her shirt was torn and she'd scratched her face and hands quite badly on splinters and nails on the boxes. When the guard, one of the surly ones, came in he was quite surprised.

'What yer bin doing then?' he asked suspiciously.

'I sleep walk you know 'said Jane quickly. 'I walked in my sleep last night and spent all the time banging into those boxes and scraping against them.'

'I see,' said the guard, who was obviously rather stupid. 'Well—don't do it again.' He banged down some plain boiled fish and a suet pudding and walked out.

Jane waited until the plates had been collected and then climbed up the boxes again and down the other side. She soon found that though she could get her hands through the vents in the tube she could do nothing else. But after feeling about for a while she found a small loose nut on the inside. After undoing this she was able to pull a corner of the vent and make a small opening. The tops of the boxes were often loose and Jane was easily able to break off a wooden strut and use it as a lever. Two hours hard work, often with loud tinny noises which made her stop and listen, and she had wrenched quite a large opening in the ventilation tube—just large enough for her to squeeze through.

She felt much too tired to do that at once, so she decided to set off the next night when she was completely rested.

The day passed quicker than usual. Although of course excited, Jane also felt rather frightened at the idea of escaping, especially into a narrow tube. She wanted to put it off. But far too soon supper was eaten and the surly guard had locked the door.

The moment his footsteps had died away, Jane plumped her blanket so that it would look as though she were still in it. It was quite difficult getting into the ventilation tube, but eventually she was lying flat out, her arms ahead, her legs pointing towards the rushing air. She had decided that the sailors would have put her and Jemima and Mrs Deal in storerooms farthest from the Mess, since they would have wanted to keep Sergeant Cobbin and Captain Thomson as close to them as possible. She also decided that the warm air came from the engine room. Therefore, to go towards the Mess and away from the engine room she must move in the same direction as the air. Then she would be bound to pass Captain Thomson and Sergeant Cobbin's storerooms.

Sometimes there was several inches above her, sometimes hardly any room at all. But she managed to keep going by humping her bottom and then pushing with her feet and pulling with her hands. It was difficult, but steadily Jane began to hump and push her way slowly down the tube. There was a faint rushing noise in her ears; every now and then this changed its note as the air rushed through the vents into a storeroom. Each time this happened, Jane felt for them on the left and said through them, softly but clearly, 'Hullo—this is Jane Charrington. Is there anyone inside?'

There was never any answer. Jane began to think she'd made a mistake. Of course, she thought, they'd put Captain Thomson and Sergeant Cobbin *farther* away from them so as not to be bothered by them. Or perhaps the ventilation machine sucked air instead of blowing it and so really she was crawling towards the engine room. But it was impossible to turn round and she'd come much too far to try and go backwards. She felt exhausted and frightened. Soon, thought Jane, I shall be too tired to go farther and then I shall just lie here till I die of thirst.

And then, faint above the rushing air, she heard a strange noise coming from in front. It was a regular purring like a cat or small fan. Very carefully and slowly she humped herself forwards.

It was someone snoring. As she came level with the next set of ventilator holes, the steady, pulsing note was unmistakable. And Mrs Deal snored.

'Mrs Deal, Mrs Deal,' whispered Jane. 'Is that you?'

There was no answer. 'Mrs Deal,' said Jane.

'Mrs Deal,' she said loudly. 'MRS DEAL, MRS DEAL, MRS DEAL,' she shouted, not caring if she woke up every sailor on Peeg.

At last there came a grunting and stirring from the room the other side of the ventilator holes. Then a deep, familiar voice muttered, 'What's that? Who's that?' It was Captain Thomson.

'Captain Thomson,' cried Jane. 'It's me, Jane.'

'What?' Captain Thomson's voice was now wide awake. 'Who's there? Where?'

'It's me—Jane. Here,' shouted Jane.

She heard Captain Thomson moving rapidly about, muttering loudly. 'No one here. I'm going mad. They're breaking me down. Once four is four. Twice four is eight. Three fours . . .'

'Captain Thomson,' shouted Jane. 'Please. You're not mad. I'm in the ventilation tube. I can't get out. Help.'

Luckily the ventilation tube in Captain Thomson's storeroom was in the open bit of wall and not buried behind boxes of explosive. She heard his voice very close to the vents.

'Is that really you, Jane?'

'Yes,' said Jane.

'Goodness me. How wonderful. Come out. Goodness,' said Captain Thomson.

'I can't,' said Jane. 'How can I?'

'Slide it back,' said Captain Thomson. 'There should be a slideable panel. Wait a minute. The devils have tied me up, but I think I can do it from this side.'

There was a lot of grunting and then suddenly a sliding noise just by her ear. Jane stretched out her arm and found it waving in space. The next moment she had struggled out and was leaping about in the darkness.

'Hurrah! Hurrah!' she cried. 'Oh it's wonderful—I thought I'd never find anyone or ever get out.'

'You're a good girl, Jane,' said Captain Thomson, and his voice sounded quite shaky. 'I'd take you in my arms if the devils hadn't tied my hands.'

'Oh you poor thing,' said Jane. 'I'll undo them.' She felt her way round him and started to work on the rope tightly binding his wrists.

'How'd you get into the ventilation tube?' said Captain Thomson. 'Don't tell me that's where the brutes have been keeping you?'

Jane explained, and once again Captain Thomson said he would have hugged her if his hands hadn't still been tied. The knots were very tight, but after half an hour and using her teeth Jane managed to get them undone. Then Captain Thomson did indeed whirl her up and kissed her several times on the top of her head.

'You may have saved our lives,' he said.

Jane could feel his beard had grown quite long. 'Why are your lights off?' she said. 'Mine are left on all the time.'

'The silly fools were trying to break me down,' said Captain Thomson. 'A spot of darkness doesn't bother a chap who's lived underground for thirty years, I can tell you.

'Now,' went on Captain Thomson in a grim voice, 'now we must plan. You wrap yourself in my blanket and lie down opposite the door. I shall hide behind it. Then—we wait.'

Trembling with excitement, Jane wrapped herself in the blanket and then sat up against the wall to help him wait. Gradually, however, she sank lower down the wall. Her long hours in the ventilation tube had exhausted her. And it was a great relief to feel she could leave everything to Captain Thomson again. In ten minutes she was fast asleep.

At first excitement kept Captain Thomson wide awake. One of his worries was that, try as he might, he had completely forgotten every lesson in the unarmed combat leaflets; all the toe-holds, arm-locks, and various ways of bending, twisting, breaking and unbalancing an enemy which he had so carefully practised with Sergeant Cobbin had vanished from his mind. 'I shall have to rely on surprise,' he thought to himself. 'Let's hope it's one of the smaller sailors.' He settled himself for a long night. But he, too, was tired. The strain on him over the past week had been great. During the whole of that afternoon Mr Tulip had argued with him trying to get him to join Pilut. His head fell onto his chest and soon his steady snores joined the gentle breathing of Jane in the storeroom.

They were both woken at seven-thirty by the light being turned on and a sailor walking in with Captain Thomson's breakfast. When he saw Jane he stopped.

'What yer doin' here? This ain't your room.'

Jane, who had forgotten where she was, stirred sleepily and said, 'Don't be silly—of course it is.'

Almost at the same moment Captain Thomson, who had also forgotten, half-fell from behind the door rubbing his eyes.

'What are you doing to me?' he said loudly. 'I won't crack. I'm going mad. Where . . .'

At the sound of his voice the sailor whirled round dropping the breakfast. Immediately Captain Thomson remembered his plans and, recovering just before the sailor, jumped up and grabbed him with his huge hands.

The sailor was neither small nor nearly as old as Captain Thomson. On the other hand he had been taken by surprise and Captain Thomson was a very big man. They immediately began fighting so fiercely that Jane ran out into the tunnel to see if she could find something to hit the sailor with. But there was nothing to be seen—it stretched empty on either side, still immaculate from Mrs Deal's last enormous clean.

But by the time she hurried back, Captain Thomson was sitting on the sailor's chest. As she came in, he seized the sailor's revolver from his belt and sprang to the door.

'Get up,' he said. 'Get up and stand against the wall.'

Dazed, the sailor staggered up.

'Tie him up,' said Captain Thomson to Jane. 'Reef not Granny. Left over right, right over left.'

When she'd finished, Captain Thomson gave her the revolver and told her to shoot if the sailor moved at all.

'Shoot to kill,' he said.

Nervously Jane pointed the heavy gun roughly at the sailor's heart. Captain Thomson went behind him and swiftly added several more knots, pulling the rope tight and then taking the end down and tying it round the sailor's ankles.

When he'd finished, they hurried out and Captain Thomson locked the door behind them.

Outside, he stopped and looking at Jane said quietly, 'Jane, this is war. We must use our surprise. Counter-attack at once, mop up the enemy, then release our friends. Follow me.'

They kept well against the rocky wall of the tunnel, stopping every now and again to listen. But they reached the place where the tunnel mouth joined the ramp without seeing anyone, and soon came to the Mess itself. It was as they were creeping along the passage which led to the ante-room that they heard someone whistling.

'The kitchen,' whispered Captain Thomson.

Outside the kitchen Captain Thomson placed his fingers on his lips, pointed the revolver in front of him and boldly pushed the door open.

Standing at the stove with his back towards them stood Bob, the only nice sailor among their guards. He stopped whistling and said without looking round, 'You've taken your time, Bill. What kept you?'

'Put your hands up,' said Captain Thomson. 'Don't move. Get a rope from the cupboard, Jane. Hands up, young man. This is war. I shall not hesitate to shoot.'

They tied Bob to one of the kitchen chairs and then Captain Thomson asked how many more sailors were on Peeg.

'Wouldn't you like to know,' Bob said in a tough voice.

'Heat the poker in the stove,' said Captain Thomson to Jane. 'Push it well in.'

'You wouldn't dare,' said Bob.

Jane thought this too, but when Captain Thomson pulled the poker out with its handle wrapped in a dish cloth, and held it glowing in front of him she became rather nervous.

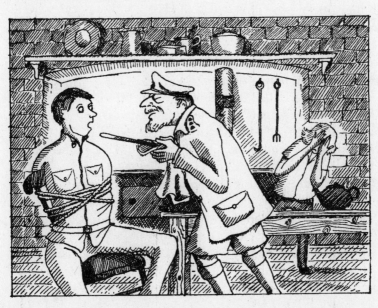

'Oh don't burn him, Captain Thomson,' she said. 'He was always the nicest.'

'I'm afraid war is never nice,' said Captain Thomson. 'It's his life or ours. Go into the ante-room if you don't like the smell of burning flesh. Better still, go somewhere where you won't hear his screams.'

But as she was walking away, Bob suddenly said, 'All right, all right, I'll talk. You can't escape anyway. No—there's only us two here.'

'When are you relieved?' said Captain Thomson.

'Twelve o'clock tomorrow,' Bob said.

'Good. We've a whole day,' said Captain Thomson. 'Do they ring up?'

'Sometimes,' said Bob.

'Very well,' said Captain Thomson. 'If they ring I shall untie you and you will say that all is well. Is that clear?'

'And if I don't?' said Bob.

Captain Thomson pushed the now cooling poker back into the stove. 'You will,' he said.

It did not take them long to find the others. They hurried back to the tunnel and after shouting a bit, traced them by answering shouts.

Jemima burst into tears as Jane rushed in and seized her in her arms.

'Oh Jane,' she sobbed. 'I've been so lonely and frightened. Have we been rescued? Oh that horrid man—he said we'd be blown up in two weeks.'

Mrs Deal was in fighting form. She had spent much of the time polishing and dusting her storeroom with a cloth, and it gleamed spotless when they opened the door.

'And not a minute too soon,' she said to Captain Thomson. 'I knew you'd get us out—but I had hoped sooner.'

'It was Jane here, ma'am,' said Captain Thomson. 'We owe a great debt to this young lady.'

'I shall tell your father and mother,' said Mrs Deal. 'Now—where's Mr Tulip? I'd like to give him the rough side of my tongue. Locking innocent young girls up—the idea! Were you alone?'

Jemima nodded, and at the memory two tears rolled down her cheeks. Mrs Deal picked her up and hugged her.

'You poor things,' she said. 'I'll give him a piece of my mind.'

Sergeant Cobbin seemed quite unworried by what had happened. He and Captain Thomson shook hands and immediately began to plan what they must do next.

'We've got our war at last, Sergeant,' said Captain Thomson.

The long years of training proved their worth. After a quick but large breakfast of dried egg, toast, tinned butter, tea, dried milk and, for a treat, some dried bananas they all set to work. Sergeant Cobbin, Jane and Jemima loaded the Peeg Special with petrol. This meant quite a long walk carrying heavy cans round the back of Mount Peeg so that there would be less chance of them being seen from *Tulip*. Captain Thomson got out his maps and tried to work out where they were and where they could fly to. Mrs Deal took the first watch at the top of the Blow-up room stairs, where their secret entrance opened on to the cliff. She was to give warning if anyone came from the submarine.

All day they worked, taking it in turns to watch from the cliff-top. The machinery to blow up the island had to be carefully checked. Warm clothes were got out of the store and tried on. 'We start at first light,' Captain Thomson had said. Maps, torches, binoculars and the engine-room compass—which had been returned while they were locked up—were all loaded into the Peeg Special's tiny cabin. Sergeant Cobbin gave them each a machine gun, a revolver and fifty rounds of ammunition. The telephone rang twice, but each time Captain Thomson seized the poker and made Bob tell them it was all all right.

By evening it was all completed. They went to bed early after a large supper.

'An army marches on its stomach,' said Captain Thomson. 'Tomorrow the outcome of the battle will be decided.'

They were up early. Jane and Jemima were so excited they woke at four o'clock and couldn't get to sleep again. But in any case, Mrs Deal came into their room at five o'clock while they were busy talking, and told them to get up quickly.

'The Captain wants to start at seven sharp,' she said.

'Gosh, how *exciting* it is,' said Jane.

'It is extremely dangerous,' said Mrs Deal in a rather disapproving voice. But when she had helped them both dress, in thick woolly underpants, khaki trousers and thick quilted wind jacket, she said, 'Well, yes—there is certainly an element of excitement. As you know, the Navy has always been my favourite among the services owing to my husband, followed closely, now, by the Army. But I've always had a soft spot for the Air Force. What do you think of these?'

She put her hand into the large pocket of her apron, which she was wearing over the same flying uniforms that Jane and Jemima had on, and pulled out a large pair of goggles. She put them on and went over to the looking glass.

'Quite becoming,' said Mrs Deal. 'It wouldn't surprise me if they became the vogue.' She turned her head sideways and patted her bun. Then she took two more pairs of goggles from her pocket and gave one each to the two girls. 'We're all to have them. In case the windows break in the Peeg Special.'

Captain Thomson's plan, as usual, was simple but brilliant. The Blow-up mechanism was to be set for a waiting period of twenty minutes. He was then going to ring up the submarine and tell them Peeg would blow up in twenty minutes. They would just have time to rescue the two sailors and escape themselves. Meanwhile the Peeg party would escape in the plane. The plan was possible because the blow-up machinery was of a very special sort. Once started it could not be stopped, not even if the Blow-up room itself was completely destroyed, because when the Blow-up room switch was pressed then a timing mechanism was started in every single storeroom. To stop the island blowing up then, all those timing machines would have to be found and destroyed, and they had all been hidden in the rock of each storeroom.

'When they come and get you,' Captain Thomson said, after explaining all this to Bob, 'you pass it on. Right?'

'Right,' said Bob, who had become quite docile.

Unfortunately there were still some adjustments to be made to the blowing-up machinery and at eight-thirty Captain Thomson and Sergeant Cobbin were still working feverishly at them. Jane and Jemima were both keeping watch at the top of the Blow-up room stairs.

Luckily it was neither raining nor snowing, but dark clouds poured across the sky hardly a hundred feet above the turbulent sea. Rising out of the waves, they could see several icebergs, some quite large, some no more than chunks, pitching and tossing like small boats.

Jane was looking lazily out, passing the binoculars back and forth over the just visible top of the submarine when she noticed to her surprise that it seemed to be rising higher and higher out of the water. When it was rough, the *Tulip* often went completely under water to pull Peeg, only coming up when it was necessary to send a boat ashore. This happened now. Before their horrified eyes, a boat was lowered from the submarine containing three tiny figures, and in a moment was roaring towards the island. Not, however, before Jane had recognized one of the men through her glasses.

'It's Mr Tulip,' she said to Jemima, as they raced down the Blow-up room stairs.

Captain Thomson was brisk and calm. 'Plan C, Sergeant,' he said. 'Mrs Deal, girls—hide a 100 yards down the tunnel. If we are captured, come and release us. Sergeant—you go inside that cupboard. I shall conceal myself in the ante-room. They will go first to the kitchen because that is where the guards have been sitting. I shall come quietly to the door and step smartly in. The moment you hear my voice,

Sergeant, step from the cupboard to complete the pincer movement.'

It all went as Captain Thomson had planned. Crouching in the tunnel, clutching their guns nervously to their chests, Jane, Jemima and Mrs Deal could just pick out the murmur of voices, among them, the high gay notes of Mr Tulip. Then after a pause they heard Captain Thomson's loud, giving-orders voice. About five minutes later Sergeant Cobbin called down the tunnel.

'Mrs Deal? You can all come back now. Job's done.'

Two new sailors and Mr Tulip were standing against the wall with their hands up. Captain Thomson, a revolver pointing at them, looked at his watch.

'Time to get cracking,' he said. 'Tie up those two sailors, Sergeant, then Jane, Jemima, you go and get the Peeg Special out.'

'What about me, darling?' said Mr Tulip. 'What dreadful fate have you in store for me?'

'You're coming with us, Tulip,' said Captain Thomson shortly. 'Sergeant—tie his hands behind his back. Mrs Deal—do you feel strong enough to guard him?'

'Oh dear,' said Mrs Deal. 'Using my—that is, might I have to fire my gun?'

'I hope not,' said Captain Thomson. 'But you know how to. Only shoot him in the legs.'

'Oh dear,' said Mrs Deal, 'I *think* I could. I'll try.'

'Plucky girl,' said Captain Thomson. 'March him to the top of the Blow-up stairs and you can watch the submarine at the same time. I shall adjust the timing mechanism, set it and then—off we go!'

Mrs Deal pointed her gun at Mr Tulip's knees. 'Quick march, Mr Tulip,' she said firmly. 'To the ante-room. Walk in front of me.'

Jemima, Jane and Sergeant Cobbin all hurried up on to the cliff and ran up to the cave where the Peeg Special had been concealed. It was very heavy but fortunately the ground sloped downhill and once they had pulled the wooden blocks away from in front of the wheels, it rolled downhill itself with Sergeant Cobbin sitting in the pilot's seat to put the brakes on.

They had just turned it round and were arranging things inside the tiny cabin when suddenly, so loud it made them all jump, there came the sound of furious shooting from farther back along the cliff-top. Sergeant Cobbin seized his gun and jumped from the plane.

'Glory me,' they heard him say. 'Mrs Deal's gorn off her rocker.'

The old-fashioned machine guns were short little guns which could fire thirty bullets one after another. They had lots of knobs and clips and used to rattle a lot. They often went wrong and in nervous hands would suddenly start firing for no reason at all and were almost impossible to stop.

This was what had happened to Mrs Deal. Looking across to the rocks and bushes which concealed the Blow-up room entrance, they saw Mr Tulip come rushing out, closely followed by Mrs Deal. Mrs Deal's gun was firing continuously, but instead of throwing it away, she was swinging it wildly about, so that bullets whirled past Mr Tulip and even tore into the ground at her own feet. The firing stopped. Mr Tulip turned and bolted back into the bushes around the Blow-up stairs door.

Mrs Deal continued running towards the plane.

But worse was to follow. The sound of the gun had alerted the submarine. As they watched the bridge rose up on its top. They could see men running about under the glass dome and then panels opened along the side of the submarine and three large boats slid out crammed with sailors.

'Go and get the Captain,' Sergeant Cobbin shouted to Jane. 'Jemima, you help me get this stuff stowed. I'll start her engines. Hurry.'

Jane shouted, 'Help Jemima and Sergeant Cobbin get everything arranged,' to Mrs Deal as she passed. But Mrs Deal, face set, her bun beginning to unravel, ran on towards the plane without answering.

When Jane reached the ante-room Mr Tulip, shaking and trembling, was on his knees before Captain Thomson. 'Save me! Save me!' he was crying. 'She's gone mad. She tried to kill me. Don't leave me. I won't do anything.'

When Jane rushed in, he gave a loud scream, and tried to crawl behind Captain Thomson's legs, only stopping when he saw it was Jane.

'Oh thank goodness, darling,' he said. 'I thought you were that lunatic. What's she doing? Re-loading?'

'Boats are coming from the submarine,' panted Jane. 'Sergeant Cobbin's starting the engines.'

'Right,' said Captain Thomson. 'I'm coming at once. Get back to the plane and help. Tulip—get up. You'll stay by me.'

When Jane arrived back at the Peeg Special its engine was roaring and it was straining against the large rocks which had been put in front of its wheels. Looking across to the submarine, Jane saw that the boats were well on their way to the island.

'Where's the Captain?' shouted Sergeant Cobbin above the roar of the engine.

'He's coming,' shouted Jane.

But there was no sign of Captain Thomson. The boats bounced and tossed on the waves, surging forward with their powerful engines. Sergeant Cobbin unslung his gun from his shoulder.

'Mrs Deal,' he called. 'Take Jemima's gun and come and help me head them off. Girls—you stay here.'

'I'm not touching one of those weapons again as long as I live,' shouted Mrs Deal, who had already climbed into the Peeg Special.

Sergeant Cobbin hesitated, then said, 'Right—Jane and Jemima, give me your guns and stay here.'

The two girls stood and watched him run to the cliff-top. The plane roared and shuddered behind them. They couldn't hear Sergeant Cobbin's gun, but the boats began to swerve and dodge. He threw away one gun and picked up another. Still the boat drew nearer and suddenly Jane heard a noise like a whip cracking above her head. The sailors were firing back.

And then at last Captain Thomson appeared from the Blow-up room. He was staggering under two immense loads; under one arm, kicking and struggling, was Mr Tulip, under the other he held a huge sack.

He and Sergeant Cobbin reached the plane at the same time.

'Help me get this man in,' Captain Thomson shouted.

'I won't. I won't,' shouted Mr Tulip, struggling violently. 'Won't, won't, won't.'

But Sergeant Cobbin seized his shoulders and Captain Thomson his legs and they threw him into the cabin. Captain Thomson bent down and picked up his sack.

'What's that?' shouted Sergeant Cobbin.

'A few rocks,' shouted Captain Thomson. 'My geological specimens.'

'We're not taking those,' shouted Sergeant Cobbin. 'We'll be lucky if we get off as it is.'

'It's thirty years' work,' shouted Captain Thomson.

'I'm not trying to take off with that,' Sergeant Cobbin shouted back.

They stood glaring at each other, Captain Thomson clutching his sack as though it were a large baby. But at that moment they heard the sound of guns above the roar of the engine. The sailors had climbed the cliff and were kneeling along its top, firing at them.

'Get in the plane,' yelled Captain Thomson, dropping his sack of geological specimens. 'Girls—this is fire and movement.' He wrenched his gun off his shoulders and sent a shower of bullets along the cliff-top. The sailors ducked down.

Sergeant Cobbin sprang into the plane and a moment later the engine died to a loud mutter.

'Jane, Jemima,' Sergeant Cobbin shouted from his cock-pit. 'Pull away the stones.'

The two girls did so and then, terrified now by the sailors' bullets,

which despite Captain Thomson's firing were still hitting the ground all round them, rushed to the plane. Mrs Deal pulled them in. Captain Thomson fired a last burst of bullets, bent down, flung his sack of rocks into the cabin on top of Mr Tulip, and pulled himself in, slamming the door behind him. The engine rose to a roar and very slowly they began to bump along the grass.

Through the tiny window Jane saw the sailors spring up from along the edge of the little cliff and start to to run after the plane. The Peeg Special trundled a bit faster, but still firmly on the ground. Faster—the sailors were left behind but now knelt and fired. Faster—the engine roaring, the cabin shaking; but still they were on the ground. Jane and Jemima, noses pressed to the windows, could see the grass whizzing by, feel the bumps as they raced over the stones and holes. They must be getting near the end of the cliff. Oh why, Jane thought, had Captain Thomson thrown all the rocks in? Faster.

Suddenly Sergeant Cobbin looked round and yelled into the cabin, 'I can't do it. I can't get her off. We're too heavy.'

It was too late to do anything. With engine roaring, the Peeg Special reached the end of the cliff and roared straight over the edge. There was a sudden sinking in their stomachs as it fell towards the sea. And then, as the waves actually broke over the wheels, it stopped falling. They raced along just above the white crests and at last, slowly, slowly, began to rise into the air. Higher and higher they rose, turning all the time, until four minutes later Sergeant Cobbin was able to fly back quite high above the island on course for Australia.

Captain Thomson looked at his watch. 'We've got ten minutes till she blows up,' he shouted. 'Keep her on full throttle, Sergeant. We don't want to be hoist with our own petard.'

Looking down on Peeg, Jane and Jemima could just make out the sailors rushing out from the Mess and running across the cliff and the beach to their boats. The submarine already looked quite small.

'They may just make it,' cried Captain Thomson above the roar of the engine. 'But they've got to cast off and then dive deep. Very deep and very fast. I doubt they'll do it.'

Jane could see where the school had been before the hurricane had blown it away. Its foundations were clearly out-lined on the turf. She could see Captain Thomson's garden. She could see the top of Mount Peeg where Sergeant Cobbin had sunbathed. She could see the foam at the back of the island where the gallant engines still forced the island on. She realized that she had grown very fond of Peeg and hardly wanted to see it blown up.

She looked at Captain Thomson. His red face was set and expressionless. Every now and then he looked at his watch. He held the binoculars to his eyes and stared back at Peeg as it disappeared behind them.

Jane and Jemima looked back too, sharing one of the little windows now, because Mrs Deal and Mr Tulip had revived sufficiently to crouch next to each other and Captain Thomson had the third. The island grew smaller and smaller. First the submarine seemed to merge with it, then the cliff became hard to distinguish. Below them the sea was grey and wrinkled, with occasional icebergs like toys on the crumpled blanket of a giant's bed. It became difficult to make out the mountain. The whole of Peeg looked like a mound in the distance. Captain Thomson looked at his watch. The mound became a loaf.

'She's going in thirty seconds,' Captain Thomson shouted to Sergeant Cobbin. Sergeant Cobbin switched the automatic steering on and turned to look back through his cock-pit window.

The loaf became a fist. 'Now!' cried Captain Thomson.

But still Peeg sat there, still distinguishable in the grey distance. For at least a minute they watched it. Jane thought—'It won't go up. They've made a mistake.'

And then, very slowly, the island began to swell. It grew twice, three times its normal size, until silently, almost gently it opened up in the middle and a vast white ball, too bright to look at, grew out of the opening. Then the white ball began to shoot upwards, creating as it went a great shaft of black smoke like the trunk of a thick tree in which flames and sudden balls of fire appeared and vanished.

They heard the first rumble of the explosion above the engine and then the plane was suddenly seized by a blast of air and whirled violently sideways. Jane and Jemima were flung together across the cabin and the plane fell towards the sea.

For five minutes they were tossed and buffeted by the winds from the explosion. Sergeant Cobbin wrestled with the controls. They caught glimpses of the island through the windows; the fire ball splitting up and expanding, the black cloud rising higher and higher. The rumbling grew fainter.

Gradually the air became calmer, the plane flew level. Sergeant Cobbin throttled the engine back to save petrol and its roar sank to a steady drone.

Jane and Jemima looked out of the little window and back over the sea. The fire and flashing of the explosion had gone. A vast, perfect mushroom cloud had formed in the sky such as they had seen in pictures of atomic bombs, and was now beginning to drift northwards, its shape slowly distorting in the winds. Of the Island of Peeg there was no sign.

10. Home Again

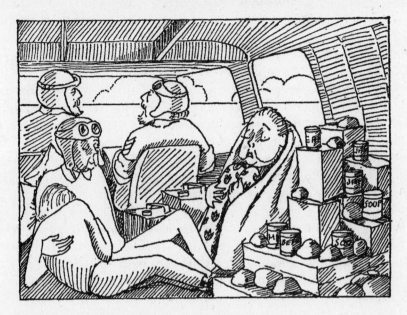

THERE is not a great deal more to tell.

The journey to Australia was long and uncomfortable. Jane sat on Mrs Deal's lap and Jemima on Captain Thomson's. Mr Tulip sat in a little space on the floor, surrounded by food, tins of petrol and pressed into by Captain Thomson's sack of rocks.

It was extremely cold at first. Luckily their clothes were very warm, but Mr Tulip soon began to shiver and shake in his thin silk uniform.

'You should wear more sensible clothes,' said Captain Thomson, who had secretly always rather disapproved of the white uniform.

'Sweetie, if I'd known you were planning this little trip I'd have put on something cosier,' said Mr Tulip irritably, his teeth chattering.

After a while, Captain Thomson put his rock specimens all round the cabin and gave Mr Tulip the sack to wrap round his shoulders.

On and on droned the Peeg Special. It began to grow dark. Sergeant Cobbin had fitted a tube from the reserve fuel tank into the cabin so that he could pour petrol down it from the cans. They had enough fuel to take them two thousand miles, but with all the extra weight Sergeant Cobbin thought it would be touch and go.

They had supper and then sat uneasily dozing, listening to the engine and trying to keep warm. At two o'clock in the morning Sergeant Cobbin clambered stiffly back from his cockpit and asked Captain Thomson to take over. Captain Thomson was a little worried, although he had been taught what to do. But nothing happened, and at four o'clock Sergeant Cobbin took over again.

At ten o'clock that morning, just twenty-four and a half hours after they had left Peeg, the west coast of Australia rose up over the horizon. Half an hour later, with one can of petrol left, they bumped to a stop in a small field outside the little town of Nornabys.

After a bath, a sleep and a large lunch, they were driven north to Perth and then flown for questioning to Canberra. Here, the first thing they insisted on doing was sending telegrams to tell everyone they were alive. Mrs Deal sent one to her brother Frank in Peeblesshire. Jane and Jemima sent one to their parents. Captain Thomson and Sergeant Cobbin said sadly that they didn't suppose anyone would remember them, but in the end they sent one to the War Office.

The police and Australian Secret Service seemed to believe nothing. But everyone in Canberra was very excited by the explosion of Peeg, which the scientists had thought was a Chinese atom bomb. Captain Thomson was able to point out on the map more or less where it had happened and this agreed with the scientists' calculations. Secret documents Captain Thomson had brought from Peeg also impressed them.

But it was Mr Tulip they were most interested in and which finally made them take everything else seriously. The Pilut organization had already been in touch with the Australian Government and they had been very worried. At first they didn't believe Mr Tulip was Mr Tulip, until photographs and other details, despite Mr Tulip's strenuous denials, proved who he was. Then their whole attitude changed at once.

'Do you mean he really did the things he said he did?' Jane asked the officer who was questioning them.

'He is a dangerous international criminal,' said the officer. 'Precisely what he's been up to it's difficult to say. But he is wanted in several countries and whether or not the rest of your extraordinary story is true you have done a great service in catching him.'

Mr Tulip was taken away from them that same evening. He looked so forlorn, and at the same time brave in his crumpled uniform, that Jane and Jemima ran after him to the door.

'Goodbye, Mr Tulip,' said Jemima.

'Come and see us when they let you out of prison,' said Jane.

Mr Tulip looked pleased and bending down kissed them each gently on the cheek. 'Thank you, darlings,' he whispered. 'But don't worry. They won't keep me long. I promise you, darlings, I'll see you before the year is out.'

When he'd gone, Mrs Deal said, 'I've a feeling we'll see that rogue again. He's a bad penny—whatever his charm.'

Their story sounded so fantastic (especially as a telegram to London had discovered that no one there had even heard of 'Project Peeg'), and at the same time was so important since it was not only about the Pilut plan to nearly destroy Australia but about British wartime secrets as well, that it was decided to fly them to London. Their presence had been kept secret and they were flown out two nights later in a large airliner, in which, to Mrs Deal's excitement, they travelled first class. Before they left they were allowed to send telegrams telling their relations when they would arrive.

Although the Australians were now very polite, Jane could see that they were still suspicious. Two policemen went with them, though they sat discreetly behind them all the way.

'They think we're part of the Pilut organization,' said Captain Thomson angrily. 'I bet Tulip's been spinning some tale.'

A great many times during their questioning he'd said sternly to the Australians, 'We are serving members of His Majesty's Armed Forces.'

'Her Majesty's,' said Jane.

'Her Majesty's then,' said Captain Thomson, impatiently swinging his goggles.

The first thing that happened at London Airport was Mr and Mrs Garing. Jemima rushed into their arms, bursting into tears, and Mr and Mrs Garing were both crying too.

'Darling, darling,' sobbed Mr Garing.

But there was no sign of Jane's mother and father, and though she asked all the policemen and airport people they said there had been no message.

'They must be in America still,' said Mrs Deal, holding Jane in her arms. 'You'll see them soon.'

'Yes I will, won't I?' said Jane, trying not to cry. And then she suddenly burst into tears, and clinging to Mrs Deal sobbed, 'I will see them soon. I will.'

There was a telegram for Mrs Deal which said: 'Thank you for telegram. Had no idea you were meant to be dead. Frank.'

'Well, I suppose I must be glad he was spared the agony of uncertainty,' said Mrs Deal, somewhat put out.

Jemima was allowed to drive from the airport with her mother and father, though they had to drive between the large black car in which the others drove, and a police car following.

'VIP treatment,' said Mrs Deal, settling back into the large comfortable seat. 'I feel quite the little pop star.'

'Pop stars aren't followed by police,' said Jane. 'We're more like famous criminals.'

'Well, as long as we're famous,' said Mrs Deal dreamily.

All the way Captain Thomson and Sergeant Cobbin were amazed at the changes, especially as they got deeper and deeper into London. 'Do you remember poor old London when we last saw her, Sergeant?' Captain Thomson said.

'The blitz?' said Sergeant Cobbin. 'She took a proper beating right enough.'

'Brave boys of Biggin Hill,' said Captain Thomson. 'Look—they've dug a hole under Hyde Park Corner.'

At Whitehall, where Jemima's parents had to stay behind in a waiting room, they were hurried through long corridors and eventually shown into a large room overlooking St James's Park. Captain Thomson paced nervously up and down.

'Brings it back, eh?' said Sergeant Cobbin. Captain Thomson nodded. Mrs Deal still had a dreamy smile on her face and was moving very slowly and gracefully. Somewhat to his embarrassment, she had given her arm to the young man who had led them to the room.

'I feel like a queen,' she'd whispered to Jane and Jemima.

They hadn't waited long when the door opened and a tall, grey-haired man in uniform, with a large red face, walked heavily in and stopped, looking at them all.

'Good morning,' he said. 'I'm General Herkenshaw. How do you do?' He looked at them rather grimly again, and then suddenly leant forward, staring at Captain Thomson. He took two slow steps, still staring, and then suddenly bellowed, 'It's Tony Thomson! Tony! My dear fellow—where have you been all these years?'

Captain Thomson was also advancing, his face red and jolly. 'Bill!' he cried. 'Bill a General. I'd never have believed it. Wonderful to see you, old man.'

They shook hands and almost embraced. Then General Herkenshaw turned to Sergeant Cobbin and said, 'No—don't tell me. Wait a moment. It's on the tip of my tongue—*Cobbin*. That's it—it's Cobbin, isn't it?'

'Sir!' cried Sergeant Cobbin, pink in the face and standing stiffly to attention.

'Sergeant Cobbin of D Squadron,' said the General.

'Sir!' yelled Sergeant Cobbin, standing even more stiffly.

'At ease, Sergeant, at ease,' said the General kindly. 'Now Tony—introduce me.'

'This is Mrs Deal,' said Captain Thomson. 'This is Miss Jemima Garing, this is Miss Jane Charrington.'

'Not the ex-Earl's daughter, not Chris Charrington?' cried General Herkenshaw, again amazed.

'Yes,' said Jane.

'By all that's wonderful,' said the General. 'I know your father well, young lady. He's due back from America soon with your dear mother. It's all very hush hush of course—as usual. But within a week. But what is all this, Tony? I was told you were possible defecting Pilut agents. Perhaps the leaders.'

'It's a long story, Bill,' said Captain Thomson.

'And you must tell it,' said the General. 'But you must be tired. You, madam—have you had a bath?'

'A bath would certainly be gratefully appreciated,' said Mrs Deal graciously.

'Where are these good people staying?' the General said over his shoulder to the Lieutenant who had accompanied him.

'Well, sir,' said the Lieutenant, 'the Minister said they were to be kept in custody.'

'Nonsense, nonsense,' cried General Herkenshaw. 'These are friends of mine. Tony and I went to Aldershot together—and then to India, eh, Tony? No—get Sergeant Cobbin, Mrs Deal, Miss Garing and Miss Charrington rooms in the Ritz. Tony, you'd better come along with me.'

'Jemima's mother and father are here, Bill,' Captain Thomson said.

'Then she must stay with them,' said General Herkenshaw, 'and no doubt, until her mother and father get back, young Jane would like to stay with them too.'

So began their two days of questioning. But it was much easier and nicer than in Australia. Captain Thomson told General Herkenshaw almost everything over their lunch, and for the rest of the time they just had to be there in case there were more questions.

It was soon discovered that the train carrying the workers who had made Project Peeg back to England had been totally destroyed by a bomb. This the two soldiers knew already. But it was then discovered that the building in which the Project would have been planned, and where all its records would have been kept, had also been totally destroyed. So secret had Project Peeg been that the only other living person who knew about it had been Winston Churchill, and they supposed, in the turmoil of war, he had forgotten about it.

'If we'd known about Project Peeg,' said General Herkenshaw, 'of course we'd have made a search. We'd have thought twice about the falling-to-bits theory the scientists suggested.'

It was also found out that the Island of Peeg had been seen at least five times in their journey south. Two ships had seen them and three aeroplanes. But when anyone tried to see the new island again it had of course moved on and no one could find it.

Then, on the second day, a copy of a short letter was found in Winston Churchill's private papers. It said, that in view of the progress of the war, Project Peeg was no longer necessary and should be discontinued immediately. The letter was dated the very day in which the whole building to do with Project Peeg was destroyed by a flying bomb.

'It must have been delivered and then immediately destroyed in the explosion,' said General Herkenshaw, 'before anything could be done. That explains why Winston did nothing more. He imagined his orders had been carried out. I thought the old boy wouldn't have forgotten something like this, which must have been very dear to his heart.'

But Captain Thomson and Sergeant Cobbin were very depressed by the discovery of Winston Churchill's letter. They felt it meant they had been wasting their time. General Herkenshaw soon cheered them up.

'On the contrary,' he said. 'Yours is the spirit which won us the war. It's what I'd have expected of you both and I hope I'd have had the guts to do the same. What is more, you have caught—you five have caught—a very dangerous criminal we have been after for some years. The man Tulip. I shall see you are rewarded for both actions.'

Captain Thomson was promoted to full Colonel, and Sergeant Cobbin, at his own request not made an officer, to Regimental Sergeant-Major. Captain Thomson was awarded the Distinguished Service Cross and Sergeant Cobbin the Distinguished Conduct Medal. Their pay was also given them for the whole thirty years they had been on the island. In addition to this, there was a reward of fifty thousand pounds for the capture of Mr Tulip, which they all shared.

'It's no more than you deserve,' said General Herkenshaw. 'And I'm glad that this little bonus, plus gratuity, demob pay, back pay and no doubt some journalist and TV fees will make you, Tony, and you, Sergeant-Major Cobbin, comparatively wealthy men.'

The news was then given to the public and for three days they were interviewed, photographed, and appeared on TV. Only Mrs Deal seemed to enjoy it.

Mr and Mrs Garing, who had been very kind to Jane, took Jemima away home soon after the questioning was over. They said that Miss Boyle had started a new school on an island called Isle Ornsay off Skye, but that Jemima wasn't going to it. They asked Jane to come and stay but she said she'd wait in London till her mother and father came back. And, two days later, they did.

When Jane met her father and mother at the airport she was so pleased and excited she forgot everything else. Mr Charrington whirled her high into the air and kissed her from the top of her head to the tips of her toes. Mrs Charrington held her close and said, 'My darling, my little darling.'

Soon it was all explained. Mr Charrington was a very distinguished space scientist. The Government had suddenly sent him on an extremely urgent and secret space mission to America. So secret and urgent was the mission in fact that the arrangements for sending him letters hadn't worked. No one knew where he was—except those too busy and secret and important to bother with forwarding letters. As a result he and Mrs Charrington had never got Miss Boyle's telegram and letter, nor Jane's telegram, and as they hadn't often read the English papers, they hadn't any idea anything was wrong at all.

'Except we did think you were writing rather few letters,' said Mr Charrington. 'But then you always do that, my sweet.'

It all came out in General Herkenshaw's flat, where they had driven from the airport. Mr Charrington was immediately furious and made several angry telephone calls. Mrs Charrington held her daughter in her arms again. 'How could you bear it, darling?' she said.

'Well, Mrs Deal would say it's a mercy you were spared the agony of uncertainty,' said Jane. 'But I'd have liked you not to have been spared all of it. You could have had a twinge and then you'd have been even more pleased to see me.'

'We *couldn't* be more pleased,' said Mrs Charrington, hugging her again.

'It won't happen again,' said Mr Charrington.

Captain Thomson and Sergeant Cobbin (or rather Colonel and RSM) were in General Herkenshaw's flat too. And soon Mr and Mrs Charrington were listening enthralled and amazed to their daughter's adventures. When the tale was ended, Mr Charrington walked over to the two soldiers and shook their hands.

'Colonel, RSM,' he said, 'you've brought our daughter through safely. I'm deeply grateful.'

'Your daughter brought us through safely,' said Colonel Thomson. 'If it wasn't for her we'd still be locked in the storerooms inside Peeg. She's a fine girl.'

'If it weren't for her I'd be at the bottom of the sea,' said RSM Cobbin.

Jane blushed modestly and then said quickly, 'Can they come and stay at Aldeburgh with us, Daddy?'

'They're more than welcome,' said Mr Charrington. 'I hope we'll see a great deal of them before we go. But that's a piece of news I haven't had time to tell you. We're off to Cape Kennedy next week for two years. You, mummy, Mrs Deal and me.'

'Oh! but they must come too,' cried Jane, suddenly realizing she couldn't bear not to see the two soldiers again.

'Don't you worry, Miss Jane,' said RSM Cobbin. 'We'll all meet again.'

They spent one more day in London and then it was time to go down to Aldeburgh.

The two soldiers came to Liverpool Street to say goodbye. As they all stood on the platform Jane felt very sad. Even if they did just meet once or twice, she felt they wouldn't meet often. The two soldiers were upset too. When the whistle blew and RSM Cobbin picked her up his face was quite red and his voice was hoarse.

'Now off you go, Miss Jane,' he whispered. 'We'll see you very soon.'

She thought she saw tears in Colonel Thomson's eyes as well.

'There's a good girl,' was all he could say as he held her in his big arms. 'There's a good girl.'

The train was moving. They were all in a first-class carriage. Jane suddenly burst into tears and pulled her head in from the window.

'We must see them again,' she sobbed. 'For a nice long time. Always.'

'We will, darling,' said Mrs Charrington gently. 'We'll have them out to Cape Kennedy for a long holiday.'

'Promise?' said Jane.

'Promise,' said Mrs Charrington, and at once Jane felt better.

'Now you come in,' said Mr Charrington. 'Don't want your head knocked off. Come and sit by me, my sweet.'

But Jane kept her head out a little longer, and went on waving and waving until the two old soldiers grew smaller and smaller and eventually, as the train went round a corner, disappeared altogether.

Jane's Adventures
in a balloon

For Tino

1. The Airship

SOON after Mr and Mrs Charrington got back from America, Mr Charrington was knighted *Sir* Christopher Charrington for services to science. So once again, to her delight, Mrs Charrington became *Lady* Charrington.

They also decided to move temporarily back to Curl Castle. The reason was that many years before, Sir Christopher had decided that as modem travel grew faster and more crowded, what people would like would be slowness and emptiness. He had therefore designed an Airship which would provide all those things.

Sir Christopher was not the only person who thought this. So did a number of rich businessmen, among them a German called Herr Grudheim. A year before, this man had agreed to build the Airship.

Sir Christopher Charrington had made one condition. Although his Airship was to be made in Germany, he wanted it put together and launched from Curl Castle.

First, a large hangar was put up in the field behind the Observatory. And soon after that, long trucks came roaring slowly up the narrow lanes loaded with bits of Airship. More and more workmen came and lived in tents just outside Inkpen village.

Jane used to go every day and watch the Airship being put together. At first all was confusion: men shouting and waving, huge pieces (but very light) of metal swinging from cranes, and nothing seeming to come together. But gradually the skeleton of what looked like an enormous whale began to appear. Her father explained that the Airship was quite small as Airships went.

'It will only be 425 feet long,' he said. 'And do you see how the body is divided into sections? Each of those will contain a separate balloon, for reasons I'll explain to you later.'

By the end of October the frame was completed and there took place what airshipmen call "The Enveloping", which is when the Airship is named.

For two days everyone worked without stopping, fixing on to the frame the enormous cover of Dacron and aluminium. When they had finished, for the first time the Airship looked like an Airship. It was towed, a gleaming, quivering sausage, slowly out into the sun. The hundred Cornish workmen stood and watched. Sir Christopher and Lady Charrington, Jane, Herr Grudheim and one or two others, climbed the steps of a small platform. Sir Christopher Charrington said, 'Now, you name her, darling.'

'But you haven't told me her name,' whispered Lady Charrington.

'Well, because you're a tiny bit of a snob,' said Sir Christopher, 'I thought we'd call her something you'd like—*Airship Ladyship*.'

'Oh darling!' laughed Lady Charrington. 'I suppose I *am* a snob. Oh dear. But you must agree it is a lovely name.'

So Lady Charrington pulled back the bottle of champagne and then said clearly and loudly into the microphone, 'I have much pleasure in naming this Airship—*Airship Ladyship*, and God bless all who fly in her.'

Then she let the champagne smash against the side of the *Airship Ladyship* and, while all the men cheered, the Airship was towed slowly back into the hangar.

Now that the enveloping had been done things went forward swiftly. The part where the passengers and crew were going to be was to be hung underneath the *Ladyship* so that wide windows and glass floors would provide the largest views possible. While this was being assembled, two nuclear engines arrived on lorries and for a week they roared and screamed, being tested at the far end of the field. A small gas manufacturing plant was built in the valley and began to make helium.

The inside of the *Ladyship* was to be decorated by Lady Charrington. At first she was rather nervous of doing it because she said the only sort of decorating she liked was what people had liked in 1930. But then she found all the smart people in magazines liked that too, so everything became quite easy.

All the cabins, with bathroom and sitting-room, were put along the bottom so that they could have large windows and glass floors. In the middle was the ballroom, and above this the dining-room and kitchen. These two had a special gyroscope so that they would stay level, however rough the winds. At the front was the control room where the pilot sat. On the outside, half-way up, there was an open promenade, with lifeboats every twenty yards.

November and December passed, Christmas came and then it was the New Year. Every day Jane hurried up to the hangar and watched the *Ladyship* grow. When the engines had been fitted in, one of the pilots, a kind man called Henry, showed her how to work the fairly simple controls. Jane wasn't sure she'd understood.

Soon after this, the twenty balloons which were to carry the *Ladyship* were fitted inside the envelope. Sir Christopher was particularly pleased

with these and explained to Jane, in almost too great detail, exactly how they worked.

'Most Airships have been raised or lowered by throwing out ballast, letting out gas, or using altitude rudders and flaps,' he said, as Jane followed him along a catwalk underneath the vast skin of the envelope. '*Ladyship* works quite differently, thanks to a little invention of my own. Each balloon is fitted with a pump, worked by hand in emergency, but usually by power, which pumps the gas out and returns it as a liquid to the cylinders you see there. If all the balloons are emptied, we fall; when they are filled again we rise.'

He stopped and looked down from the catwalk to the top of the movie theatre 40 feet below. Jane, little realizing that all this information was later to save her life, began to feel rather bored.

'The balloons are filled with helium,' boomed her father. 'Why?'

'Because it doesn't burn,' said Jane automatically. He asked her this question at least three times a week.

'Excellent,' said Sir Christopher. 'Now, here's another interesting thing about the balloons. Each one supports the segment of Airship immediately below it. In the event of an emergency, each section of the *Ladyship* can be instantly sealed off and then automatically released. The *Ladyship* can in fact be considered as twenty separate compartments, each supported by its own balloon, all joined firmly together, the balloons covered in an hermetic skin.'

'Yes, Daddy,' said Jane.

The weather grew colder. Radar scanners and sonic height indicators were fitted and the cabins became sufficiently furnished for Mrs Deal to come in and start to supervise the cleaning. At the end of January a date was fixed for the launch.

It had to be postponed. When the balloons were filled with helium several pumps were found to be faulty. Also the computer, which really ran the *Ladyship*, had to be reprogrammed. The heating system broke down and Jane wore overcoat and gloves as she ran about inside the Airship, or helped Mrs Deal, desperate to finish, as she raced up and down the promenade on a mobile floor polisher. A new date was fixed.

It, too, had to be postponed. One of the nuclear reactors sprang a tiny leak and instantly sealed itself. A mile of beige carpet was sent to Scotland by mistake. But now, journalists and reporters had got interested and Jane gave several interviews. It snowed for three days.

Finally, Sir Christopher announced that all faults had been mended. Every system was checked and rechecked. Nothing went wrong. The day of the launch was announced for Wednesday, February 14th.

But, although mechanically all was well, even two days before the launch much remained to be done. All day and far into the night the hundred

workmen swarmed round the *Ladyship* like ants round the most enormous ant egg. Drills buzzed, bolts were tightened and large tankers discharged their cargo of liquid helium. In the middle of all this, seeming
to need no sleep at all, Sir Christopher rushed hither and thither, gal-
vanizing, encouraging, scolding.

And the activity outside the *Ladyship* was equalled by that inside. In
fact, surpassed. Although, of course, no one expected the decorating to
be finished in time for the launch, Lady Charrington was determined
it should be as near finished as possible. Martin Newall, the famous
designer, came down to help and all day and far into the night the two
of them whirled from Curl to *Ladyship*, from *Ladyship* to Curl, trailing
yards of swag curtains or panels of mural, their arms full of plans and
sketches, their mouths full of pins.

But even their activity was as nothing compared to that of Mrs Deal.
Earl Mountbatten, an old friend of Sir Christopher, had agreed to
launch the *Ladyship*. His position as an Admiral of the Fleet and First Sea
Lord, was enough to raise Mrs Deal—a great admirer of the navy—to a
state of near frenzy. She prayed for some catastrophe to delay the launch
another week, and was even tempted to prick a balloon, so that she
would have time to get everything clean enough to satisfy the great man.

Then at lunchtime on the day before the launch, Sir Christopher
ordered that all work was to stop.

'I want everyone to go and rest, ready for the big day tomorrow,' he
said. 'And I mean *everyone*—including my darling wife, you Martin, and
especially you, Mrs Deal.'

It was a long time before Jane could get to sleep. Her father had said
that she could fly the *Ladyship* for some of the time the next day, and
she tried to remember what the pilot Henry had told her about the
controls. Perhaps there would be an accident, though Sir Christopher
said Airships were really the safest way to travel. Finally, she slept.

It was still dark when she woke up. From the coldness, she guessed
it must be before 4 o'clock which was when the central heating turned
itself on. Sure enough, a little later the big clock in the hall went bong-
bong-bong-bong. Four hours to wait till breakfast.

Suddenly she thought she'd go and look at the Airship. She was far
too excited to sleep any more, but more particularly she wanted to look
at the controls again. She'd woken up even more worried about flying
the Airship than when she'd gone to sleep.

It was dark and very cold when she crept out of the kitchen door
and, pointing the torch ahead, hurried up the path towards the hangar.
There were no stars in the sky so Jane guessed it must be cloudy, which
her father had hoped it wouldn't be. There was a light wind.

The Airship filled the hangar. The arc lights, blazing from all round and above it, quite dazzled Jane when she came through the doors, already open for the launching.

She walked quickly across the concrete floor towards the middle tower. Her footsteps echoed, but so vast was the hangar that the echo was quickly lost. It was very still, very cold, also very empty, which was odd. Where was big, bearded John Coleman, the guard who watched the Airship at night?

She came to the middle tower and, feeling a sudden pang of fear, she stepped into the lift and pressed the top button. The lift rose swiftly and stopped opposite a door in *Ladyship*'s side.

It was very warm in the Airship. Jane at once felt safer. She took off her coat and then set off up the corridor to the pilot's cabin. 'I shan't touch the controls,' she said to herself 'That would be dangerous. It would be terrible if I drove *Ladyship* out of the hangar. I'll just look at them, then go and have some breakfast.'

Five minutes after the door in the side of the *Ladyship* had closed automatically behind her, a second figure, in gum boots, appeared out of the darkness and, after pausing at the hangar entrance, hurried across to the middle tower. It was heavily muffled in a large grey duffle coat, the hood completely hiding the head. It stopped at the tower, looked quickly round, then stepped into the lift, shot up and in a moment had disappeared into the *Ladyship*.

At the precise moment—so precise, it might have been arranged—that the small duffle-coated figure had appeared at the front of the hangar, John Coleman disappeared through a door in the back. And just four minutes after the duffle-coated person had gone into the Airship, John re-appeared through the same door, accompanied by five rough-looking men.

Once inside, they split into pairs and ran to the three tall towers which held the Airship to the ground. A moment later, quite silently on their large rubber tracks, the towers began to move slowly out of the hangar.

It had begun to grow a little lighter outside. It was just possible to see the line of trees at the edge of the field and the solid mass of grey cloud moving slowly across the sky.

The towers stopped. The *Ladyship* swung a little in the light breeze. And then quite gently, with no warning, no visible sign of release, she began to rise silently into the air. As she floated up, like a huge grey grub ascending from the bottom of a pool, she swung round and started to drift south. Higher and higher, her long sausage shape now clearly outlined, her size appreciable; higher and higher and now less easy to see in the grey light of dawn, her own greyness beginning to merge with the grey clouds; higher and higher, really very difficult to tell apart from the clouds, until, like a ghost, the *Airship Ladyship* quietly disappeared from sight.

2. The Crash

It was ten minutes before Jane realized that anything was wrong. Deep inside the *Ladyship* the movement was so small as to be hardly noticeable, and when she did wonder if she felt a swaying, she thought it was probably a wind blowing in the hangar. Also, on the long walk to the pilot's cabin in the front, there were so many new things to look at: new furniture, a little room with fruit machines and a roulette wheel for gambling, and also the children's play room, now fully equipped.

It was when she noticed that all the swings in this room were swinging gently from side to side that she realized something was wrong. 'It can't be blowing as hard as that in the hangar,' she thought. 'I must go and investigate.'

She hurried out and ran down one of the sloping ramps which led to the cabins. The door of the first one was open. Jane walked over to the window and pulled back the curtains.

Nothing. She could see nothing—no hangar, no arc lights, just greyness, as though another curtain had been drawn outside.

Her heart beating hard, half frightened, half excited, Jane sat on the bed and thought. Obviously, someone—or more probably several people—were trying to steal the *Ladyship*. And she, it was obvious, was the only person who could stop them. But how? The first thing to do was to arm herself, and Jane remembered that only the week before, her father had received from London a case of 24 light hunting rifles which were to be put in the lifeboats in case of shipwreck.

It took her over ten minutes to get one. Not because they were far away, but because now she had to creep round the *Ladyship* with great care, lying flat on her stomach to peer round corners, and all the time keeping an eye open for signs of men. Because Jane was fairly sure the *Ladyship* was being stolen by a gang. There had in fact been rumours of something like this happening, which was why her father had ordered that the Airship be guarded so carefully. John Coleman had been armed. No doubt he had been overpowered and probably beaten up.

It was thoughts of this sort that made Jane grow more and more frightened as, hunting rifle now held in front of her, she crept towards the pilot's control room. Her plan was that since one at least of the gang must be driving the *Ladyship* she would go and hold him up and force him to drive the Airship back to Curl before the rest of the gang noticed.

But when at last she was standing outside the closed door of the control room, it all seemed much more difficult. She wasn't at all sure how to use the rifle. Was it even loaded? And suppose there were four men, or six? Jane bent towards the door and listened. But there was no sound at all. The Airship was totally silent. Jane was amazed how quiet the engines were; her father would be delighted.

At last, heart beating hard again, she pulled herself up. She was the only person who could save the day, she must be brave. She put on as fierce a face as she could, opened the door and stepped in with the gun at her shoulder.

'Hands up,' she said in a loud, trembly voice. 'Don't move or I shoot.'

The control room was empty. There was nowhere for any one to hide, and not even any sign that someone had been there; the two high swivel chairs standing on their single legs at the control panel in the front were set straight, none of the dials or screens on the computer, which covered most of the back wall, were moving.

What on earth had happened? If the computer wasn't working, then nor were the engines. No wonder it was so quiet. But where, Jane wondered, were the robbers. Surely the *Ladyship* hadn't just floated out of the hangar by herself—if she had, she had certainly floated quite far and quite high.

The front and sides of the control room were built entirely of thick glass. These bulged out to give the pilot as wide a view as possible. Though Jane could still only see mist, she thought it was much lighter than before. Now it was streaming down past the glass in tatters and streamers and looking up she thought she saw indistinct patches of blue.

Probably, she thought, something had gone wrong with the engines and the men stealing the *Ladyship* were trying to mend them. Once finished, one at least of them would return to drive the *Ladyship*. She would hide outside the control room and catch them as they came in.

But she was too late. While she had been planning this, her eyes fixed on the thinning cloud and growing areas of blue, the door of the control room had been opened five inches and the long barrel of a rifle poked carefully but quickly through. Now the door was pushed wide and a voice said loudly, 'Hands up. I have a gun.'

Jane jumped with fright, dropped her gun, and quickly put up her hands. Then she turned round. Framed in the door was one of the oddest sights she'd seen in her life.

It was Mrs Deal. Despite the power of the *Ladyship*'s central heating, she was wearing a large duffle coat. The hood had fallen forward, disturbing her bun so that a length of grey hair appeared below her chin. It had also knocked her spectacles on their ribbon off her nose so that she was pointing the large rifle, with difficulty, at what Jane knew could only be a dim blur.

'What on earth are you doing, Mrs Deal?' she said. 'Have you gone mad?'

'Miss Jane?' said Mrs Deal in a surprised voice. 'Is that you, Miss Jane?'

'It certainly is,' said Jane. 'Put that gun down and put on your spectacles. You might kill me.'

Mrs Deal put the rifle on the floor. Then she pushed back her spectacles and stared at Jane. At last she said, 'Well, you've really done it now and no mistake, Miss Jane. What your father will say I dread to think. Driving off in his Airship! And that nice Mr Grudheim. You're old enough to know better.'

'But I didn't, Mrs Deal,' said Jane. 'It's nothing to do with me.'

'I've caught you at the wheel red-handed,' cried Mrs Deal. 'How can you say such a thing? Your poor mother!'

Quickly Jane explained how she had come out to the *Ladyship* because she couldn't sleep and after wandering about looking at things for about ten minutes had suddenly discovered she was airborne. 'In fact,' said Jane, 'I'd come here to catch the thieves. What do you think we should do now? Perhaps as there are two of us we could search the whole Airship.'

'There's no one else on this Airship,' said Mrs Deal, 'of that I'm sure.' She explained how she too had been unable to sleep. She had been worried that the *Ladyship*'s rooms would not be up to the high standards of Earl Mountbatten and had come over for a last whisk round. 'I've been into every cabin and over all the state rooms,' she said. 'I did the galley, the engine room and even had a peep at the superstructure. There's not a room I haven't looked at. In fact it was with looking so carefully I missed that we were floating. But a man I wouldn't have missed.'

Despite this, however, they did thoroughly search the *Ladyship* again, each carrying one of the hunting rifles. But Mrs Deal was quite right, there was no one but themselves aboard. It was very mysterious.

'Well how did we get up here then?' said Jane, once they had returned to the control room. 'And how are we to get down?'

'How we got up I don't know,' said Mrs Deal. 'But I have no doubt the Royal Air Force will be here directly to take us in tow. They won't let a great big thing like this Airship float about for long, blocking half the sky. Now, don't you touch the instruments. I've work to do and I don't want a nasty crash before we're rescued.'

However, once Mrs Deal had left the control room, this was exactly what Jane did. Very relieved to find that they were not in the hands of brutal robbers, and that the *Ladyship* had in some mysterious way floated off by itself, she realized that somehow she would have to fly them back on her own.

This was not in fact as difficult as it sounds. Sir Christopher had carefully designed the controls of the Airship to be as simple as possible, so that even the stupidest passenger could be allowed a turn at the wheel. Strapping herself into one of the high swivel chairs, she started to press in turn all the buttons in front of her. At the seventh button, the Airship shuddered slightly, she heard a low hum, and all the dials and little lights flicked into life.

Now, thanks to Henry, Jane knew more or less what to do. She set their speed for 100 mph and, seeing that their height was over 8,500 feet, she thought she would bring the Airship down a bit to see if she could find out where they were. With a confident gesture, she pushed the small manual descend/ascend lever as far forward as it would go.

The result was startling. With a surge of power the nose of the *Ladyship* began to plunge down, the tail rose up and within four seconds she was racing down through the clouds at 100 mph. Jane was flung forward on to the controls and only kept in her seat by the safety straps.

Frantically she groped for the descend/ascend lever and pulled it as far back as it would go. At once the nose shot up, the tail shot down and the Airship began to climb almost vertically upwards. Jane hung back in her straps, her short arms unable to reach the lever. It was only by pulling herself forward by the accelerator knob that she was able to get to it, and put the *Ladyship* on an even keel again. She had forgotten Henry's warning that the instruments were extremely delicate and had, without thinking, made the Airship perform a highly dangerous manœuvre, only to be attempted in an emergency.

But if the effects had been surprising in the control room, down in the body of the Airship they had been catastrophic. Mrs Deal had been in the main state room, putting the finishing touches to the already ice-like slipperiness of its parquet flooring with one of the large mechanical polishers. All at once, to her horror, the floor began to tilt downwards. In an instant it had turned into something much more like an enormous playground slide. Letting go her handle, Mrs Deal turned and, arms and legs whirling, tried desperately to reach the door behind her. The floor tilted lower. Mrs Deal stretched frantic hands. 'Help!' she called. 'Help, someone!' And then suddenly she collapsed on her stomach and with a high doomed cry began to slide swiftly down the state room.

It seemed for a moment that nothing could prevent her crashing with tremendous force into the chrome and gilt walls at the far end. But no sooner had her slide gained speed, than abruptly the Airship changed direction. What had been down now became up, but so fast had Mrs Deal been travelling, carried on the soft folds of the duffle coat, that she continued onwards till she was only a few feet from one of the gold-rimmed mirrors. Then, gently at first, but with ever increasing speed, she started to slither back again. This time there was no escape. The Ladyship continued to point straight up, Mrs Deal continued to slide straight down until, with a last despairing shriek, and at high speed, she shot through the door she had been trying to reach in the first place.

Some echo of these terrible events reached Jane in the control room. When she had got the *Ladyship* level again, she set off, feeling rather worried, so see what had happened.

The scene in the long corridor which led from the state room along the bottom of the Airship was one of considerable confusion. Fortunately the state room itself had been cleared for the launching ceremonies and, apart from Mrs Deal and the polisher, there had been nothing to slide about. The corridor, however, was strewn with a jumble of little sofas, brass spittoons, gilt chairs, smashed vases and lamps and tiles and all the other things Lady Charrington had lovingly collected. Amongst all this

Jane found Mrs Deal. The lucky chance which had sent her hurtling through the open door had caused her to land in the middle of a fragile silk-covered *chaise-longue*. The *chaise-longue* had broken in half, but Mrs Deal was unhurt, if extremely upset, by her experience.

'Oh, Miss Jane, how could you?' she said as she was helped from the wreckage. 'I've never had such a fright in my life. I felt I was flying. And the mess in the cabins! I'll be up all night.'

'I'm dreadfully sorry,' said Jane. 'I promise it won't happen again. I see now you have to be very gentle.'

'I don't know about gentle,' said Mrs Deal. 'Look at it all. Talk about a bull in a china shop. I'm right back to square one.'

Once in the control room again, Jane decided that she must try and find out where they were. She set the automatic descent lever to 'Level descent—half speed', and then sat back, looking anxiously out through the glass and every now and then at the altimeter.

Swiftly the numbers clicked back. As the *Ladyship* went down it grew darker again, the grey cloud pressing close, wrapping them in its damp cotton wool.

At 1,000 feet she moved the automatic descent lever to 'Slow'. The computer hummed, drops of water formed on the glass, the Airship sank slowly down: 500 feet, 450, 425, 400—Jane stared out and down, expecting at any moment the dark hump of a hill to loom blackly up through the swirling greyness. 370, 350, 325—nothing.

And then suddenly they were out, as abruptly as though they had emerged through the bottom of a pancake.

'The sea!' cried Jane aloud in her astonishment, and moved the lever to 'Stop'.

There, about 25 feet below the Ladyship, its heavy calm surface as grey as the cloud they had sunk through, were the moving waves of the sea. For an instant she saw it and then, impelled by her nervous hand, they were up in the cloud again. It might have been a dream.

The sea. Where on earth could they be? Had they been blown far out over the Atlantic Ocean, headed for America? Jane tried to remember in what direction the wind had been blowing when—how long ago it seemed—she had set out from the Castle to the hangar. She seemed to remember it had been blowing towards Inkpen. That was north, in which case the *Ladyship* would have been blown north too. That would mean they were over the sea above Cornwall. All she had to do was to go south. She spun another dial and turned the big Airship round until a large green S appeared in the direction finder. Then she pushed the airspeed control to 200 mph and at the same time moved the 'Level ascent' lever to bring them up above the cloud. This, now she was moving under her own power, the *Ladyship* did quite quickly; the numbers on the altimeter flicked past, the thick grey fog lightened, became a mist, a trailing of tatters and wisps and then suddenly—she was out!

It was one of the most beautiful sights Jane had ever seen. The control room was filled with bright sun, but a sun not just blazing in an empty blue sky, but flowing in from all sides, reflected off an immense white carpet, a vast tranquil ocean whose gentle tussocks spread away on all sides as far as she could see, a cloud that covered the world.

Jane stood and stared, dazzled by the snowy distances. Then, after a while, she turned and pressed a button marked 'Lock', at the same time moving the airspeed control to 250 mph. The *Ladyship* was now on automatic pilot and would continue to fly due south at 250 mph until her position was altered. The computer would correct for wind and would also, fed information by its rotor scanner, avoid any obstacles in the Airship's path. None of this, of course, did Jane know.

She had decided to go and look at the promenade deck. The view from here was as magnificent as it had been from the control room. And for the first time Jane could see they were moving. Stretches of the deck floor were made of glass, and through them she could see the long black shadow of the Airship passing over the whiteness below them.

It was the sight of this swiftly moving shadow after half an hour which made Jane suddenly think she ought to go and see where they had got to. Hurrying back to the control room she stopped the *Ladyship* and moved the automatic descent lever to half speed descent.

The dense cloud that day was covering most of Western Europe. It was not till 500 feet that the *Ladyship* suddenly emerged into clear air and Jane saw the ground rising swiftly towards them. She stopped the Airship and then stood up in her seat, the better to see out. Below was an undulating countryside with, directly underneath, a small village.

Quite by chance Jane recognized it. She was almost sure it was the little village of Porthcurno at the far western tip of Cornwall. It was a favourite spot of her mother's. That meant they were about 75 miles from Curl. All she had to do was to drive the Airship due east.

Below her, people stared up and waved. As they watched, the giant Airship, still headed south, rose vertically into the clouds. It was the first time she had been seen since she had disappeared.

This sighting both hindered and helped the enormous search operation which had been started the moment that the *Ladyship* was found to have disappeared. The search was hard enough as it was, because of the thick cloud. But it was made harder because all the villagers said the Airship was heading south, whereas the moment she was in the cloud Jane had set course east.

The search was helped because it was the first definite information anyone had had about the *Ladyship*'s position. This was quite different from what Jane believed. The wind that morning had in fact been blowing from Inkpen to Curl, that is from the north, and the sea she had seen had been the Channel and not the sea near Bristol. Instead of being above Cornwall, as she believed, they were in fact over the little village of Les Bouchettes, in France.

When they broke out of the top of the clouds again Jane put the *Ladyship* on the automatic control and also set the speed at 400 mph. Now she knew where they were, and since they had all the afternoon to get back, she thought it would be fun to go and have a look at Aldeburgh. After this she went off to find Mrs Deal and suggest they had some lunch.

Mrs Deal was slumped disconsolately in one of the smoking rooms, a duster trailing from her hand. She explained that, though there was not too much broken, every cabin was in disarray. The *Ladyship* had never been meant to dive or climb at the angle achieved by Jane. Everything not fixed to the ground (though a great deal was fixed) had slid and fallen.

'It's too much for one pair of hands,' said Mrs Deal wearily. 'I don't know what your father will say, or the Lord High Admiral, but it'll have to wait till we get home.'

However, on learning that this would take place towards the end of the afternoon, she soon cheered up. 'Fancy mastering a monster like the *Ladyship*,' she said admiringly. 'You have some of your father's mechanical skill, I see.' Jane felt very proud and together they set off to see about some lunch.

They found the kitchen, thanks to its gyroscope, in perfect order. The steaks and vegetables laid out and ready for the launch banquet were to hand, as were cheese and trifle and fruit. Mrs Deal was a good cook of the simple English sort and soon they were sitting down to a delicious meal. Mrs Deal, to celebrate, as she said, their imminent return, even opened a bottle of red wine and became quite merry.

And all the time the *Ladyship* sped eastwards, a gleaming white cigar against the snowy wastes of cloud.

After lunch Mrs Deal said she thought she'd have forty winks. The central heating made her drowsy. Jane went up to the control room to bring the *Ladyship* down for another look.

Gently they sank, the altimeter flicking off the figures, drops of water condensing on the bulging glass of the control room. The cloud seemed even thicker than before and when they still hadn't emerged at 300 feet, Jane slowed the Ladyship almost to a stop and then stood up in her chair to see better, one hand resting on the automatic ascent/descent lever. Her heart was beating.

Once again they came out with startling suddenness—to a sight so astonishing that Jane gave a cry of horror and flinging herself forward onto the control panel pressed hard on the Emergency Lift button. The helium flowed into the balloons. The nuclear engines discharged a direct down thrust. The Airship soared straight up.

It had been a mountain, a steep, rocky mountain only 50 feet below the *Ladyship*, with jagged rocks and a few fir trees. Jane thought she had seen snow.

So where on earth could they be? Not Cornwall certainly. It reminded Jane a little of Scotland, but they had gone south so it couldn't be Scotland. Perhaps it was France. Jane had been to France once when she was five but it somehow didn't seem like France, and if it wasn't France then they were lost.

At that moment the *Ladyship*, still impelled by Emergency Lift, burst through the top of the clouds and out into the sunshine. Jane stopped her rising further and continued their course eastwards, but at only 25 mph.

The fact that she was lost didn't really worry her at all. Indeed, the idea of quite a lot more flying at first excited her. The *Ladyship* had enough fuel to last two years, and food enough for weeks. She would fly around until the cloud disappeared and then come down and ask where they were. Then she would fly back using the map, or else she'd ring Curl, reversing the charges. But before this it might be fun to go on a little trip. She decided that every half an hour or so she would bring the *Ladyship* very carefully down and try to see where they were.

But as the Ladyship flew steadily on above the cloud, Jane grew more and more uneasy. First there was a buzz and then a red warning light began to flash in the middle of the computer control panel. 'Computer fault', 'computer fault', 'computer fault'.

Jane stared at it. What sort of fault? But since she hadn't the faintest idea how to mend a broken computer—and was quite certain Mrs Deal hadn't either—she decided the only thing she could do was nothing.

It was from this moment that the computer began to make a series of mistakes which were to prove disastrous. It started by lowering two special Emergency Explosive Grappling anchors at the back of the Airship. Then the altimeter began to register incorrectly and the radar scanners stopped working. But Jane, of course, was unaware of all this and flew on, 'computer fault', 'computer fault' winking pleadingly but in vain behind her.

Other things however increasingly worried her. She suddenly remembered that they hadn't got all that much food because the emergency rations had not yet been loaded and the kitchens had only been stocked with enough food for the launch banquet of 50.

But what frightened her most was the loneliness and emptiness of the sky, the unbroken surface of the cloud. Now that she was lost, the whiteness below, glaring in the afternoon sun, seemed less friendly. It was like the desert of snow at the North Pole, only here it was a desert beneath which Jane knew were steep and dangerous mountains.

And the silence. The *Ladyship* made no sound as she sailed majestically through the air; she hardly trembled. Trapped on the ground by cloud, no companionable aeroplanes roared over or beside them. Jane felt suddenly too small and too young to be in charge of such a huge craft. She wished she wasn't alone. She wished Mrs Deal would appear, but she knew Mrs Deal was asleep somewhere deep in the empty Airship behind her.

After half an hour, she stopped the *Ladyship* to go and look at the ground. She strapped herself in securely and then lowered the Airship carefully into the great sea of cloud. They sank very slowly. Jane kept on stopping and looking out, and watched the altimeter all the time.

Disaster, when it came, was so swift and unexpected, so violent, that afterwards Jane was never able to remember exactly what had happened.

Several times on the way down, the *Ladyship* had bumped and shaken a little. Suddenly, however (and when according to the altimeter there was still 1,000 feet to go), there was the most tremendous lurch. If it hadn't been for her safety belt Jane would have been flung to the floor. At the same time there came two muffled explosions from somewhere at the back of the Airship.

What had happened was simple. Instead of being 1,000 feet above the ground they were in fact only 40 feet above it. The Explosive Grappling anchors had just touched, exploded and driven deep into the earth. The *Ladyship* was now firmly attached to the ground at the back.

Jane peered frantically through the glass at the whirling mist. But she could see nothing. The altimeter still registered 1,000 feet; the radar screen showed nothing.

Then all at once the mist cleared. There, not twenty feet below, were the tops of pine trees waving in the wind on the side of a steep mountain—pine trees which were growing quickly closer as the *Ladyship* drifted towards them.

Jane at once pressed hard on the Emergency Lift button. At the same time she braced herself in her chair. There was a violent shaking and then slowly the Airship began to tilt backwards. Tethered securely to the ground, she was unable to take off. Instead, the engines were driving her to stand on her tail.

Up and up went the front. Jane's chair spun away from the controls. Now she could see in front of her the winking light—'computer fault', 'computer fault'. Up and up, back and back, until they balanced vertical, the engines roaring below them.

But the *Ladyship* didn't stop there. Now twisted sideways as one anchor was wrenched partly from the rocky earth, she slowly, but with increasing speed, began to fall backwards. Jane glimpsed blurred pine tops rushing up towards them, mist whirling aside, and then with a tremendous crash and shuddering force the *Airship Ladyship* dashed her ponderous length upon the mountainside.

There followed, for what seemed hours, but was in fact only six minutes, pandemonium. The screech of tearing metal. The roar as the nuclear engines, self-sealing fortunately, tore loose from their moorings and plunged down into the forest. The smashing and cracking of tables and structure, the rush as the swimming pool emptied, sizzling and spitting as it did so, on to the hot elements of the nuclear-powered central heating.

And then it died away and there was almost silence except for a sighing which could have been the wind in the pines. It was the gentle hiss of escaping gas.

3. Out of the Frying Pan, into the Fire

ALTHOUGH Jane was not actually knocked unconscious by the crash she was so jolted and deafened and frightened that it was ten minutes before she knew properly what was going on.

She found that she was hanging upside down from her chair in the wrecked control room. Below her, about four feet from the top of her head, the torn trunk of a large pine tree had thrust through the broken glass, and turning from side to side Jane could see other pine trees and Airship wreckage. On the trunk underneath her she could see snow. It was very cold.

Jane took hold of the edge of the seat with one hand and with the other pulled the release buckle of her belt. It fell open and she swung easily down on to the pine trunk. The weight of the Airship had brought the tree and those round it close to the ground and it was a simple matter to scramble out onto the snow.

Despite the mist which still hung about the trees, thinning and thickening in response to a slight breeze, the sight was incredible. The *Ladyship* had smashed down along 200 yards of steep, pine-covered mountain. In the front where Jane had been it was still partly held up by the trees; but in the middle it had squashed them completely flat and, breaking open, scattered its contents over a wide area. As she walked towards this, her breath curling up in the cold air, she came upon chairs and bedspreads, strips of chrome, struts of wood and trails of wire. It was eerily quiet, except for the hiss of escaping gas and the creaking of the pines as the front of the Airship settled deeper into them.

Looking at it and shivering with cold, Jane breathed a deep sigh. 'Golly, Dad's lovely new Airship,' she said. 'Whatever will he say?'

Unexpectedly the answer came at once, from just five feet above her head, where the towering body of the *Ladyship* was now almost touching the ground.

'Your father will be extremely angry,' came the voice of Mrs Deal, sharp with disapproval. 'As will Lady Charrington. From what I can tell, this aircraft is quite beyond repair. You have a lot to answer for,

Miss Jane; though I must bear part of the responsibility for letting you take the controls.'

Looking up, Jane saw the tousled head of Mrs Deal looking crossly down through the broken window of a cabin. So far from being surprised by the crash, she had expected it, or at least prepared for it. Before sinking into a heavy slumber, she had piled the bed with extra blankets and then strapped herself in with the storm straps for extra protection.

'And another thing,' she said, fumbling behind her, 'you'll catch your death if you stay out there like that. Look at you shivering. Now put this round you at once,' and she threw down a blanket which Jane gratefully wrapped round herself.

Mrs Deal then undid the storm straps and lowered herself gingerly to the ground. She tucked her hair back into her bun and looked about her. 'Where are we then?' she said. 'This isn't Cornwall.'

'I don't know,' said Jane.

'You don't know!' cried Mrs Deal. 'But I thought you said we'd be back by the end of the afternoon. And how did it happen? Didn't you see this great mountain?'

Jane explained that the computer had gone wrong and so she didn't know where they were and that was probably why she'd hit the mountain. This explained the whole thing to Mrs Deal.

'I never did trust these computers,' she said, 'not since my brother in Peebleshire got a Water Rate for a million pounds. No wonder we're in such a pickle. The quicker we get off this mountain the better.'

Jane said it might be more sensible to climb back into the Airship, see if they could find any food, and spend the night in one of the least damaged cabins. The sun was already starting to set and at least in the Airship they would be warm and safe.

Mrs Deal wouldn't hear of it. 'I'm not going back into that *Ladyship* and that's flat,' she said. 'Wild horses wouldn't drag me back for all the tea in China. If ever a craft had a jinx on it, it's the *Ladyship*.'

As if in answer to her words, there came a sudden series of cracks and crashes from the front of the Airship. Made heavier by the loss of helium it was settling lower in the trees, breaking them down and spilling more of its contents on to the ground. Jane too, although she knew Mrs Deal was wrong, felt there was something unlucky and even sinister about the battered remains of the *Ladyship*.

'In that case we'd better go down hill,' she said. 'That's where the houses will be.'

So they set off together down through the pine trees. It was not easy. Once away from the destruction of the crash, the snow became thick and Jane's trailing blanket caught in the fallen branches. Now that the sun had gone it was much colder and more difficult to see.

'Are there wolves still in places like this?' said Jane after a while, panting a little with the effort of getting through the snow.

'No,' said Mrs Deal without much conviction.

'When the moon gets up we'll hear them howling,' said Jane, 'then we'll see their gaunt forms gather . . .'

'Nonsense,' said Mrs Deal. 'No wolves and no tigers, either.'

'Tigers?' said Jane.

'I can't stand tigers,' said Mrs Deal. 'I'd rather a wolf than a tiger.'

As it grew colder, Jane's hands became numb from holding the blanket round her shoulders. She and Mrs Deal struggled on in silence. It was less steep here but there seemed to be more branches. The snow gleamed in the gathering darkness, the bigger branches criss-crossed black against it.

For the next two hours they stumbled down in a darkness which grew thicker and thicker, until they could scarcely see the snow, and the branches and pine trees disappeared altogether. They bumped and tripped, and Jane began to feel she couldn't go on much longer.

And then at last they found the path. They were swaying and struggling over a large pile of pine branches buried in snow, when the ground dipped into a steep bank in front of them. At the bottom was a path—quite wide, two inches deep in snow, but a little easier to see.

'A path means people and people mean houses,' said Mrs Deal, her voice loud in the muffling silence of the snow. 'Come on, best foot forward.'

As they hurried down the winding path, and she grew tireder and colder, Jane felt more and more like a little girl again. Mrs Deal, whom she often teased and often, though she was very fond of her, did not take seriously at all, seemed to grow stronger and more grown-up. She put her duffle coat round Jane and drew her close.

But even this did not keep out the piercing cold. Jane's feet became numb and then her hands. There was no sound except the occasional soft plop as snow fell from a branch, and the muffled sound of their footsteps as they walked, ever more slowly, down the path. Jane felt sleepier and sleepier. She began to dream and several times would have fallen but for Mrs Deal's arms.

And then suddenly Mrs Deal said, 'Look, Miss Jane, a light! We're saved!'

Jane, who had been almost asleep, shook her head and peered ahead through the darkness. There, sure enough, twinkling not far below them, were the lights of a house. And sniffing, she thought she smelt wood smoke.

Now she and Mrs Deal began to run. The path turned and turned again, the lights were hidden, reappeared, were gone, and almost at once they were out of the trees and standing below the little house, looking up some steep wooden steps which led to its front door.

'Up we go,' said Mrs Deal.

At the top was a small veranda, with light streaming out from two small windows on either side of the door. Mrs Deal raised her hand and tapped politely.

The door opened, light poured out and was then blocked by a tall, stooping figure.

'Who's there?' said a deep but gentle voice. 'Good heavens—a child! What on earth are you doing? Come in, come in. Mind the step.'

Almost fainting with cold and relief, Jane stumbled in, followed by Mrs Deal.

The house (or chalet rather, because they soon learnt that they had crashed in Switzerland) belonged to Mr Sydney Saxton, an elderly Englishman. He wasted no time when he saw how tired and cold they were. Saying that all explanations could wait till the morning, he hurried Jane into a hot bath and then sat her in front of the large stove covered with pale blue tiles. Then while Mrs Deal had a bath he prepared some hot soup.

Jane nodded off several times while she sat, wrapped in his large dressing gown, and ate her soup. But as she was climbing into the little bed he had showed her, she heard Mrs Deal begin to tell him what had happened.

'Such an experience,' she heard her say, 'thank you, I think another little nip would do me good. The Airship belonged to Miss Jane's father, Sir Christopher Charrington of Curl Castle.'

As Sydney Saxton's deep voice rumbled in reply, she fell fast asleep.

In the morning, when she came down to breakfast, Sydney Saxton had evidently heard the whole story.

'I understand you had a narrow escape,' he said, handing her a plate of porridge. 'I heard an explosion up the valley but imagined it was one of the avalanche prevention squads. It's time they got busy. And Mrs Deal tells me you piloted the Airship yourself. Very clever.'

'Not really,' said Jane, modestly. 'Daddy made it very simple to drive and Mrs Deal was busy dusting. Tell me,' she added politely, because her mother said it was polite to make conversation, 'what do you do here?'

Sydney Saxton was a tall thin man of 75, with a lot of grey hair brushed well back, a hooked nose, long jaw and deep blue eyes under curly bushy grey eyebrows. He stood up and smiled at Jane.

'I'm writing a book,' he said. 'Or rather I'm sorting out my notes, arranging the material, and hope to start in a week or so. It's a long business.'

There was a pause. Then Sydney Saxton stretched out his arms and said, 'Now, what's it to be—eggs and bacon?'

But at that moment Mrs Deal, who had overslept for almost the first time in her life, came down the stairs. 'You leave that to me, Mr Saxton,' she said briskly. 'We've dropped in on you out of the blue and I won't have you put out on our behalf.'

'Come Mrs Deal,' said Sydney Saxton. 'I can easily manage. I've cooked for myself these last eight years since my wife Veronica died. You must be tired after your ordeal.'

'I'm as fit as a fiddle. I slept over the clock and I'm as right as rain,' said Mrs Deal, who with her grey jersey dress and her bun tied carefully looked just as she always did. 'No doubt you'll be wanting to get on with your work. I know you literary gentlemen.'

Sydney Saxton cast a reluctant eye towards a table in the corner of the room, which Jane saw was deeply buried in sheets of paper covered in neat handwriting. Along shelves in front of the table were piled boxes which were bursting with papers.

'No doubt you're right,' he said in a gloomy voice. 'Though at my age . . .'

His voice tailed off as he walked slowly towards the table. On the way, however, he became distracted by the large, blue tiled stove and bending down opened its door to throw in several logs.

'I was telling Mrs Deal last night,' he said over his shoulder, 'you may both have been saved from the frying pan only to land in the fire. It's quite possible we'll have an avalanche in the valley soon.'

'What fun,' said Jane. 'Will we be able to see it?'

'I fear it's more dangerous than that,' said Sydney Saxton. 'It could well sweep right down over this house.'

While Jane ate her eggs and bacon, cooked by Mrs Deal, he explained that his was the only house in the valley. Each year he was completely cut off for three months. But every few years the wind would blow in from the west and not change. If it continued for long enough, snow would build up and up at the top of the valley and eventually come roaring down, destroying everything before it. Already the wind had been in the west for one entire week without change.

'Do you mean we're doomed and trapped?' said Jane anxiously. 'We must tell Mummy and Daddy.'

'Oh, I don't think we're doomed,' laughed Sydney Saxton. 'I don't want to alarm you too much. I don't suppose the wind will continue. It often blows for a week or so like this and then changes. Yesterday, for

instance, though the wind blew from the west, there was hardly any snow. It takes a good fourteen days of continuous snow and continuous west wind before the situation becomes frightening.

'As to being trapped, I fear we are my dear. But I have plenty of food and as soon as I can I'll get news out to your parents. If I were ten years younger I'd ski out and get help. But though I'm strong for seventy-five my heart's not too good and it's beyond me now.'

While Sydney Saxton wrote his book, or, to be accurate, prepared and sorted his notes, read old notes and made new notes, before starting to write his book, Jane explored. The chalet was built against the steep side of the valley, so that when you went upstairs to the three small bedrooms and looked out of the back windows it was as though you were still on the ground floor. Just below the windows was a small, snow covered lawn and then the pine forest stretching up. In the front, you could see right across the valley. Downstairs there was the kitchen, a small bathroom and the living-room. To the right of the stove were the stairs; on the wall was a large dial to show which way the wind was blowing.

From the outside the chalet looked exactly like a cuckoo clock, except that on top of its steeply sloping roof there was a small platform on which Sydney Saxton said he sunbathed in summer.

There was one curious thing about the way it was built. Although it was very strong, made of thick logs bound together with rods and loops of iron, it was attached relatively feebly to four tall poles.

'The idea,' explained Sydney Saxton, 'is that when an avalanche comes the stilts will be swept away and the chalet will ride on the surface of the snow like a raft.'

'Does it work?' asked Jane. 'It sounds rather fun.'

'It sounds quite exciting, I agree,' said Sydney Saxton. 'I believe it has worked for very small avalanches, but usually the snow comes too fast and there's far too much of it. We'd be crushed like a matchbox here.'

He had had the area under the house, where it stood on its four stilts, closed in with boards and in the large room this made were kept the food and fuel and all the stores which had to carry him through the three months of winter.

Fortunately Sydney Saxton had a grandchild not much older than Jane, and she was able to dress up warmly enough to go outside. She made a snowman. She explored the store-room and made a house out of some cardboard boxes. All afternoon it snowed and the wind blew in the same direction, though whether it was from the west or not Jane didn't know. But though it snowed too hard to be able to see right across the valley, she found that where the path was protected by the pines she could use the sled.

At teatime she mentioned this. 'I think it's lovely here,' she said, 'except it would be fun if someone could come sledding with me, Sydney.' (He had asked them both to call him Sydney, which Jane at first found embarrassing. Mrs Deal seemed to find it impossible.)

'I'm glad you like it,' said Sydney, 'because I'm afraid we're in for a long winter. I'm a bit old for sledding, I fear, but when the snow lets up I'll show you some interesting places in the woods. Also I'd be very interested to take a look at the Airship.'

After supper Sydney settled down with tweezers and screw driver to mend the wind indicator. Mrs Deal had found some crochet hooks and wool and asked if she might use them. They sat peacefully in front of the stove, its door open, and Jane, who couldn't think of anything to do, asked Sydney some questions.

'Don't you sometimes get lonely here in the winter?' she said.

Sydney looked up, tweezers poised. 'Not really,' he said. 'When Veronica died eight years ago I was lonely, but very seldom now. I have the wireless and my books and my writing.'

'Tell me a bit more about that,' said Jane.

'Well, I've always kept a journal,' said Sydney. 'I shall put in about your arrival.' He went on to tell Jane about some famous people he had known and showed her photographs of them or paintings and drawings by them on the walls. Though she didn't always follow what he said, Jane enjoyed listening to him and found his deep voice gentle and soothing. Nor was she alone in finding this. After a while it sent Mrs Deal into a deep sleep and it was the rattle of her crochet hooks falling to the floor that made Sydney see it was time they all went to bed.

As Mrs Deal undressed Jane and put on her pyjamas, she said, 'A thoroughly nice gentleman. We couldn't have fallen into better hands.'

'Yes, he is nice,' said Jane. 'He knew Virginia Woolf, you know.'

'Who's she?' said Mrs Deal.

'I don't know,' said Jane. 'But she was very important.'

She climbed into bed, snuggling up with her hot water bottle and listening a moment to the quiet sounds of the night before falling asleep. Downstairs the big blue stove crackled and glowed, pouring out steady waves of warmth. Outside the snow fell softly and swiftly, streaming up the valley and settling deeper and deeper upon the chalet, the path and the pines; the wind made a deep sighing sound like the sea and blew, as it had blown all day, from the west.

The next ten days, especially compared to the hectic months which were to follow them, were some of the calmest and most enjoyable Jane could remember. Each morning, while Mrs Deal prepared breakfast, she would help Sydney collect the wood for the stove. To do this they had to roll back the carpet in the living-room, lift up a trap door and then lower a basket on a rope into the store-room below. Jane would then go down and fill the basket, which Sydney would pull up.

After breakfast, Mrs Deal would dust and polish and scrub until the little chalet gleamed and shone, said Sydney, as it had never shone before. Sydney himself would slowly settle to his work, grumbling and irritably fluttering his long bony fingers among his papers. Mrs Deal did the housework on tiptoe during this time and Jane was not supposed to go into the living-room. Instead, she would play in the snow around the house or in the store-room. She couldn't go far from the chalet because it snowed continuously. Not only was it difficult to see far, but large drifts were blown up in exposed parts of the pine forest and at the edges of the paths. Nevertheless, she still managed to have fun sledding, and Sydney began to teach her how to ski on his grand-daughter's skis.

And all the time, night and day, making its melancholy music in the pines, the wind blew from the west. Sometimes it was quite gentle, just a breeze, so that Sydney would look more cheerful and say they'd soon have a change. But at other times it would blow hard, bending the pines, laden as they were, making the chalet tremble on its stilts, the stove roar, and driving the snow almost straight up the valley to gather and compress in an ever-growing mass upon the steep, high slopes of the mountains at its end.

At first the direction of the wind was only one of many things in their lives, but it soon became the only thing they could think or talk about. Jane noticed that Sydney gave the arrow of the wind indicator, which had pointed stiffly in the same direction ever since it was mended, a tap before he went to bed. Then he began to tap it in the morning, at lunch and in the afternoon; soon he was tapping it all the time as though by persistence he could tap the wind round to a new direction.

By the end of the week, they were listening to every weather forecast in the hope of hearing that the wind was going to change. But instead there began to be avalanche warnings and reports of avalanches in other valleys nearby. On the first day of their second week, Sydney turned the wireless off after the lunchtime news looking very serious.

'I fear it's getting worse,' he said. 'There was a bad avalanche in Grissalp last night—ten kilometres from here. Three people lost. The last time they had a bad slip was six years ago. We had one four days later.'

'Oh dear, Mr Saxton,' said Mrs Deal, who up till now had supposed that Sydney would somehow deal with the avalanche question. 'Perhaps we'd better pack our bags and be off. Lady Charrington would never forgive me if Miss Jane was carried away in an avalanche.'

'I know,' said Sydney. 'But what can we do? I'm afraid escape is out of the question. A fit man would find the pass choked with drifts and a blizzard blowing. I'm seventy-five and not the man I was. Jane is only a child, though you are very enterprising, my dear. And I don't suppose you can ski, Mrs Deal?'

'I'm a strong swimmer,' said Mrs Deal helpfully.

'I fear that's of little use,' said Sydney gloomily, pulling the long bony fingers of his left hand. 'Little use. No, we are trapped here at the mercy of the elements.'

That night, as the wind roared overhead and she lay tucked up warmly under the thick blankets and fat eiderdown of Mr Saxton's grand-daughter, Jane thought about the problem. But hard as she thought, nothing seemed any good. Perhaps, after all, the chalet would be all right, and would just have the stilts knocked from under it and then go whizzing down on top of the avalanche like a sled. But Sydney had said that the avalanche would send a great blast of air in front of it which would blow the chalet into little bits before the snow even reached it. She fell asleep still puzzling.

During the night she dreamt once more that she was in the *Ladyship* again. As usual, they were crashing. Jane pressed buttons and pulled knobs but all in vain. The *Ladyship* rose higher and higher on her tail, engines roaring, dials spinning, and finally, with a terrifying crash, fell back on to the pine trees and lay still. Jane woke in the darkness and lay panting, her heart beating. But at that moment she realized she'd found the solution—of course, the *Ladyship* was the answer.

4. The Avalanche

AT BREAKFAST the next morning, as soon as they were all sitting down, Jane said excitedly, 'Sydney, I've had an idea.'

'Yes, my dear, what is it?' said Sydney, his face as usual gloomy after the Swiss News and a fruitless tap at the rigid wind indicator.

'Well,' said Jane, 'if the avalanche is going to come down the valley, why don't we move out of its way? I'm sure the *Ladyship* crashed quite a long way from here. Why don't we move up there and camp in the cabins? We could take up the stove and gas cylinders and stores. I'm sure if we piled things on to the sled we could carry up enough in the next few days to last the winter.'

Mrs Deal, in whom the somewhat late realization of their danger had been working all night, spoke first, in fact almost at once. 'Saved by a slip of a girl!' she cried delightedly. 'What do you say, Mr Saxton? A doomed craft the *Ladyship* may have been, but perhaps she'll save us yet.'

But Sydney shook his head. 'I'm sorry to disappoint you both,' he said, 'and it was a very intelligent suggestion, Jane, but the shape of the valley makes it impossible, I'm afraid. The heights all along this side are packed with snow. Avalanches can and will start anywhere and come down the sides at anypoint, even though the one that starts at the top is likely to be the biggest. No spot is really safe.'

After that gloom descended on the breakfast table and they all grew gloomier as the morning wore on. Mrs Deal took a duster and some floor polish upstairs and began to do the wooden boards of the landing. 'At least,' she thought to herself, 'I can die with a duster in my hand.'

Sydney sat at his desk trying to write. He wanted to put into a last note a farewell, a summing up in a few paragraphs of the fruits and lessons of a long life. But what were the fruits and lessons of a long life? He stared at the wall in front of him, his mind blank. Jane sat near the stove and listlessly did some crocheting.

The final blow fell after lunch. As usual Sydney turned on the news, but instead of hearing it through, he stood up in the middle and turned it off.

'That's it,' he said quietly. 'What I feared has happened. That was an avalanche warning for this valley. At most we have two or three days.

Not even a change of wind is any good now because the warning means that there is already enough snow on the heights to cause an avalanche. I fear we're lost.'

When Sydney had finished speaking there was a long silence. Mrs Deal sat twisting a duster in her hands. At last Sydney walked to the window and spoke, looking out over the valley.

'It's my fault,' he said in a low voice. 'I got this chalet cheap because of avalanche danger. It never pays to be mean.'

'Nonsense, Mr Saxton,' said Mrs Deal, who had become very fond of him. 'Generous to a fault, I'd say.'

'No, there's a careful streak,' said Sydney. 'It's not myself I mind about. I've had a long life, with all its fruits and lessons. But you Mrs Deal, cut off in your prime. And Jane here, scarcely begun. That's what I mind. Though I'm sad, of course, that I'll never finish my book.' He turned and looked across the room at his table. 'Or rather,' he added after a pause, 'never begin it.'

There was a long silence. The wind moaned, Mrs Deal's face grew red, Jane remembered her mother saying you should always break a silence. And it was while thinking of something to say that she had her second idea.

'Sydney,' she said excitedly. 'I've suddenly thought of something. Daddy made the *Ladyship* specially so people should be able to escape in trouble.' Quickly she explained how Sir Christopher had constructed the Airship in sections. In an emergency, any section could break away and carry the passengers to safety. He had been particularly concerned with crash landings in remote places when the rest of the Airship would have been too damaged to take off.

'And you see,' she finished, 'it doesn't matter if there is no power, because the pumps which put the helium in and out of the balloons can be worked by hand. Don't you think we ought to go and look. It is a chance.'

Sydney wasted no time. 'Jane, you are a very intelligent little girl,' he said. 'Now, all get warm clothes on and we'll start at once. Are you coming, Mrs Deal?'

'I'd best be there to keep an eye on you,' said Mrs Deal, to whom the whole idea sounded extremely dangerous.

Soon Sydney was leading the way up a path through the pine forest. They each carried a shovel to clear snow from the wreckage. The wind seemed to have dropped a little and for once it was scarcely snowing.

Although it had taken Jane and Mrs Deal nearly four hours that first evening to reach the chalet from the Airship, the return journey, even though uphill, was far quicker. Sydney had guessed from their descrip-

tion roughly where they had crashed and within 40 minutes they were gazing once more on the disaster.

Over 100 yards of forest had been almost completely flattened, and because of this, the wind had been able to blow over the wreckage and prevent the snow from settling. The torn Airship, its broken pieces looking sometimes like monster bones, some times like rippings from giant tins, the debris of panels and furniture, were only thinly covered. It was a strange and desolate scene.

'What a fine craft she must have been,' said Sydney, after they had looked for some time. 'I get an inkling of the conception even in its ruin. But we must get to work. Let us start at the front and work down to the back.'

They worked for two hours, Jane pointing out balloons, cylinders and extractor-inflator pumps. Sydney quickly saw how it all worked and he and Jane were soon scrambling about the wreckage, shouting to each other to come and see when they found an undamaged cylinder, balloon or pump. Mrs Deal looked for cleaning equipment and occasionally a distant cry of triumph would reach them when she found a brush or an unbroken can of floor wax.

By the end of that time it was evident their position was hopeless. One way or another there were plenty of balloons and cylinders; the trouble lay in the sections. Those in the middle and back had all been so badly damaged, it was plain that none of them were even remotely safe. There were four at the front which were less damaged, but these were so pierced and tangled with pine trees that it would obviously have taken a week or more to cut them free.

'And we don't have a week,' said Sydney. 'We have two days, or at the most three. I'm sorry, Jane. It was a good idea but we have been defeated by circumstances.'

They stood sadly, looking at the remains of the *Ladyship*. The light was fading and snow had started to fall heavily again, making it impossible to see to the end of the open space. Once again, flowing in from the west, the wind began to moan in the pines. Jane watched Mrs Deal stagger towards them, laden with cleaning utensils.

'Not a bad haul,' she panted. 'And there's more besides.'

'Sydney says it won't work,' said Jane. 'The *Ladyship* is too badly broken.'

'Well—our fate is sealed then,' said Mrs Deal. 'But we must be thankful for small mercies. This can of floor wax is as good as new.'

'Come on,' said Sydney. 'We don't want to walk back in the dark.' He and Mrs Deal set off slowly, picking their way through the debris. But Jane couldn't move. For some reason she had remembered a story she used to tell herself when she was a little girl and somehow, though she couldn't imagine how, she felt it had something to do with their escape.

'Come on, Jane,' called Sydney. 'We must get down the mountain and up into the chalet.'

And it was then, when he said 'up into the chalet' that Jane had her third and most brilliant idea. In a flash, she saw how her childish dream might save them from the avalanche.

When she was seven or eight she and her parents and some friends of theirs went to Westmorland every summer for a holiday. They stayed in a small farmhouse called Banks and the two mothers did all the cooking while her father went fishing.

It was often wet and windy in Westmorland, and when she was put to bed in her little room with its candle and thick white-washed walls, Jane used to tell herself a story. While their parents were out she and her friends suddenly discovered that Banks could fly. If you pulled the riddling knob on the Raeburn cooker, the little farmhouse slowly rose into the air. They floated up from the hillside out over the beck (the Westmorland name for the little stream in the valley) and so away, to have amazing adventures which Jane always fell asleep before she could think of. Really it was just the idea of a flying farmhouse which gave her pleasure, of opening the little window in her bedroom and looking down at the ground far below; of people looking up and waving; the idea of travelling to strange lands.

Perhaps it was the sound of the wind which reminded her of Westmorland, or something about the handy size of the chalet, but when she suddenly thought of it again and of the story she used to tell herself then, she saw how they might just be able to escape.

'Sydney, Sydney!' she shouted, running after him and Mrs Deal. 'I know you'll think this mad, Sydney,' she said, 'but why don't we tie one of the balloons to the chalet and get out like that? You said it was meant to break away from the stilts.'

'Now that's enough of that,' said Mrs Deal crossly. 'Who ever heard of such an idea?'

'What's so odd?' said Jane. 'Your floor wax isn't going to help.' Sometimes Mrs Deal irritated her.

'It's a daft idea,' said Mrs Deal, a note of alarm in her voice. 'How would we get the things down there for a start?'

'We've got sleds,' said Jane. 'And Daddy made every thing specially light. You know three men could lift one of those balloons when empty.'

'We are not three men,' said Mrs Deal. 'It's dangerous even to suggest such a thing.'

'Dangerous it is and daft it may be,' said Sydney, speaking quietly from nearby. 'But we are drowning men Mrs Deal, and drowning men must clutch at straws, even if they seem daft. I think it's just possible it could work.' And turning round he set off down through the pines with long, careful, old man's strides into the gathering gloom of the evening.

When they reached the chalet, Mrs Deal renewed her protests.

'Fly up in this cockleshell?' she said, shaking the veranda balcony. 'What'll hold us together? You might as well take to the air in a teacup.'

'Come now,' said Sydney soothingly, 'it's by no means decided. I have a lot of things to work out. But if we attempt it, you can rely on the chalet. Some of these logs are thicker than a man's thigh and the whole is cross-welded with steel joists to keep it in shape. Because it was built to ride an avalanche—which it may still have to do—it won't be damaged by being lifted into the air, I can promise you that.'

'How will we guide it or steer it?' said Mrs Deal. 'We'll be at the mercy of every puff of wind.'

'So long as it gets us out of the valley, I'll be satisfied,' said Sydney. 'We'll come down to earth again as soon as we can.'

In the time left before supper and for an hour after it, Sydney worked at his table. Then he called Mrs Deal and Jane and spread out some sketches.

'I think it's worth a try,' he said. 'It's a risk. That is,' he added hastily, as Mrs Deal raised her hand in alarm, 'there's a possibility we won't succeed, but the risks of staying here are far greater.

'Now, I am assuming two things: first that we are able to get the balloons and gas cylinders down here; second, that the balloons will lift the chalet. Assuming these two things to be possible, our first step is to fetch them and install the gas cylinders in the living-room.'

'In here?' broke in Mrs Deal. 'They'll be veritable dust traps.'

'They are quite clean,' said Jane. 'They'll just have some snow on them.'

'Puddles,' said Mrs Deal.

'We'll brush them down first,' said Sydney rather briskly, with the air of a man being sidetracked. 'Next, we'll have to attach the balloons to the chalet. That will be our hardest task. I seem to remember some netting round the balloons.'

'That's right,' said Jane. 'I think it's spun nylon.'

'Good,' said Sydney. 'We'd never get the empty balloon up on to the roof. As Mrs Deal said, we are not three men. What I propose is this.' He pulled one of the sheets of paper towards him so that, standing round his chair, Jane and Mrs Deal could see. His idea was simple but masterly. He proposed that they should lay the empty balloon out flat on the lawn behind the chalet. Because the mountain was so steep this was almost level with the top of the roof. They would pull the bottom of the balloon across to the roof and fasten it there. Then they could take Sydney's 200 yards of nylon climbing rope, and any other rope they found, and fix it firmly into the netting round the balloon, and then tie it again round and under the chalet. Sydney's garden hose would take the helium up from the living-room to the roof. As the balloon filled, it would tend to pull the chalet over, but this way it would just pull it into the mountain and not forward on to its face.

When he had finished, Sydney sat back, his lined face glowing.

'I *am* enjoying this,' he said. 'I don't think I should have been a writer at all. I should have been a balloonist. I don't know whether your idea will work, Jane—and *what* a clever idea it is—but at least it will keep us occupied till the end.'

Jane was delighted by Sydney's praise and lying in her little bed she found she was too excited to go to sleep. But, leaving her room to fetch a glass of water, she accidentally overheard something from the landing which made her worry again.

'Before we go to bed, Mrs Deal,' Sydney was saying, 'there's one thing I must tell you. You know I have a dicky heart?'

'Now you are not to over-do things,' said Mrs Deal firmly. 'If there's any heavy work to do in this hare-brained scheme of yours, you leave it to me.'

'I'll take great care, of course, and I'm usually all right with these digitalis pills here,' said Sydney, 'but if I should have an attack, you will find a full syringe next to the Slogodon sleeping pills in the medicine cupboard in my room. You must at once give me an injection.'

'How?' said Mrs Deal resolutely. 'Where?'

'Just push the needle anywhere into my leg and press the plunger,' said Sydney.

Jane returned to her room and got into her warm bed again, and a little later, lulled by the wind blowing monotonously up the valley, she was asleep.

Unfortunately they met with an early delay. Woken by Sydney at 7 o'clock, they were up at the *Ladyship* by 8.30. But when they arrived, they saw at once that the helium cylinders were far too big for anything but the large sled.

The large sled was too big to take up the small path and had to be pulled up the main path. It took nearly an hour and another twenty minutes to drag it through the forest to the flattened clearing.

As they stood panting at its edge, Mrs Deal, panting herself, came up to them with her arms full of coiled rope. Her eyes were sparkling.

'At least one has the sense of tidying,' she said between gasps. 'And there's more than one might think. I found a fine coil in the remains of one of the lifeboats.'

Sydney, his tall thin frame bent against a tree while he got his breath, looked up. 'Excellent, Mrs Deal, excellent. But put them down for a moment. We need every assistance with the cylinders.'

The helium cylinders were six foot long and three foot round, with the manual pumps fixed to one side. The first one, which had conveniently fallen undamaged from one of the middle sections, appeared completely immovable. But at last, having driven three poles under one side, they got it to roll reluctantly over.

'I think we'll have to roll it down on to the sled, won't we?' panted Jane. Sydney could only nod.

And so they worked. Their breath spurted in long white plumes, their backs ached, they were boiling hot but with freezing hands. And of them all, none worked harder than Sydney. His bushy eyebrows dripped with beads of sweat; when one of the helium cylinders started to slip it was Sydney's old, thin but still sinewy arm which steadied it; Sydney it was who held back the laden sled as they started slowly down the path. And even that night he wouldn't let them stop.

'A man of your age,' said Mrs Deal in a worried voice. 'You'll kill yourself.'

They had managed to get two helium cylinders down to the chalet and a third had been taken as far as the path. Jane had never worked so hard in her life and even Mrs Deal, muscles hardened by years of polishing, confessed to feeling tired.

But after a quick supper, Sydney got them going again. 'Tomorrow is our last day,' he said.

While he was hanging a block and tackle above the trap door, so that they could pull the cylinders up from the store room below, Mrs Deal and Jane carried up stores and piled them in the bathroom.

After several journeys, Sydney said, 'That should be sufficient, Mrs Deal.'

'If you'll pardon me, Mr Saxton,' said Mrs Deal, whose earlier gloom had returned, 'I'll get a few more in. I see no reason why, if you ever get this claptrap into the air, it should ever come down again. I'd like to have something put by.'

'I hope we won't be up more than a few hours,' said Sydney. 'Besides, I need help.'

'I'll be back directly,' said Mrs Deal going out with her torch. 'Come on, Jane.'

Jane felt too tired to take sides and in any case a little later Sydney agreed they should go to bed. One cylinder had been pulled under the trap door and roped up ready for raising. Sydney himself looked grey and exhausted. Jane didn't even bother to wash, but just put on her pyjamas, got into bed and was almost at once asleep.

She was woken at 7 o'clock by Sydney. 'Come on, my dear,' he said, gently shaking her. 'An avalanche could come at any moment now and there's still a lot to do.'

She discovered that Mrs Deal had already been up an hour, carrying stores. It was almost impossible to get into the bathroom.

After breakfast, they set off up the path. It was snowing hard again, thick rapid flakes blowing into their faces and making it difficult to see and walk. The last cylinder of helium was fairly easy. By 10 o'clock it was lying in the store beside the others. It was the balloon itself which took them too long.

They found it surprisingly easy to detach one of the spare, empty balloons from a smashed middle section of the *Ladyship*, and by folding it onto the sled layer by layer it wasn't too heavy to handle. The trouble was it was too large. It flopped over the sides and down the back, and piled right up, it reached Sydney's chin. It could only be kept on if held up at either side. Again and again, as they slowly made their way down through the pines and eventually the path, it toppled over and cascaded over the snow. Then they had to stop and heap it up again. It was after 2 o'clock when, exhausted, they reached the chalet.

By now Sydney was growing desperate. He allowed them only twenty minutes for a lunch of fried eggs and bacon and then hustled them out into the driving snow.

'It's life or death now,' he said. 'We must get on.'

'I don't think I *can*,' said Jane.

'It's like the war,' shouted Mrs Deal, unexpectedly stimulated, her duffle coat flapping in the wind.

They secured the block and tackle to a pine tree above the snow-covered lawn and then very carefully pulled the balloon up the slope. Once there, they pulled it out all round until it was flat. Swiftly the driving snow began to cover it. It was 3.30 and already growing darker.

Next they took the block and tackle up on to the roof, secured a long rope to the bottom of the balloon and prepared to pull it across and fasten it to the sunbathing platform. Mrs Deal went indoors and began to join together the various lengths of nylon rope she'd collected. The rope slipped twice from the bottom of the balloon and twice Jane and Sydney had to re-fix it. Finally, the light fading fast, it was done.

Now they had to tie the balloon firmly to the chalet. Sydney, moving very slowly, fetched the 200 yards of nylon rope from the store and, bent double against the wind, brought it to where Jane stood on the lawn.

'We'll thread it down through the net on either side,' he called, throwing her an end. 'Secure it to the platform and then take it round the chalet.'

But they were beaten. The snow had already covered the balloon and had to be brushed away before the rope could be pushed through the meshes of the spun nylon net. Their hands were frozen and several times Jane stumbled and fell. Even Sydney fell once, though it was so dark now that Jane couldn't see him.

After twenty minutes, she felt an arm on her shoulder. It was Sydney beckoning her to follow him down.

When they came in, Mrs Deal looked up from her knotting. 'Finished already?' she said. 'My, what workers!'

Sydney walked over to his table and sat heavily down.

'It's no good,' he said. 'We're finished, done for.'

'Oh no, Mr Saxton,' said Mrs Deal. 'Done for? The end?' She stopped, and reaching for her duffle coat groped in the pocket for a handkerchief.

After a pause, Sydney said, 'If I'd been younger we might have done it. If. . . .' He paused and then said, 'But there it is. I'm sorry.'

There was a long silence. Mrs Deal twisted her handkerchief in her hands. The snow on their clothes began to melt and drop on the floor;

Jane noticed that snow, or it might have been tears, was running down Sydney's worn, tired cheeks. And all at once, as long ago on the island of Peeg when she and Mrs Deal had nearly died of thirst, she felt rising in her a hot, obstinate anger. Why should they just sit and wait for the avalanche? She felt very tired, they all did, but they could still move, they weren't dead. At the same time she felt very sorry for Sydney, sitting there so old and sad. Getting up, she went and put her arm round his shoulders.

'Don't give up, Sydney,' she said. 'Don't worry. It's because we're all tired. You remember, Mrs Deal, when the Island of Peeg sailed away, how miserable you were and then it was all right? You've always said 'Never say die'. We've *got* to go on. We *mustn't* give up.'

'That's right, Mr Saxton,' said Mrs Deal, drying her eyes. 'If you desert us we've no hope, and Miss Jane's quite right. While there's life there's hope.'

Straightening his shoulders, Sydney looked at them. He stood up. 'You are both right,' he said quietly. 'Age makes us cowards. Come, Mrs Deal, let's get these clothes off and have a hot meal. There may be little time left, but what there is we'll use.'

They changed their clothes, built up the stove and ate a huge stew. Sydney and Mrs Deal had a little gin and then, refreshed, they set to work. The block and tackle were brought down from the roof and for two hours they hauled and heaved and pushed and rolled, and eventually all three helium cylinders were standing in the living-room along the wall beside the front door. Finally, Mrs Deal insisted that they pull up four small cylinders of gas for the cooker, bundles of candles, more tins of food and a crate of gin—'just in case'. The bathroom was now full and she began to heap things around the kitchen and in her bedroom.

After this Sydney sent Jane to bed. Lying warm in her blankets, she heard him clumping up the stairs and then up the steps to the trap door which led to the roof. The noise of the wind grew as he lifted it. She guessed he was fixing the garden hose to the balloon.

Before she fell asleep she thought, if there is an avalanche I'd rather die cosily in my bed like this at night than up and dressed, during the day.

But still the avalanche didn't come. Indeed, when Jane was woken by Sydney the next morning it seemed further away than ever. There had been a dramatic change in the weather. The clouds and the wind and the snow had gone. Instead it was completely calm, the sky blue and the air so clear you could see right across the valley, picking out individually the dark pine trees with their covering of snow and sometimes even a single icicle flashing in the sun.

When she came down she saw the hose, which she had heard Sydney fixing, hanging down from the roof to the cylinders.

'It couldn't be simpler,' Sydney said. 'To fill, you just turn those screw handles at the top. To empty the balloon, you pump.'

Mrs Deal had carried up several baskets of wood for the fire and piled the logs neatly in her bedroom.

Jane was surprised, when they hurried out after a quick breakfast, how gloomy Sydney seemed.

'Isn't it lovely?' she said.

'Yes, the weather's changed,' he said. 'But it comes too late. This is more dangerous than ever. We'll have a north wind, there will be a slight thaw, then—a slip. It could happen any minute.'

Jane looked at his grave face and then out over the valley. Suddenly the strange stillness, instead of being calm and peaceful, became menacing. It was as though everything were waiting for something to happen.

They all three worked very hard and by 1.30, three ropes had been fixed round the balloon and passed round and under the chalet (Sydney had bored numerous holes in the wooden walls of the store-room through which they threaded the rope).

At 1.45 Jane and Sydney were just starting to fix the fourth and last rope when disaster struck. Sydney had picked up the edge of the balloon to fold back. He bent, began to pull and then suddenly raised his arms and with a low moan crumpled into the snow.

'Sydney!' cried Jane, and rushed over to him.

His face was white, a pasty white against the blinding snow; the skin around his mouth was blue. He was breathing very fast and one thin bony hand pressed against his chest. But Jane didn't wait to look again. Racing down the slope, she shouted, 'Mrs Deal! Mrs Deal! Sydney's had a heart attack. Quickly, come quickly.'

Mrs Deal acted swiftly. She hurried upstairs and came down a moment later with the syringe. Together they ran out and up the lawn again.

'He warned me of this,' said Mrs Deal grimly. 'Poor man. Pray God we're not too late.'

She knelt by Sydney and, without even bothering to pull up his trouser leg, thrust the needle straight through it into his thigh. Then she pressed home the plunger.

The effect was immediate and wonderful. Sydney's breathing gradually steadied, the blue colour faded round his lips, and Jane, who was holding his head on her knees, felt him relax.

'Poor man,' said Mrs Deal. 'We must get him into the chalet this instant. He'll catch his death.'

They slid him carefully down the slope and then, helped a little by Sydney becoming half-conscious for a moment, managed to get him on to Mrs Deal's back. Jane supported and pushed and together they staggered and swayed up the steps through the living-room and somehow, nearly falling several times, got him on to his bed.

'Weighs no more than a sparrow,' gasped Mrs Deal as they undressed him. She found the Slogodon where he had said. 'His sleeping pills,' she said to Jane. 'That's what the poor man needs, a good rest. I'll mash five up in some warm milk. You can't have too much of a good thing.' Mrs Deal enjoyed anything to do with ill health.

When she came down into the living-room again, having taken Sydney a hot water bottle and, as she put it, having 'got his Slogodon down', she said. 'He still doesn't look too well at all. If he dies, he's killed himself for us—a martyr. Not,' she added, 'that it really matters now which of us goes first.'

Her words reminded Jane, with a thrill of terror, how terrible their own danger still was.

'Come on, Mrs Deal,' she said. 'We must finish. Sydney said the avalanche could come at any moment now.'

It was much harder and slower without Sydney. The nylon rope had to be woven through the snow-covered meshes of the balloon's huge net, every so often tied to it by strips of cord. When at last this was complete, Jane tried to throw the ends over to Mrs Deal on the roof.

They missed lunch and worked on into the afternoon. Jane kept on dropping the short cords which fastened the rope to the net; Mrs Deal seemed unable to catch the rope ends and missed them ten times; they grew tired and had to stop more and more often for a rest. Jane kept on thinking she heard distant rumblings. Over the dead, ominous stillness of the valley the sun began to sink. Having been too hot, they became cold again. Mrs Deal could hardly get her fingers to tie the thick nylon rope.

But by 4 o'clock it was finished. They hurried out of the store, where the last knot had been tied, and Mrs Deal ran up the steps to the veranda. But Jane hesitated and then turned, drawn by the beauty of the valley below them.

The pale sky was a little darker now and the sun, just dipping below the mountains, swept the snow with pink, making it glow, not dazzling as it had been all day, but dream-like and gentle, even the black charcoal marks of the pine trees looking soft and blurred. But beautiful as it was, Jane found it frightening. It was unreal, too much like a dream. In the great silence, the trees seemed to wait and listen, all facing one direction, up the valley. They too were watching. And the wide wash of the sun was like a spotlight in a theatre, itself turned up the valley the better to light some fearful drama that every thing knew was about to take place.

She shivered and then Mrs Deal called, 'Come in, Miss Jane. Whatever are you doing?'

In the chalet, she found to her surprise that Mrs Deal was starting to prepare a meal.

'There's no time for that,' Jane said. 'We've got to escape.'

'I don't know about that,' said Mrs Deal from the kitchen. 'That's not my province.'

'Look,' said Jane. She got a chair, stood it by the cylinders and, after a nervous pause, resolutely turned the round handle until it would turn no further.

'I don't think you ought to touch those things,' said Mrs Deal. 'We ought to wait for Mr Saxton before meddling with his cylinders.'

'There's not time,' said Jane. 'I'm going up to my bedroom to see if anything's happening. When I call, turn on the other cylinder.'

She ran up the stairs and leant out of the window. At first she noticed nothing. The balloon lay flat on the lawn, the snow which had covered it churned by their feet. To her left, it sagged across to the roof where the ropes from its end were joined to the sunbathing platform. But quite soon she noticed small ripples flowing down it, disturbing the snow. These grew until they were steady waves, as though someone were flapping their sheets and filling the end of a bed with air.

She ran to the top of the stairs and called down to Mrs Deal, 'She's filling. Turn on the next cylinder.'

'I don't like to,' answered Mrs Deal.

'Go on, Mrs Deal,' said Jane. 'Mr Saxton fixed them himself.' She saw Mrs Deal stretch out a nervous hand and give the screw handle a few quick turns as though it were red hot. 'More!' she shouted and ran back to her room.

Now, instead of waves and ripples, there were large bulges moving and swelling inside the balloon. Still on the ground, it heaved like a whale, a shifting heap of mounds and hillocks. Minute by minute it grew and grew, the bulges merging together, becoming rounded mountains, and all at once it gave a jump, a shift backwards and with a loud crack, throwing Jane to the floor, the chalet was heaved after it and, as Sydney said it would, fell heavily against the little cliff into which it had been built. Jane heard Mrs Deal cry out and the sound of tables and chairs sliding and crashing about.

She scrambled up and clutched on to the window again. The chalet was being pulled backwards and sideways, groaning and creaking. And

now the balloon, still not quite balloon shaped, but loose and flapping and filling rapidly, started to sway and lollop into the air, pulling the chalet even more violently.

As it did so, Jane thought, but wasn't sure, that she heard a low rumble from far up the valley. At the same time a light breeze blew in her face. This caught the balloon and helped it swing upright.

'Faster, Mrs Deal,' Jane shouted. 'More gas!'

The rumbling was definite now, not so distant after all. The chalet lurched sideways, backwards, and then, as the filling balloon was caught by the wind, was suddenly wrenched forward and with a sound of snapping and breaking wood was pulled off the stilts that held it up.

For a sickening instant, as she overbalanced back on to the floor, Jane thought they were simply going to crash into the ground. But at last enough gas had flowed into the balloon. For a moment they sank, then, with a great gust, they were seized by the wind and hurled forwards and outwards over the valley. The air began to shriek. The chalet was blown outwards and at first downwards too, shaking and swaying, every timber straining. Then the vast lifting power of the helium took charge. Jane felt the shaking grow less. They were rising steadily, leaving her stomach behind. Pulling herself across the floor, she eventually managed to drag herself up and look out of the window again.

There below her she saw one of the strangest and most terrifying sights she had ever seen in her life. The whole top half of the valley, now about 800 feet below, was filled with a swirling cloud of whiteness which, writhing and spreading, emitted a continuous roar. In front of this, an invisible hand seemed to be scattering and flattening the trees, blasting out a path. Then, as Jane watched, the rising mass of whiteness went underneath her and with a deep, reverberating rumble the avalanche, millions upon millions of tons of rushing snow, passed down the valley, sweeping everything irresistibly before it.

Far above, the chalet rose smoothly into the pale sky.

5. The Mountains of
the Moon

FOR FIVE minutes Jane sat on the floor of her bedroom, recovering.
When she eventually came down into the living-room there was a scene
of considerable confusion. All the furniture had slid towards the front
door when the blast from the avalanche had first thrown them forwards, and then slid back and forth, ending up all over the place as,
whirling and buffeted, the balloon had carried them swiftly upwards.
Books and ornaments had shot from shelves, pictures had fallen and
broken or were hanging askew, Sydney's notes were everywhere. Also
the ropes cannot have been tied quite accurately because the chalet was
tilted up towards the kitchen.

'Well, we've done it,' Jane called to Mrs Deal, who was clinging to the
door of her kitchen. 'Isn't it thrilling?'

'I don't know about done it,' said Mrs Deal, in a quavery voice, 'you've
nearly done for me.'

But Jane was too excited to try and cheer her up. Hurrying through
the furniture she went to the nearest window and opened it.

The air that came in was thin and very cold. The deep blue sky, in
which there were already one or two stars, was cloudless. And when
you looked down past the remaining planks of the store-room . . . with
a start Jane pulled back. It was terrifying. Gripping the window ledge,
she looked slowly out and down again—terrifying but beautiful.

Far below, evening had already fallen on the valleys and low mountains. In the semi-darkness it was just possible to make out the smudged
masses of pine forests against the snow; in some of the valleys she could
see the lights of towns or villages; and here and there, but growing
more numerous to the left, great peaks rose up out of the gloom, their
flanks and tops still twinkling, like the chalet, with the golden glow of
the setting sun. It was silent, except for the faint creaking of the chalet's
wooden structure as it swung beneath the balloon.

Jane drew in her head. She felt quite dizzy. 'Have you seen the
aneroid?' she asked Mrs Deal. 'I think I'd better see how high we are.'

'If you ask me we're quite high enough,' said Mrs Deal.

Jane looked past her into the kitchen. She could just see some smashed plates on the floor. 'At least we're safe Mrs Deal,' she said. 'The chalet is still together, the ropes are holding OK.'

'We'd soon know if they weren't,' said Mrs Deal. 'And look at the mess. It will take a week to get straight. And my kitchen! Scarce a cup that could call itself by name. Did you see Mr Saxton on your way down?'

'No,' said Jane, 'but I expect he's still sleeping after all those pills.'

'I must go to him at once,' said Mrs Deal. 'Poor gentleman, too weak to call out.' Inch by inch, holding on to overturned chairs and walls where possible, she tiptoed across the kitchen floor. 'We don't want a glissade,' she said.

As she went, Jane suddenly saw the aneroid and, probably because they had fallen off the table together, the large map of Italy and Switzerland which Sydney had been working at.

It looked to her as though the aneroid showed just over 6,000 feet. That seemed quite high, so she took a chair and put it against the helium cylinders. One dial registered empty, the other a quarter full, with the spare one still full. Jane turned off the one showing a quarter, and went back to the table to look at the map.

Sydney had marked it with thick circles, one round Rotbad, their valley, the other round all the high peaks and ranges nearby. As far as Jane could see, the highest near them was 7,200 feet, and she wondered whether she should turn the cylinder on again. But the aneroid now showed 6,649 feet. They were still rising.

But where were they? It was impossible to tell; when Jane looked out of the window it was even impossible to see if they were moving. The chalet was now too far above the ground to judge their movement against it. After a few moments, she shut the window and went and looked at the map again. Since she didn't know in what direction they were moving, if indeed they were moving, it was impossible to tell which of the peaks ringed by Sydney were dangerous to them.

'It's an ill wind blows nobody any good,' called Mrs Deal cheerfully from the landing. 'He's sleeping like a baby.'

Suddenly Jane remembered that Sydney had said they would have a north wind. That meant a wind blowing from the north, in which case the chalet must be moving south. She looked at the map again. Sydney had only put his rings in quite a small area around their valley, since he had expected to land almost as soon as they were free of it, but it seemed to her that none of the mountains to the south were higher than 8,300 feet. She looked at the aneroid again—7,100 feet. If they were still rising at 9,000 feet, Jane thought, she would pump some gas back into the cylinders until the balloon stopped going up.

'Yes, sleeping like a child,' said Mrs Deal again, walking with more confidence up the sloping floor. 'Poor dear, his room was in a dreadful state. His bed had slid right over against the window but fortunately he hadn't stirred. It's getting awfully cold up there. Come to that,' she added, 'it's very cold in here, too.'

It was true. Rising (though slowly now) through the rarefied and freezing air at nearly 8,000 feet, the temperature in the chalet had been dropping steadily. Now they were both actually shivering. Mrs Deal opened the stove door.

'Nearly out,' she said with chattering teeth. 'And just as well, no doubt. A fire would blow us all to Kingdom Come with so much gas about. We'll freeze and like it I suppose.'

'Helium doesn't burn,' said Jane. 'I'll get some logs. Where are they?'

'In my bedroom,' said Mrs Deal. They found her bed, like a sinking raft, just visible amid a turbulent sea of logs and tins and other items she had carried up from the store-room. Together they carried down several loads of logs and soon had the stove roaring again.

While Mrs Deal cooked some supper, Jane stood at the window. The earth below was now almost entirely covered in darkness. Only a few giant mountains still had their peaks touched with golden light; as indeed were the balloon and the chalet until, to Mrs Deal's surprise and relief, they stopped rising at 9,480 feet, and floated steadily in the black, clear night. Supper, eaten by lamplight, was fried corned beef hash, with tinned new potatoes and ending with tinned peaches. After it, they both went up to bed.

As she lay in bed, listening to the creaking and groaning of the chalet as it gently swung beneath the balloon, Jane thought how odd it was to be nine and a half thousand feet high, warm and safe, with nothing between them and the snow-covered mountains far below but freezing empty air. Soon she fell asleep.

Lulled by the gentle motion of the chalet and worn out by all the excitement and work, Jane slept late. Mrs Deal, however, had been up several hours by the time she eventually came down. The stove was burning, breakfast was laid and the sun streamed through the windows on to a living-room neat as a new pin.

'I've quite come round to these cylinders,' said Mrs Deal when she saw Jane. 'See how nicely they take a shine. Now sit down and have your cornflakes and I'll do you a nice egg and bacon.'

But first, Jane hurried to the windows. Unfortunately, high as they were, the view this time was a little disappointing. Stretching away miles below them were scattered rafts and streamers of cloud; the ground she could see between these distant clouds was little more than a grey-blue blur.

'At least we seem clear of the mountains,' she called to Mrs Deal, shutting the window against the piercing air. 'I think after breakfast I'll try and take the balloon down a bit and see if we can find out where we are.'

Mrs Deal put her head round the kitchen door and spoke above the sound of frying. 'I hope you're not going to touch the controls my girl—remember what happened in the *Ladyship*. Wait till Mr Saxton comes down.'

'The *Ladyship* crashed because of the computer,' said Jane, feeling this was unfair of Mrs Deal. 'I shan't do anything dangerous. But how is Sydney?'

'Still sleeping peacefully,' said Mrs Deal. 'We'll leave him till one o'clock then I'll take him up a light lunch. Couldn't be better for him.'

After breakfast, while Mrs Deal added a final scintilla of luster to the already gleaming helium cylinders, Jane studied the pumps.

The way they worked, like everything Sir Christopher invented, was simple and ingenious. A long handle was attached to each cylinder. When a small knob on the top was turned to 'Deflate', the gas valve was opened and the handle pumped back and forth. Gas was then sucked back from the balloon, re-compressed into liquid in a compression chamber inside the pump and forced back into the cylinder.

Jane waited until Mrs Deal went upstairs, then fetched a chair and the aneroid and carried them over to the cylinders.

'Just you watch how you go with them things, Miss Jane,' called Mrs Deal from the landing. 'I don't fancy a repetition of events in the Airship.'

'I'll be very careful,' said Jane.

The pump was effective but very slow. After ten minutes' hard work there was still no movement on the aneroid. Jane wondered if it was broken. She knew that in an emergency she could always pull the cord, as Sydney had showed her, which let out gas. But this of course meant gas was wasted.

She pumped on, her arms aching. Upstairs she could hear bumping as Mrs Deal arranged the logs and tins in large neat piles around her room. The chalet swayed gently to and fro. Jane changed hands and then changed back again. And then, suddenly, the needle of the aneroid flickered.

Jane picked it up and was surprised to see that in fact they had been very gently sinking for some time. The needle registered 8,700 feet.

But when she looked out of the window and down through the cold air it was difficult to see if they were moving down at all. The islands and layers of cloud were more numerous here, yet they seemed to remain the same great distance below. It was just as cold. Only the creeping needle of the aneroid showed that they were in fact slowly descending.

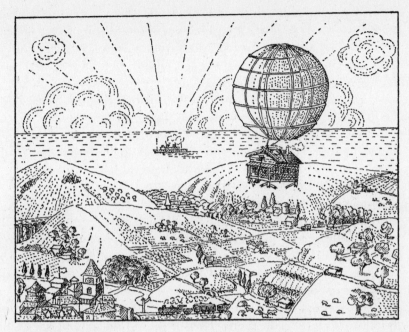

At 5,000 feet, when at last it was noticeably warmer, the chalet sank into the first mound of cloud. At once the situation changed. It was now possible to see that they were gently falling. Wisps and chunks of cloud rose up past the window. Jane put out her hand, trying to catch them.

At 3,000 feet, the chalet dropped abruptly out of the bottom of the cloud and the sight below was so startling that Jane flung back her head and shouted, 'Mrs Deal! Mrs Deal! Come and see where we are!'

The chalet was floating down and over rounded hills covered in bluey-grey scrub with occasional pines. Jane could see tiny villages and houses, and small winding roads along which even smaller cars slowly moved, and beyond it all the sea.

'Well, it's a relief to see solid earth again,' said Mrs Deal, who was standing beside her, 'though 'see' is no doubt all we'll have of it. There's no telling where we are. The cars drive on the right. That might be a clue.'

'Not really,' said Jane, remembering one of Miss Woolley's classes at Inkpen School. 'They only drive on the left in England and Hong Kong and we know we're not there.'

'Well, there can be no question of landing,' said Mrs Deal. 'We'd be dashed to smithereens at this speed.'

It was true that the wind must have been quite strong. Already the pine-covered hills had been left far behind, and they were skimming above flat fields crossed by straight roads. Effortlessly, the balloon carried them along, gradually dropping lower.

'I think that's a palm tree,' said Mrs Deal, who was getting interest-ed despite herself. Jane went and fetched Sydney's binoculars so that they could read any large notice, and for ten minutes they leant out of the window pointing things out to each other and trying to read sign-posts and advertisements. Mrs Deal said they looked like Greek to her. It was partly because they became so absorbed, and partly because the chalet had swung round to face the hills, that they did not see until too late the danger towards which they were being carried.

Blown by the wind, the chalet swung round again so that they could see the main road again, below them to the right.

'Look, they're stopping and waving,' said Jane, waving back. 'I expect they think we're in a film.'

'And there's the sea!' cried Mrs Deal. 'How lovely.'

At the same time, too late to do anything, they realized what was happening.

'We'll be carried out to sea,' said Jane. 'Quick. we must land. I'll pull the emergency rope.'

But she was too late. Little villas with neat gardens were passing swiftly not 600 feet below them. Then it was a thin strip of grey sand and shingle. Then the grey, flat waves gleaming in the occasional sun; and in a moment the shore was receding behind them and they were being blown out to sea.

Oddly enough, Mrs Deal seemed neither worried nor surprised.

'As I told you both,' she said, 'I knew we'd be up for weeks. Fortunately there's plenty to eat. I managed another load before Mr Saxton's collapse. Which reminds me. It's time the good gentleman had some lunch.'

While Jane switched the knobs on the cylinders to 'Inflate', and allowed helium to flow back into the balloon and bring them gradually up again from a sea now perilously close beneath them, Mrs Deal went to wake Sydney. It took some time to rouse him from his Slogodon sleep, but when eventually she did, he insisted on putting on his dress-ing gown and being helped downstairs.

'I don't think it was a heart attack,' he said weakly, 'probably a severe palpitation. But you say you gave me an injection Mrs Deal? Without that I've no doubt I should have had an attack. And I deserved one. Very conceited to think I could do so much at my age.'

'Nonsense, Mr Saxton,' said Mrs Deal, supporting him under one arm. 'As clear a case of self-sacrifice as ever I've seen.'

Once settled in front of the stove with a bowl of soup and a rug, Sydney began to recover. Principally he was amazed and delighted at the success of the balloon. He made them go over every detail.

'And you did it alone, you two. It's truly remarkable. Though I must confess to a feeling of pride that it worked so well.'

After lunch, while Sydney sat by the window, well wrapped up, and held the aneroid, Jane worked the pumps and they practised rising and falling. They became quite good at it and found that it was easy to rise fast, but took longer to start going down. When they had finished this, Sydney stabilized the balloon at 5,000 feet, just above the clouds. He then got out his maps and tried to work out where they might be. But beyond a guess that they had probably crossed the coast some where in the region of Genoa, he said he'd have to wait till they saw a landmark before he knew exactly.

He and Mrs Deal went to bed very early, Sydney because he still felt weak and rather drugged. Mrs Deal herself, after a glass of medicinal gin, taken to restore her strength, confessed that she had actually got up at 4 o'clock in the morning to begin tidying, and she wasn't, as she said, as young as she had been.

When they had gone, Jane cleared all the tins and packets and parcels out on to the floor and ran a full deep bath. The water surged backwards and forwards with the swaying of the chalet and if she didn't interrupt its rhythm would gradually mount up and spill over both ends. She splashed and washed and eventually pulled out the plug, imagining how odd it would seem to a sea captain far below if a lot of hot, soapy rain suddenly fell on his ship.

So normal did it now seem to be living in a house that floated 5,000 feet in the sky, that she never remembered that all regular supplies like electricity had been cut off. Her bath had probably used practically all the water the chalet had left.

Jane learnt that this was, in fact, exactly what had happened the moment she came down to breakfast.

'No water,' said Mrs Deal, looking for some reason rather pleased. 'Not a drop. Instead of the sea, it's a waterless grave for us. I knew it would get us in the end.'

'What do you mean, 'it'?' said Jane, feeling irritated as well as rather guilty.

'I mean what I say,' said Mrs Deal mysteriously, 'you mark my words.'

'Well anyway, the water is my fault,' said Jane. 'I had a bath.'

'It would have happened sooner or later,' said Mrs Deal. 'You were just the instrument of fate, an unwitting tool.' She went into the kitchen, while Jane started what she had to admit was a rather dry breakfast—cornflakes without milk, toast and marmalade.

However, Sydney, when he came down in his dressing gown after his own breakfast, said things weren't as bad as they seemed. All they would have to do would be to let the chalet sink below the level of the clouds and hope that some of them contained rain. He suggested that they pull the drainpipe outside the bathroom window away from the wall and direct it into the bath.

This he managed to do fairly easily with his walking stick, and that very afternoon they descended through a thick blanket of cloud and found themselves in a heavy rainstorm. By the time it had finished, the bath was well over half full and Jane and Mrs Deal carried the water to the roof and emptied it into the tank.

Sydney recovered rapidly and was soon his old self again. He decided that he would abandon his book and instead keep notes of what happened to them every day. This seemed a great relief to him and Jane thought she had never seen him go to his table with so much pleasure. He also tried to work out where they were.

'We are being blown pretty steadily south-south-east,' he said, a direction Jane had never heard of. 'That means we'll pass over Sicily, or close to it.'

He was soon proved right. The very morning after the rainstorm they saw their first land. It was a group of small islands far ahead of them and a little to the left. Standing on the sunbathing platform under the swelling balloon, Sydney was able to identify them through his binoculars.

'The Lipari Isles, north of Sicily,' he said. 'With any luck we'll see Stromboli tonight.' Sure enough, soon after darkness had fallen, they saw some distance from them the orange glow of the volcano.

So they skimmed gently south (or rather, south-south-east). Mrs Deal settled into one of her cleaning, polishing, dusting routines. Jane became rather bored. She tried bringing the balloon down just above the sea and fishing from it with bits of food stuck on a pin tied to some string. But it was difficult to keep the chalet at a completely even height and it kept jerking her line out of the water. She caught nothing. Sydney used the occasion to throw some small logs in and try and work out how fast they were going.

'If we keep on like this we should strike the coast of Libya tomorrow night or the next morning,' he said.

'Well, the sooner we land the better I'll be pleased,' said Mrs Deal. 'We've plenty of food and fuel that's one mercy, but I'm tired of being blown hither and thither, as if I were no more than a cloud.'

It grew warmer as they were blown south and they didn't need the stove during the day. At night, however, they always took the balloon up to 10,000 feet (a job Sydney left entirely to Jane, who had become very good at it) in case they should be blown to a place where there were mountains. A fire was very necessary at that height, and so it was always lit and filled with logs. They also managed to duck under two more rainstorms which completely filled the tank and the bath.

Then on the sixth day, they sighted land. It was Jane who saw it first. The chalet was quite low, about 1,000 feet, and she was lying on the platform under the balloon, sunbathing. She sat up to turn over and brown her back when—there it was! A thin low rim to the horizon, grey or sand-coloured. Jane looked very carefully and then came running downstairs.

'There's something very like land on the horizon,' she said excitedly.

Sydney got up from his table, where he had been catching up on his notes. 'Well done,' he said. 'Mrs Deal, where are my binoculars?'

'Don't strain yourself,' warned Mrs Deal, handing him the heavy leather case. 'Rest them on the window sill.'

Sydney looked for a long time, then he said, 'Take her to 5,000 feet, Jane. I think you're right.'

Now there was no doubt at all. Even without binoculars they could see, crescent-shaped, the coast of Africa curving far ahead and below them.

'Yes, that's Libya all right,' said Sydney, lowering his glasses. 'We should make it tonight.'

'Heaven be praised!' cried Mrs Deal. 'Solid earth beneath my feet at last.'

But during the afternoon the wind gradually died away. By evening the chalet hung, almost motionless, a mile or so from the shore, where they could plainly see the white houses and breakwater of a small port. At one time a gentle breeze even began to blow them out to sea again.

'How warm it is,' said Jane feeling it on her face. 'It actually feels hot.'

'It's blowing off the Fezzan Desert in the middle of Libya,' said Sydney, who was examining the little port through his binoculars. 'One of the hottest places in the world even at this time of the year. It's the reason this is one of the few coasts where you can get an onshore wind after dark—though I fear it will come too late for us.'

'How do you know?' said Jane.

'I think that must be El Awegia,' said Sydney, putting down his binoculars. 'Well, nearly fifty years ago now, I was ADC to General Herkenshaw, the High Commissioner at Benghazi.'

'General Herkenshaw?' cried Jane. 'But I know General Herkenshaw. You know, Mrs Deal, that nice friend of Daddy's.'

'That would have been his son William,' said Sydney. 'They were both generals. Quite rare. Anyway, I know the country round here quite well—or did at one time. I think that will be El Awegia, or one of several similar ports hereabouts.'

Night fell, a few lights twinkled on in El Awegia, but the now invisible shore remained as tantalizingly far away as ever. Then, as Sydney had said, they began to move towards it. The wind grew stronger. Soon, looking down, Jane thought she could see waves breaking.

'Will you bring her down, please, Jane?' said Sydney.

'How far?' said Jane.

'You're not going to try and land in the dark?' cried Mrs Deal, pulling her head in sharply from one of the windows. 'In this inky blackness? There could be a herd of tigers down there.'

'They don't have tigers in Africa, Mrs Deal,' said Sydney. 'Just bring her down a few hundred feet Jane. I want to see if it's El Awegia or not.'

'No tigers in Africa?' cried Mrs Deal. 'Fiddlesticks!'

But Sydney was leaning too far out of the window to hear what she said. 'A bit lower, Jane,' he called.

Unfortunately the balloon had been blown too far down the coast and he was unable to find out any more.

'I shall assume it's El Awegia,' he said, walking to his desk.

'Shall we go higher?' said Jane.

'Yes,' said Sydney. 'We needn't go too high. Stop at 3,000 feet. There are no mountains near here. Or rather,' he added, 'not very near, and I certainly hope we shall be safe on land long before we have to think about them.'

'Hear hear,' said Mrs Deal from the kitchen, where they could hear a savoury corned beef hash frying.

At one time in the night the wind must have been quite strong, because Jane woke up to hear the chalet groaning and creaking, and she could feel it swinging under the balloon.

It was this wind which started them on their journey to disaster. When Jane got up, she thought at first they had been blown back over the sea again. But it was not the sea they had been blown out upon but a vast, desolate desert. And as they floated motionless above it, Jane could already feel waves of heat being reflected of the sands below.

It was the Fezzan Desert, as she learnt from Sydney when she came down into the living-room. He was very worried.

'We could be stuck here for weeks,' he said. 'They have calms that last a month at least.'

'Why don't we land, Mr Saxton?' said Mrs Deal. 'At least we'd have our feet on firm ground.'

'We'd hardly last a day, Mrs Deal,' said Sydney. 'Even at this time of the year, the heat during the day is terrible. It's one of the hottest places in the world. And at night—fierce cold. If I'd guessed this was going to happen I might have risked a night landing.'

'I think it blew quite hard last night,' said Jane.

'It must have,' he said, frowning and going back to look at the atlas on his desk. 'We've been blown all of three hundred miles.'

For two days they hung above the Fezzan Desert. No matter how high or low they went, they could find no wind. The heat was so strong that it streamed up in shimmering waves, making it impossible to see clearly to the horizon. While this lasted, throughout the day, they fixed the balloon at 8,000 feet, where it was pleasantly cool. The night, however, was as cold as the day had been hot. They would bring the balloon down to 500 feet, stoke up the fire with wood from Mrs Deal's bed room, fill hot water bottles (whose water was carefully returned to the tank each morning) and pile blankets on their beds. The first evening, Sydney, who was becoming increasingly anxious about their chances of escape, made Jane bring the balloon down to 30 feet so that he could leave a message in a bottle.

'It's a slender chance,' he said, 'but a caravan might pass this way.'

'Do you think so?' said Jane, rather mystified. 'I doubt it.'

'An Arab caravan,' said Sydney. 'A string of camels.'

On the third day, a slight wind started up, which freshened until by lunch time Sydney estimated they were being blown along at twenty miles an hour. But this pleased him no more than had their not moving at all. He looked constantly at his atlas, and then went and stood at the window with his binoculars, muttering, 'I don't like it.'

'Why?' said Jane.

'I won't tell you because I could be wrong,' said Sydney. 'The scale of this atlas is very small and my memory may be faulty.'

'I knew this venture would end in disaster,' said Mrs Deal. 'We should have stayed put and trusted in the Lord.'

All night the wind blew, and in the morning they learnt what Sydney feared. He had taken them up to 2,000 feet to avoid the dust and sand coming up from the Fezzan Desert. When Jane came down he was standing at the window, gloomy and taciturn, looking down at swirling grey clouds puffing across the flat surface far below.

'It's the Tiran,' he said. 'It's the worst thing that could have happened.'

'But I thought we wanted to get off the desert,' said Jane.

'Yes, but not due south,' said Sydney. 'Come here both of you and I'll show you why.'

Jane went and stood beside him, and Mrs Deal came from the kitchen, nervously polishing an egg-timer. Sydney opened the window wide and stood back so that they could both look out. 'What do you see?' he said, pointing.

Mrs Deal drew back. Jane looked out. 'Hills,' she said.

'Exactly,' said Sydney, 'and do you know what those hills are?'

Neither of them answered. Sydney paused, while Jane looked again at the low grey hills plainly visible in the distance. 'Unless I'm very much mistaken,' he said, 'those are the foothills to the Mountains of the Moon.'

'Oh, mercy on us!' cried Mrs Deal.

'Why, do you know about them Mrs Deal?' said Sydney, interested.

'No,' said Mrs Deal. 'But I don't like the sound of them. They sound eerie.'

'Yes, perhaps eerie is the word,' said Sydney, thoughtfully walking over to his table. 'Strange certainly. Come round here and I'll explain.'

Then, pointing occasionally at the open atlas, he told them about the Mountains of the Moon. They were a ring of mountains rising abruptly from the southern edge of the Fezzan Desert. The mountains were very high—none lower than 20,000 feet—and their sides were almost vertical. The circle they formed was unbroken. On the inside, the sides fell just as steeply and the ring of mountains surrounded a deep valley. From aeroplanes, it could be seen that this valley was covered by a dense tropical jungle with a lake towards one end. But the Mountains of the Moon were stranger than this, for they themselves were surrounded by another, outer ring of mountains which, though not as high as the ones they encircled, rose in places to 16,000 feet. And in between these two vast rings of mountains there was a mile-wide gap, a deep canyon filled with a rushing river, which protected the Mountains of the Moon like a natural moat.

'A formidable barrier,' said Sydney, 'and one which has never been penetrated. Or rather, from which no expedition has ever returned. Before the war, five assaults failed on the steep, ice-covered climb up. After the war, two expeditions are believed to have got down into the valley, but they never got back.'

'Does anybody live in the valley?' said Jane.

'Nobody knows,' said Sydney. 'There are legends in the surrounding tribes of course: that the Mountains are hollow and that sort of thing. But a barrier which has so far resisted the best equipped of modern mountaineering expeditions is unlikely to have been penetrated by savages. No, I think we can be sure that there are no people in the valley.'

Two hours later, the outer rampart or ring of mountains came into view. Terrifyingly high, they stretched the entire length of the horizon. The hot, dry Tiran blew the chalet swiftly along, high above the barren gullies, empty water courses and grey rocky hills of the outer desert.

Sydney, who was looking ahead through his binoculars, suddenly said, 'There they are! Look Jane! Tilt the binoculars quite high. The Mountains of the Moon!'

Jane put the binoculars to her eyes and immediately the first ring of mountains jumped close. They seemed to rise straight up from the foothills—cliff upon cliff, tumbling ravine, sheer crags, rising steeper and steeper until snow appeared, flashing in the sun. Jane moved the binoculars from side to side. There was no end to them.

'Higher,' said Sydney. 'Point the binoculars higher. You're only looking at the outer ring.'

And suddenly Jane saw them. They towered above the outer ring like a man standing by a boy. All white from snow and ice, she had at first thought they were some trick of the sun on high cloud. They rose sheer, distant, implacable, icy perpendiculars stretching for the sky.

'The Mountains of the Moon,' whispered Jane. 'Sydney—we'll never get past those. We'll be dashed to pieces.'

'Well, we must make a decision,' said Sydney. 'We can try and land in the foothills now, though we must remember that the Tiran is blowing at a good forty miles an hour now. I doubt we'd survive the crash. And if we did, our chances of being picked up by one of the nomadic tribes are remote and not necessarily pleasant. Or we can attempt to cross the Mountains of the Moon, a hazardous undertaking whose dangers I need hardly point out. What do you think, Mrs Deal?'

'It doesn't seem to me to furnish one with the materials of a proper choice,' said Mrs Deal. 'It's either crashing and being eaten by cannibals and tigers now, or crashing into those mountains and falling to our death in a few hours' time. I leave it to you, Mr Saxton.'

'I think we should try and cross them,' said Jane.

'On balance, I agree with you,' said Sydney. 'Now—we must prepare.'

First, more gas was let into the balloon. But, urgent as it was to start rising, Sydney only let in half a cylinder. At the enormous height they were going to try and reach, he explained, the gas would expand. If they put in too much now, the balloon might burst later. Nor could they put in a lot of helium now and pump it out as they rose because the lack of oxygen as they got higher would certainly make them muddled.

'I shall probably become unconscious,' said Sydney. 'If I do, give me some digitalis, cover me up and we must hope for the best.'

'The worst, you mean,' snorted Mrs Deal. 'A speedy end and a tidy one, not lingering on some snowy peak or amidst the bubbles of a cannibal's pot.'

They stoked up the fire to prepare for the cold and put on their warmest clothes. Sydney put a syringe of digitalis on his table, a blanket over his chair, and spread paper to take notes of the ascent. Chairs, books and other liftable objects were placed by the windows to be thrown out if they had to rise in a hurry.

And all the while, they floated steadily higher. But, thought Jane, surely not high enough. They were now within three miles of the outer ring. Though these did not rise as sheer as they had at first seemed to, they were extremely steep. Great shoulders and knees of mountain thrust up from the barren foothills. They towered above the little balloon, blotting out the Mountains of the Moon behind them.

'Won't we be blown against the sides?' asked Jane anxiously.

'I don't think so,' said Sydney. 'Watch.'

As they came within a mile of the outer mountains, the wind gradually changed direction. Soon they were being blown along beside them.

'Nine thousand feet,' said Jane, who was holding the aneroid.

A few minutes later, Sydney, who was standing behind her at the window, pointed ahead and down. Far below, Jane saw the flashing and foaming of a river.

'That is the river which over millions of years has cut the great circular canyon between the outer ring and the Mountains of the Moon,' he said. 'In a moment we will see the gorge it has made in the outer ring. I rather fancy we will be carried through that.'

This was what happened. The balloon and the chalet were now gathering speed, and at the same time seemed to be drawing closer to the precipitous sides of the mountains. Jane could clearly see pockets of glistening snow. Frightened, she shrank back against Sydney, whose bony hand rested comfortingly on her shoulder. Then, just as it seemed they must crash, the side of the mountain disappeared, the balloon was swept round the edge and was blown through a great gorge which opened out in front. But magnificent as this was, it was the Mountains of the Moon at which they stared. Now only a mile or so away, they rose sheer into the sky, so steep that Jane had to tilt her head far back to see their peaks, and so dazzling where the sun caught the ice and snow, it was difficult to look. They were a splendid and terrifying sight.

Now began one of the strangest and most frightening journeys Jane was ever to make. Later, when she tried to remember what happened, it seemed vague and confused, like remembering a dream—or a nightmare.

Once through the gorge, the wind fell away and the balloon began to drift to the right, towards the gloomy canyon between the inner and outer mountains. It grew darker and darker. Soon it became impossible to see the rushing river far below. Six or seven thousand feet above them a narrow band of light showed where the outer ring came to an end. It also began to grow very cold. Mrs Deal, moving heavily, opened the door of the stove and threw in some logs. At first, innumerable cascades and fountains of water had sprung from both sides and plummeted down into the darkness, making no sound. But now the balloon, rising ever more slowly, passed only ice and snow. They were at 13,000 feet, which was as high as the aneroid would register.

Jane put it down and felt her way through the semi-darkness towards the window. Drifting in the great void between the vertical walls, rising through the extraordinary silence, the balloon sometimes came within a few hundred feet of the glistening, ice-covered rock. With a surge of sluggish fear, she wondered what would happen if they were to hit the side. She sat down and pressed her forehead against the icy window pane. The balloon drifted closer. Her head nodded back and then fell forward against the cold glass. It did not wake her.

How long she dozed she did not know, but when her eyes opened the balloon was so close to the glistening rockface that she felt she could have touched it with a broom. She stared out, trying to wake up, trying to remember where they were. And then, as the balloon drifted a little further away, she noticed that it had stopped rising. Through the gloom she could see that they hung opposite exactly the same place in the canyon.

They were trapped. The ice-covered rocks loomed over them oppressively. Sooner or later they were bound to touch them, the balloon would burst and they would fall to their deaths. With thudding heart, Jane opened the window—wincing at the freezing air it let in—and with enormous effort lifted a chair and threw it out. She threw out another, and two of Sydney's books, and then had to sit back panting and exhausted. It took her ten minutes to throw out four chairs and all of Sydney's books, including, unfortunately, all the notes for the book he had been writing.

Still the chalet hung steady, now once again drifting in the half-darkness towards the sharp, ice-covered rocks. With growing panic, Jane realized there was only one thing to do. She must risk more gas. Panting, her head aching, she dragged herself across the room and turned the second cylinder full on. Moments later she felt the balloon rising again, and rising fast.

It was now that she noticed that Mrs Deal and Sydney were both unconscious. Mrs Deal had slid to the floor and fallen on her side. Sydney had sprawled forward over the table, his pen still resting between his fingers. With a final effort, feeling in a dream, Jane pulled herself over to him. She arranged the blankets around his shoulders and catching sight, in the rapidly growing light, of his syringe, she pushed it unconcernedly into his arm and pressed home the plunger. Then, feeling somehow that her task was done, she lay on the floor in front of the stove and closed her eyes. At this moment sunlight flooded through the windows, as the balloon finally lifted them above the first stage of their journey, the outer rim of mountains. Then it continued to climb steadily higher, up and up and up into the silent, freezing, oxygenless air, with the chalet and its unconscious cargo swaying gently beneath it.

Jane never knew what woke her. Perhaps it was the sound of a giant rock falling into the chasm. Perhaps it was some determination buried deep within her. Whatever it was, it is certain that had she not woken they would all have died.

The little room was freezing cold and bright with sun. Sydney and Mrs Deal lay unconscious, their breath so shallow as to scarcely show in the icy air.

With immense effort, each pull causing her to gasp, Jane dragged herself up and staggered across to the window.

The sight was amazing. The balloon had now lifted the chalet almost to the top of the Mountains of the Moon (they were in fact floating at 22,574 feet). Far below Jane could see a dark line where the outer rim of mountains formed their chasm with the Mountains of the Moon. And beyond this outer rim, and yet further below, a dim haze concealed what must have been the Fezzan Desert.

But the scene beside her had changed entirely. Instead of the sheer and icy walls there were broken slopes, covered in snow, leading to the peaks of the Mountains of the Moon. As she watched, the balloon moved steadily in towards one of those gleaming ridges.

Now they were so high, the balloon had once again stopped rising. At the same time, at this great height, they seemed to have been caught in a stratospheric stream of swiftly flowing air. The chalet was moving quite fast. Not far below, Jane could see the snow being whipped from the sides of exposed rocks. Not at all far below. In fact, the balloon seemed to be falling. Not fifteen feet below she could see their huge shadow; the snow was whirling off the sides of the ridge. Sluggish, feeling sick, Jane looked for something to throw out. They mustn't crash.

Immediately, with a violent tilt and the sound of smashing crockery and sliding furniture, they struck the ridge. Jane was flung to the ground. Then the chalet gave another lurch, she felt a sinking feeling in her stomach and all at once they began rising quite fast into the air.

With a great effort, panting and numb with cold, she pulled herself up and looked out of the window. It was clear what had happened. The chalet had been carried against the top of the ridge. But instead of being dashed to pieces, only the long planks which had once been a wall of the old store-room underneath had been broken off. Relieved of this weight the balloon had started to rise again.

And in a few minutes its rapid ascent revealed the most extraordinary sight. They were now being carried quite fast above the broken, icy rocks which covered the peaks of the Mountains of the Moon. Suddenly, looking ahead, clinging weakly to the ice-covered window-sill, Jane saw that the ground had begun to fall. A moment later she was looking down slopes, not vertical as on the other side, but certainly extremely steep. Down, down, down she looked, through huge ravines, over precipitous, curling glaciers, over cliffs and farther down, past clouds, small hills and a running river, thin as a thread, until, no larger than a book, 24,000 feet below, she saw a dim, shimmering green, the pale vegetable haze of the jungle which filled the large round valley encircled by the Mountains of the Moon.

But above this immense void, the balloon, with the chalet swinging beneath it, was still swiftly rising.

Her head swimming, almost asleep, Jane knew what she had to do. Stumbling against the few remaining chairs, she staggered across the room and up the stairs on hands and knees. At the top, hanging down through the trap door in the roof, was the rope attached to the emergency gas escape valve on the balloon. Wearily Jane reached up and with the last of her strength pulled down on it.

How long should she hold? Was it a minute—or ten? Sydney had said something about not too long, or was it not too short? Jane felt her eyes closing. Her whole body was without feeling. Her heart was fluttering and no breath seemed to satisfy her. Slowly, with a little sigh, she let go the rope and slipped unconscious to the floor.

Above her, inaudible in the icy and indifferent air at 25,200 feet, the emergency valve snapped shut.

6. The Jungle

BY THE time Jane had fainted, a good deal of gas had escaped and the balloon was falling swiftly through the thin air. As it sank lower, however, the speed of its fall became slower. A buffeting wind carried it away from the cliff edges and far out into the middle of the enormous bowl into which it was sinking. The air became thicker. And at 8,000 feet, when Jane became conscious again, it was just possible to feel currents of warm air rising from below, still further slowing the chalet's fall.

Leaning weakly against the ladder leading to the roof, Jane looked down into the living-room and saw Sydney and Mrs Deal still lying unconscious near the stove, their legs entangled as though they had fainted while dancing. The room, swaying slightly, was in chaos. But there was no doubt it was warmer. The ice on the window panes was melting. Her breath was only just visible when she breathed out. As quickly as her stiff legs and numb fingers allowed, she stumbled down the stairs and over to the window.

Once more the view had completely changed. All round the valley, but quite distant now, the Mountains of the Moon rose to their jagged snowy peaks. And below, covering the whole vast floor and rising some way up the sides, was an enormous jungle. Jane found the aneroid, now registering again, and watched their descent. 8,000, 7,000, 6,500, 6,200 feet—ever more slowly the balloon sank towards the green carpet below. The mid-afternoon African sun became strong again. At 4,000 feet Jane could just hear a confused sound—a jumble of cries and screeches as from a distant zoo. She began to pick out trees from the green background; some distance up the valley there gleamed a vast lake. We'll be landing soon, thought Jane.

She hurried to the helium cylinders, switched to the third and last one, and let gas flow up into the balloon until the hand on the aneroid was scarcely moving. She had just turned off the cylinder when there came a low moan from in front of the fire.

Sydney, though his colour had returned, was still lying unconscious. But Mrs Deal had opened her eyes and was staring at the ceiling. She did not blink or even move her eyes when Jane gently shook her and waved the aneroid in front of her face.

'Look Mrs Deal,' she said, 'only two thousand feet. We're safe. We're going to land soon.' But, eyes fixed, Mrs Deal just groaned again.

There was no time to bother about Mrs Deal. The chalet was still sinking too fast. Jane let another surge of gas out of the cylinder and then, when the needle of the aneroid was completely steady, went to the window.

They had stopped about 50 feet above the trees. These were enormous, and so tangled with huge creepers and clusters of thick leaves that it was impossible to see the ground. Every now and again, among the waving greens, were flashes of gold and red and blue, as brightly coloured birds flew calling from the shadow of the chalet drifting over them; Jane saw some monkeys, who also fled chattering; but she saw nothing else. There were no clearings or river banks, no hills rising above the trees where the chalet might have landed; for twenty minutes they were gently blown above a jungle that seemed to stretch unbroken to the Mountains of the Moon.

And then at last Jane saw a break in the trees. It was ahead of them; a small clearing where, if they were not to miss it, they must land at once. With beating heart and wishing Sydney were there to do it instead of herself, she rushed up to the landing and pulled the rope which opened the emergency valve.

The chalet began to fall almost at once. The noise of the birds and insects and monkeys grew louder. Looking across the landing, Jane suddenly saw a treetop through Sydney's window, and she let go the rope so that they would land lightly.

They nearly did so. But at the last moment a gust of wind caught the balloon and carried it against one of the trees. The chalet gave a violent lurch and then hung for an instant, leaning steeply forwards. Jane was hurled against the bannisters, catching a glimpse as she fell of Sydney and Mrs Deal rolling over and over through the confusion below. The air was full of the sound of sliding furniture, breaking branches and tearing balloon; the chalet tipped wildly up and down, shuddering and creaking, descending in a series of colossal jerks until it hit the ground with a final thud, tilted gently to the left and was still.

In the silence Jane heard, as weeks before on the mountain in Switzerland, the gentle hiss of escaping gas, and then the raucous hubbub of the jungle surged back.

Oddly enough, it was Mrs Deal who recovered first. Jane heard bumping from downstairs. She pulled herself up and peered over the banisters.

The scene below was one of total chaos. Broken furniture was piled everywhere, papers, tins of food from the kitchen and smashed crockery over it and under it; the windows were broken and ash from the fire, long since burnt out, was settling in a fine dust; and over the jumble, like a lumberjack on a log jam, Mrs Deal was clambering to the door.

'Mrs Deal!' called Jane. 'Where are you going?'

Mrs Deal turned and looked up, propping herself on the angled floor with the broom she was carrying. Her grey hair hung on either side of her forehead, where a large blue bruise was already visible, her skirt was torn, but her jaw was set and her eyes fierce.

'I've had all I can take, Miss Jane,' she said. 'I've had more than I can take. I was never all that keen on the air force, brave lads though they were, and this craft has more than fulfilled my worst fears. You have done your best. Now it's time for an adult to take a hand. I shall make for the nearest outpost of civilization and return with help.' So saying, she turned round, stumbled over the kitchen table, forced open the door and disappeared into the sunlight outside.

'Mrs Deal!' shouted Jane starting down the stairs. 'Stop, Mrs Deal! You're mad. You can't leave us.' Her bruises forgotten, she climbed swiftly over the furniture. Behind an overturned table, she thought she saw Sydney trying to sit up. Then she was out on the veranda, had jumped down into the grass and was blinking in the sun.

The clearing was not large; the size of about three tennis courts surrounded by jungle. At one side there seemed to be a pool, but the grass was as high as Jane's waist and it was difficult to tell. The broom upright in her hand like a staff, Mrs Deal was already half-way across.

'Mrs Deal, Sydney will be cross,' shouted Jane, starting after her.

'I'd rather risk that good gentleman's wrath than that cockleshell taking wing again,' called Mrs Deal without pausing. 'I know my duty and now there's dry ground and solid under my feet I'm not flinching from it.'

'You'll get lost,' shouted Jane. 'It's dangerous—gorillas, buffaloes, snakes!' Mrs Deal strode relentlessly on. In a moment she'd be gone. Suddenly Jane remembered what she had to say.

'Tigers!' she screamed. 'Mrs Deal there are tigers! You'll be eaten alive by tigers!'

Mrs Deal stopped. At the word 'tigers' she stood quite still and stared ahead. When Jane reached her she found she was trembling.

'Thank goodness you called to me, Miss Jane,' she said. 'Another minute and I'd've been gone.'

'Sydney said they were man-eaters,' said Jane, hoping Mrs Deal would not remember what he had in fact said.

'You needn't tell me,' said Mrs Deal. 'All tigers are man-eaters. Come, we must hurry back to the chalet.'

As they walked back she told Jane that when she was a little girl she had seen a man mauled by a tiger in a zoo. It was not a thing she liked to talk about. She'd had nightmares for years. Crunching the man's arm as though it had been a stick of rock. The tiger's teeth! The thought of it made her want to scream aloud.

At the chalet, Mrs Deal hurried Jane up on to the veranda. 'I only hope we're safe here,' she said. 'I'll have to do something about those windows.'

'Why don't you just close the shutters?' said Jane.

'Shutters,' said Mrs Deal scornfully. 'It'll take more than shutters to keep the ravening beasts at bay.'

When they came into the living-room they found Sydney, weak but conscious, leaning against the wall. He smiled and raised his hand.

'Are you all right?' asked Jane anxiously.

'I shall be as right as rain in a few hours. I'm still a little weak now. But what happened? Where have we landed?'

Briefly and modestly Jane told him everything. Sydney listened with growing interest and excitement.

'You acted with great bravery and skill,' he said, when she had finished, 'and it was also your idea which got the chalet into the air in the first place. A remarkable achievement.'

'Something of a mixed blessing in my view,' said Mrs Deal.

Nor did Sydney seem particularly upset by the loss of his book. Indeed Jane thought he seemed almost relieved. He said he'd been working on it so long that he could write most of the notes from memory. 'Besides,' he added, 'what has happened is far more exciting. I told you that no expedition had ever returned from the Mountains of the Moon. Possibly none has even succeeded in getting inside them. We may be the first human beings here for thousands of years. I shall keep a full account. There could be some very interesting plants and animals.'

'Interesting, Mr Saxton?' said Mrs Deal. 'I'd hardly call tigers interesting.'

Sydney put his hands against the wall and slowly pushed himself upright.

'Tigers?' he said, panting. 'Tigers are animals we won't see. There are no tigers in Africa.'

Mrs Deal stared at him. 'No tigers in Africa? Come, Mr Saxton. Africa is famous for her tigers.'

'Oddly enough, you only find tigers in Asia,' he said. 'India is famous for tigers. Not Africa.'

But Mrs Deal refused to be convinced. She went into the kitchen, her face was set in an expression which Jane knew well, saying clearly, 'There *are* tigers in Africa.'

Weak as he was, and though the light was beginning to fade, Sydney was eager to have a look outside. They helped him over the furniture and soon he and Jane were standing beside the chalet. Mrs Deal, her face still obstinate, had decided to remain inside.

First they examined the damage to the balloon and chalet.

The balloon had been caught by several long branches of one of the taller trees. These had torn it badly, as the weight of the chalet had pulled it down; but apart from broken windows, the chalet itself seemed unharmed. Its stout timbers had withstood the terrible journey without shifting.

Next Sydney looked round the clearing. Walking slowly to its edge with his hand on Jane's shoulder, he explained that in his years as ADC to General Herkenshaw he had often taken trips to explore the jungles of Central Africa. Already, he recognized a wild orchid, and behind the pool he thought he saw a mangrove. As they forced apart the thick ferns and grasses which choked the space between the massive trees, there came the sound of loud hammering from the chalet. Mrs Deal must already have begun the task of reconstruction.

But once they had parted the undergrowth and were able to peer into the jungle properly, it was quite different. Nothing grew in the deep gloom cast by the giant trees. But as Jane's eyes grew used to it, she saw the darkness was hung with long creepers and crossed with fallen trees. It was swarming with insects and had a strong, damp, mushroomy smell. It was also rather frightening. Although she could see none, she knew ferocious animals were hunting in the jungle.

It was almost dark when they climbed into the chalet again. Bats were swooping across the clearing. Mrs Deal had lit four candles and was busy making the supper. She had also nailed pieces of broken chair across all the windows and the room now had the aspect of a fortress. Jane thought this was going too far, but Sydney, seeing that it comforted Mrs Deal, praised her.

'A good idea,' he said. 'One can have a bit of trouble from inquisitive monkeys.'

'The great cats could break them at a blow,' said Mrs Deal, 'but at least we'd have some warning.'

Supper was delicious: baked beans, fried eggs (which had not broken), and a pudding of Angel's Delight made with condensed milk. Sydney said that even though Mrs Deal had succeeded in bringing nearly the entire four months' supply of food, they might well be in the jungle very much longer than that. The next day he would set about getting food.

When they had finished they went up to bed. They were all exhausted after their extraordinary journey, especially Sydney. While Jane wearily made her bed, which had been scattered all over the room, she heard Mrs Deal next door hammering something across her window. A little later came the sound of heavy furniture being shoved in front of her door.

For a while, hot even though she had only a sheet on top of her, Jane lay dreamily listening to the jungle. Screechings, honkings, croakings filled the night air, and every now and again she heard a muffled roar, like distant traffic, instantly cut off. Lions? wondered Jane, or elephants? Tigers she knew it couldn't be because she was sure Sydney was right. As though from far away, she heard Mrs Deal hammering again. A mosquito was somewhere near her. She was asleep.

Jane was woken next morning by the hot African sun shining through the window. Her first thought was that it had some how succeeded in setting light to her. Her face, her arms, in fact her whole body felt on fire. Sitting up, she discovered she had been bitten all over by mosquitoes in the night; red, swelling lumps covered her.

When she came downstairs, she found that Sydney and Mrs Deal had also been badly bitten; but they looked even odder because they seemed to have covered their faces in flour.

'Poor child,' said Mrs Deal, hurrying towards her, shaking a bottle. 'Luckily I had some calomine put by. Here, let me dab a little on.'

'It's *tyrannus nox*,' said Sydney, 'the night mosquito. I shall have to improvise some netting.'

The soothing calomine quickly calmed the itching, and by the time Jane had finished her breakfast she could hardly feel it.

'Now,' said Sydney, 'there's a lot to do. The first essentials are to find water, food and fuel. Later on, we can start to think about how to get out of here. Now—just wait here a moment, Jane, while I go to the box-room for some things.'

He returned about ten minutes later having changed and looking pleased.

'Not at all bad,' he said. 'I don't suppose the box-room has been cleaned for years. I think I can protect us from mosquitoes and I've found my old gun, cartridges and this topee here. Also, by a piece of luck, not one bottle of the dozen gin has been broken.'

'Medicinal gin?' called Mrs Deal from the kitchen. 'That's a blessing. I should imagine the jungle is alive with fevers. I've found some cooking brandy here, if the worst comes to the worst.'

'Excellent,' said Sydney. 'Oh, Mrs Deal?'

'Yes, Mr Saxton?' said Mrs Deal coming from the kitchen holding the brandy.

'While Jane and I go and look for food and water, I wonder if you could gather some wood. We must save as much fuel as possible.'

There was a short silence in the hot chalet. The air was loud with the noises of the jungle. Then Mrs Deal said in a quiet but determined voice, 'I'm sorry, Mr Saxton, but I am not leaving the shelter of this house.'

'Why ever not?' said Sydney.

'I wouldn't put my head outside that door for all the tea in China,' said Mrs Deal. 'One snap of the giant jaws and . . . ugh!' She shuddered and closed her eyes. 'As I see it, our first priority is to make this craft safe from the big cats.'

Her fear of tigers was so great that there was plainly no point in arguing with her. Indeed, they had barely left the chalet before the sound of violent hammering leapt into the hot air.

Sydney led the way, the large white topee on his head, and wearing white shorts and a shirt, which, though both very clean and beautifully ironed, were yellow with age. A strong smell of mothballs drifted back to Jane who followed him. Sydney had given her one of Veronica's large floppy hats and although this came well below her ears it kept the sun off. She followed him closely, feeling safer the nearer she was to the hefty-looking shotgun on his shoulder and the belt of bright red cartridges round his waist.

At the other side of the little clearing they found a small pool of stagnant water. It was thick with reeds, the water seething with insects and choked with rotting leaves and branches. As they approached, three huge, green, lumpy toads leapt from the grass and plopped into it. Large, oily bubbles rose all over it, bursting gently with a smell of bad eggs.

'This will be where the mosquitoes come from,' said Sydney. He looked thoughtfully at the black water popping in the sun. 'I wonder,' he murmured.

'What?' asked Jane.

'Nothing,' said Sydney. 'Something I'll have to think about later. Come on, we must start to explore the jungle. Pools like these can lead to rivers.'

Sydney chose a spot a little to the left of the pool and began to force a way in. Jane squelched after him.

It was not easy. Creepers as thick as Jane's leg hung in festoons from the tangled branches above and were themselves tangled with fallen branches below. These were heaped and wet and slippery, the ground was boggy, and it was dark enough for quite a number of *tyrannus nox* to think it was night and rise stinging from the water. Several times Sydney's topee got knocked off, his gun caught on branches, and his long bony legs became so knotted among the creepers that Jane had to help him get free.

And then suddenly they reached the end. One moment they were struggling under the cavernous twilight of the trees, the next they were out in the open air again, the sun on their faces. They were standing on the bank of a small river.

'What a piece of luck,' whispered Sydney. 'Look—a watering place.'

To their left, Jane could see that the bank of the river had been trampled down and the flattened mud was churned and marked with the prints of dozens of animals.

'They'll come here to drink, morning and night,' whispered Sydney. 'Let's hide ourselves.' He drew Jane back and crouched down, the gun across his knees. From beside him, she peered out through a thick green fern. The little river was pale mud-grey and hardly seemed to flow. The trees alongside it soared gracefully up, creepers like tresses of hair hanging down and trailing in the water. Against the dark tangled green of the huge trees and ferns, butterflies as big as envelopes swooped and dipped—velvet black, with large gold and scarlet circles on their wings. Above the river, giant dragonflies whirred past, darting ahead, then stopping, whirred backwards, upwards, sideways, transparent green and gossamer blue.

So fascinated did she become that she was unaware of Sydney raising his gun. Suddenly, so loud it seemed to be inside her own head, there was an immense explosion. Jane uttered a cry, which was immediately echoed by a perfect tornado of shrieks and screams as birds, parrots and monkeys panicked in the trees. There was another explosion, and Sydney was running from the trees. He had killed a small pig-like animal. Even as they came up, its short back legs kicked sharply, and then lay still.

'A young wart-hog,' said Sydney with satisfaction. 'Delicious.'

'Oh—poor, poor thing,' said Jane.

'I know my dear,' said Sydney. 'But we must eat.' He began to inspect the deeply churned mud at the river's edge, and after a while said, 'Well, I think I can recognize anteater, porcupine, a number of the pig family, and possibly a waterbuck.'

The journey back was almost impossible. Jane carried the gun, while Sydney embraced the wart-hog. Sweat streamed down their faces, the mosquitoes bit, and their loads grew heavier and heavier. Several times Sydney fell so that his immaculate white clothes were soon covered in mud; blood from the wart-hog drenched his shirt. It took them nearly an hour and when they finally staggered into the clearing again they looked quite frightening.

They certainly frightened Mrs Deal. When she opened the door to them, she gave one loud scream and then put her hands to her mouth and stared at them, speechless and trembling.

'It's all right Mrs Deal,' panted Sydney, 'we are quite all right.'

'But the blood,' whispered Mrs Deal.

'Sydney killed a wart-hog,' said Jane.

Gradually Mrs Deal grew calmer. They took off their clothes and used a little of the precious water to get clean.

'I heard the shots,' said Mrs Deal, sponging Sydney's back. 'Naturally I was terrified. I thought it was an encounter with the King of Beasts at the very least.'

'The lion is the King of Beasts,' said Jane. Mrs Deal's excessive fear was beginning to irritate her.

'Not for me, Miss Jane,' said Mrs Deal. 'Oh no—tiger tiger burning bright.'

Sydney skinned the wart-hog, and soon six thick chops were frying in the pan. Mrs Deal opened a Swiss packet called *Pomme* and made some mashed potato.

Her own morning had also been strenuous. All the windows were now heavily nailed against possible attack, and she had done a great deal of tidying. The living-room looked almost as neat as it usually did, if emptier from the furniture Jane had had to throw out. After lunch Mrs Deal announced that she intended to begin on the top rooms.

'It's a regular tonic,' she said. 'We're going to have a damp problem so I must get everything aired.'

Sydney told Jane that he would start cutting a path through to the river and would also fetch some water. He wanted Jane to collect wood.

'We can't go on squandering gas,' he said. 'I know Mrs Deal brought all the cylinders, but we must save as much as we can of those in case we're still here in the rainy season.'

When Mrs Deal protested that it was dangerous for Jane to go anywhere near the jungle alone, he gently but firmly told her that he insisted on it.

'We have a lot to do,' he said. 'There are no tigers in this jungle, Mrs Deal. There are no tigers in Africa. Jane will be perfectly all right.'

The afternoon passed quickly. Jane pulled slimy branch after slimy branch from the jungle and leant them against the chalet to dry. She was touched to see that Mrs Deal continually peered through a crack in her barred and shuttered window to see that she was all right. Across the clearing, the sound of axe blows marked Sydney's slow progress towards the river.

At 4.30 the sun vanished behind the Mountains of the Moon. Exhausted, Sydney and Jane returned to find that Mrs Deal—still energetic despite the heat—had put some more of the warthog in to roast. She strained and boiled the bucket of water Sydney had brought from the river and, after cleaning themselves up as much as they could, they sat down to supper.

Sydney said they should save candles, and since they were in any case all very tired they went to bed soon after eating.

One last thing had to be done. Sydney had found a roll of cheesecloth which his wife had kept for making cream cheese. There was just enough for him to nail two large piece of this over the planks with which Mrs Deal had covered his window and Jane's. For Mrs Deal herself he had an even more effective protection against the mosquitoes. This was an old bee-keeper's veil, a tent of thick black net which went over her head and reached well below her waist. Mrs Deal was delighted with it.

'Veils are quite the vogue now, you know,' she said, turning and lifting it elegantly at the hems. 'Help me upstairs, Miss Jane. It's a little difficult to see with just the one candle.'

Jane thought she looked rather odd, but didn't say so. In fact when they reached Mrs Deal's room, she said politely, 'It suits you.'

'You really think so?' said Mrs Deal, pleased. She groped her way to the mirror, but the enveloping shroud was too thick for her to see anything. 'Nevertheless, that's a sweet thing to say, Miss Jane,' she said. 'Now it's high time we were all in bed.'

Already they were becoming used to the many noises of the jungle at night, and instead of keeping them awake, the shrill cries, the honkings and croakings, the sudden barks and occasional distant roar, soothed them like a lullaby. Four minutes after she had slid into bed, Jane was asleep, and not long after that, muffled and soft from the thick folds of bee-keeper's veil, Mrs Deal's gentle snores were sounding through the chalet.

Every day they rose when the sun appeared above the glistening peaks and went to bed when it sank behind them. This not only saved candles, but allowed them to work in the coolest time of the day. Mrs Deal was the luckiest. The chalet, with its thick wooden walls and windows completely planked over, was the coolest place to be. And Mrs Deal refused to leave it. The furthest she would go was on to the veranda, to break wood, hang out clothes and, later, to sit stitching up the holes in the balloon. She boiled the drinking water, cooked the food on the living-room fire to save gas, mended and cleaned their clothes, and kept the chalet gleaming and neat.

But though Mrs Deal was fairly cool, Jane and Sydney, until they got used to it, felt permanently too hot. The first things they did each day were to get water, food and wood. Every morning they set off down the narrow, winding path which Sydney had cut. The bushes at the end of the path had been left to act as a screen and they would creep into these and sit watching the watering place. Sometimes they had to wait half an hour or more. In the end something would appear which Sydney knew was good to eat and he would shoot it. In this way they ate numerous wart-hogs, porcupines, waterbuck, an okapi and some guinea fowl. Many animals came which he didn't shoot: hippos, bands of chattering monkeys, a mongoose, the toothless scaly anteater which came regularly and the wrinkled grey crocodiles which lazed in the mud.

When he had shot an animal, Sydney would skin it—throwing the skin into the river—and carry it back. Jane meanwhile would fill one of the buckets and slowly carry it back to the chalet. Six buckets lasted them a day, and all the water had to be strained and boiled by Mrs Deal. After this, Jane would collect more wood to lean against the chalet. Sydney by now would be gathering fruit or edible berries and roots from the jungle or else cutting the grass in the clearing. He had cleared this on their third day, partly to calm Mrs Deal who said tigers could crawl through right to their very doorstep, but mainly to let the ground dry out. The ground did indeed soon become much firmer and drier, but the grass required almost continual cutting.

On their fourth day Sydney decided they would try and get the balloon down from the tree. At first it looked as though it might be difficult. The ropes round the balloon had caught in some branches half-way up one of the largest trees and seemed thoroughly tangled in them. Also it was plain that only Jane would be able to climb the tree. Mrs Deal as usual refused to leave the chalet; and Sydney, after climbing a few shaky feet off the ground, had to confess he wasn't up to it.

However, when Jane, carrying the bread knife, started up it she found it quite easy. Its vast leaves cast a cool shade like an enormous green tent. The branches were as thick as the trunks of most English trees, the trailing thick creepers made climbing very simple, and she soon reached the branch in which the ropes at the top of the balloon were mostly caught. She wedged herself safely and began to saw through every rope in sight. She cut two, and then edged further out and sawed again. She could not see the ground, but she could see across to the trees on the other side of the clearing and that made her feel how high she was. She stretched her hand as far as she could and was about to cut through another coil of nylon rope when it suddenly disappeared. At the same time her branch swung upwards, there came the noise of branches cracking under her and a cry from Sydney below.

When she got down she found the balloon collapsed down one side of the chalet. Once released from the top, its weight had been sufficient to rip it clear from the other branches, some of which were still sticking out of it. An hour of strenuous pulling and cutting finally had the balloon stretched out in the clearing. Once it was laid out, they could see the damage was considerable. Six or seven enormous rips stretched almost the length of the balloon and there were numerous holes.

'But what I don't understand,' said Jane, as they stared at it in the fading light, 'is what's the point of mending it? We've only got about half a cylinder of helium left.'

'Ah, I have a plan for that,' said Sydney, walking with her slowly to the chalet. 'It's risky, but it's our only chance.'

As they ate their supper—of porcupine roasted in clay then peeled to remove the prickles, and an egg-shaped fruit called borassus—he explained. His plan was simple but brilliant.

They would have observed, he said, or Jane would have, the bubbles which surged continuously to the surface of the stagnant water at the edge of the clearing. This was methane or marsh gas, and it was lighter than air. That is to say, if you filled a balloon with it, the balloon would float. In the box-room Sydney had a roll of transparent plastic sheeting with which he now proposed to make a tent over the stagnant water. Into the top of the tent he would fix a length of tube leading to one of the empty gas cylinders. The tent would gradually fill with marsh gas; when it was full they would pump it into the gas cylinder with Sir Christopher Charrington's pump. Eventually they would have enough to raise the chalet.

'But even then I don't understand it,' said Jane the next morning, as she helped Sydney put up the marsh gas tent. 'Suppose we do get the balloon mended and full again. If we tie it to the chalet it will just get caught in the tree again and be punctured. We'll never be able to pull the chalet into the middle of the clearing.'

'Pass me that length of nylon,' said Sydney in a strained voice. He was leaning out over the pool, tying the poles together to form a frame for the marsh gas tent. 'We'll cross that bridge when we come to it,' he said when he'd finished his knot. 'It's possible we may have to build some sort of raft to float up in.'

'Don't tell Mrs Deal,' said Jane.

They carried and rolled one of the empty helium cylinders across the clearing and attached the hosepipe to the pump. Mrs Deal unpicked the bottom of the balloon and with the long terylene threads began to mend the tears and rips. Every afternoon she would sit on the veranda forcing Veronica Saxton's largest embroidery needle through the tough fabric.

'Though goodness knows,' she said, 'I've no desire to take flight in that coracle again. I'm simply helping to prepare my doom.'

As the days passed Sydney grew stronger and happier. As a young man he'd loved the jungles of Africa and gradually his old knowledge and skills returned. Each day he'd set off to explore, coming back with roots and berries for Mrs Deal to cook. Some things surprised him—he found sugar cane and a wild baobab, evidence that parts of the valley might once have been cultivated. But there was never any sign of human beings and Sydney said it was almost certainly empty.

In the evenings, before the light vanished and they went to bed, while Mrs Deal quietly finished her stitching, he would look up from his notes and tell them some story of his adventures as ADC to General Herkenshaw. Or else he would tell them of the famous writers and painters he and Veronica had had to stay in Wiltshire. Neither Mrs Deal nor Jane had heard of any of them, but some of the names had a magic ring to them, like those of jewels or strange creatures—Bells and Garnetts and Partridges, Gertlers, Brenans, Woolfs. And remembering and talking about his youth, Sydney seemed to grow younger.

And then, two weeks after they had floated down from the Mountains of the Moon, everything changed.

The day began well. As they set off for the river, Sydney noticed that the marsh gas tent was bulging at the sides. Hurrying over, they found that it was straining quite noticeably at its ropes. At once Sydney opened the valve on the cylinder and began to pump vigorously. Gradually the restless tent grew still, the bulges and ripples subsiding. As soon as they had done so, Sydney stopped.

'Go on,' said Jane, 'there must be masses more gas there. It's been bubbling for over a week.'

'I know,' said Sydney, panting a little and taking off his topee. 'But methane gas and air form a highly explosive mixture. We must take great care not to get any air into the cylinder. Now that the tent is fairly full, we'll keep a close eye on her and pump away as soon as she bulges again.'

In the afternoon something even more exciting was to happen. For several days Mrs Deal had been hinting that under certain, very special circumstances, she might consent to a short trip outside the chalet. The night before, after three glasses of medicinal gin, she had revealed what the circumstances were. It was to be in broad daylight. She was to be accompanied by Sydney with his gun and Jane carrying a large stick. She would on no account leave the clearing, or even go near its edge. And the door of the chalet was to be left open all the time, in case she felt the need to bolt.

In fact, it took her nearly a quarter of an hour to leave the veranda. For minutes she clung to the railings, peering fearfully into the surrounding jungle and sniffing the air. Twice she made as though to step down and twice darted back into the chalet.

'Oh come *on*, Mrs Deal,' said Jane irritably. 'You're the biggest coward I've ever seen.'

'You haven't seen the beasts in all their savagery,' said Mrs Deal. 'I saw a man savaged nearly to death. I was scarred for life.'

Sydney was more patient and eventually, holding him tight with one trembling hand, while the other gripped Jane, she moved with faltering steps out into the clearing.

Gradually she grew more confident.

'Quite a little lawn,' she said, eyeing the grass. She confessed it was a great relief to be out, after two weeks in the chalet. Raising her eyes a fraction, she noticed the marsh gas tent and while she disapproved of its object, she had to admit it was a clever idea. She was much impressed, from a distance, by the path to the river.

On the way back to the chalet she became quite cheerful. 'I shall take a turn every day,' she said. 'Perhaps I have been over-anxious. Give me your stick, Jane; you can let me walk alone Mr Saxton.'

They were over half-way back, Mrs Deal was walking at her usual brisk pace, looking confidently about her, and Jane was about to leave them, when Mrs Deal suddenly stopped. Her face had turned quite white and she began to tremble violently. As Sydney and Jane looked at her anxiously, she slowly raised two shaking arms and pointed into the trees above the chalet.

'Look!' she whispered. 'Look!'

The sight was indeed horrifying—and strange. Crouched along the big branch that reached over the chalet was the most enormous tiger Jane had ever seen. At least ten foot long, its smooth satin fur, striped orange and black, seemed to glow in the sun; wrinkled black lips were pulled back from great curving yellow fangs. But it was not alone. Astride the broad back, strong legs wound under its middle, was a nearly naked black boy about Jane's age, holding a short spear in his hand.

It was a frightening sight—and one that proved too much for Mrs Deal. For an instant longer she pointed, petrified, then raising her arms to heaven and closing her eyes upon her fate she gave a low moan and, falling back with a thump on to the soft ground, fainted dead away.

At the same time, Jane turned, started for the chalet, caught her foot in a tussock and fell on her face. As she did so, she heard almost simultaneously two terrifying noises—the double crash behind her as Sydney fired both barrels of his gun, and, a fraction later, the furious roar of a springing tiger.

7. Mub

ALL JANE could remember later about the attack was confusion. She said afterwards that she probably fainted too. There was a thud as the tiger landed, then a lot of scuffling, shouting, snarling, much more shouting from the boy in a strange language, and at last—silence.

Very slowly, Jane raised her head. Beside her, Mrs Deal lay flat on her back, her arms outstretched and her bun, as usual in time of crisis, unwound over the grass. Some way in front of them stood the tiger and the young boy. Sydney had obviously missed them because neither looked hurt and the boy had his foot on the gun. In one hand he held the spear; the other gripped a short lead attached to a collar round the tiger's neck. Every minute or so, as the tiger snarled and tugged forward, he pulled this and said something sharply in his language.

But the oddest sight of all was Sydney. He was sitting up on his elbows and staring at the boy with an expression, not of fear, but of amazement. As Jane watched, he suddenly began to speak swiftly in the boy's language

At once the tiger stopped straining at the lead and sat back with its ears pricked. The boy looked astonished and then quickly answered.

Sydney replied, the boy answered, the tiger purred and soon they were talking away as if they had known each other for years.

After a while, Sydney stopped and said to Jane. 'This is the most extraordinary thing that could have happened. I think we've discovered the legendary Barabou tribe—the Tiger Men. This young fellow speaks one of the Mahali dialects—like all the tribes round here. But there are traces of Indian words—mostly in Hindustani, which fortunately I speak too. This is a book in itself.'

Before Jane could ask a great many questions, a second extraordinary thing happened.

'I speak English little bit,' said a voice in front of them. 'You English, you welcome, Malou take you see Massa Surely little while now tomorrow.'

It was the young black boy. Smiling and waving his arms, so pleased that he quite forgot to hold the tiger, he took a step towards them and said, 'How do you do, good-bye, you come see Sahib Mub in Stockade, great chief Mub. You welcome Malou chief's son.'

Jane in fact was not all that surprised. It always seemed odder to her to find that some people could not speak English then to find that they could. But Sydney was even more amazed than he had been by the appearance of Malou, if that was his name, and the tiger, in the first place. He stood up and peered down at the little boy as though he were some astonishing new plant. Then he began to speak to him very quickly.

They spoke together for about ten minutes. Jane soon got restless, and thought she'd better see how Mrs Deal was, but as soon as she moved, the tiger, which had been peacefully licking its paws, gave a low growl and showed its teeth to her. Jane stopped nervously.

Malou spoke sharply to the tiger, turning his head from Sydney. Then he smiled at Jane. 'He let you go now,' he said.

Jane smiled back and, still keeping an eye on the tiger, went and knelt by Mrs Deal.

'Mrs Deal,' she whispered, 'are you all right? Mrs Deal—don't worry. It's a *nice* tiger.' But Mrs Deal did not answer. Eyes closed, breathing calmly and evenly, she seemed to have fallen into a deep sleep; only a slight flush on each cheek made Jane wonder if she was quite well.

Sydney now turned to her with great excitement.

'It'll take some time to get to the bottom of this,' he said, 'but as far as I can gather they *are* the Tiger Men—the Barabou.'

'But I thought you said there weren't any tigers in Africa,' said Jane. 'No wonder Mrs Deal's fainted.'

'Nor there are,' said Sydney. 'However, there have always been certain legends in this particular district. I'll tell you them later, but I thought it better to keep them from our good friend. But there's more than that. As far as I can understand young Malou, this valley is ruled by a great Chief— a man called Mub. There is also someone called Surely, a white man who, if I understand him correctly, taught him and is teaching him English. I think he said Surely is a doctor. Malou seems particularly frightened of this Mub. 'Mub' is a word in their language; roughly it means 'No Face' or 'Faceless One'. Apparently if anyone penetrates the valley—virtually unheard of—they must be brought to see Mub in his Stockade at once. Malou says we must go to his village now and then be taken to the Stockade tomorrow. There is of course a difficulty.'

'Mrs Deal,' said Jane.

'Mrs Deal,' said Sydney. Together they looked for a moment at the flat figure. 'Malou suggested we tie her to the back of his tiger, but I'm afraid, unconscious as she is, that would not be safe. She might slip off and I don't like to think of her reaction if she came to on the back of a tiger.'

Jane did not actually agree with him about the unconsciousness. She had been surprised to see one beady eye flick alertly open when Sydney had suggested tying her to the back of the tiger and as quickly flick shut again. However, if she was awake, Mrs Deal would certainly refuse to be tied to, or even go anywhere near a tiger, so Jane said nothing but just nodded agreement.

Malou had obviously been trying to understand their conversation. He had been looking from Jane to Sydney and now, as though he realized they spoke about her, down at Mrs Deal. As they all stood silently, he suddenly said, 'Little girl come with me. By and by come my father Chief Hassou, fetch lady, big white man.'

Sydney spoke to Malou for a moment, then he said, 'He wants you to ride with him on the back of his tiger. Could you do it, do you think?'

'Couldn't I stay here?' said Jane, looking with fear at the great beast stretched in the sun.

Sydney spoke to Malou again. 'He says one of us must go,' he said. 'Mub will be angry.' He mentioned some dreaded place called Death Stockade.

'He must go very slowly,' said Jane. '*Extremely* slowly.'

Malou smiled at her and held out his hand. 'Malou go very slowly,' he said. 'Come. Not afraid.'

And so for the first time in her life Jane climbed on to the back of one of the great tigers of the Barabou. Later, though never becoming quite as skilled as the Barabou themselves, she came to love riding them, and learnt to go for long expeditions alone through the trackless jungle. She became far more at home on them than ever she had been on the ponies at Curl Castle.

Now, however, she felt frightened. Malou had pulled the tiger to its feet and was already astride it. For the first time Jane noticed its tail. This was much longer than an ordinary tiger's tail, and at the end it spread out in a large fan of yellow and black fur about a foot across.

'Look at its tail, Sydney,' said Jane. 'It's huge.'

'I know,' said Sydney. 'Some sort of selective breeding. Fascinating.'

As Jane walked nervously up to the tiger it turned its head and looked at her with its large marble-like yellow eyes. A single thick slimy blob of saliva fell from its jaws and slowly sank to the ground on the end of a glistening thread. Then she swung one leg over the smooth satiny side, warm from the sun and carefully humped herself on to the tiger's broad back, Malou took her hands and pulled her arms round across his stomach and suddenly—they were off! Not slowly at all, but into a long flowing bound, Sydney's voice shouting 'Good luck!' behind her, and then bound after rippling bound, tail streaming, and in a moment they were across the clearing and had vanished into the depths of the jungle.

* * *

She learnt later that she had been quite right about Mrs Deal. No sooner were they alone than she sat up and asked Sydney indignantly whether, had she not pretended to be unconscious, he would have insisted on her being tied to the back of the horrible beast.

'I'd rather have died, Mr Saxton,' she said. 'In fact I almost certainly *would* have died.'

Next she asked him how he could have had the heart to tell her that there were no tigers in Africa, when there quite plainly *were* tigers in Africa—as large as life and twice as terrible.

Sydney explained that, on the contrary, he had been quite correct. There are no tigers in Africa—or nowhere else in Africa. He had known about the legends of the Mountains of the Moon, which it is true did mention an animal like the tiger, but he had thought it would be unkind to worry her with stories which at the time had seemed little more than fairy tales.

This made Mrs Deal feel much better. She respected Sydney and had not liked thinking he had tricked her. Also, she was just beginning the fever which was to keep her in bed for the next six days. Her throat ached and she was shivering; when they got back to the chalet, Sydney took her temperature and found that it was 103.2°. To help her sleep he gave her a handful of his Slogodon sleeping pills and then Mrs Deal slipped into her bee-veil and went up to bed.

While this was going on, Jane was speeding through the jungle. Narrow paths threaded it, often quite dark, the light cut out by the trees meeting overhead; sometimes the paths widened, so that she could see the sky. And down them, guided by Malou, the big tiger swiftly cantered. Jane found that it wasn't too difficult. The movement was smooth and rhythmical, the great muscles of the hind legs seeming to thrust them forward in a continuous and apparently effortless glide. Only when they sometimes turned rather abruptly into a new path did she have to tighten her arms round Malou. And once, when some jungle animal ran terrified in front of them and the tiger gave a great leap, six feet up and fifteen feet along, she slipped half-way down its side and only Malou's tightly gripping legs kept them both on.

For an hour they sped through the jungle, and then the tiger turned into a much wider path. They cantered down this for five minutes and then, gently, the tiger stopped. Jane looked round Malou's shoulders and saw one of the strangest and most beautiful sights she had ever seen.

In front of them the road widened into a large space 60 or 70 yards across and perhaps 100 yards long. Down each side there was a single row of little mud huts, each surrounded by a low mud wall so that they

looked like two rows of bowler hats with up-turned brims. But the space was not a clearing. There were no trees at the far end. Instead it opened out on to a wide lake, golden now in the slanting rays of the sun about to sink behind the Mountains of the Moon. On the far side of this, about half a mile away, the jungle swept round the lake again, a thick green fringe growing to its very shores. And beyond this again, still further off, though nearer than they had looked from the chalet, rose those same great Mountains.

But it was the scene immediately before her that interested and surprised her most. In front of the little houses, all down the village to the lake, were gathered the tribe of the Barabou. And among them, around them, sometimes in the case of little children, even on top of them, there were more tigers than Jane had ever seen in her life before. There seemed to be hundreds: big tigers, old tigers, glorious golden bounding tigers, rolling and fighting together, tiny fluffy baby tigers lying on their backs while little tots of two or three tickled their stomachs. The air was full of their grunts and purrs and roars (so that was what I sometimes heard at night, thought Jane); she noticed, too, that all the tigers had the same large tail, with its flat, spreading, bushy end, as Malou's tiger. And the tigers were not just lying there; they were being used. A young woman trotted across the village, her legs tucked up astride a rather slow old tiger; another tiger passed with some logs strapped across its back; a third was pulling a mat on which sat a man with his leg bandaged up.

Jane stared and stared and then, as one aspect of this strange scene struck her with ever-increasing force, she murmured, 'Poor Mrs Deal. What *will* she do? She'll be terrified out of her wits. Oh dear, oh dear.'

'You like?' said Malou, smiling at her. 'Come—me see mother brother sister.'

In fact, mother brother sister, and a great many other relations besides, were already hurrying up to them. Malou greeted them, waving his arms at Jane and in the air to explain the balloon, and generally telling them what he had found. The excitement grew. In all the hundreds of years the Barabou tribe had lived within the Mountains of the Moon, people from the outside world had only managed to enter three times. Soon the whole village was gathered round them in the dusk, feeling Jane's clothes and smiling at her. And not just the people, the tigers too. Jane couldn't help feeling rather nervous as the rough black noses sniffed about her, furry muzzles brushed her legs, and yellow-green eyes glowed in the growing dark.

Suddenly, Malou took her arm. 'Father,' he whispered. Jane looked up and saw in front of them a man rather taller than the rest, before whom the villagers stood back. He asked Malou some brisk questions, listened intently to his answers, and then took charge. He raised his arms and into the silence called out a few commands. At once the Barabou started back to their huts, calling the tigers sharply after them. Then Malou's father (after Mub, he was the Chief of the Barabou) called several men by name and began to give them orders. In fact, the first order was something to do with Mub, because Jane heard the name several times when he spoke rapidly to a young man who immediately leapt on to a tiger and vanished into the night. 'To tell that strange being,' she thought, 'that white gods have come from the sky.' She imagined Mub as someone fat and oily, perhaps because his name rhymed with tub.

The rest of the night was like a dream. Men appeared with long sticks, their ends flaring and flaming with smoky yellow flames. By their light, five men and five tigers were lined up and Malou's father (called Hanou she later discovered) said a few words to them. Next, to her amazement—and yet she was not really amazed, because nothing is surprising in a dream— two small elephants were led out of the darkness. Not more than seven foot high, they stood blinking and wrinkled in the light of the wildly flickering torches, each carrying what looked like a large basket on its back.

Now Malou came running over to Jane. 'Come?' he asked her, smiling his wide smile. 'You come?'

'I come,' said Jane.

One of the little elephants was led forward and sank ponderously and carefully, like her grandmother weeding, on to its knees. Jane was helped into the basket, which was lined with animal skins, and they set off.

The journey that had taken her and Malou an hour, took nearly four hours by elephant. Principally this was because the paths down which a tiger could speed with lithe ease now had to be forced much wider apart. Men shouted, the torches flared, the elephants swayed and crashed forward—but Jane noticed very little of it. After they entered the jungle she found the only way to avoid being hit by branches was to snuggle down at the bottom of the basket. Quite soon she fell asleep.

She awoke when they reached the chalet. From her basket, she saw Sydney standing under the torches on the veranda talking excitedly to Hanou and waving his arms about. A moment later they entered the chalet, followed by three men; and ten minutes after that they re-emerged, carefully carrying a blanket-wrapped bundle. One end of the bundle, Jane saw, was a head in a bee-veil. The Slogodon, together with the aspirin and some medicinal gin, had plunged Mrs Deal into a sleep from which it would have been difficult, if not impossible, to wake her.

Soon Sydney was climbing into Jane's basket, orders were shouted, and they were off again.

'Brave girl,' he said. 'How was the tiger ride?'

'Great fun,' said Jane. 'But Sydney, who do you think these people are? Who are the Barabou? How did they get here?'

'I'm not at all sure,' said Sydney, 'but do you notice how fine their features are? And these elephants—surely much smaller than African elephants. I've got an idea, but I'll tell you what I think in the morning.'

Jane rather wished he'd tell her then, but already the rocking of the elephant was making her feel drowsy. Soon the branches forced them both to crouch down in the basket and quite quickly she was asleep again.

She was still asleep three and a half hours later when they arrived in the village. Dawn was breaking on the mountain peaks when Hanou lifted her down and carried her across to one of the huts. She was just aware that she was being tucked under another large, soft animal skin and that lying next to her was Malou.

One final thing she noticed before her eyes closed again. If she pushed out her feet her toes touched the warm hard back of Malou's tiger lying stretched along the floor at the foot of their bed. And already Jane thought it was one of the safest and most comforting things she had ever felt.

It was clear next morning that Mrs Deal was far too ill to accompany them on their visit to Mub. Her temperature had risen, she tossed feebly to and fro on her bed of skins, and she was too weak even to remove the bee-veil. Looking at the small figure trapped in its black folds and weakly moaning, Jane felt quite worried. But after feeling her pulse and tapping her chest, Sydney said he thought it wasn't too serious, but that she must certainly stay in bed a few days. He also gave her three aspirin and another Slogodon.

'Is this an outpost of civilization?' asked Mrs Deal in a groggy voice.

'In a way,' said Sydney soothingly.

'Safe at least from the great cats?' asked Mrs Deal, raising herself anxiously on her elbows.

'Safe as houses,' said Sydney.

Malou and his father were also worried by Mrs Deal. They were talking earnestly together when Jane and Sydney came from her hut, carefully replacing the skin which hung in front of the door, and Hanou at once came up to them and took Sydney by the arm. After some discussion with him, Sydney turned to Jane and said, 'He says Mrs Deal ought to see their Medicine Man. We're going to see him now. These fellows often know a great deal about natural remedies—the bark of special trees, beneficial berries and so on.'

This may well have been true; unfortunately the Medicine Man looked so strange and terrifying that even Sydney, who had been expecting something of the sort, stepped back in alarm as he emerged from his hut.

It looked, for a moment, as though an enormous tiger with three heads was standing on its back legs facing them in the sun. One head covered the Medicine Man's like a mask; the other two were secured on top of it. The tawny, striped skin was drawn across his chest and his arms were thrust into the fore-legs, ending in long yellow claws. When he saw them, he opened the jaws of the tiger's head and give several loud, life-like roars.

'Oh dear, no,' said Sydney hurriedly, first backing away and then stepping forward, with a vague idea of not hurting the Medicine Man's feelings, and trying to shake one of his paws. 'Oh, I'm afraid that wouldn't do at all. That would finish Mrs Deal off for good, I fear.'

There followed another long conversation with Hanou, in which Sydney explained that on no account was Mrs Deal to see or, if possible, even hear a tiger. Tigers, he said, were in a way why she was ill. He also asked about this Doctor Surely that Malou had told them about.

Hanou was amazed to hear that anyone could feel anything but delighted to see a tiger, but agreed to give orders that they should be kept from Mrs Deal's hut. And yes, he said, certainly they could ask Massa Surely to come and see the poor white woman; in fact that was an additional reason to hurry to see Mub in his Stockade, where they really should have gone first thing in the morning.

'They are obviously frightened of this Mub,' said Sydney, as they swayed together on top of one of the little elephants. 'It will be interesting to see what he's like. Some got-up monster like the Medicine Man, I expect.'

As they went through the jungle he explained to Jane what he knew and what he guessed about the Barabou.

'It is very little,' he said. 'There have always been very old stories that many hundreds of years ago one of the local tribes set off north in a time of famine. They were gone for a hundred years, and when they returned their faces had changed and they brought with them strange striped animals like lions which they called Barabou. From the descriptions these animals were plainly tigers.

'Some of the stories ended there. But there were others which said the Barabou—as the tribe came to be called—had learnt the secret of the Mountains of the Moon. These mountains were supposed to be hollow. One day—rather like the Pied Piper of Hamelin—the Barabou were supposed to have vanished inside them. They and their striped animals never came back.

'Now, of course, when I was out here in the twenties as ADC to old Herkenshaw, we none of us believed a word of it. There were no tigers to be seen, here or anywhere else in Africa. All the other stories about the Barabou were equally absurd; for instance, I remember one was that their animals could fly. As for a few natives getting inside the Mountains of the Moon, the idea was ridiculous. As we know, three fully equipped modern expeditions have tried—and never returned. And the idea that the Mountains were hollow was even less likely.'

'And yet here they are,' said Jane, fascinated by Sydney's tale.

'Here they are,' said Sydney. 'Obviously there was a lot of truth in the old legends. Certainly, these tigers—or their ancestors rather—came from India, because all tigers come from there, or from Asia. And actually tigers are very good animals in jungles. I don't know if an African tribe went north to India, or some Indians travelled south to Africa. I should think they probably came from India in the first place.

'Anyway,' he went on, 'since the tigers are true, and since there is a tribe here, we must suppose some truth in the other legends; for instance, in the story about the Mountains of the Moon being hollow. I am almost sure this elephant is an Indian one too. Now it couldn't climb these mountains any more than a tiger could. Obviously the mountains are not hollow, but the legend probably refers to some ancient pass through them: a ravine so deep it almost seemed like going through a tunnel. Probably in later years an earthquake or large rock-fall blocked the ravine and the Barabou found they were trapped for ever.'

They swayed on in silence for a while. The path wound gradually upward and as they went the jungle seemed to be getting less thick. Looking up at the Mountains of the Moon slowing coming closer, Jane suddenly had another idea.

'Perhaps one of the expeditions nearly succeeded,' she said. 'Only one man survived, the brave Dr Surely. He staggered down the mountain to be greeted as a god by the fat chief Mub. Then he stayed here for years and years and had a lot of children.'

'It's possible,' said Sydney, smiling at her. 'Frankly, anything's possible now.'

'But how long do you think the Barabou have been here?' asked Jane.

'Impossible to say,' said Sydney. 'Legends can continue almost unchanged for hundreds of years. I should think they have been here a good while. They have obviously learnt how to tame the tiger and that must have taken some time. And then you'll have noticed the tiger's tails. It must have taken quite a long time for that to happen. There is no reason why they shouldn't have come here a thousand years or more ago.'

Before she could ask more questions, their elephant suddenly stopped. Jane noticed that the air was much cooler. Without her properly realizing it, the jungle had faded away and they had been travelling for quite a while through long, coarse grass and scrub. Malou and Hanou, who had been trotting in front, had stopped too. Now Malou turned round and came cantering back. Jane was surprised to see that his face had turned pale. He pointed ahead.

'Mub,' he said in a low voice. 'Mub there. Now you must see.'

He was frightened—and yet Jane thought not only frightened. She felt in some way he was angry too, angry and defiant. But before she could think further, their elephant moved forward again and she looked ahead to their destination—the dwelling of the dreaded Mub and his henchman, the sinister Dr Surely.

About half a mile in front the ground rose sharply into the first of a series of high cliffs which formed the beginnings of the Mountains of the Moon. At the bottom of one of these, in the very middle, a high wooden stockade had been built out to form a semi-circle. At either end there were wooden towers.

As they came nearer, Jane saw that the tall wooden gates in the middle of the Stockade were guarded by two huge black men, and there was also a guard in each of the wooden towers. The gate guards, she noticed, were armed with rifles; a fact which also seemed to surprise Sydney. Leaning forward, he looked at them sharply from under shaggy eyebrows.

'Most odd,' he murmured.

'Odd?' said Jane.

'Very odd to find rifles here at all,' said Sydney. 'But I think I recognize the make and that makes it odder still.'

After a few words with Hanou, one of the guards opened the gates, while the other walked through them leading the elephant. Jane was just able to wave back to Malou, and then the gates closed behind them.

The space inside the Stockade was not as large as it seemed from the outside. An area of bare earth about the size of four tennis courts contained three small wooden buildings, a large one in the middle, and behind them all, a sheer cliff.

The elephant followed the guard to the largest building. There were six enormous dogs tied to rings in the wall and these strained and growled when the elephant knelt down and Jane and Sydney climbed to the ground. Jane took Sydney's hand nervously.

'Wolf-hounds,' said Sydney. 'This gets more and more extraordinary.'

Beckoned by a third guard, they walked to the door. He opened it in front of them and stepped aside to let them pass. They were face to face with Mub.

Jane was only to see Mub six times altogether, yet she remembered his face with horror for the rest of her life. He was sitting at a table in front of them and looked so tall Jane thought he was standing up until she saw his long thin legs bent underneath it. He was dressed in a white robe which flowed down to his ankles and was fastened tightly round his scrawny neck. And above this was his face. It was as though someone had taken a piece of old dead skin, stretched it tightly over his skull, and then poked three holes in it, two for the eyes and one for the mouth. The skin was pure white, as white as chalk or flour. It was completely smooth. The eyes had no eyelids. There was no nose. The little round mouth had no lips. He had no hair and small stumps of dead white flesh for ears. It was the face of a monster.

Jane stared so long that eventually the monster spoke.

'Little girl,' said Mub, in a hard voice, with an accent Jane could not recognize. 'You are looking at a miracle of plastic surgery.' Then dabbing the holes which were his eyes, he turned to Sydney. 'Who are you?'

'My name is Sydney Saxton,' said Sydney. 'My companion is Miss Jane Charrington. And whom do I have the honour of addressing?'

'You will call me Mub,' said Mub. 'How did you get here?'

Sydney explained, and while he did so Jane looked at the three other people in the room. Two of them were black guards, who stood stiffly on either side of Mub's chair. But the third was white; a little old man, about 60 or even 70, Jane thought, with a wrinkled, kind face, a wispy moustache and a white robe like Mub's, only baggier and a bit untidy looking. He seemed very nervous, fidgeting about and looking anxiously from Mub to Sydney as they spoke, and pulling at his fingers so that every now and again one of his knuckles gave a loud crack. Could this be the brave mountaineer, Dr Surely?

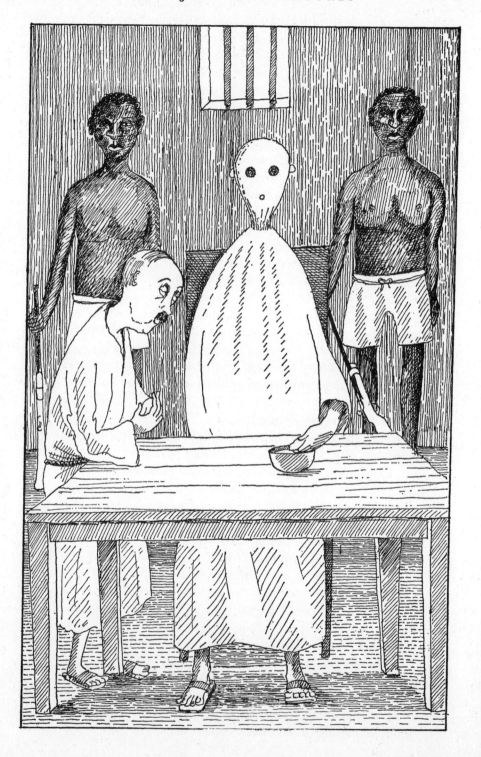

'How do you propose to return?' said Mub.

When Sydney had explained, Mub sat in silence. 'How likely are you to succeed?' he said.

'Most unlikely, I'm afraid,' said Sydney. 'But I imagine there is no other way out?'

'Only the mountains,' said Mub.

'I thought perhaps the legend of the hollow mountains . . .' began Sydney.

'A legend only,' Mub interrupted briskly. 'You are unlikely to succeed. Nevertheless I should like your word of honour as an English gentleman that you will not attempt to leave this valley without telling me.'

Sydney looked rather surprised. 'I should naturally not dream of trying to leave without coming to say goodbye,' he said formally.

'I wish for your word of honour,' said Mub.

'I have said it would be discourteous to do otherwise,' said Sydney.

'Mr Saxton,' said Mub. 'I rule this valley. Give me your word.'

There was a pause and Jane felt suddenly nervous. In the silence, she heard two knuckles go crack. Then Sydney said in a cold voice, 'You have my word.'

'Thank you, Mr Saxton,' said Mub. 'Surely, you will inspect this chalet regularly and report to me.'

'Certainly sir,' said the little man, his face twitching. 'Of course, sir. Certainly, sir.'

'We were wondering whether Dr Surely would be good enough . . .' began Sydney, about to ask help for Mrs Deal. Once again Mub interrupted him.

'*Doctor* Surely?' he said. 'Surely is not a doctor.'

'Just a humble mister,' said the little man quickly. 'No doubt you were misled in the village. Aspirins gave me a reputation, quite unjustified. I must apologize.'

'Not at all,' said Sydney. He smiled at Mr Surely and then turned to Mub again. For some reason he did not pursue the subject of Mrs Deal.

'Tell me—er—Mub,' he said with a slight effort. 'May I ask how you and Mr Surely came here?'

'We are the remains of the partially successful expedition of nineteen forty-six,' said Mub. 'Mr Surely and myself were the only ones to survive the descent into the valley.'

'And you have stayed here ever since?' said Sydney, amazed.

'Our oxygen was lost, our food supplies and much of our equipment,' said Mub. 'I doubt we could have managed the return trip. But there was another reason. Despite the miracles of modern surgery, my operation also was only a partial success. I prefer to remain anonymous and invisible in this quiet place. Mr Surely also had his reasons.'

'Oh dear me, yes,' said Mr Surely, giving his knuckles several loud cracks.

'I didn't know rifles were part of mountaineering expeditions,' said Sydney.

'Despite your knowledge of the legend of the hollow mountains, your knowledge of these people is not complete, Mr Saxton,' Mub said. 'There were rumours that we might find a warlike and hostile tribe. It appeared advisable to arm the party. A fortunate move, as it turned out. Mr Surely and I had to fight for our lives.'

There was a short silence. Mr Surely fidgeted about and gave several little coughs. Sydney stroked his chin. Jane looked at the dark holes of Mub's eyes; drops of water hung on the smooth dead white skin of his cheeks. At last Sydney spoke.

'You must have discovered a good deal about these people, Mr— er. . . .'

'Call me Mub,' interrupted Mub again.

'Mub,' said Sydney. 'I should be most interested to know what you think about where they came from and so on.'

But Mub had had enough. He stood up. 'Talk to the Headman, Hanou,' he said. 'He knows as much as I do. Mr Surely, accompany them to their chalet and report back to me. Remember Mr Saxton, I have your word of honour as a gentleman. Good-day.'

Watching his thin figure sweep out of the door at the back of the room, Jane remembered her Uncle Ewan, who was very tall. Mub, she thought, must be at least six foot seven inches high.

From outside the Stockade, they could see the jungle stretching below them; dense green. It filled some 70 square miles of the bowl-like valley, with the lake silver towards one end. They could see the midday sun glinting on the snow of the surrounding peaks.

'A fine view,' said Sydney, 'and this drop in temperature is a great relief.'

It rose quickly as they descended into the jungle. Malou and Hanou rode ahead on their tigers, with Mr Surely in between them, sitting on a rather old, gentle tiger going grey about the muzzle. As Jane and Sydney swayed behind on their elephant they discussed Mub.

'Poor man,' said Jane, 'to have such a horrid, terrible face. It will haunt my dreams for the rest of my life.'

'I fear plastic surgery and his face are the most genuine things about him,' said Sydney grimly. 'I know the legends of the Mountains of the Moon as well as anyone living, and anything about a hostile tribe is not among them. I think his accent was Prussian.'

'Why the rifles, then?' said Jane.

'I don't know,' said Sydney. 'If I'm not mistaken, they were British rifles of the Second World War. There is some thing definitely phoney about him. You saw the wolf-hounds chained up outside—I am quite certain those weren't found in the valley. I've never heard of a mountaineering expedition taking wolf-hounds with it before. I shall look in my files in the chalet. I was doing book reviews for the *Daily Telegraph* just after the end of the war and I have kept a good many copies. I shall see if I can find any record of a nineteen forty-six expedition here.'

'Why didn't you tell him about Mrs Deal?' said Jane.

'Something else occurred to me,' said Sydney.

Mrs Deal was their first concern when they reached the village. Sydney explained the situation to Mr Surely, laying particular stress on her fear of tigers.

'Oh dear,' said Mr Surely, 'it's true I have some slight knowledge of medicine, sir. In the war. . . .' He stopped, a worried expression on his face. 'Well, when we first got here,' he said, 'it was really a case of castor oil and keep your fingers crossed, sir, if you know what I mean. I'm afraid the last of that went twenty-five years or more ago. However, I'll do my humble best.'

He was a long time with Mrs Deal. When he came out, he seemed much merrier.

'Would you believe it, she knew Lady Somerlyton,' he said to Sydney. 'I was in service before the war, you know, sir; butler to the Somerlytons for four years, and numerous other posts. We'll have a lot to talk about when she's well again.'

'She's not too ill, then?' said Sydney.

'Oh, it's simply a fever you get here, sir,' said Mr Surely. 'There's a juice they get from the bark of one of the trees that clears it up in two or three days. And I think I helped to reassure her about the tigers, which do seem to prey on her mind, as you said, sir. I explained that the roaring she heard was in fact the bull monkeys. In my humble opinion, she should rest here till she is better and then be taken back to your residence.'

This was what they did. After three days of bark medicine, Mrs Deal was so much better that Sydney became nervous she would get up, wander out and discover Mr Surely's kindly deception about the tigers. She was already complaining.

'Those bull monkeys are a perfect pest,' she said to Jane. 'I can't think why they are allowed to wander about roaring like that. As soon as I'm stronger I shall go out myself and shoo them back into the jungle where they belong.'

On the third night, Sydney gave her an extra three Slogodon and two tumblers of medicinal gin, which he had brought back after showing the chalet to Mr Surely. Then, wrapped in blankets, her head enveloped in the bee-veil, Mrs Deal was lifted on to a bed strapped to the back of one of the smaller elephants. When she woke up, she was safe in the chalet again.

8 . Death Stockade

FOR THE next two and a half months Jane lived almost entirely in the company of Malou and his two tigers, Anrap and Antrim. Malou's English improved rapidly, and soon they could talk easily together.

The tigers were the most important thing in the lives of the Barabou. A few days after a Barabou was born, it was given its own baby tiger. The two babies slept together, played together, ate together. At first, the mother of the Barabou child would feed both her own baby and the tiger; but as soon as their little masters or mistresses were old enough they would feed their tigers themselves, and Jane loved to watch a little Barabou boy aged three staggering up to a fully grown tiger, his tiger brother with whom he had been brought up, dragging an antelope leg or a crocodile's head for supper.

The only lessons the Barabou children had were with their tigers. Before they could walk, they were riding them about the village. By the age of five they could make them come when they were called, sit, jump, trot or go full speed, swim, and fetch and carry things. By the age of seven they were able to go hunting on their tiger—lying flat on its back while it crept closer and closer to some unsuspecting jungle boar, until, at a touch of the foot, it would spring into the air and seize its prey in giant jaws or rend it with ferocious claws.

Much of this, patiently taught by Malou, Jane became very good at. First he taught her how to grip the tiger round the middle, feet tucked hard in behind the front legs. For trotting and walking you sat upright; for the swift bounding runs and leaping you lay flat, one or both arms round the tiger's neck. Leaping was what Jane liked best. First three feet, then six feet, and before long she was able to stay on for the gigantic fifteen or twenty foot spring of the full-grown tiger. It was now she realized why they all had such large tails. When they leapt they stretched their tails behind them like squirrels do, and the wide flat ends of the tails spread out and steadied their flight.

When Jane could stay on for a full twenty-foot leap, Malou taught her how to take her tiger tree-running. Tigers don't in fact really like going up trees, they prefer to stay on the ground; yet, once trained, the Barabou tigers were almost as agile and clever in the air as cats or squirrels.

'Up,' Jane would say sharply to her tiger in the language of the Barabou, at the same time tapping him lightly on the left shoulder. Her tiger would pause, reluctant as always to take to the trees. 'Up,' Jane would say again, giving a firmer tap. Her tiger would run lightly to the nearest of the closely packed trees and, as Jane lay forward and folded both arms round the thick neck, spring with a rolling ripple of muscle into the branches. And now would begin one of the most exciting experiences in the world—the tree-running of a highly trained Barabou tiger.

Trotting and then galloping along a broad lower bough, the tiger would gather itself and then leap. Its tail would stretch out, the end fanning. There would be a flash of sunlight, and then shade again as they landed in the next tree. Trot, gallop, leap—flash of sun—the tearing vegetation and grunt as the tiger broke their fall on the next-door tree. Gradually the speed would quicken, the leaps become longer. Sometimes the tiger would have to climb higher and then, as it sprang out across a 30 or 40 foot gap and the sun flashed, Jane would see the jungle 150 feet below her, perhaps glimpse a startled antelope, and then, the wind rushing in her hair, they would fall with terrifying speed towards the next tree, land with a crash, the tiger's claws scrabbling for a hold, fall perhaps to a branch below and then—they were off again. Leaping, falling, racing up the wide smooth path of some fallen giant, spring into space, to run and leap and crash again, on and on until the tiger began to tire or the sun to sink below the mountains and it was time to go home. It was the closest to flying that Jane had ever been. Indeed, so like flying was it that Jane explained to Sydney it really more or less *was* flying. So one more of the ancient legends turned out, in a way, to be true.

Malou rode Anrap; Jane rode Antrim. At the age of nine, all the Barabou were given a second tiger to train and get to know, in preparation for the time when their first tiger would die or become too old to hunt. Antrim was Malou's second tiger, and soon he became almost as fond of Jane as Anrap was of Malou.

There were only two things about Malou which puzzled Jane. The first was that he would never tell her anything about Mub. Perhaps he knew nothing, because when she asked him that is what he said. But once, when he was trying to explain about a very dangerous cliff and warning her not to go there, he said, 'It is terrible—terrible like Death Stockade.'

'What's Death Stockade?' asked Jane. But Malou refused to say anything more and in fact, later, refused to admit that he'd even said the words 'Death Stockade'.

The second thing was that every three weeks he would suddenly disappear for three or four days and when he returned would refuse to tell her what he had been doing. He would only say it was something to do with being the Chief's son, some magic he couldn't tell her and, on Sydney's advice, she did not press him any further.

If Jane's life was spent all over the jungle, Mrs Deal's was quite the opposite. Once back in the chalet she resolved never to leave it again. She did not, it is true, stay all the time in the chalet itself, as she had before. Oddly enough, now that she had seen a tiger, Sydney was able to persuade her that there were no tigers actually wild in the jungle. She would sometimes take little walks round the clearing and twice went as far as the river. Further than this she would not go.

But though her life was confined to one place, this did not mean she had too little to do. As the chalet stayed longer and longer in the damp warm air of Africa, green moulds and luxuriant yellow mosses began to spread up its walls, over books, blankets, beds and furniture. Mrs Deal fought back with grim energy. Each day a supply of fresh water, meat, vegetables and fruit arrived from the Barabou. These had to be prepared and cooked. There was the balloon to mend, a task made easier by a continual supply of waxwood torches also supplied by the Barabou. And as well as all this, Mrs Deal liked to keep the grass in the clearing trim and neat with a pair of Veronica Saxton's old garden shears. All day she worked, far into the night she stitched, and sometimes, when she at last struggled up to bed, she was almost too tired to pull the bee-veil over her head against the mosquitoes.

Though Jane and Malou dropped into the chalet every three or four days (always tying Anrap and Antrim some way off so as not to alarm Mrs Deal) and Sydney spent at least half his time there, she might have been lonely had it not been for one thing, and that was her friendship with Mr Surely.

As soon as Mrs Deal had recovered from her fever, Mr Surely began to pay her regular visits. At first he pretended these were to inspect the progress of the balloon, as Mub had ordered him to do. But it soon became obvious that he really came to gossip with Mrs Deal about the old days. After a brief look at the bulging plastic marsh gas tent, which he didn't understand at all, he would climb on to the veranda, gratefully accept a cup of tea, and settle himself to talk about one of the several grand houses where he had been butler, and which Mrs Deal had either visited or knew about. Only two things did he find it difficult to talk about. The first was Mub. Always a gentle, timid man, whenever he mentioned Mub, Mr Surely became terrified.

'He's a hard man,' he would say, making his knuckles crack nervously. 'Oh, he's been a hard taskmaster to me, I can tell you that.'

'I can see he has, Mr Surely,' Mrs Deal would say soothingly. 'Have another cup of tea.'

'Thank you, Mrs Deal,' Mr Surely would say. 'Yes, I've had to eat a great deal of humble pie in my time. A *very* great deal of humble pie.'

The other subject was Mrs Surely. Only gradually did Mr Surely reveal he had been married. 'She could be dead,' he said. 'But there again I doubt it. Although she was ten years older than myself, Sarah Surely was as strong as a horse.' Mrs Deal learnt that his wife had also had a very bad temper and had nagged him all the time. Indeed it was Mrs Surely who had made it easier for him to endure the long years of exile in the jungle.

'It's true I've often had a longing to get back to good old England,' he said to Mrs Deal one day, 'but then each time I've realized that if ever I found myself back with Mrs Surely—God help her, she's her own worst enemy—I'd just be wishing I was back here again.'

Apart from these two subjects, nice timid Mr Surely enjoyed talking to Mrs Deal more and more and more. First he came twice a week, then three times a week, and soon he took to calling every day.

While Jane stayed with the Barabou and Mrs Deal remained in the chalet, Sydney divided his time between the two. He discovered that his guesses about the Barabou had been nearly right. They had indeed come from India and probably, from the legends that Hanou told him, nearly a thousand years before. But one thing he could never discover, and that was how they had managed to cross the Mountains of the Moon. Hanou just laughed when Sydney asked him about the stories of the mountains being hollow.

'They are made of rock,' he said.

At the chalet, Sydney spent several days after their return from Mub reading through old copies of the *Daily Telegraph*. He could find no account of any 1946 expedition to the mountains, but a number of copies were missing so he could not be certain no expedition had taken place. Sydney became engrossed in the old, moldering pile of papers—particularly in his own book reviews, a number of which he read out to Mrs Deal.

'I can't think why I never collected them into a book,' he said.

'Now's your chance, Mr Saxton,' said Mrs Deal.

But on the fourth day, Sydney discovered something that seriously upset him. He came down the stairs from his room, white and shaky, holding up a copy of the *Daily Telegraph*.

'This is terrible,' he said, 'terrible.'

'What is?' said Jane, who happened to have dropped in that afternoon.

But Sydney would not tell her. He walked slowly past her and, muttering, 'It's a bad business,' left the chalet. He was gone for two hours. When he came back, to a by now very anxious Jane and Mrs Deal, he was not carrying the paper.

'I have destroyed it,' he said. 'I could be mistaken. If I am right, we may be in some danger. If I am wrong—then all is well. Either way, we can do nothing about it.'

However, Sydney cheered up quite quickly. There was much to occupy him round the chalet. Botanizing expeditions to collect plants, slow, exploring rambles in the jungle to see what he could find, household chores like wood-collecting and sharpening the shears; and in the evenings he would talk and write his notes.

There was also the marsh gas. Day by day it bubbled up into the tent, and week by week Sydney pumped it out into the cylinders. Gradually they filled. By end of the first month one cylinder was full and the second had been connected to the tent. Another month, and this was full. The third cylinder was already half full of helium and after a fortnight on the tent this too was full.

At the same time Mrs Deal completed her repairs to the balloon. Each tiny hole, each tear, however small, had been minutely drawn together with neat cross-stitch; for the larger rips down the sides she had used a more robust herringbone. 'I only hope it holds,' she said, 'I've done my best.'

'It looks lovely, Mrs Deal,' said Sydney.

The next problem was how to get the chalet out into the middle of the clearing. This, however, proved unexpectedly easy. Sydney had noticed how skilful the Barabou were at moving large objects. All they did was harness the elephants and pull them over rollers made from neatly cut tree trunks.

So it was with the chalet. Early one morning two elephants were loaded up with rolling logs and long coils of creeper rope and then, accompanied by most of the village, set off for the chalet (tigers, of course, were left behind). They roped it to the elephants and pulled it slowly into the middle of the clearing—all with much shouting and laughter and cheering, and with Mrs Deal urging them on from the veranda.

Only Sydney seemed unaffected by the general excitement. Jane, who had seen him more than usual during the last few days, had noticed he had seemed particularly silent and serious. Now, he immediately asked Hanou to have the three full gas cylinders put into the

chalet. He also explained that he wished the chalet to be securely tied
to the ground so that it would not be pulled over when the balloon was
filling. The creepers were to be wound round the chalet and tied in a
single large knot outside, above the door on to the veranda. It would
then be possible to release the balloon by a single blow, cutting the knot.
While this was going on, he directed another group of men to lay the
large balloon out flat on the grass at the back, re-thread the ropes and
fasten them round and under the chalet. He himself went up on to the
roof and connected up the gas hoses.

'But we're not going this minute, are we?' asked Jane in dismay.

'Unfortunately not,' said Sydney. 'I gave my word as an English gentleman to the man Mub that I would tell him before we left and I suppose I must do so. I must say I regard the idea of behaving like an
English gentleman in these circumstances as completely ridiculous, but
it's hard to lose old habits.'

'Really, Mr Saxton,' said Mrs Deal in a shocked voice.

'If Mub is who I think he is,' said Sydney, 'he, at any rate, is certainly
no gentleman.'

'But who *do* you think he is?' said Jane. 'And do you really think he
might stop us going?'

'I really don't know,' said Sydney, in a worried voice. 'But if he does,
I want to be able to leave at once in case he changes his mind.'

'I don't know why we are talking like this,' said Mrs Deal, whose sense of reality had returned with its usual pessimism at the talk of going. 'You won't get far in that thing.' And indeed the chalet, balancing lopsidedly on the rolling logs in the middle of the clearing, festooned in creepers and its wooden walls more than half covered by extravagant mushrooms and mosses, did not look a very reliable vehicle.

Once started on this subject, Mrs Deal could not leave it. All her old fear of flight returned. When Sydney suggested she came with him and Jane to see Mub, she immediately refused.

'Certainly not,' she said. 'I've enough to do as it is without coming to parley with some heathen savage. If we're going to take to the air in this gimcrack of yours Mr Sydney then I'd best prepare. If crash we do, and I've no doubt we will crash, then at least I'd like the craft in a respectable condition.'

Accordingly, Jane and Sydney set off together accompanied by Hanou and the rest of the Barabou. Jane collected Antrim who, with Anrap, had been tied to a bush well away from the clearing, and she and Malou left the main party to go careering through the great trees, soaring and plunging out of shade and into sun, in and out, gripping the bodies of their tigers in what Jane feared might be the last real tree-run she would ever have.

Their inverview with Mub was soon over. They had stayed the night with Hanou and his family, and arrived outside the Stockade as the early morning mists were drifting up through the trees.

'Good-day, Mr Saxton,' said Mub, when they were led before him. He sat just as before, tall and thin behind the table, his hideous, nose-less white head rising from a white gown. 'What do you want?'

'We have come to say good-bye,' said Sydney. 'I have now collected sufficient gas to try and lift the chalet. You asked me to tell you when it was ready. I have now done so.'

'So soon?' said Mub. 'I had no idea. Mr Surely has not been reporting to me accurately.' He turned and spoke to one of the guards beside him. Then turning to Sydney he asked, 'What are your chances?'

'I should say fifty-fifty,' said Sydney. 'But it is our only hope.'

'It is a risk you will not have to take,' said Mub. 'Had you said you had one chance in twenty, I might have allowed it. Fifty-fifty is likely to succeed. You will stay here.'

'What on earth do you mean?' said Sydney.

'Ah, Surely,' said Mub, as an anxious Mr Surely hurried into the room. 'You did not tell me the progress Mr Saxton had made. Why not?'

'I humbly apologize, this very morning, I was humbling to apologize and tell you sir, but it is a rather technical bubbling gas for me to fol-low, I beg. . . .' babbled Mr Surely, frantically pulling his fingers. He looked terrified.

'I wish the chalet to be destroyed,' Mub interrupted him. 'Today. Now.'

'Smashed? Ruined?' cried Mr Surely, looking more and more miser-able and frightened. 'If you really wish it sir, yes sir, of course sir.'

'Have you gone mad?' said Sydney in a cold, furious voice. 'You can't do that.'

'I can do what I like,' said Mub. 'Like me, you can remain in this val-ley for the rest of your life. There is no escape. Surely—take some men from the village and go and burn the chalet this instant.'

'But you can't do this to a young girl,' cried Sydney, putting his arm round Jane's shoulder. 'I am an old man. At least let this young girl go.'

'No,' said Mub. He stood up. Jane saw that two red spots had appeared on Sydney's cheekbones. There was a long pause, as he and Mub looked at each other. Suddenly Sydney spoke.

'I know who you are,' he said. 'You are a monster in more than face. I promise you, if I get out from this valley, I shall see that you are brought to justice.'

Mub turned abruptly and walked to the door. There he stopped and spoke rapidly in Barabou, then turned to them. 'If you know who I am, your fate is sealed. You will be taken to Death Stockade. Surely, don't stand there. Go and do as I told you.' He waved his hand to the guards and was gone.

They were seized roughly and hurried out of another door. They were taken across to the back of the cleared space and through into a smaller Stockade enclosing a space right against the sheer cliff. Here they were thrown into a small wooden hut. The door shut with a thud and Jane heard three bolts being banged home. Then silence.

9. Mrs Deal's
Finest Hour

AS SOON as the men had gone, Jane jumped up and ran to the door. It was impossible to open. There were no windows, only narrow slits in the thick, tree-trunk walls.

Jane went and sat down by Sydney, who was staring gloomily and blankly at the ground. 'Cheer up, Sydney,' she said, 'something will happen. Listen, tell me who you think Mub is. Is he going to kill us?'

There was a long pause, then Sydney, who looked suddenly much older, raised his head wearily. 'I fear so,' he said. 'If I am right, I fear so. While I was looking through the old copies of the *Daily Telegraph* I came upon a curious piece of information. In January nineteen forty-six, Von Bummhausen, the monster of Marmlein Concentration Camp, escaped from his military hospital near Dusseldorf in Germany. Just before he was captured at the end of the war, he tried to avoid punishment by killing himself. Instead, by some mistake, he nearly destroyed his face. He was recovering from plastic surgery, when he managed to escape. He was traced to the north coast of Africa and then he disappeared.'

'I'm sure it's him,' said Jane excitedly. 'You can tell he's really wicked.'

'It certainly explains certain things,' said Sydney. 'It explains the British Second World War rifles, it explains his face, his desire to remain here and his refusal to let us go. I should add that Von Bummhausen was an extremely tall man, over six foot five inches.'

'I wonder when he'll kill us,' said Jane. 'We must escape.'

But if Mub—or Von Bummhausen—did plan to kill them, he was in no hurry. Day followed day and nothing happened. They had three meals brought to them by one of the guards; for an hour each afternoon they were allowed to exercise in Death Stockade. This was not much larger than two tennis courts. At its back, the cliff rose straight, with a number of large rocks fallen at its base. In front, the wooden stockade was over 30 feet high. Quite obviously, in front or behind, escape was impossible.

To one side at the back, against the cliff, there was a row of 22 six-foot-long mounds, each with a rock at its head.

'Those are graves,' said Jane to Sydney. 'I expect they are the victims of Von Bummhausen's savage cruelty. Our own tortured bones will soon rot there.'

On the fifth day, they were visited by Mr Surely. He came tiptoeing in, carrying their evening meal. He was also carrying two warm goatskins over his arm.

'Mr Surely!' cried Jane, running towards him. 'Oh, Mr Surely, please get us out.'

'Ssssh, Miss !' whispered Mr Surely nervously, looking over his shoulder. 'No one knows I'm here. I've brought you some nice venison.'

Sydney came over to him and drew him aside. 'Tell me one thing, Surely,' he said. 'Is Mub Von Bummhausen? At least tell me that?'

But Mr Surely looked quite terrified at this. 'Ssssh—please Mr Saxton! It's more than my life's worth to say that name. I won't say he is, but this I will say—I won't say he isn't. But Mub he is now, and Mub he must remain. Now—let me go sir, I beg you.'

'What can we expect?' said Sydney.

'He keeps his own evil counsel,' said Mr Surely cracking his fingers. 'But you've seen them mounds out there. . . .' His voice died away and he looked fearfully behind him again.

'Well, if he wants to kill us why doesn't he get on with it?' said Jane.

'That's his cruel way, Miss,' whispered Mr Surely. 'He likes to think of the agony of anticipation. Eight or nine days is his usual. One thing I'll tell you—your chalet's safe and well. As is Mrs Deal. Now I must go. If he were to know I'd been here—why, I've no doubt I'd join you.'

Day followed day, but now to the boredom of doing nothing, was added the fear that they had in fact not all that long to wait. Sydney sank into a deep gloom. Jane during the day felt mostly bored, but at night the fears raised by Mr Surely came to the surface. Outside in the main Stockade she could hear the wolf-hounds baying. She thought of those silent mounds against the cliff, she dreamt of Curl Castle and her sweet mother, and she woke in the darkness crying, burying her face in her arms so that her sobs would not disturb Sydney.

They had little or no hope of escape. As Sydney said, their hopes could only rest on Mr Surely and Mrs Deal, and they were very wobbly foundations for anything to rest on.

Mr Surely was certainly wobbly. He felt he was plunging deeper and deeper into some deep bog of lies and disobedience which would shortly be discovered and he would be instantly shot.

Having started by not telling Mub—or Von Bummhausen, rather,

because of course Sydney was quite right—having begun by not telling
Von Bummhausen about Mrs Deal, he certainly did not dare do so now.
He had also decided not to burn the chalet. He knew Mrs Deal would
be extremely unhappy staying with the Barabou so he had decided to
leave her the chalet. In the old days such disobedience would have
been unthinkable. Von Bummhausen himself would have ridden down
on a tiger to see that his orders had been obeyed. Now, though it terrified him, Mr Surely thought he could risk it.

Nor had he told Mrs Deal that Jane and Sydney had been locked up.
He pretended they were just staying away for the weekend. But Mrs Deal
could see something was wrong. Mr Surely had become very nervous
recently; whenever Mub or Jane or Sydney were mentioned he looked
rapidly at the jungle, lowered his voice and tried to change the subject.
On the sixth day she decided she must find out what was going on.

'I think I shall pay a visit to Mr Mub tomorrow,' she said to Mr
Surely, as they were sitting on the veranda drinking tea.

Mr Surely began to tremble, so that his cup and saucer rattled together.

'You can't do that, Mrs Deal,' he said.

'Why not?' said Mrs Deal.

'Mub wouldn't like it,' said Mr Surely nervously.

'Why ever not?' said Mrs Deal. 'It's high time I met him. Besides I
can't think why Mr Saxton and Miss Jane are staying so long.'

'They're just there for the weekend,' said Mr Surely.

'Six days is a very long weekend,' said Mrs Deal. 'I should never forgive myself if something happened to Miss Jane. I shall go tomorrow.'

The thought of Mrs Deal arriving at the Stockade, no doubt men-
tioning the chalet in her first breath, exposing all his deceptions, made
Mr Surely feel faint and sick. He realized he would have to tell at least
part of the truth.

'Mrs Deal,' he said, 'I fear, out of nervousness, I haven't told you the
entire truth. Things are not quite what they seem.'

'I thought as much,' said Mrs Deal. 'Now you just relax with another
cup of tea, Mr Surely, and tell me what's going on.'

Mr Surely explained that his master was a strange and violent man.
He was given to curious actions, difficult to explain. He had locked Mr
Saxton and Miss Jane up.

'But why?' cried Mrs Deal, amazed. 'He must be mad.'

'He is mad,' said Mr Surely. 'He doesn't want them to leave the valley.'

'Why ever not?' said Mrs Deal. 'And what about me? Doesn't he mind
if I leave the valley?—not that I'd trust myself alone in this wooden
deathtrap.'

Mr Surely hesitated. At last he said, 'He doesn't know of your existence.'

'Doesn't know of my existence?' cried Mrs Deal in astonishment. 'Why ever not?'

'He just doesn't,' said Mr Surely, looking embarrassed.

'But didn't you inform Mr Mub of my presence?' asked Mrs Deal, more and more surprised.

'No,' said Mr Surely.

'Why not?' said Mrs Deal.

'I don't rightly know,' said Mr Surely. 'Somehow an opportune moment never arose.'

'Well I don't know, I think it's very odd,' said Mrs Deal, feeling faintly irritated. 'Still, it may turn out to have been for the best. This Mr Mub of yours is plainly unhinged. I'll have to rescue Mr Saxton and Miss Jane somehow and then we'll fly off. I rely on you, Mr Surely, to help me get them out.'

But at this Mr Surely began to tremble again, so that he had to put down his cup and saucer. 'Don't ask me to do that, Mrs Deal,' he said. 'Please, not that. I've toed too many a line to step over one now. If you put all the lines I've toed end to end, they'd stretch. . . .' His voice faded miserably away and he looked down at his feet. 'Please, Mrs Deal,' he said.

But Mrs Deal was still feeling rather cross that she had not even been mentioned to Mr Mub, much less introduced. 'The worm turns, Mr Surely,' she said. 'Perhaps it's time the worm turned now.'

'I've turned as far as I dare,' said Mr Surely. 'Von—that is Mub—wanted this chalet burnt and I've not burnt it. I've kept your presence a secret. I've visited Mr Saxton and Miss Jane when I shouldn't have. If I do any more turning I'll be turning in my grave.'

'Well don't you worry, Mr Surely,' said Mrs Deal, suddenly feeling sorry for him. 'I'll find a way somehow. But why is your Mr Mub so strange?'

Suddenly, Mr Surely wanted to tell her everything. For 28 years he had lived shut away in the valley with no friends, no one to talk to, no one to love him. Often he had been frightened and lonely, often, despite Mrs Surely, he had longed for England. At the sound of Mrs Deal's kind voice, at the sight of her kind face as she leant over to pour another cup of tea, he felt himself relax.

'Mrs Deal,' he said. 'Mub is not quite what you think he is.'

Mrs Deal, who had imagined him as a sort of fat savage, with a ring in his nose, said, 'Well, it's true I didn't expect a gentleman, but insanity I didn't bargain for.'

And then Mr Surely did tell her more or less everything. He explained that Mub was really Von Bummhausen, the brutal concentration camp monster. When his face had been badly burnt, Mr Surely had been one of the medical orderlies helping to look after him in hospital. Von

Bummhausen and six other Germans had escaped, forcing Mr Surely at gun point to accompany them. They had fled to Africa and thence to the Mountains of the Moon. Here Von Bummhausen had set up his kingdom. He had killed all the people in the other two expeditions which had penetrated the mountains, and several times he had almost killed Mr Surely. He had frequently had him beaten and sometimes tortured a little. Only now that he was an old man was Von Bummhausen less cruel, out of tiredness not because he'd become any kinder.

Mr Surely spoke so fast, after his years of silence, that some of what he said was rather confusing. Mrs Deal asked a number of questions; among them, hoping to find some method of escape which might make the balloon unnecessary, she asked if he could remember the exact route Von Bummhausen had taken over the mountains.

'I'll tell you later,' said Mr Surely, hurrying on.

'You've had a terrible time, Mr Surely,' she said, when he'd finished. 'Enough to break the stoutest spirit. Of course you'd be reluctant to put yourself in further danger.' But she was not, as Mr Surely had expected, in the least frightened to hear who Mub really was. On the contrary, she was stimulated. 'A Nazi is he?' she said. 'A nasty German war criminal? Well, we did for them then and we'll do for them now. Just let me get this place straight and I'll tackle this Von Mub or whatever he's called.'

'I shouldn't delay, Mrs Deal,' said Mr Surely. 'I don't know what you can do, but he's decided to kill them, I'm sure of that.'

'Well, I must have help,' said Mrs Deal. 'What about that Malou boy Miss Jane used to bring here? He seemed a lad of spirit.'

'Poor young Malou,' said Mr Surely. 'When Jane and Mr Saxton didn't return from the Stockade, the village thought they'd been done to death. He's been alone with his grief ever since.'

'Well you tell him privately they are not dead,' said Mrs Deal. 'Then send the lad to me. I'll work something out with him or my name's not Doris Deal. Now off you go Mr Surely. If this chalet is to take to the clouds again I've got my work cut out.'

Mr Surely was terrified of telling Malou that Jane was still alive. Once more he was secretly going against Von Bummhausen; in fact, in Mr Surely's view, it more or less amounted to the worm turning completely. At the same time he felt very guilty about not doing more to help. He finally decided it was the least—and at the same time the most—that he could do.

Accordingly, when he reached the village, he had Malou, his eyes red and swollen from weeping, sent to him in the hut he used for passing Von Bummhausen's instructions on to the Barabou. Then he explained. Jane and Mr Saxton were alive, imprisoned in Death Stockade. Mrs

Deal was going to rescue them, goodness knows how, and Malou was to help. *No one*, not even Hanou, was to know about this. As Malou jumped and skipped in silent delight, Mr Surely grew more and more agitated. Fear made him angry. 'You look unhappy when you leave this hut, young Malou, or I'll tan your hide,' he said. 'You look unhappy or my goose is cooked.'

Mr Surely himself found it only too easy to look unhappy as he started apprehensively back to the Stockade. 'I shall be found out,' he thought to himself. 'I shall be found out and roasted alive.'

Malou managed to keep a straight face until he had ridden Anrap slowly out of sight of the village. Then, with a wild whoop and bringing his hand down with a crack on the animal's powerful rump, he took to the trees.

Mrs Deal greeted him warmly and then, worried by Mr Surely's saying she mustn't delay, got down to the business of planning. She was delighted to find that Malou not only said he could get into Death Stockade, but knew how to get out too. There was one difficulty. Mrs Deal asked what it was. The difficult was that she, Mrs Deal, would have to ride a tiger.

Mrs Deal did not even allow herself to think about it. She simply said no, and dismissed the horrifying idea from her mind. She was sorry, but there could be no question of it. She wouldn't. Malou could explain his plan to her tomorrow, but she was quite sure some other animal would do just as well.

'Those nice elephants who pulled the chalet,' she said. 'Ask your father to lend us one of them.'

'Mr Surely said no talk to my father,' said Malou.

Mrs Deal looked thoughtful. 'Did he?' she said. 'He's a clever man, Mr Surely. He may have eaten more humble pie than is good for a man, as he says himself, but he is good and he is clever. No doubt we could borrow an elephant without telling Mr Hanou.'

'Elephants no can climb,' said Malou.

'We'll cross that bridge when we come to it,' said Mrs Deal briskly. 'Now I've a lot to do here. You can explain the whole thing to me tomorrow. Go and borrow an elephant and come and fetch me tomorrow early.'

Mrs Deal had a light supper and then packed her overnight bag to be ready for an early start. Apart from a clean night dress and spongebag, she put in the Slogodon in case the bull monkeys should be troublesome and two bottles of medicinal gin for emergencies. She packed a nice romantic novel, *The Laughing Cavalier*, that she was reading, and two candles and a box of matches. The bee-veil, into whose hot but protective folds she finally wrapped herself, could go in last thing.

Malou borrowed an elephant by saying he was exercising it, and arrived very early, when the dew was still dripping from the branches and the sun had not yet risen. But Mrs Deal had already been up for an hour, burnishing the gas cylinders, changing Sydney's sheets and generally putting the last touches to the chalet, before, as she confidently expected, they tried to escape in it the next day, or at the latest the day after.

It never occurred to her that anything could go wrong. The fact that Von Bummhausen was a German and that Britain had won the war had somehow convinced her that she would rescue Sydney and Jane without difficulty. She found she enjoyed riding on the back of an elephant very much. It seemed a safe, zoo-like way of travelling. As she said to Malou, this was her first real outing in over two months.

Her awakening was sudden and terrifying. Malou had carefully remembered to leave Anrap tied up at home so as not to frighten Mrs Deal. It had not occurred to him to warn the rest of the village to do the same. It was as they came into the village of the Barabou that Mrs Deal first learnt, with a shock that nearly caused her to faint, of the full extent of what she afterwards described as the tiger problem.

The broad open space between the round huts was, as usual, packed with tigers. Big, little, old and young, leaping, growling, playing, the marmalade-coloured mass seethed and swarmed in the hot midday sun. The elephant stopped. Mrs Deal half rose to her feet, then fell back, her eyes bulging and her finger pointing.

'Look Malou, look,' she whispered. 'What's happened? What *are* they? Am I mad? Are they—*tigers*?'

Hanou at once ordered all the tigers out of sight, and Malou coaxed her into a hut to recover her composure. It took her a long time to calm down, but slowly she became unexpectedly brave. The reason was that she had seen some of the tigers playing with small children, and even babies. Now Mrs Deal loved little children and babies. If the tigers didn't hurt babies, she thought, they would be unlikely to hurt her.

She questioned Malou closely. She learnt that tigers had been with the Barabou for as long as anyone could remember, living with them, eating, sleeping and serving them.

'But why did no one tell me these great beasts looked after the children?' she said at the end. 'Like them I never shall, but if I'd known *that*, it might have removed some of the terrible dread which naturally attaches itself to the Monarch of the Glen.'

Next Malou explained in detail his plan of rescue. Mrs Deal listened carefully and it soon became clear to her that it could be done on tiger-back or not at all. After a long silence, when he'd finished, she said, very well, she would ride a tiger. But she must be strapped on, the overnight bag by her hand, and then she would just lie there. Malou must guide the tiger and control it.

She spent the rest of the afternoon sitting at the door of the hut, peeping round at the tigers and children, who soon re-emerged, playing in the sun. Although she was already beginning to wish she hadn't said she'd go on a tiger, and indeed felt steadily more frightened as evening drew near, the sight of the tigers not eating or even hurting the children did do something to calm her.

When it was dark, she lit one of her candles and tried to read *The Laughing Cavalier*.

It was not till then that Malou began stealthily to make his preparations. Gradually a pile of wax-wood torches, creeper ropes, food and so on, grew in the back of the hut.

Mrs Deal ignored it. It reminded her of what was in store, and that she found more and more terrifying. Her own preparations were quite different and much more simple. Malou had said they would leave at 12 o'clock, when it was darkest and they could expect some cloud over the moon. Mrs Deal had decided that the only way she possibly could really ride a tiger was if she were completely unconscious. At 10.30, therefore, she poured a full tumbler of medicinal gin and took two Slogodon; at 11 o'clock she had another tumbler and another two Slogodon and at 11.30 the same again. At 11.45 she had a final half-tumbler of medicinal gin, one more Slogodon for luck, then put the gin bottle and Slogodon box back in her bag, pulled the bee-veil over her head and shoulders so that she should see nothing, and fell happily back against the wall.

When Malou arrived at 12.15 she was decidedly groggy. He had brought Rotha for her to ride, a very gentle but powerful tigress ten years old. To Rotha's back he had secured a light bamboo litter which was used for carrying sick people. But Mrs Deal could hardly stand. She staggered and tottered, and then leant against the wall of the hut, laughing weakly.

'Sssh!' whispered Malou, grappling with her. 'Please, ssh, Mrs Deal!'

At last he managed to get her stretched out and tied on to the litter. He also tied her overnight bag by her right hand as she had asked. Then he swiftly tied the rest of the things he had collected to the two tigers and arranged Mrs Deal's bed of skins to look as though someone were in it. All the time, from Rotha's back, came the sound of muffled but distinct snoring.

Malou took them to the back of the village and then round through the jungle in a wide circle to avoid disturbing the other Barabou tigers; once they were on the trail again, he urged the beasts to a steady canter.

It was a strange journey. The clouds before the moon made it very dark, but the tigers sped on, sensing before they saw them the animals which sometimes blundered into their path. Mrs Deal surfaced again and again from her sleep, groping each time she half woke for the Slogodon. She was jolted when Rotha sprang to avoid a small wart-hog, and woke again when, faint through the bee-veil, some jungle creature screeched or snorted as they passed. Each time, she sank back into her dreams again.

It was just after 2 o'clock when they reached the plateau of Von Bummhausen's Stockade. Malou headed the two tigers straight for the cliff, keeping as far from the Stockade as he could. The guards he knew he could avoid, but only distance would prevent them being heard or smelt by the tigers or fierce wolf-hounds inside the compound. At the bottom, instead of turning, Malou urged Anrap straight on. With hardly a pause, the tiger sprang at it and began to climb, followed by Rotha. Mrs Deal felt herself slip a little. We're climbing Death Stockade, she thought. She felt dizzily for her overnight bag.

Malou's plan was brilliantly simple but very dangerous. About 100 feet above the ground a narrow ledge or fault ran along the cliff, parallel to the ground. It continued round the Stockade and on beyond it. At the smaller Death Stockade it dipped a little. This was where they would enter.

Only two Barabou tigers, and two of the very best at that, could have done it. In places the fault was no more than a few inches wide, and quite invisible in the thick darkness. Yet, yellow eyes blazing, soft, black, padded feet delicately feeling, not dislodging so much as a sliver or pebble of rock, the great cats crept along the narrow ledge. At times, where the cliff wall bulged out, they seemed almost to stick to the rock face. Malou shut his eyes and held his breath.

Then, all at once, round a corner, there was the Stockade far below him, the tall, sharp-pointed tree-trunks casting their shadow from eight vast torches blazing at the door of the main hut, Von Bummhausen's dwelling. And by this light, Malou could also see two silent black guards standing on the steps. But he and Mrs Deal were too high for the light to reach them. Invisibly, the two tigers crept on in shadow round the cliff face. And now the fault began to tilt downwards a little. The distance from the ground grew gradually less. In five more minutes they were directly behind and above Death Stockade.

It was a fearsome height. So far was it that Malou could not even see the ground. The pointed stake-tops of the Stockade itself looked far away, the guards small and insignificant; surely, thought Malou, it is a mad long way to jump.

Without thinking and at once, so that he would have no more time

to think, he smacked Anrap on the side. The tiger quivered, hesitated an instant, then sprang. And as he disappeared, out and down into the darkness, Rotha gathered her great haunches and sprang too. But Mrs Deal felt none of it, for, as Rotha plummeted down, tail spread to its fullest, thick and wide, all four legs braced out, the air now rushing past, roaring past, the ground hurtling up—as they dropped like rocks out of the night, Mrs Deal fell finally, deeply, unalterably asleep.

Jane and Sydney had gone to bed that night early and gloomy as usual. But they had also been frightened. It was now exactly a week since Von Bummhausen had locked them up, and eight or nine days, Mr Surely had said, was his 'usual' time before an execution.

Sydney himself was quite sure this night was their last. Two guards instead of one had brought their evening meal and though he had been unable to hear exactly what they said, he gathered from their mutterings that something was afoot.

Jane did not question him. It was the fact that she should die so young that made him more unhappy than anything, and she tried to avoid the subject. She also tried to avoid thinking about it herself, but this was almost impossible. Would they shoot her? Or cut off her head? Or hang her? Jane tried to think of Curl Castle, even of school, of anything except her own death, but it was very late before, tired and frightened, she fell asleep.

She woke abruptly at 3 o'clock. Someone had shaken her. She sat up, heart beating, and listened.

'Who's that?' she whispered. And then, from quite close beside her, she heard Malou.

'Quick, Jane. It me, Malou.'

'Malou!' She reached out, felt his shoulder and flung her arms round him. 'Malou!'

'Quick! We go now,' whispered Malou. Immediately, Jane turned back, reached into the darkness again and shook Sydney.

'What is it?' whispered Sydney. He, too, thought the guards had come for them.

'It's Malou come to rescue us,' whispered Jane excitedly.

'Good God!' said Sydney. 'Are you sure, Jane? You're dreaming, my child.'

'Sssh, Mr. Saxton!' whispered Malou, in the darkness. 'We go now.'

They both slept in their clothes and in a moment they had pulled on their shoes and hurried outside the hut. Here it was just light enough to see the dim forms of two tigers. Malou re-bolted the doors and then set off into the night.

He led them only a short distance, to the cliff face behind the hut. Here it was darker than ever and Jane could hear him scuffling and feeling among the rocks. All at once he grunted and she heard a grating sound. Suddenly Malou was close beside them again. 'Mr Saxton, you hold Rotha here. Jane, you follow, holding Rotha's tail.'

With the other hand held out to feel for obstacles, Jane let herself be led forward by the tiger. She had the impression they were passing through a large hole in the cliff, the ground under her feet was suddenly knobbly rock and not the hard earth of Death Stockade. From behind her came the grating sound she had heard before, and then the darkness grew even thicker, so that she could not even see her hand when she held it up.

But now Malou spoke in his ordinary voice. 'Now we have light,' he said cheerfully. 'Mr Saxton—you have your magic fire, please?'

'My lighter?' whispered Sydney, still unable to believe they had escaped. 'Yes. Where are you?'

Malou brushed past Jane, Sydney's lighter clicked and flickered and then with a rapid spreading of resinous smoky flame one of the waxwood torches took light and showed them where they were.

It was a low, rocky tunnel, which led steeply up into the cliff. It was so low that Jane could easily touch the roof and Sydney had to bend with one hand on his knee. Two tigers blinked their huge yellow eyes in the light from the flaring torch: one was Anrap, the other Jane didn't recognize, and this one was carrying a strange bundle.

'Whatever's that?' said Jane, pointing. But even as she spoke she recognized the bee-veil. 'It's Mrs Deal,' she said. 'Look Sydney, Mrs Deal on a tiger!'

'So it is,' said Sydney. Then he said to Malou. 'She's not ill, Malou?'

'No. She asleep,' said Malou laughing.

It was true. Not even the violent shock of Rotha's landing from the tremendous leap had stirred Mrs Deal's deep sleep. They looked at her, and listened.

'What a brave woman,' said Sydney. 'It must have taken a great deal of courage for her to face a tiger.'

'And I expect quite a lot of medicinal gin,' said Jane.

'Very wise of her,' said Sydney, tucking one limp arm back beside Mrs Deal's sleeping form.

'Quick. We go now,' said Malou. He went up to the front with the burning torch and Anrap, Jane came next, then Sydney, bent double; Rotha with Mrs Deal on her back brought up the rear. The low tunnel lasted only a hundred yards or so. When it ended they came suddenly upon one of the most magnificent and extraordinary sights that Jane had ever seen.

They were standing on a small ledge half-way up one side of a vast cavern—a cavern so large that it was impossible to see its top, its bottom or either end. Jane had the feeling of enormous space in front of her, almost like standing, at night, on the edge of the sky. And this impression was strengthened because the ledge on which they stood, and other ledges along the walls as far as she could see before they vanished into the darkness, were covered with what looked like long icicles, sticking straight up, or hanging down, glistening yellow, orange and purple in the flame of the torch.

For a long time they stood and gazed, then Sydney said in a hushed voice, 'So—the Mountains of the Moon are hollow after all.'

'But how?' said Jane. 'No one dug this out, surely?'

'No. It was hollowed out over millions of years by water,' said Sydney. 'This is limestone. Notice those stalactites and stalagmites—formed drop by drop over the ages. I'm quite sure the whole range of mountains isn't limestone. There is probably an extensive tunnel system which may lead right through them. I wish we had time to explore.'

But Malou was once again becoming uneasy. 'Mub follow,' he said. 'Come!'

From the ledge a narrow path, which Sydney said looked as though cut by man, led down until, after half an hour, they reached the bottom of the cavern. Here they found an underground stream, very clear and cold, which bubbled swiftly away into the darkness. Malou now followed this upwards and steadily they began to climb up and up into the Mountains of the Moon.

As they climbed, Sydney talked to Malou. Apparently only a thirty-mile-long stretch of the mountains contained the massive limestone vein, but this was simply riddled with caves and caverns, tunnels and underground rivers. They were considered magic and their secrets were known only to the Chief of the Barabou, who passed them in turn to his eldest son. Every three weeks since he was very small, Malou had had to spend three days exploring the caverns. Now he knew them almost as well as he did the jungle.

'So that explains where he used to disappear to,' said Jane. 'But isn't it very easy to get lost?'

'Very easy,' said Sydney. 'But there are tricks, Malou tells me. All the caverns which are not dead ends, come out finally at a place somewhere in the middle of the mountains. This must be the watershed, I think, and is about eight hours ahead of us. If you get lost, you climb uphill and should eventually reach it.'

'But where are we going?' said Jane. 'We can't just go and live in this watershed place for ever.'

'On the other side of the watershed,' said Sydney patiently, 'another series of caverns leads down and eventually out of the other side of the Mountains of the Moon. You remember that river we saw below us when we crossed over? We'll come out there. That will have to be crossed and then there's the desert.'

'I'd've preferred the balloon,' said Jane. 'I was looking forward to that—to see if our marsh gas worked and everything. Actually, what I didn't understand, Sydney, was where we should have got to. Wouldn't the winds have just blown us south, further down Africa?'

'No,' said Sydney. 'At this time of the year they blow north. We'd have reached the coast all right, if the balloon had floated, which I can tell you now I very much doubt.'

Up and up they went. The stream had long since vanished, and they climbed through narrow underground gorges, through twisted tunnels worn smooth by long dead rivers, out into giant caverns, echoing, dripping, glistening with huge stalactites. But nowhere, as Sydney pointed out, did the pathway ever get too narrow for an elephant.

'Think of that first journey, a thousand years ago,' he said, 'when the Barabou first came here—because undoubtedly one of these cavern routes was how they came. Think of the great elephants, the torches, the caged tigers, the frightened hustling Indians—it's a sight I'd like to have seen.'

'And Von Bummhausen—do you think he came this way?' asked Jane.

'I imagine so,' said Sydney. 'It would explain much, the wolf-hounds, for instance. But I can't think how he discovered it. Malou thinks he is evil magic. He says his father says he just appeared—over the mountains, out of them or just snap! like that. Like a demon in a pantomime.'

Malou was certainly frightened of pursuit. He kept on urging them to go faster. As they climbed higher Sydney got more breathless and soon he had to sit astride the large tiger most of the time. Every two hours or so they stopped to rest, have something to eat and light a fresh torch. At these times they examined Mrs Deal, but she was still deeply asleep.

'Much the wisest course,' said Sydney. 'We'll make no attempt to wake her.'

'I don't think you could if you tried,' said Jane.

On they went, twisting up the ancient riverbeds. Jane thought it would never end, but at last Malou said they were on the final stretch.

This was in fact one of the strangest parts of the whole journey. The river had at some time in the distant past gouged out a huge groove inside the mountain. Up this they slowly climbed. But to their right was a cliff falling away into an enormous, deep hole. Though she could see nothing but blackness, Jane sensed its awful presence. Malou said it was about 300 yards across and it must have fallen sheer, nearly a mile into the mountains. When, now nearly at the top of the watershed, they stopped and threw a large rock in, Sydney counted 28 measured seconds before, deep in the earth, they heard the rumbling echoes of it striking the bottom, and these echoes themselves continued to sound and roll for about a minute.

'Here we are,' said Malou. 'In a minute—all downhill.'

And then, following so close upon it that for a moment Jane thought it was the final effect of the falling rock, there came a shattering report. A stab of flame flashed in the darkness, and then two more reports echoed and there were two more flashes. Almost at the same time a line of flaring torches appeared along the ridge in front of them, held aloft by advancing men, and in their middle, tall, terrifying, his white robe dazzling in their light, strode the figure of Von Bummhausen.

'Stop!' he shouted harshly. 'Stop—or I shoot.'

Events after that moved very quickly. By the light of the torches Jane saw Anrap leap forward, teeth bared, claws reaching for the tall white figure in front of them. She heard the tiger roar, and then heard the answering roar of Von Bummhausen's gun, saw Anrap fold up in mid-flight and fall on to the path. The next instant, Malou's arm was round her waist and running with her to the edge, he sprang out into the blackness. There was the roar of another gun behind them and Jane felt a rush of air past her ear and then they were falling—falling faster and faster, and yet, as they fell, Jane could hear screams coming up from below them, scream upon scream upon scream.

10. The Worm Turns

'AND WHO is this woman?' It was Von Bummhausen speaking. He, Sydney, Mr Surely, Mrs Deal still peacefully asleep, and seven of the guards, were all standing in the main yard of the Stockade. It had taken them four hours to descend from the watershed by the same more direct route Von Bummhausen had used to reach it.

'Why have I not seen this lady before?' said Von Bummhausen, twitching the bee-veil angrily. 'Surely—who is this?'

Mr Surely looked at the familiar figure and felt his heart sink. Now it would all come out, the concealing of Mrs Deal, the non-burning of the chalet, everything. He clicked his knuckles.

'Well—I—perhaps . . .' he said nervously.

'Yes?' said Von Bummhausen. 'Out with it.'

'I,' said Mr Surely, and then he stopped, staring terrified at the tall white figure. 'I didn't,' he whispered.

'He means he has never seen Mrs Deal before,' said Sydney, suddenly realizing the difficulty Mr Surely was in. 'Mrs Deal became ill after our descent in the chalet and was attended to in one of the huts of the Barabou. I saw no reason to inform either you or Mr Surely of her presence.'

'Why not?' said Von Bummhausen.

'Look here, Von Bummhausen,' said Sydney, suddenly straightening with anger. 'You have caused the death today of two innocent children. Goodness knows how many other murders you are responsible for. I promise you this, that if I ever escape from here—and I shall not stop trying—you will pay for your crimes.'

Von Bummhausen did not even bother to deny who he was. He motioned his guards towards them and said, 'You are lucky to be still alive, Mr Saxton. You were to be shot at dawn this morning—which is why I discovered your escape so soon. I guessed at once you might have had help and taken some road unknown to me through the mountains. It is obvious the Barabou helped you. I shall take two hostages and shoot them, together with you and this Deal woman, in three days from now. Meanwhile, you will be locked inside the Stockade in the room next to me. Take them away, Surely.'

Sydney did not answer. He was very tired after the long march up and back in the mountain. Also he could see little chance of escape. Forcing himself to walk upright, he followed an equally dejected Mr Surely and the still sleeping Mrs Deal towards the largest building in the stockade.

Jane and Malou fell for fifteen terrifying feet and then landed with a thump on a broad ledge sticking out into the blackness. Immediately Malou seized Jane and pulled her back against the cliff face, and it was as well he did so, for a moment later the light from several torches waved over the front of the ledge as Von Bummhausen's guards leant out and tried to see what had happened.

Malou made them wait for thirty minutes after all was silent. Then taking her by the hand he led Jane up on to the main path again.

Once they were there, still in pitch darkness, she at last dared to speak. 'But Malou,' she said, 'what were those screams?'

Malou laughed. 'You know that trick,' he said. 'You hear that a moment ago. Listen.' He leant out and shouted, and immediately, echoing eerily back from ledges and jutting cliff face, down and down until eventually it was sounding faintly from the very bottom, she heard 'Jane, Jane, Jane' flung back successively from the immense black depths. It did indeed sound as though someone were calling out her name as they fell.

'Well,' she said, 'now what do we do?'

'First we go down. Then by-and-by we kill Mub. Yes,' said Malou, 'he kill Anrap. By-and-by, we kill him.'

The journey down was one of the most terrifying and exhausting trips Jane had ever done. It was cold and in the darkness often danger-ous, but Malou's knowledge of the caverns was extraordinary. He told Jane that one of the tests for the Chief's eldest son was to wander for seven days, alone, in darkness, inside the Mountains of the Moon. Eventually, after six hours, they reached the end.

It was dark when they stumbled out into the jungle. Relieved as she was, Jane was too tired to do more than long for sleep. They climbed high into one of the great trees and, as they had done many times before, made a small platform where three branches joined, covered themselves with some large leaves and were soon fast asleep.

They were woken by the sun and the familiar din of the jungle. Jane had never thought the sound of screaming, chattering and croaking could sound so delicious. They climbed swiftly down the tree and gath-ered some berries and roots for breakfast.

They had come out of the mountains by way of a small underground river which ran quite close to the village of the Barabou. Malou said he would go there at once to see what help he could get, and also to tell his father and mother he was not dead.

Jane accompanied him some of the way and then, coming upon a large clear pool, and because it was already very hot, she said she'd have a swim and try and wash herself a bit, and Malou could meet her later.

She was scarcely out and dry before Malou arrived back. He was riding a very old tiger Jane hadn't seen before (and she knew most of the tigers in the village) and his face was grave.

'Bad news,' he said. 'Mub come. He very angry. He take my father and uncle. No one help us. All frightened.'

By careful questioning, Jane discovered that that very morning Mub had arrived in the village with five of his guards. He had seized Hanou and his brother and they were to be imprisoned in the Stockade and shot, together with Mrs Deal and Sydney, in two days' time. He had left three guards in the village. Luckily, just before he reached it, Malou had met his cousin Alou out for a walk, who had described everything to him. Alou, very surprised to see him alive, had said all the Barabou were far too frightened to do anything to help and warned him to keep away. His cousin had managed to smuggle out one very old tiger, Shala, the mother of Antrim (to have brought Antrim himself would have been far too dangerous), and had promised to tell Malou's mother that he was alive, then he urged him to go deep into the jungle and hide for ever—or until Mub was dead.

'Now it is all over,' said Malou. 'Now nothing we can do. Mub too strong.'

'Nonsense,' said Jane. 'We haven't even tried yet. The first thing to do is to go somewhere they won't find us. I think the best place is the chalet. They won't dream of going there because Von Bummhausen thinks it's been burnt. And once there we can get Sydney's gun.'

As they jogged through the jungle, Malou told Jane all he knew about Mub's first appearance among the Barabou many years before he was born. At first they had received him kindly—indeed some of them thought he was a god—but quite soon his demands for servants, food, tigers, wives, etc., became so great that Malou's grandfather, the old chief, had decided he must be taught a lesson. He had gone to visit Mub in his large hut, taking six leading tribesmen with him. For an hour they had talked sternly to him about good manners. Mub had listened, and then shot them all. For a week after that the six Germans (but not Mr Surely, which was one reason they liked him) had waged war on the Barabou, and had killed so many of them that they had been forced to surrender.

They reached the chalet a little after lunchtime. Jane felt quite cheered to see it standing in the middle of the clearing, a bit lopsided on the rolling logs. The grass had grown more than a foot, and inside the chalet, though all was neat and ready for take-off, green and yellow fungus had begun to appear on walls and furniture and curtains. The three gas cylinders were streaked and discoloured.

'It would break Mrs Deal's heart,' said Jane.

They had a quick lunch of baked beans, spaghetti rings and some tinned rice pudding. Then they began to plan. It became rapidly clear that they were in a very difficult, if not impossible, position. What, after all, could two young children, with an old shotgun, do against a gang of armed men? As they talked deep into the afternoon, and suggestion after suggestion, plan upon plan, appeared too dangerous or impracticable, Jane began to despair. There seemed nothing they could do without help—and the only help was the Barabou, too frightened to do anything at all.

Believing themselves to be perfectly safe, the two children made no effort to keep their voices quiet, nor did they keep guard. All at once, however, the tiger Shala gave a low growl and half sat up, the fur along her back bristling.

'Sssh!' hissed Malou. 'She hear something.'

They listened intently, but could hear nothing; or rather heard too much, because it was impossible to distinguish anything from the roar of the jungle. Jane put two cartridges in Sydney's shotgun. For five minutes they sat with beating hearts, straining their ears, and then at last they heard what Shala had heard. There came the unmistakable squelch, squelch of someone crossing the clearing.

Had they known what Von Bummhausen was like, they would have realized that the chalet was in fact the most dangerous place they could have chosen to hide. Once he thought the Barabou had helped Malou break into Death Stockade he began to imagine all sorts of plots against himself. He wondered if any of his orders recently had been carried out. The chalet, for instance, had that been burnt? Probably not. To find out he sent the one guard he trusted completely, the only person he knew would never disobey him. And as Jane stood up and levelled her gun steadily at the door, and Shala backed with bared teeth against the stove, a head came slowly into view. Wearily, miserably, Mr Surely appeared, climbing the veranda steps.

'Mr Surely!' cried Jane, lowering her gun.

'Miss Jane!' cried Mr Surely, clutching his heart, and then grabbing the veranda rail to stop himself toppling backwards. 'Miss Jane—what a fright you gave me. Gracious me! And young Malou, too. Well, and I thought you were dead, both of you. Mrs Deal will be pleased, and Mr Saxton; so will Hanou and his brother. It will be some comfort to them all at the end.'

Mr Surely sat panting and gasping. He mopped his forehead, smiling kindly at Malou and Jane.

'There's not going to be an end, Mr Surely,' said Jane. 'Mr Surely, you've got to help us.'

'Oh dear,' said Mr Surely.

'You've *got* to,' said Jane. 'How can you leave Mrs Deal to her fate? You said once that if you were sure Mrs Surely had passed on you'd ask Mrs Deal to become Mrs Surely. You can't leave someone who's almost your wife to *die*.'

'You don't understand, Miss Jane,' said Mr Surely. 'I've sat too long below the salt to change now. That terrible man—I'm frightened of him.'

But he sounded uncertain. Jane's words had only echoed what he had already been thinking—how indeed *could* he leave Mrs Deal to her fate? And yet, how could he prevent it, weak as he was, against Von Bummhausen and his guards? But despite his fear, deep inside him he felt the stirring of a most unusual excitement.

'Perhaps,' said Mr Surely slowly, 'perhaps I needn't help you, but I could just not stop you. I could turn a blind eye.'

'You've got to *help* us,' said Jane. 'You've got to fight to save Mrs Deal.' At the word 'fight', Mr Surely jumped, but again, rippling through him, he felt a strange surge of excitement.

'You my friend,' said Malou. 'You taught me speak English. You help.'

Suddenly Mr Surely stood up. 'Perhaps I could help you,' he said. His heart was beating hard. 'Yes I could and perhaps I will. Yes,' said Mr Surely, now very excited, walking up and down, 'I *shall* help. I shall deceive him and trick him. I shall be meekness itself. Not,' he added, 'that I'm not always meekness itself, but I shall eat more humble pie than ever before, toe every line, I shall *abase* myself.'

'I shouldn't eat too much humble pie,' said Jane. 'He might suspect something. I should just be normal.'

'Normal *is* eating too much humble pie,' said Mr Surely bitterly. 'But he won't suspect anything. He thinks I'm a spineless weakling. I hope he will find he is wrong.'

Jane had never seen anyone change so quickly. Mr Surely was as bright and quick, as jolly as when he used to drop in for cups of tea with Mrs Deal.

They began to plan at once. Jane said she supposed the best thing would be to try and rescue them at night. But Mr Surely said no, oddly enough the morning would be best. He would order all the guards to go out hunting. Then he would give a signal—a white flag run up the Stockade flagpole—and Jane and Malou would come over from the jungle and help him capture Mub.

'Can you get tigers from the village?' he asked Malou. 'We shall need four—for you and Jane, Mr Saxton and Mrs Deal. Your father and uncle will be all right on their feet.'

Malou was not sure. The Barabou were very frightened. His mother might help. He would try.

There remained only to decide where to go if they managed to free the prisoners. Jane at once said that of course they must come to the chalet. Mr Surely secretly agreed with Mrs Deal that the chalet seemed a most unlikely vehicle. However he was still too frightened of Von Bummhausen to consider the alternative, which was to hide away somewhere in the valley and wait their chance to escape through one of the caverns in the Mountains of the Moon.

Shortly after this they parted. Jane and Malou loaded a bag with tins of food, took the gun and a box of cartridges, and set off for the village. They stopped about a quarter of a mile from it just as the sun was setting. While Jane built a platform high in a large tree, Malou went to talk to his mother.

He was gone a long time. Jane ate her share of the food, and then curled up close to the comforting warmth of the old tiger Shala. She lay listening to the noises of the jungle and trying to see the stars through the leaves above her. She was nearly asleep when Malou appeared silently out of the darkness and crouched beside her on the platform.

His mother had been very frightened but had promised to help. His cousin Alou would bring three old tigers (young ones would be missed) to a special pool nearby, early next morning.

Malou ate his food and snuggled down close to Jane. Before they went to sleep she thought, Tomorrow our fate is decided.

They woke before the sun had properly risen above the mountains. There was some dew and a faint mist hung among the branches. Jane and Malou shared a tin of cold baked beans and then, shivering a little, climbed down and set off to find Alou.

He was already at the pool when they arrived, the three old tigers beside him. He was extremely nervous. As soon as they appeared, he thrust some long bandage-like ropes which Malou had asked for into their hands, wished them luck, and disappeared into the jungle.

In order to rest the tigers for their work later in the day they walked, so it was 10 o'clock before they reached the plateau and could see across the scrub to where the Stockade stood out against the cliff, menacing and still. Jane sank down and leant against Shala, Sydney's gun across her knees.

For a long time nothing happened. The Stockade appeared deserted. Perhaps Sydney and Mrs Deal have already been shot, Jane thought, and this is a trap. Von Bummhausen and his guards are slowly creeping up on us. Nervously, she opened Sydney's gun, put in two cartridges and shut it. Still nothing happened.

Suddenly, Malou jumped up and pointed at the Stockade. 'Look, Jane!' he whispered.

A tiny figure was on the roof of the main building. As they watched, a white flag was run up the flagpole and fluttered from its top.

'Now,' said Jane excitedly. 'This is it.'

Malou told the tigers fiercely to wait, then he and Jane, carrying the gun between them, set off at a trot into the chest-high savannah grass.

They were met at the small side door, as they had arranged, by a terrified but at the same time highly excited Mr Surely.

'Oh, what a business,' he whispered, whisking them in and shutting the door. 'I'm all of a shake, but it's going according to plan. Mub himself found me sending them all off and asked me what I was doing. I nearly called them back on the spot, but I managed to say we were completely out of meat and I would guard the prisoners. I didn't know I had it in me.'

'What shall we do now?' asked Jane. 'Where is Von Bummhausen?'

'There's not a moment to lose,' whispered Mr Surely nervously. 'He's in with the prisoners now, gloating. The sooner we get him under lock and key and make ourselves scarce, the better. Don't hesitate to use that gun, Miss Jane.'

Jane, who found the gun almost too heavy to hold, hoped this would not be necessary. Fortunately Mr Surely was carrying one of the rifles, though she noticed that even his hands were trembling.

They hurried across a narrow stretch of bare ground and then Mr Surely, crouching low, led them down the side of one of the smaller huts. At the end he stopped, peered round it, then dropped on his hands and knees and began to crawl with great speed towards the back of the largest building. Jane and Malou crawled after him.

Mr Surely was panting loudly when they reached him at the door; but he had already opened it and they followed him a few yards along an empty corridor down which he tiptoed. He stopped outside a door and standing beside him they could hear plainly the high cruel voice of Von Bummhausen.

'You have given me the most trouble, Mr Saxton. It will give me great pleasure to have you shot last. I shall do it personally. It is a long time since I have looked forward to something so much. This woman will be shot before your eyes.'

The voice became almost shrill with pleasure. Jane's arms suddenly stopped aching; she felt very angry. Poor Sydney, poor sweet Mrs Deal— the horrid beastly man. Mr Surely reached a shaky hand towards the door. For the first time in 28 years, the worm was about to turn.

'The two Barabou will be tortured before being shot.' Von Bummhausen still had a faint German accent. 'You will also watch that, Mr Saxton.'

Mr Surely closed on the handle and pressed it down. He took a deep breath and stepped firmly through.

But Jane was in front of him. Holding the heavy gun as high as she could she ran into the room and said furiously, 'How dare you speak like that. Put your hands up. Don't move or I shoot.'

Out of the corner of her eye she saw Sydney, Mrs Deal, Hanou and his brother, who were standing in a row chained to the wall, start forward with expressions of amazement. But her attention was fixed on Von Bummhausen. The tall white figure stood quite still for a moment and then whirled round.

He took no notice of Jane or Malou, but simply stared coldly at Mr Surely.

'What are you doing?' he said. 'Is this some kind of joke, Surely? Answer me.'

'Not exactly a joke sir, dear me no,' said Mr Surely. 'I have decided . . . that is . . . we have an expression—the worm turns . . .'

Von Bummhausen stared down, and then suddenly raised his fist and stepped forward. 'You treacherous little coward,' he snarled. 'You will be shot, I . . .'

Jane raised her gun to shoot. I'll shoot off his big toe, she thought. But before she could pull the trigger, Mr Surely's rifle exploded deafeningly beside her.

Everyone jumped violently and Von Bummhausen staggered back. But he was not hurt. Indeed, a small jagged hole in the ceiling showed where the bullet had gone, and as they all recovered there was a click as Mr Surely re-loaded.

The explosion seemed to have given him strength. He stepped towards Von Bummhausen and pointed the rifle at him. 'The next one won't miss. You can't have forgotten I was a soldier once.' He voice was trembling. 'I've stood this for twenty-eight years,' he said, 'and I'll stand no more. Do you remember the times you've had me beaten? The time you pulled my nose in front of the guards? You've made me toe the line just once too often; my toes are toeing no more. I've been

bullied and harried till I've had my fill. I'll eat no more of my words, that I won't. No, nor swallow them neither, and no more humble pie or humble crust or dog's dinners,' cried Mr Surely, more and more wildly, the metaphors of his humiliation crowding in upon him. 'I've sat below the salt long enough. My spirit's been broken once too often, I've cooked my goose till I'll cook no more. You can walk over my grave till you're batty, and stuff yourself with humble pie till you burst—the worm is turning with a vengeance now,' shouted Mr Surely, 'and you can like it or lump it!'

There were several moments of astonished silence and then leaping forward, her chains clanking, Mrs Deal cried, 'Hurrah for Mr Surely! Spoken like a man—and I'm not surprised.'

'Jane,' said Mr Surely, panting but in command of himself again. 'Jane, take the keys from my left pocket and undo them all.'

While Jane did this, he kept his rifle pointed steadily at Von Bummhausen. Sydney and Mrs Deal, rubbing their wrists, embraced Jane, while Hanou picked up his son Malou and held him tight. Swiftly they chained Von Bummhausen to the wall, and then hurried from the room. All this time the tall German had said nothing; but Jane thought his silence, with his glowing eyes and monstrous scarred face, more sinister than any words.

As they pushed towards the jungle, Mrs Deal once more praised Mr Surely. 'I wish I'd given that unpleasant man a piece of my mind before we left,' she said. 'You took him down a peg and no mistake, Mr Surely.'

'I should have done it years ago, Mrs Deal,' Mr Surely called back over his shoulder, from where he was leading the procession, astride one of the tigers from the Stockade. Jane and Malou brought up the rear, carrying Sydney's heavy shotgun between them. Sydney and Mrs Deal were in the middle, being helped by Hanou and his brother.

And they needed help. They had been badly tired by their journey down through the caverns, and tired still further being chained to Von Bummhausen's wall. Stumbling slowly, each supported by an arm from the Barabou Chief and his brother, it took them half an hour to reach the jungle.

When Mrs Deal saw the four tigers waiting meekly round the large tree, she gave a deep groan. 'I suppose I'm expected to ride one of those man-eaters again?' she said gloomily.

'Come Mrs Deal,' said Sydney, 'remember your finest hour.'

'My finest hour it may have been,' said Mrs Deal. 'Remember it I cannot. The whole episode is just a blur to me.'

However, she made remarkably little fuss as they strapped her on to the oldest and gentlest of the tigers. As she explained afterwards, she couldn't really have cared less then if she'd lived or died. Indeed died, had she been allowed the choice, would probably be what she'd have chosen.

They were just strapping Sydney on to his tiger when there came the first sign that their escape was not going to be as easy as it had at first seemed.

Mr Surely was just saying, 'We should have a good five hours' start, Mr Saxton. We can take it nice and easy,' when a strange booming sound, a gong or giant bell, came from the direction of the Stockade. Looking across the waving savannah grass, Jane saw a sight which froze her blood.

Standing on the roof of the largest building, clearly recognizable despite the mile or so between them, stood Von Bummhausen, his white robes blowing in the wind. It looked as though he were searching the edges of the jungle with binoculars.

They all drew rapidly deeper into the trees.

'Oh dear oh dear oh dear,' said Mr Surely, 'he's freed himself. That gong will bring the hunters back within the hour. We must be off at once.'

As they finished tying Sydney on to the broad back of his old tiger, Hanou came up and said something rapidly to Mr Surely.

'Very sensible,' said Mr Surely, turning to explain to Jane. 'He and his brother will lay a trail in the opposite direction to delay the pursuit. Now, off we go.'

Jane was to remember that journey as one of the most frustrating she had ever made. Malou explained to her that Von Bummhausen's huge wolf-hounds were specially trained for hunting.

'They go very quick,' he said.

'Then we must go faster,' said Jane.

But the tigers were too old. Shala was still capable of a sustained gallop; the others could only trot, or occasionally canter. Hour after hour they threaded their way through the narrow tracks of the hot damp jungle. A few parrots fled screaming as they passed, monkeys swung and chattered angrily, sometimes clouds of *tyrannus nox*, the vicious mosquito, floated round them, stinging, when the ground grew boggy. Several times Malou led them along small streams to make it more diffïcult for the wolf-hounds to follow. The sun rose to its height, and began to sink; all the time it was trot-trot-trot, and Jane could feel the pursuit behind them, the terrible, furious figure of Von Bummhausen at its head.

At 3:30, just half an hour before the sun would start to disappear behind the Mountains of the Moon, Malou heard very faintly the sound he had been listening for since they'd started—the high baying of a wolf-hound on the scent of its prey. Ten minutes later, Jane heard it too.

'What's that, Malou?' she said.

'The dogs. They get close,' said Malou, once more steering Shala into the course of a shallow river.

Now fear was added to the frustration and discomfort of their flight—fear which made them forget their hunger and smack and kick their tigers in a desperate effort to go faster. But the animals were too tired. Jane's tiger stumbled and nearly fell. Behind them, the baying grew closer. Malou led them down another stream and then on to the track again. Sydney's tiger stumbled. There were the hounds again. They would be caught.

And then suddenly—there was the clearing! A few more weary strides, and they stopped beside the chalet. Jane leapt from her tiger and ran to Mrs Deal. But Malou was there before her. With swift strokes from his long-bladed knife he cut her loose and as she rolled off her tiger he and Mr Surely caught her and together carried her up the steps. Jane took Malou's knife and cut Sydney's straps.

'Thank you, my dear,' he said, stretching and rubbing his legs and arms. Then very slowly hobbling to the steps and pulling himself up on to the veranda, he said, 'Well, we must see if this thing works,' and disappeared inside.

Now Malou was standing beside her in the long grass.

'Good-bye, Jane,' he said.

'But you must come too,' said Jane. 'You must come. Please Malou—we've had such fun.'

'I stay with my people,' said Malou gently. 'You go. I watch you go—and one day you come back.' He bent and kissed her and Jane flung her arms round him and held him.

'Yes Malou,' she whispered, 'one day I'll come back. Good-bye.'

Then he sprang on to Shala, the tiger whirled round and with a bound vanished into the large tree near the path leading to the jungle.

'Come on Jane!' shouted Sydney from the chalet. Very slowly, tears pouring down her cheeks, Jane climbed the veranda steps.

Inside the chalet, all was bustle. Even Mrs Deal had somehow managed to prop herself up in the kitchen to make tea. Mr Surely was standing by the window, his rifle in his hands. He was looking intently towards the entrance to the clearing. On the table beside him lay Sydney's shotgun. Sydney himself was standing by the gas cylinders, watching their dials.

'Run and see how the balloon is filling,' he said as Jane came through the door. 'We must get out of here.'

Jane ran up the stairs and climbed out on to the roof. It had begun to grow dark. As she emerged she heard the wolf-hounds baying in the jungle. She had almost forgotten Von Bummhausen. How long had they got?

The grey-white shape of the balloon stretched out behind the chalet, draped over the ropes which were to hold it upright when—or if—the balloon began to rise. Already ripples of gas were pulsing through it, little pockets and bulges appearing in its flatness.

She ran downstairs. Sydney was standing by the window beside Mr Surely. He was holding his shotgun and also had a knife beside him on the table.

'It's filling,' said Jane. 'How long will it take? Do you think it will work?'

'I don't know,' said Sydney. 'We must hope so. I'm worried about the lifting power of methane. I should say it will take about twenty minutes. We may have to fight it out with Von Bummhausen.' He smiled at Jane. 'Don't worry,' he said. Like a captain returning to his ship, being once more in the chalet seemed to have restored his spirits.

Outside, the wolf-hounds bayed again. 'I think they've been held up by that last stream we went down, sir,' said Mr Surely. 'I should say we have ten minutes.'

'In that case we'll have to fight,' said Sydney grimly.

The minutes passed. Both men were sweating. Jane ran up to the roof again and saw that the balloon was now swelling and bulging right along its length, the gas surging in it like a sea. She suddenly thought, How can we fight him? He's only got to fire one bullet into the balloon and it will burst. We'll have had it.

The shadows now covered the clearing. A small yellow and blue bird swooped across it and then once more came the sound of the wolf-hounds, much closer and yelping with excitement. Jane ran down into the chalet and stood by the window. They could hear men shouting now, and frenzies of barking. Suddenly, Mr Surely pointed.

Cantering slowly into the gloom of the clearing was one of the old tigers they'd ridden from the Stockade. It did not stop but disappeared heavily into the jungle on the other side. A moment later one of the wolf-hounds appeared, barking furiously, and disappeared after it. At the same time, the chalet gave a great lurch backward and then tipped forward, the creeper ropes which held it upright creaking loudly.

'At last,' said Sydney, and leaning forward pointed out of the window. Jane looked up and saw that the vast, unwieldy bulk of the balloon now swayed above them.

But still it was not full enough to lift the chalet. Sydney left the window and stood with raised knife by the single knot of creeper he had to cut to release them. They rocked noisily to and fro. By now the whole jungle seemed full of baying wolf-hounds and shouting men. All at once Jane felt the floor jarring and heard bumping as they began to bounce on the rolling logs underneath them.

At once Sydney said, '*Now!*' and with one sweep sliced through the tangled creeper above his head. There was the sound of rending wood, the chalet leant forward, righted itself, and then very slowly, foot by foot, began to rise from the ground.

As it did so, Jane saw an enormous tiger spring into the clearing. Sitting astride its tawny back was a tall, white-robed figure carrying a rifle—Von Bummhausen! They were too late.

She could scarcely follow what happened next. She saw Von Bummhausen leap to the ground and raise his rifle; she also felt rather than saw Mr Surely raise his rifle beside her.

Neither was quick enough. Even as they moved, there was a flash of gleaming gold, a roar, and another tiger landed full square upon the white-robed man, lashing furiously at him with its claws. From its back, a thin brown boy plunged downwards twice with a long knife. Then the tiger with its rider turned and sprang back into the jungle.

At the same time, the chalet rose slowly above the tops of the trees towards the light, was caught, still rising, in a gentle breeze and drifted sideways. In a moment, the clearing had disappeared from view.

11. Home Again

THERE IS not a great deal left to tell.

The balloon, with the chalet swinging beneath it, rose steadily into the pale blue sky. As they climbed, they left the evening darkness behind and it grew lighter and lighter.

'It works,' said Sydney with satisfaction. 'I never thought it would. Of course, we're rising much more slowly than before; methane hasn't the lifting power of helium.'

Jane looked down into the shade from which they were rising, at the green jungle, threaded with glinting streams and rivers, and at the huge lake gleaming at one end. Beside it, she could just see the little village.

'Did you see Malou?' she said. 'Wasn't he brave? He killed Von Bummhausen. He had his revenge for Anrap.'

'A very brave boy, certainly,' said Sydney. 'It is fitting that one of those noble people should free them from the tyranny of that terrible man. We must return and see them all.'

'Oh can we?' said Jane, excitedly. 'Please let's!'

'Well, I'm thankful to see the back of the place,' said Mrs Deal, who had limped from the kitchen to join them. 'It's taken twenty-five years off my life as it is.'

As they rose higher it began to grow cold. Jane asked Sydney if she should light the fire, but he said that marsh gas, methane, was highly explosive and it would be too dangerous, so they wrapped themselves in blankets and closed all the windows. Mrs Deal said she missed the bee-veil, left behind in her overnight bag at the Stockade.

'It was much warmer than it looked,' she said.

'I thought it did look quite warm,' said Jane.

At 10,000 feet Sydney took some digitalis, his heart medicine, and went to bed, in case he should become unconscious as he had the first time; Mrs Deal also went to bed. Now Jane and Mr Surely, who had had the cylinders and everything explained to him, were alone.

At 13,000 feet the aneroid could show no higher, and the chalet met the northward blowing winds and began to swing to and fro under the balloon. Hampered by their blankets, Jane and Mr Surely shuffled to the window.

Far below them in the jungle floor of the valley it was already deep night; up where they were the sun was shining brightly on the snow-covered Mountains of the Moon. Dizzy and freezing cold, Jane stared at their glistening points and sheer icy sides. She guessed they must be about 16,000 feet up now.

'Mr Surely,' she said after a while. 'We're being blown towards them.'

'I know, Miss Jane,' said Mr Surely, in a worried voice. 'And we are hardly rising. The ballooon doesn't seem able to get any higher.'

Fortunately, however, they soon saw they were being blown towards a gap in the mountains, a deep V-shaped slice between two soaring peaks.

Slowly they drew nearer; then they were passing over the snow, only ten feet above it, the steep slopes of the cleft rising on either side. It was completely silent.

The minutes passed. Jane and Mr Surely sat with their heads on the table, dozing. Then, all at once, there came a jolt, and a sound of breaking wood. They staggered to the frost-covered windows and tried to look out.

It was plain what had happened. At the end of the high valley along which they were being blown, the ground rose a little and the bottom of the veranda had struck it a glancing blow. Now they were some way out, crossing over the giant chasm which circled the Mountains of the Moon like a moat. But this time, instead of being blown round it, they carried straight on over the farther range of lower mountains which formed the other side of the chasm.

Twenty minutes later, Jane and Mr Surely started to pump gas back into the cylinders. They continued until the chalet had descended to 6,000 feet. After that Mr Surely cooked them a light supper of tea, spaghetti rings in tomato sauce, and tinned pears. Mrs Deal and Sydney were fast asleep, so he pushed hot water bottles down their beds, prepared two more for Jane and himself and they went to bed.

For three days they were blown north over the desert. Mrs Deal, faced with a chalet that had not been properly cleaned for weeks, soon recovered her strength. Mr Surely helped her, remembering many old butler tricks in the process. Sydney busied himself with his notes.

On the morning of the fourth day they slowly approached the coast and soon they could see below them a large town which Sydney said was Benghazi. The wind was very light that morning and the chalet hardly moved through the clear hot air. Pumping gas carefully back into the cylinders they floated gently down and at half past eleven landed lightly beside a road just outside the town.

A large crowd of excited Arabs quickly gathered, one in a battered old taxi. They climbed into this and Sydney told it to go to the British Consulate.

The Consul, by an extraordinary and lucky coincidence, turned out to have been at the same school as Sydney and knew him well. He was amazed at their story, but not quite as amazed as they expected.

'You won't believe this, Saxton old fellow,' he said, 'but I had a telegram from Christopher Charrington only yesterday.'

And then they learnt that just three weeks before, some wandering Bedouin had found the bottle Sydney had left in the desert with its message so long before. The Arabs had brought it to the Consul, and he in turn had sent it to Sir Christopher, suggesting that his daughter might yet be alive and well.

That afternoon they sent telegrams: Jane to her father and mother, Mrs Deal to her brother in Peebleshire, Sydney to his daughter in France; only Mr Surely did not send one. He did not know where his wife was, or even if he had a wife. He was also beginning to worry about the army.

'After all, in a way I'm a deserter,' he said.

'Daddy will look after that,' said Jane.

Early next day they flew back to London. Sir Christopher and Lady Charrington were at the airport.

'Daddy!' shouted Jane. 'Mummy!' She raced towards them and leapt first into her father's and then her mother's arms.

'Darling!' cried her mother. Tears were pouring down her cheeks. She could hardly speak. 'My sweet precious girl. I thought . . . I thought . . .' But she could only sob and hold Jane tightly.

Sir Christopher was crying too, his large kind red face redder than ever.

'The message gave us hope,' he said. 'I was mounting an expedition. Due to set out in two days' time.'

Jane introduced Sydney and Mr Surely, and then explained about Mr Surely and the army.

'We'll go and see General Herkenshaw at once,' said her father. 'As you know, he's an old friend of mine.'

General Herkenshaw was delighted to see them all once more, and particularly pleased to see Sydney, whom he remembered from the days when Sydney was his father's ADC. When he'd heard the facts about Mr Surely he was most reassuring.

'You couldn't have done anything else, Corporal,' he said. 'You were

abducted, you didn't desert. And you, together with the others, are partly responsible for the death of this monster Von Bummhausen. There is a handsome price on his head. All of you will share it.'

It was not until they had flown back to Curl Castle in Sir Christopher's private plane, and were sitting eating crumpets in the blue drawing-room, that they were able to tell the whole extraordinary tale.

'I want to hear *everything*,' said Sir Christopher.

So they told him everything. Jane and Mrs Deal explained about the Airship floating away ('A gang of casual labourers with a grievance,' said Sir Christopher. 'They were caught a week later.') They described the crash. And then, in turn, they told how they had escaped the avalanche, crossed the desert, and all that had happened in the Mountains of the Moon. They talked all afternoon and evening.

When they had finished, Sir Christopher Charrington stood up.

'It's the most amazing story I've ever heard,' he said. 'I congratulate you all—for your bravery, your resource, your skill. Now, what are you going to do now? You Mr Surely—I imagine you'll want to find your poor wife?'

'In a manner of speaking, sir,' said Mr Surely. 'But I was wondering sir, I would esteem it a great honour sir—that is, if you had need, or space, for a butler sir, I would be most willing to buttle.'

'I would be delighted,' said Sir Christopher. 'What about you, Saxton? You'll stay here of course as long as you want. I shall insist on a month at least. Have some more port.'

'That's very kind,' said Sydney. 'I accept both offers. But later, after I've rested a bit, I shall return to Switzerland. My friends are there now. I took out substantial avalanche insurance. And once there, I shall write a book.'

'A book? How interesting!' said Lady Charrington. 'What will it be about?'

'I shall postpone my old book,' said Sydney, 'and write a new one. I shall write an account of the adventures we have just told you.'

'A splendid idea!' cried Sir Christopher. 'Splendid, Saxton. What will you call it?'

'Well, if she doesn't mind,' said Sydney, smiling at Jane, 'I'd rather thought of calling it *Jane's Adventures in a Balloon.*'

At this there was a silence. Sir Christopher and Lady Charrington beamed, and Jane beamed. She thought it a perfect title. Mr Surely, too, agreed.

'I played a very humble role,' he said. 'I see no reason for my name to appear.'

'Well I do,' said Mrs Deal, who had been somewhat nettled at being left out. 'You stood up to Von Bumini or whatever he was called, at the end. And what about my part I'd like to know, Mr Saxton? What about my finest hour, as you described it yourself?'

'Perhaps it is a bit unfair,' said Jane guiltily. 'After all, even if he never actually went up in the air, we'd never have got away if it hadn't been for Malou.'

'Most certainly it's unfair,' said Mrs Deal. 'Credit be where credit's due. Your name must figure, Mr Saxton. We should all be mentioned.'

'All right, all right,' laughed Sydney. 'I'm very sorry. How about this, then: *Mrs Deal's, Mr Surely's, Mr Saxton's, Malou's and Jane Charrington's Adventures in a Balloon?*'

Everyone agreed this was an excellent title, and that, if titles today weren't so ridiculously short and small, is what this book would really have been called.